POSSESSION

CAMP HAVEN

A. ANDERS

CONTENT NOTES

Camp Haven is a safe space where everyone from experienced kinksters to curious newbies can live out their fantasies. But beware, this all-inclusive festival of delights, includes Power Exchange and Impact Play and Hostage Parties (oh my!), along with role-playing, Primal Kink, Consensual Kidnapping, and a sub Auction. If any of these themes are tough for you, please tread carefully.

For a full list, please visit www.adrianaanders.com

*To everyone who's ever been shamed for how they look:
you are beautiful, you are loved, you are perfect just the
way you are.*

*And to Ozan, my ride or die:
"No matter what happens, I'm glad I came with you."*

AUTHOR'S NOTE

Dear Reader,

In my experience, some books are easy to write and some are difficult, some are an enjoyable challenge and others are like pulling teeth, every step of the way. Writing Possession was a little of everything. And, now that my author's journey is over on this one, with a little distance, it seems fair that this book gave me all the rough things and the good things and everything in between. A wild ride, but also tough and emotional and raw.

Zion and Twyla came to me fully formed. Zion, for those who've read *Kink Camp: Hunted*, was a whole, real person since he first hit the page. Like Athena, who sprang fully grown from Zeus's head, he came out ready and roaring. I could see him, feel him, read his thoughts with unerring precision. The problem with Zion was that he didn't want to be pinned down. It wasn't in his nature at all to settle with any one person, or even several. Finding him someone to love was a challenge.

And then came Twyla. I won't ruin things by telling you about her. I'll let you meet her yourself.

First though, please know that these two get up to many, many things at Camp. I ask that you please read the above content notes with care. As you saw, there are quite a few.

Also know that it is very important to me, as someone who has attended a camp much like this one, that you understand just how clear the rules are. Nothing happens without the explicit agreement of all parties involved. Camp—and my personal experience of the kink community—isn't a place of hatred and fear. It's a place for love and acceptance and being who you truly are. It is my greatest hope that this book conveys that spirit.

Happy reading.

Adriana

When you come to the end of your rope, tie a knot and then hang on.

    - FDR

BONUS PROLOGUE

Twyla

I arrive at the premiere without a hint of foreboding. Not an inkling of how my life's about to blow up.

I'm excited. I mean, who wouldn't be when they're about to walk their first red carpet with a handful of the world's biggest and brightest?

I step out of the limo, gliding past the screaming fans who strain against the barriers surrounding the walkway. I'm guided between swaths of photographers and industry people, approaching the red carpet as if in a dream. The excitement crescendos and I soon realize why: Zion Mason is up in front, larger than life, smiling that devastating smile as the cameras go off, his muscular build caressed by the elegant lines of his tux.

The man's a mega star. A legend. The most amazing part, I found out on-set, is that he's a good person, too. A Hollywood unicorn. Private, but friendly, respectful, and kind to everyone. The consummate professional. Honestly, I didn't know beautiful people could be like that.

I step onto my own little corner of the carpet, floating on a euphoric blend of nerves and excitement. Half of this feeling comes from the dress I've got on, which not only fits my body right, but makes me feel like a queen. It's this deep, rich scarlet that offsets my dark eyes and hair and gives my skin a burnished glow. But it's the way it celebrates my big curves rather than trying to hide them that made me cry when the stylist turned me to face the mirror.

I just wish, now that I'm here, surrounded by the buzzing fans and the flashing photogs, that it wasn't quite so tight around the chest. Breathing's a bit of a challenge, but then it's the tightness that lets me get away with not wearing a bra. I can live through this for the next three hours.

For the split second that I picture how good it'll feel to shed all of this at the end of the night, I relax enough to give the crowd an honest to goodness smile.

But then I feel a tug and realize that the tip of my toe has snagged on the too-long trail of the dress. I quickly work out my foot, narrowly averting disaster, hoping nobody noticed. Adrenaline spikes in my veins, making me a little woozy.

Thank God the crowd's mostly focused on Zion and his co-star up front, because I'm really messing up this red carpet debut.

Not that anyone cares, of course. I only played a supporting role in the film. For me, this has been a big break. For the paps, I don't exist.

I steady my gait and push ahead, head high, shoulders back, smile in place. Let them focus on Zion and Mala. I'm just happy with the paycheck.

"Twyla! Over here!" a photographer calls from the stands. Surprised that anyone knows my name, I pause and turn, posing the way I've practiced at home these past few weeks.

I take a deep breath in, channeling the voluptuous, sexy woman I saw in the mirror this afternoon. My hair's this luscious fountain of waves flung over one shoulder, my make-up's understated, but soft and flattering. I almost feel like I *belong* here.

Up ahead, the cluster of Zion and Amber, our director, along with Mala and a few other actors, comes to a stop. I edge up to join them, noting Zion as he heads over to chat with a journalist.

"Over here, Twyla! Give us a smile!" I jolt, recover, and swivel again, chest out, the way I've learned: smile in place, chin down, eyes in what I hope is a sultry half-squint. I'm on edge still, but feeling pretty good.

"More! More!"

I push the smile and breathe deep. The bodice tightens.

Someone moves closer. Zion, I think. I flick him a look and see what might be appreciation in his eyes, although I'm probably imagining it, just like I imagined him staring at me a few times on location. The man's always made a point to be friendly with me, but he's never once flirted.

Those weird eye contact moments were wishful thinking.

"Come on, show us what you got!" someone screams. At me? I can't tell. It's confusing and loud. I don't think I'll ever get used to how relentless these people are. One man in particular keeps saying my name like he knows me. Like I owe it to him to smile.

Is this what it feels like to be famous? My expression thins at the edges and, rather than get caught looking anything but calm and pristine, I take in another deep breath and move. In my peripheral vision, I see Amber waving. Farther along, Zion's answering questions. He looks over as I turn and his gaze lingers on my face.

I force myself to move on and take a step, another, getting a little resistance from my dress on the third. It's my shoe again. Something frantic starts to build in my chest as I work to get the thing undone without looking awkward, but the pointy toe is really jammed in there this time. It's as if I'm trapped in a net and then, out of the blue, the tightness just...disappears.

For one second, with the flashing lights and screaming paps, I'm relieved not to feel like I'm suffocating anymore. And then dread rushes in, because what had been a low, but still acceptably modest neckline, is quickly becoming Not Safe For Work and—

Fabric rips, releasing my foot, and the momentum sends me sprawling.

Oh, no. Oh, god.

There's this suspended instant when my palms hit the hard carpet and I twist to keep my face away from the paps. I'm on my hands and knees and the goddess dress is ruined, the hem speared clear through by my spike heel, and just as it feels like nothing could possibly be worse than this moment, the cloth drops another inch and one whole boob literally flops forward, out the top of my bodice.

There's no sound in my head. No shouting or questions. No horrified gasps.

I blink.

I don't know if I breathe. I don't think I move at all. The single clear thought I've got when my brain comes back online is that *anything* would be better than this.

Rewind, rewind, rewind, some part of me is screaming, while I scrabble, one-handed, at my dress, trying to hold it together and drag it up, but my knees and the damn heel have got it pulled too taut to move.

I want to die. Sink into the floor. Blend into the red carpet and disappear.

And then, a body bends over mine, big and warm. It surrounds me, covers me, hides me from the crowd.

Zion?

He makes quick work of removing his jacket and drapes it over my shoulders, then, with gentle hands, takes the offending shoe off, then the other, tugs at the dress's bunched fabric until I get it high enough to cover my chest and stuff my breast in place. It's kind of amazing how he accomplishes all this with a sort of easy grace, as if he helps women back into their clothes in front of audiences every day.

As if that weren't enough, he stands and picks me up without breaking a sweat, my sparkly shoes dangling from one hand.

I'm held tight to his chest now, every part of me covered and properly put together.

The seconds—maybe minutes—that follow go by in a series of chaotic flash-frames. Popping lights, yelling, people running around us. Assistants with shocked expressions. The rest of the cast, Amber, the writer. They gather around.

Farther away, there's laughter, but it doesn't hurt as much as it would outside of Zion's arms.

I hide my face against the soft tux covering his shockingly wide chest, trying to curl up and die, while part of my brain focuses on how unlikely—even shocking—it is that Zion Mason's the one who saw me and stepped in. Me, a nobody, as far as most of the world's concerned. Why was he even looking at me? It's baffling that he, of all people, noticed my emergency.

His big arms tighten around me. "You're good, Twyla," he says, the words vibrating low and solid under my ear, like a heartbeat. "I got you. I got you."

He smells good. Like soap, expensive, fragrant, fresh. A hint of some herbal cologne, so bright and lemony in contrast with the LA exhaust and dust and the perfumes of every person out here.

He whispers, "Mind if I distract them?"

I stare numbly up at his hard, freshly-shaven jaw, his neck, his Adam's apple. "How?"

He swallows, hard, his pupils blow wide. The way he's breathing sounds nervous, almost shaky, but when he clears his throat and speaks, his voice is as solid as ever. As sure. "You good with a kiss?"

I peek out at the crowd, catch sight of that one man laughing—the creep with the mustache who shouted at me—and, without thinking it through, I nod.

Before I've had time to prepare, Zion says. "Tilt your head back," and leans in for the kiss.

Except it's more than that. God, so much more.

First, is the look. It's not steady the way I've seen him look on-screen. It's a quick, almost eager flickering over my face. Against me, his chest is moving up and down, the cadence almost wild. When his gaze finally settles on my mine, there's intensity there, so much emotion.

"Watch me," he urges. "Come on."

His eyes are so fierce and possessive it hurts to hold his stare. And then there's the way his stare slides down to my lips, where it lingers, getting hungry, hungry...

When he leans in, my whole body tightens up in anticipation of the kiss I know is coming.

But then it doesn't.

Maybe it would be too obvious for what he's got planned. And yes, I remind myself, this is all a plan. It's for show. He's a master seducer. A man who knows his way around a camera like no other.

But when he puts his nose to that place in the crook

of my neck—between my ear and my shoulder—and sniffs, I can't help but get goosebumps.

It's stronger than me. More visceral than anything I remember experiencing. And I know, beyond a doubt, that this moment will stay imprinted on my brain forever.

And ever.

I swear everything goes silent at this point. Not a sound from the fans, the paps, even passing cars fade to nothing. In the hush, Zion Mason turns and brushes his lips to mine, waits, and presses in. Lush lips, warm tongue, the oh-so-human scrape of a tooth.

I feel it *everywhere*. Because the man knows how to kiss. And he most certainly knows how to sell it for the cameras.

When he pulls away, I feel alone, cold. His expression is so soft, so real... But I know better than to believe it. When he gives me his signature grin, I dredge up a smile of my own and let him carry me inside like some prize he's caught in the wild.

He sets me down and I'm surrounded by helpful people and put back together, still a mess inside, but somehow saved from ruin.

Hours later, back in the safety of my little one-bedroom, my best friend and agent, Gigi comes over and combs through every single thing that's been shared on-line. "He's a genius," she says as she scrolls. "A goddamn magician."

"What?"

"Not a single nip shot."

"Seriously?" the fear that's kept my chest tight and

my stomach roiling dissipates the tiniest bit. "Let me see."

And here's the thing.

The pictures do show me wretched and ruined on the red carpet, but there's not a single one of my boob. That's how fast Zion got to me. And the other photos? The ones taken with him? He's somehow made it look like I'm some prize he's just won in a...a...gladiator tournament or something.

And the kiss?

It's the most movie-worthy kiss I've ever seen. It's... beautiful. Heartwrenching.

"Look at you. Preciosa," she says, with a sigh. "Better not let your mama see this or she'll have you married by next month."

I'm incapable of ungluing my attention from the screen to respond.

There's not a bad angle, not a body part out of place. The kiss is smoldering hot and looks planned and rehearsed and like it was shot eighty times before being retouched in some studio and also somehow totally spur-of-the moment.

It felt...good. I mean, fine. You know, a screen kiss. Nothing more.

Yeah, right.

Even now, it feels like I'm looking at true love. Zion's the hero, I'm the damsel. He's all hard muscles and deep intensity and I'm lush, flushed innocence and the two of us together are pure romance.

"Shit, babe," Gigi says, sounding as awed as I feel. "This is gonna change everything."

Who could have predicted just how prophetic that statement was?

1

I'm about to kidnap my wife.

No, that's not a euphemism. And no, it's not a joke.

But we're playing here, acting out just one of her many—it turns out—fantasies.

Doing it with a stranger: check. Impact play: check. Pushing every one of her limits: check.

I've yet to find the thing my wife doesn't want and I'll tell you, keeping up with her is killing me. In a good way.

Mostly.

Something snaps under my foot and I go still. Blade, the person I've handpicked to be my wingman, stops beside me. I've known him for years. He's quiet and dependable. Steady and solid and up for just about anything.

Around us, the woods are busy, loud, teeming with life and sounds and the smells you get when it hasn't rained in way too long. There's a heaviness to the air, like maybe a storm's coming.

I hope so. Anything to relieve the tension that's been building since my wife got here.

"That her?" asks Blade, indicating a hint of color shifting between the trees up ahead.

I nod, staring hard at the shocking red of her dress as we set off again, quieter now, careful not to give ourselves away.

The closer we get, the more details I can make out— the dress looks like something Marilyn Monroe would've worn, low cut with a nipped in waist and a skirt that fluffs out all around her. That's where the resemblance ends. She's bigger than Monroe, her curves fuller, softer, her hair a rich, dark brown, and her skin the color of warm sand. She looks like a polka dotted cake and I want to devour every curve and dimple and scar on that sweet, round body. I want to lick her smooth skin and bite into those thick thighs, while my fingers twist into that mound of loose, dark curls. I want to make her squirm.

I'm shocked at how on edge I am going into this. I don't get nervous. Not here, at camp, and not when it comes to my body.

Now that Twyla's in the picture, though, I'm nothing but nerves. There's a whole useless, messed up bundle of them writhing in my gut. Fear and excitement so tightly entwined I'm not sure I'll ever figure out which is which.

Up ahead, she moves a step closer and I come to a sudden stop, close my eyes, breathe in, deep. Beside me, Blade waits. Finally, when I've gotten back at least a little of my normal calm, I look at him and nod. "Definitely her."

How do I know?

I'd recognize her anywhere. Her smell, her taste, and those little sounds she makes. I picture those warm, brown eyes, unfocused in pleasure.

Her shape's clear—short and thick, with tiny ankles and knees and wrists, her waist cinched in and the rest of her gorgeously plush. I want to spread her apart and press my face into all that goodness.

I'm dying to play with her again, even though I had her just this morning.

And the thing about Twyla is that, though her beauty's undeniable, it's the rest of her that pulls me in—her mind, her heart, her sweet, sinful soul.

"Just look at all that," I say, unable to hold my admiration inside.

Blade grins. He knows better than to dwell too long on how good my wife looks, traipsing around in that puffy little dress, those dimpled thighs just begging to be bruised, her throat already showing marks where I held her.

All consensual of course. Everything we've done this week's been just dandy with her—my sweet, clueless little newbie.

The irony in this whole wild thing is that I'm the experienced one and yet, I'm the one who's been torn apart by it. Every exchange, every interaction's shown me that I can't control myself when it comes to Twyla

Hernandez. I'm the one who hungers and wants and chases, while she—

Bends down and picks a flower, brings it to her nose and sniffs.

"She's so cute, man. I'm jealous." Blade throws me a grin that I'd wipe off his face if I didn't need him.

Because Twyla—the woman I married not for love, but for appearances—didn't want just one man to take her and make her do unspeakable things. She wanted two.

That decision alone was a message. A bratty, little nose-snubbing that resonates deep in my bones.

"She's mine," I tell him. It's a warning. A promise. A threat.

"I know, man."

He can touch her, today, but that's it.

Her head tilts at the sound of my voice, though I'm not sure she can actually hear me from the clearing. She doesn't have to, though, not with the connection we've got. She could say my name from a mile away and I swear, I'd break into a sweat.

I don't look at Blade when I start moving again, and I don't wait to make sure he's beside me. He either is or he isn't. Doesn't matter.

"Mine," I growl as we stalk my sweet little wife, giving her exactly what she wants. "She's mine."

All that matters is Twyla. Now, forever, always.

2

FIVE DAYS EARLIER...

Zion

"You..." Twyla's mouth works while she searches for an adequate word. "Are an asshole."

I can't say it's not deserved. "I know. I'm sorry."

"That's it? That's all?" She stops shoving her stuff into her bag and turns to me, all out of breath and pissed off, brown eyes glowing, cheeks flushed. She's beautiful, even angry. Especially angry.

"Not much to say, Twyla. I fucked up." I manage to sound calm and collected, despite how shitty this feels.

"Do you know how many days it's been since we got married?" She lifts one plump hand in the air and wiggles her ring finger, as if I've somehow forgotten that we *just* tied the knot. With difficulty, she yanks my rings off and drops them on the table, where they spin before settling. "Twelve days. That's how long it's been since we entered into this ridiculous *fiasco* of a marriage. Less than two...*freaking* weeks. Must be some kind of record, right?"

Right. Definitely. And it's entirely my fault. I wish—

Her purse starts vibrating for what's got to be the thousandth time today. She stares at it like she wants to punt the damn thing over to the next county. Instead, she drops her head into her hands, closes her eyes, and breathes in, long and slow and deep. "Right." When she looks back up at me, all that fiery emotion's just...gone. Snuffed out like a flame. Her eyes have gone flat, her lips tight.

I don't like this bland version. At all.

Her voice perfectly modulated now, she says, "I'll talk to my team about starting the divorce proceedi—"

The front gate bell goes off again. It's a low, classy chime, chosen by whatever fancy-ass decorator did this place up. I want to grab a hammer and smash the damn thing.

"You going to get that?" Twyla asks, her face still perfectly composed, aside from a slight flaring at her nostrils.

"No," I say. "Security people'll call when they're close. That ain't them."

"Where *are* they, dammit?"

"Stuck in beltway traffic."

The blip of a cop siren out front makes Twyla jump. We both turn to look at the living room windows, where blue and red flashing light seeps in around the heavy curtains. I don't have to head over there to know that it's a complete shitshow outside the tall front wall. There's screaming and chanting and drums and some asshole playing what sounds like the soundtrack to one of my first movies. Probably on a boombox held over their head.

All it took was one goddamn mistake—one leaked video—and we've got what sounds like half the DC population out there either praying for my godless soul or begging for a chance to jump my bones. And, while I'm all for a little action, random, over-the-top fans are not my preferred play partners.

"Come on," I say to Twyla, who's now standing still in the middle of the room. "Let's get outta here."

"Out? And how do you propose we do that?" I follow her into the cold, white-marbled, chef's dream of a kitchen, where she throws open the family-sized fridge and pulls out a bottle of water. "Are you going to strut out and distract them with your..." Her eyes flick down to my crotch, widen, and return to my face, as if she really didn't mean to do that. "Um, stellar personality?" she finishes, her cheekbones flushing a darker pink.

It brings up images I really shouldn't be picturing—tender, hot, red-stained flesh, jiggling from the smack of my hand. Or a paddle. How would a paddle sound against that ample, soft, dimpled—

"Ziooooooooon!" someone screams, so damn loud they've got to be using a megaphone and then, to really dig into my wife's embarrassment, they go on, joined by what sounds like a horde of people, chanting, "Be my daddy! Breed me! Breed me! Breed me!"

"Oh my god." Now, Twyla's skin, usually this warm, rosy beige, has gone grey and unhealthy-looking.

"You can't stay," I do my best to cover the screaming. "It's a goddamn siege. And the security team's nowhere near us." I watch her try to twist the top off the fancy glass bottle. Like everything else, the water itself is a statement: we're rich and special and we accept only the very best. Fucking slow-melted high-altitude mountain-top mineral water, mined by rainbow unicorns and flown in on only the finest Dalai-Lama-blessed aircraft, to be poured straight from elf-blown crystal bottles into our rarified movie star throats. Of course it's not a screw top.

Irritated by the whole thing, but also feeling real shitty about what I've done, I swipe the bottle and knock the cap off on the edge of the counter.

I'd use my teeth like Dad taught me back in third grade, but this set cost me a fortune.

When I hand her the bottle, Twyla rolls those big, expressive eyes. "I'll wait."

"For what? The clown army to breach the wall?"

"I'll be fine."

"You'll need to eat at some point, Twy. I've noticed you get hungry around this time of day."

"You've noticed that?"

"I pay attention."

After a pause, she puts a hand on her belly. "I can't eat. My stomach's a mess from the stress. Besides, casting directors are always telling me I'm too hea—"

"They're pricks." Sudden anger turns my voice low and mean. And sure, this marriage is a twelve-day-old sham set up by our PR teams, meant to keep me out of trouble and to help her rise to fame. We're basically colleagues hanging out in the same house, but there is not a goddamn thing wrong with Twyla Hernandez. Not her sharp brain or voluptuous body or the face that stopped me in my tracks the first time I saw her. She's beautiful on-screen and off it.

Although hell if I know what it is about her that works. Her face is a thrilling combination of round and soft, sharp and smart. Definitely not the look cameras usually like. Not anymore at least. There's something old-fashioned about her that I like. She's got these big eyes that swallow you up and lips that make you want to lean in and touch, they look so goddamn soft.

And the rest of her? Generous hips, round belly, tiny wrists just begging to be wrapped in leather. If she was really mine, I'd...

"Well, I'm fat."

"Nothing wrong with that."

She scans my face as if looking for some underlying meaning to what I'm saying. "I know," she says.

"Good. Cause you're fuckin' *perfect*, Twyla."

Her eyes go wide, her pupils blow open.

My body reacts like she's thrown a switch. I lean in to tell her all the things I think about doing to that dreamy body, when my phone buzzes in my hand. It takes my eyes a second to focus on the screen, a couple more for my brain to kick in and read the text from the security team. "Traffic's at a stand-still on 495. Company's calling in a second team."

"Shit," she mutters, turning away. Good. Distance is good. Last thing we need is another complication.

In the meantime, the volume's dialed up out front, like the crowd's gotten bigger or closer, or more rabid. Feels like everything's closing in, like one of them could breach our front wall and make a break for it any second or find a way through the neighboring properties into the back, which would leave us completely open.

"Come on." I reach for her arm. "We're goin'."

She steps back. "Going where? How? Are you calling a cab? Sending out a bat signal? Everyone's scrambling to handle this catastrophe and you're talking as if you'll just fling on your cape and forge a path through the circus out there. Meanwhile, you're acting like your...*sexcapades* aren't that big of a deal and I'm—"

"Sexcapades?" Referring to the video that was just leaked as a sexcapade is like calling a genocidal dictator a *vewy, vewy* bad boy. "I'm a Dom, Twyla, a power-hungry pansexual, open for pretty much...anything."

Her eyes go a little wide and vague. I can almost imagine that it's curiosity I'm seeing. I push back the wishful rush of... Shit, I don't know what this is. From the second we met, I've never been quite straight in my head when it comes to this woman.

Hardening myself, I go on. "You know what all that means?"

The frustration rising up inside me isn't her fault, it's mine. Or maybe a little bit the fault of the reporter willing to go to such impressive lengths to entrap me. That was true dedication to their trade. And, honestly, it wasn't even worth it. The sex was mediocre, the entire experience empty. Just a little run-of-the-mill power exchange that I barely got it up for.

And now this. The end of a career, the end of a perfectly good fake marriage.

"Pansexual means I'll fuck anybody I feel like, Twyla." Why am I doing this? Why am I rubbing it in? Trying to hurt her. Maybe push her away. As if I need any more help doing that. The thing is, I've got no idea why I'm saying this shit. She's leaving, we're splitting up, our made for the media marriage is over before it started, so... There's no reason to push her buttons. And yet, I can't seem to stop myself. "Sex is sex. And kink is kink. And as long as they're human and I'm into it, I don't care about bullshit things like gender, shape, size. I like cunts and dicks and hot, bruised skin. I like watchin' willing people getting hurt and fucked. I care about—"

"You care about your..." Her eyes flick down to my crotch again. This time, the bastard twitches, more instantly attracted to my pissed-off wife than the person who led us into this hellish situation to begin with. Maybe it's the dumpster fire I've created here, but suddenly all my rock solid lines are blurring. "Why are we even discussing this? It's none of my business."

Dropping my head, I inhale, long and slow, one hand coming up to rub the back of my stiff neck.

Couldn't I just have kept it in my pants another couple weeks? Just a few more days of appearances, and I'd be diving head first into the free-for-all paradise that is Kink Camp. The one place in this world where I can be myself. Not an actor on a set or a PR Ken-doll smiling for flashing cameras at red carpet galas, and definitely not a fake husband to this woman.

My gaze latches onto Twyla's, slotting into place in a way that makes my body go still and blows the breath from my lungs.

This is it, the feeling I got the first time our eyes met. Or even before then. It's—hell, I don't know—recognition, on a base level, almost...molecular. *I know you*, it says.

But the feeling isn't real. It's a lie. She's not mine. For the very simple reason that I don't do vanilla.

No kissing, no relationships, no love.

I'm just not built for it. Never have been, never will be.

And I'm perfectly happy this way. Romance and all the bullshit surrounding it just isn't for me.

Twyla Hernandez and I are just two colleagues, friendly near-strangers, who entered into a mutually-beneficial agreement.

That my dick had to go and ruin.

And I've got no clue how to fix it.

3

Twyla

This is all a terrible mistake.

I shouldn't be here—in this rich person's house, living a celebrity life, dealing with famous person problems.

I belong back in my affordable apartment, going from one half-decent acting job to another, praying that someday I'll get the call for something bigger and better until I'm big enough and influential enough to make films of my own. I've got projects, dammit. I've got plans.

Sadly, no matter how hard I wish things back to where they were, I'm still right here, standing in the fanciest house I've ever even seen. Outside, we're surrounded by paps and religious zealots and deranged fans trying to get to the literal Sexiest Man Alive, who just happens to be my fake husband.

Or, real husband, I guess. We are legally married, after all. There's just no *relationship* behind the marriage.

It's all a business deal, meant to help our respective careers. Both of which he's gone and blown up with his—

No. No, nope. Absolutely not. I cannot allow myself to think about his body parts or that video. Not again. Especially not in *front* of him. It was bad enough earlier in the car ride over, when I first saw the video and went from feeling sick to my stomach to having to squeeze my thighs together and slow my breathing because it literally turned me on.

I was apparently so obvious that the driver asked me if something was wrong.

Wrong? Of course there's nothing wrong. Not my fake husband getting caught on camera doing things with a stranger, not me squirming and breathing fast while looking at the pictures, and above all, not me, filled with anger and excitement and shame, fighting the urge to race home and touch myself.

Talk about mixed signals. Even I can't get my own feelings straight.

Why oh why did I let things get complicated? Why did I let him get to me, with the way he sets my body off and makes me laugh, or the way, in the short time we've known each other, he's always made me feel so cared for.

Yeah, well that was clearly an act. Which shouldn't surprise me, right? I mean, the man's an actor, after all. And this relationship isn't real.

I think of the kiss. And the way we were on the couch the other night. It felt so—

Ugh, I can't even *think* it right now or I'll cry. And that's the last thing I want to do in front of him. My only goal at this point is to get the hell away from this, pride intact.

I mean, what else can I grasp at, now that the person the whole world knows as my brand-new husband has gone and had a seedy encounter with some other woman?

The saddest part, though, is that it hurts. Like actual chest and stomach pain. I'm holding it in, doing my best to hide it, but really, I just want to collapse on the sofa with a soft blanket and a gallon of Neapolitan ice cream and something to drink that will erase my brain for a while.

Although no way could I do it on the comfy upstairs TV room sofa, because that one's been forever ruined by what we did on it. Or didn't do.

Yeah. It's not just the embarrassment—though *my god*, did he have to let her film it?—it's the other thing. The part where I thought he kind of liked me...a little? And if there's a vein of jealousy running through it all, well that's not something I'm ready to look at head on. I clearly misunderstood what happened up there. *Clearly*.

I'm the fool who liked him too much. Hell, the contract even stipulated that there'd be no sexual relationship between us. Of course, it also made extramarital affairs explicitly against the rules. By signing the damn thing, we both basically agreed to having no partnered sex.

At least we were allowed to masturbate. I assume.

Never mind that he's starred in all my fantasies lately. Doing, as it so happens, a few of the things he did to that woman in the video, an irony which is a little too sad for me to process at this moment.

Slapping my hands to the cold marble counter, I make my breathing slow, force my emotions down, and do my best to look completely unbothered by the whole thing. This calm act is all I have right now.

I can't cry. Crying would show weakness and I am *not* weak. Twyla Hernandez doesn't do weakness. No unrequited crushes, no unwise attraction, no feeling sorry for myself. None of it.

You don't survive this industry by giving in when things get tough.

I've survived by using every challenge as a stepping stone. The mean kids at school, the constant pressure to change my looks and my body, to be thinner, less Ecuadorian, more American, not to mention the type-casting I thought I'd never get away from. I've survived it all.

I'll survive this, too. Hell, maybe one day Gigi and I can even laugh about it.

I watch Zion cross to a window and pull back the curtain to look outside. Even betrayal can't take the man's good looks away. In jeans and a well-cut T-shirt, he's all lean, tall grace, light skin tanned to a pale gold, and muscles that dance when he moves. He's Newman's easy smiles, McConaughey's deep, careless dimples, an accent that makes women cream their panties, and lazy blue eyes that go sharp at the worst possible times.

I hate how gorgeous he is, but really, truly, more than anything, I hate that he did this to me, his *friend*.

Okay, so not a great friend. Our romance was a whirlwind, fabricated by a skilled team of PR people. I mean, we were friendly on set and, when we started fake dating, after the red-carpet fiasco, I thought we'd gotten to know each other a bit, but clearly it was only surface level. At least for him.

Gigi knows what kind of sexual stuff I'm into and I know about her proclivities. I mean, we talk, right?

Real friends talk and get to know a bit more about each other than Zion and I have. Also, possibly real friends don't look at their friend's ass and feel all squirmy in their belly.

Probably not, right? I also doubt that real friends wind up in the TV room, all wrapped around each other.

"Nobody's made it into the backyard yet." He drops the curtain and turns back to me, all tall, blond earnestness. God, he's gorgeous. "Come on, Twyla, let's get you someplace safe."

Feeling absolutely foolish for even letting myself care, I lean against a barstool. I'd like to sit on it, but seeing as how it was made for tall, model-types, it would be a struggle and, right now, I've got very little to my name but my pride. Scooching it back, then stepping onto the rung to squeeze my bulk between it and the too-high counter is just a little more effort than I care to show this man.

Besides, he'd totally swoop in to help. I *know* he would, which is so confusing right now I could scream. He'd rush over and pull it out, give me a hand up and help me settle in with those gentle, careful hands.

A sense-memory floods me, curling low in my belly.

His hands aren't gentle at all, are they? They're rough and mean and bossy.

Who the hell is Zion Mason? Who is this man? Is he the nice guy with whom I've cohabitated these past couple weeks or is he the man from the video? Can he be both? Truly? Can you be kind and thoughtful and easy-going one second and then turn into something totally different the next?

I thought we were friends, but we're not.

I need to remember that now.

I don't know him at all. Like millions of fans, I only know what Zion's chosen to show me.

Until now, I suppose.

Unbidden, an image rises up. That woman all stretched out, her limbs cuffed open—even her thighs. The way he smacked her when she wiggled—no gentleness there. The way he shoved his fingers in her mouth until she gagged—

I shut my eyes tight, willing my body not to react, telling my own debauched libido to stand down.

It doesn't want to, though. Neither my body nor my twisted little brain, if I'm being honest, can forget what he did. The thing is, if someone had written up a concise summary of my inner sexual self and recorded it, it would be pretty darn close to that video. The manhandling, the crass, humiliating talk, the idea that she had no power, that he *made* her do those things, turned her into nothing but an object for him to take and use and—

Yeah.

I swallow hard, looking anywhere but at Zion, who,

willing or not, now stars in my late-night masturbation reel. It's not something I seek out in real life, because god forbid anyone find out that I—a young, struggling, Ecuadorian-American actress with a wide ass and lots of opinions—have a penchant for the naughty stuff. But it's the kind of thing I think about. A lot.

The problem is, as a woman, you don't get taken seriously in this industry if you admit to liking sex. Or even having it. Or, you know, getting turned on to images of your fake husband doing it with a stranger.

The thing is, even after two weeks of cohabitation, I don't know Zion. At all.

The man in that video? He was an absolute *beast*.

I force myself to look at him now, pacing the hardwood floor with all that loose, gilded, tiger-in-the-sun strength, and layer that other person on top of this one. The monster from the video, spreading that woman out, tying her up, making her take the blows he gave her. Making her beg.

I swallow.

He catches my gaze, his eyes go wide, then narrow, compounding that predator thing. I just barely keep from shuddering.

"What? What is it? Are you okay?" His voice is low, concerned. Not a tiger. "Here, sit down."

See? He's pulling out the chair, taking care of me. Like he gives a crap.

I ignore it, hating the emotion dripping in to taint my resolve.

This Zion's hard to stay angry at, though. He's the

man I met on set. So kind. So real. Just a good person, to everyone. Every actor, every crew member and catering person. That kindness, from someone as untouchably famous is rare, and all the brighter for it.

Zion Mason was nothing like I'd expected. I mean, he definitely was the hot, 34-year-old blond charmer with a Texas accent and a smile that people fell for like flies. He also had a bit of a reputation for being a bad boy, but in reality, everyone loved him.

And I was a nobody. Or a pseudo-nobody. I got work. In Hollywood, that's miraculous. I certainly didn't expect to get *that* job, which gave me on-screen time with America's leading man.

Then, at the LA premiere, everything changed.

It was my first big red carpet event. I arrived in this deep, rich scarlet dress that celebrated my curves rather than trying to hide them. It was a little tight around my chest and a little long, but I could handle it for three hours. My hair was this luscious fountain of waves flung over one shoulder, my makeup understated, soft, and flattering. Despite the fact that I teetered on the shoes and nearly tripped on the dress twice, I felt almost like I *belonged* there. Almost.

I remember stepping out of the limo, gliding past the screaming fans who strained against the barriers surrounding the walkway. I was guided between swaths of photographers and industry people. The excitement crescendoed and I realized why: Zion Mason was up there, larger than life, smiling that devastating smile as the cameras went off, his muscular build caressed by the elegant lines of his tux.

I continued, floating on a euphoric blend of nerves and excitement.

"Twyla! Over here!" a photographer called from the stands. Surprised that anyone knew my name, I paused, turned, and smiled, chin down, eyes in what I hoped was a sultry half-squint.

"More! More!"

It was confusing and loud, the photogs relentless. One man in particular kept saying my name like he knew me. Like I owed him a smile. I pushed the smile and moved on, breathing deep, the bodice tightening. With my first step, I got a little resistance from my dress. I paused, tugged the skirt out, and moved on. With the next step, the toe of my shoe got fully caught in the gauzy under-layer. With every attempt to free it, the snag seemed to get worse, until, in nightmarish slow-motion, I fell.

Even trying *not* to picture it now, I get sweaty. The dress being yanked down, speared by the shoe. My boob popping out the top and flopping down.

I don't know if I breathed. I don't think I moved at all. The single clear thought I had when my brain went back online was that *anything* would be better than this.

Rewind, rewind, rewind, some part of me was screaming, while I scrabbled, one-handed, at my dress, trying to drag it up.

I wanted to die. Sink into the floor. Blend into the red carpet and disappear.

And then, a body bent over mine, big and warm. It surrounded me, covered me, hid me from the crowd.

Zion.

He made quick work of removing his jacket and draping it over my shoulders to shield me from view. With gentle hands, he took the offending shoe off, then the other, and tugged at the dress's bunched fabric until it was high enough to cover my chest. I unceremoniously stuffed my boob back inside.

Finally, he stood and hefted me up without breaking a sweat, my shoes dangling from one hand. He held me like that, tight to his chest, every part of me covered and properly put together.

The seconds—maybe minutes—that followed went by in a series of chaotic flash-frames: popping lights, yelling, people running around us. Assistants with shocked expressions. The rest of the cast, the director. I hid my face against the soft tux covering Zion's shockingly wide chest, trying to curl up and die, while part of my brain focused on how unlikely it was that Zion Mason would be the one to save me from my horrifying wardrobe fail. It was baffling that he, of all people, noticed my emergency.

His big arms tightened around me. "You're good, Twyla," he said, the words vibrating low and solid under my ear, like a heartbeat. "I got you. I got you."

He smelled amazing. Like soap, expensive, fragrant, fresh. A hint of some herbal cologne, so bright and lemony in contrast with the LA exhaust and dust and the perfumes of every person out here.

He whispered, "Mind if I distract them?"

I stared numbly up at his hard, freshly-shaven jaw, his neck, his Adam's apple. "How?"

He swallowed, hard, his pupils blown wide. The way he was breathing sounded nervous, almost shaky, but when he cleared his throat and spoke, his voice was as solid as ever. "You good with a kiss?"

I peeked out at the crowd, caught sight of that one man laughing—the creep with the mustache who'd shouted at me—and, without thinking it through, nodded. Before I had time to prepare, Zion said. "Tilt your head back."

And then he leaned in for the kiss.

Except it was more than just that. God, so much more.

First, there was the look. It wasn't steady the way I'd seen him on-screen. It was a quick, almost eager flickering over my face. Beneath me, his chest moved up and down, the cadence almost wild. When his gaze finally settled on mine, there was intensity there, so much emotion.

"Watch me," he urged. "Come on."

His eyes were so fierce and possessive it hurt to hold his stare. And then there was the way his gaze slid down to my lips, where it lingered, getting hungry, hungry...

When he leaned in, my whole body tightened up in anticipation of the kiss I knew was coming.

Except it didn't. Not right then.

That's when I remembered that he was a master seducer. A man who knew his way around a camera like no other.

But when he put his nose to that place in the crook of my neck—between my ear and my shoulder—and sniffed, I couldn't help but get goose bumps. It was stronger than me. More visceral than anything I remember experiencing. And I knew, beyond a doubt, that the moment would stay imprinted on my brain forever.

And ever.

I swear everything went silent. Not a sound from the fans, the paps, even passing cars faded to nothing. In the hush, Zion Mason turned and brushed his mouth to mine, waited, and pressed deeper. Lush lips, warm tongue, the oh-so-human scrape of a tooth.

I felt it *everywhere.* Because the man knew what he was doing. And he most certainly knew how to sell it for the cameras.

When he pulled away, in contrast, I felt alone, cold. His expression was so soft, so real... I knew better than to believe it. When he gave me his signature grin, I dredged up a smile of my own and let him carry me inside like some prize he'd caught in the wild.

Later, when my friend and agent Gigi and I pored over every video out there, Zion's mastery became even clearer. With my back to the photogs and the way he swooped in to hide me, the cameras didn't catch a single shot of my nip slip.

And the kiss?

It was the most movie-worthy moment I've ever seen. The kiss that launched a million TikToks, that spawned a full-fledged career for me and, well, a fake marriage for the two of us.

There's not a bad angle, not a body part out of place. Our embrace was smoldering hot and seemed planned and rehearsed and shot eighty times before being retouched in some studio and also somehow totally spur-of-the moment.

It looked like true love. Zion was the hero, I was the damsel. He was all hard muscles and I was lush, flushed innocence and the two of us together were pure, pure romance.

It felt…good. I mean, fine. You know, a screen kiss. Nothing more.

Right.

So, that was the moment. No doubt about it.

The very next day, I got offers, interviews, designers offering—no, *begging* for—collaborations where they'd design whole plus-size lines in my image.

How could I say no to that?

Everything changed because of that kiss. And not just for me. I got inundated with messages from kids, telling me I'd changed their lives. Little fat girls, Latina teens. Moms and dads telling me I'd made all the difference in their babies' lives. Just by being me. By being beautiful.

And, yeah, the idea that it all stemmed from a kiss still doesn't sit right, but, as Gigi said: We'd be fools to turn away from this chance to do something good.

Even Zion's career wasn't immune to that red carpet miracle magic. His people went on and on about ratings, about reputation, about how that kiss—and the idea that the two of us were together—turned his dubious personal reputation squeaky clean. And the roles he was being offered suddenly changed.

The savior thing, it turned out, wasn't entirely one-way. He helped put me on the map and I gave him the kind of gravitas his career had been missing.

"You know Zion, I wish—" Snapping out of my memory of that night, I flounder, unsure of what I'm even about to say to him, but it's probably unwise and embarrassing. It'll probably make me cry.

Whatever it is, I don't get a chance to say it because that's when the front window smashes in with a deafening crash and the tinkling shatter of glass. Right behind it, the confused ruckus from the street outside comes rushing in and it's *loud*.

"Brick!" Zion has to yell through the noise. "Shit! They got over the wall."

I don't understand. There's police out front, holding people back. How did someone get through? It's a numbers thing, I realize as the screaming pulses in through the gash in the window. Too many people, too much hysteria to keep out. Under pressure, the dam broke.

Fear swoops in. Before it can engulf me, Zion grabs my purse and computer bag, leaving my suitcase on the floor. "Come on," he says, leading the way to the back door.

Our surroundings blur as we race out into the small, walled courtyard behind the house.

Without hesitation, Zion grabs my hand and sprints to the far wall, bends to give me a leg up, then follows me over. Through a garden, left, then over another wall. A manicured yard, green and pristine. Another wall into a wilder, more tropical garden. Everything smells like grass and exhaust and chlorine from a pool we barely miss falling into.

It's a scene from a million movies, only there's no musical soundtrack to make it exciting and every single fence is a struggle I'm not sure I'll get over.

Another wall and we drop down to the terrifying sound of barking.

Only, when we turn to look, it's one of those fluffy little white dogs that looks more bunny that canine, with a black face and long ears. It squeals up a storm until Zion picks it up and whispers into its ear and sets it down again, upon which the tiny thing follows him around like he's a god. No different from everyone else, I suppose. As soon as we clear the gate, it starts yapping again, more annoyed with our departure than our arrival.

Just one more being on this earth who's instantly obsessed with Zion Mason. Whatever.

By the time we run out onto a smaller side street, the crowd's roar from our place has faded, my lungs are pure fire, and my sandals have rubbed my feet raw.

Zion puts a hand out to stop me. "You okay?"

"Fine," I just manage to gulp out between breaths. Sweat's streaming down my face.

We've walked maybe a dozen feet up the road when Zion's phone buzzes. He answers, gives our location, and then pulls me back into the shadow of an overgrown azalea. "We've gotta wait," he says. "He's around the corner."

I nod in acceptance, watching every car that passes, frightened that they'll see us, recognize us—or Zion, at least—and start the whole nightmare over again.

It takes a while for me to catch my breath and stop shaking from the adrenaline rush and, sad sack that I am, I can't help but wish he'd put his arm around me, because I'm cold and I'm tired and scared. At the same time, I hate myself for wanting that from him. Wanting anything at all.

"What can I do? What do you need?" nice guy Zion asks, looking caring and concerned. Looking like he means it.

"Just get me outta here." I don't trust my voice not to break, so rather than tell him how betrayed I feel, I wave him back and step farther into the shadows.

Maybe two minutes go by, maybe five, while I stand hunched, only a couple feet away from Zion, but somehow as far from each other as two humans can get. He barely looks at me and doesn't talk and I can't help but feel remorse for pushing him away.

Although I didn't have to try that hard. The deeper we get into this nightmare, the more convinced I am that I imagined the closeness between us.

Isn't that pathetic?

When a huge, dirty pickup turns onto the road, it's so different from every other car that's passed that it sends my nerves rocketing again and even Zion's arm slipping around my shoulders doesn't help. I wish he wouldn't touch me. I wish my body didn't enjoy it quite so much.

Finally, the truck comes to a stop directly in front of us. The passenger door creaks open. "Get in," comes a deep voice from the dark interior.

Zion grabs my hand. "Come on."

4

Zion

We're quiet as Liev King—one of very few people in this world I give a shit about—calmly negotiates Friday night Georgetown traffic, avoiding the massive mess around our place, and gets us the hell out of DC.

Once on the highway, Liev relaxes back in his seat and glances at Twyla. "Evening."

"Twyla Hernandez, Liev King."

She offers him a tight smile. "Thank you. For showing up when you did."

"Of course. Anything for my bestie and his wife." Liev sends me a smirk, just visible under the passing street lights. "I'm glad to meet you, Twyla. If you two hadn't gone off and eloped, we might have met already." He flicks me a quick look, one eyebrow raised. "What's the plan? Am I taking you both to camp?"

"No," I say, nowhere near fast enough to cut him off.

"Camp?" she asks.

Liev looks straight out at the road.

"Liev's house. I go there every summer. We just call it camp."

"Camp? Sounds fun." Her voice is light, completely uninterested. I guess it's back to the ice queen routine.

I still don't like it. I like the smart, snarky Twyla I've gotten to know. A woman who's as serious as I am when it comes to work, who respects my privacy, and gives me space. On the other hand, just the other night, she laughed so hard she almost pissed her pants. At a cartoon. On the sofa in the cozy den upstairs. With popcorn.

That was the night I realized what a terrible idea this whole marriage thing was. Not because I didn't want my sweet, vanilla wife, but because I wanted her way too much.

So I went out and really fucked it all up.

"You're welcome to come," says Liev, ignoring my glare.

"I appreciate that," she tells him, shifting a little in the seat between us. "But I'd better find my own way."

She squirms again, the movement releasing a warm, floral scent into the air. Not like perfume so much as an actual flower. Except that's not it either, 'cause it's not like I picture a bouquet when she's this close. I picture her warm skin, smooth and soft and shiny with oil. I picture rope burn and bruises and deep red handprints. I can almost hear the way she'd—

She glances up at me and I start guiltily, easing right to keep my quickly-hardening cock from going anywhere near her.

Just then, her phone rings and, to my relief, she puts it to her ear, voice low, though I hear most of what she's saying. It's her agent, I'd guess.

My phone buzzes a few minutes later. The security team. They're close. After a quick exchange, I hang up.

"Next exit," I tell Liev quietly, while Twyla continues her murmured conversation.

He pulls right, driving the way he does everything—smoothly, well, entrenched in his own deep sense of calm.

I cast a quick glance down at my wife.

Wife.

Not for long.

Her leg moves against mine—soft and strong and warm—and that movie night comes back to me again. I remember the wide-mouthed, low bellied laughs she let out, and then the way she hid under the blanket when I convinced her to let me watch *The Thing* after the *Ice Age* credits rolled. She fell asleep there, all wrapped up next to me. And, fuck, her little round, solemn face, the freckles scattered across her nose, making her look young and sweet and innocent, when she's actually got one hell of a dark sense of humor on her.

She shifts again, settling her round booty deeper into the truck's center seat and—*hell*—now I'm thinking about the scattering of freckles I spotted right at that line between her ass and thigh when the blanket fell back and her sleep shorts were all bunched up at her waist and I spent a full 45 minutes wondering if she had panties on under there. Then she woke up, looked at me with those soft, sleepy eyes and I had to—

Yeah. The whole marriage as a way to keep people away plan sure fucking backfired.

Drawing in a deep breath, I look out the window. "Park and ride, right lane," I tell Liev, careful not to disturb Twyla's intense-sounding call.

"That them?" He pulls the truck to a stop a few spaces from a dark SUV.

"Probably."

Twyla looks up. "I'd better go, okay? Touch base tomorrow."

I try to catch her eye. She avoids me.

My gut's heavy when I get out of the truck and head over to the SUV. "Y'all are right on time," I tell the security people, after they've shown me ID. "Let's get my wife to a safe place, okay?"

They watch her with a little too much interest as she walks over. I give them a hard stare and a split second later remember that I've got no claim on this woman—not even a fake one.

They nod through greetings and explanations with Twyla, who appears totally unfazed now. Cool as a goddamn cucumber.

Once she's slid into the backseat of their car, I put up a hand. "Give us a sec, y'all."

The two men back away. She flashes me a narrow-eyed look. Of course she resents me. Hates me. It's not like I don't deserve that.

"All right," I lean on the open door, careful not to box her in. "I guess this is it."

She nods and looks away, probably wishing me gone already.

Regret rushes in to swamp me. "Hey, Twy, listen." I bend and lower my voice. "I'm sorry. Truly." A real husband would reach for her hand or something. Goddamnit, I want to, but everything about her body language is telling me to back the hell off.

"Are you?" Her eyes meet mine, huge and dark, her expression shifting somewhere between hurt and accusatory.

"Of course. I didn't mean for... I'm sorry it happened."

She snorts. "Sure you're not just sorry you were caught?" Oh, there's the anger again, sharp and bright.

"I mean it. I fucked up. Problem is, the shit's only just hit the fan, it'll get—"

"Shittier?"

"I'm sorry. Truly." I want to grab her hand or hug her, but she's so prickly, she'd probably bite me. Not that I'd mind. "Anything you need, I'll make sure you get. Anything."

"Thank you." Her eyes search my face, maybe looking for something redeemable in my expression. Apparently coming up empty, she turns to the security team. "I'd like to get a rental car, please." She reaches for the door as if I'm not here.

I close it for her, nod at the driver, and watch them take off.

Minutes later, I'm back in the truck beside Liev, going west on 66, windows wide open, damp early summer wind blowing through my hair, like the first taste of freedom.

Only tonight it's not like that. I swallow. Tonight, it's like something's missing. Like Kink Camp's not where I'm supposed to be headed, although I know for a fact it is. It's my escape every single summer. The one place I'm real. Me.

"Want to turn back?" Liev asks, not looking my way.

"What? No. No. Why would I?" I stare out at the quickly changing landscape, where buildings and houses and intersections give way to woods, low rolling hills growing steadily in the distance. "Easier this way."

He shakes his head and sighs.

"What?"

"Easier's not always better, man. You know that."

"It is in this case," I say. And then, as if I've got to convince him—or someone—I go on. "It absolutely is."

5

Twyla

I'm finally alone.

An hour later, I drive out of the rental car lot, follow the first highway sign I see, and take a random right, which leads me south. Fine. South, north, whatever. I just need space. To cry, maybe yell a little, feel sorry for myself in privacy, and then figure out what comes next.

My phone's been blessedly silent for a while now. This doesn't seem like a problem until I reach into my purse and come up empty, check my computer bag. No phone there either. Uh oh.

Panic starts to build.

I pull over at the first place I see—a fast food place— park next to the building, and empty both bags onto the front seat of the car.

There's all kinds of useless crap, including six freaking lip balms, crusty, loose ibuprofen pills, a pen top, and a half-wrapped tampon. But no phone. Frantic now,

I lean back and concentrate... When did I last use it? Not with the security teams, definitely. Crap. And, with the number of calls I was getting, I turned on Do Not Disturb, so it wouldn't ring, even if I had some way of finding it. My last call, I remember, was with Candace, who does my PR.

The phone is in the pick-up, with Zion.

Great, just great. What am I gonna do without a phone? I'll be cut off from—

My eyes land on my laptop.

With a squeal, I open it and log in to the restaurant's wifi. Three seconds later, it starts ringing. Gigi. Thank god.

I answer and my screen lights up on my best friend and agent, also in a car, clearly on the freeway. It's still daytime in LA and she is so perfectly Gigi—gorgeous light brown skin, pristine, perfectly-shaped brows, massive mirrored sunglasses, and crimson lips—that I want to cry.

"Oh my god, you're alive." Her attention flicks from the phone to the road and back, her expression finally landing on puzzlement. "Where are you? Why haven't you answered my calls and... Wait. Are you hiding under a bridge or something? Oh my god. Did the paps corner you? I thought the security team got you to—"

"I'm fine," I interrupt, stemming her flow of words before they turn into a tidal wave. "I'm just hangin' in a McDonald's parking lot. You know. Old times."

"What?" She grimaces. "We never did that."

I snort. "I know." The relief of seeing her loosens

something in my throat and, before I know it, tears are trying to force their way up and out. I can't, though. Not yet. Not until I'm all cocooned someplace safe. If it starts now, it'll never stop.

"Oh, TeeTee, babe. Don't do it. You know how I am. If you start, I'll lose it and then we're fucked." I hiccup out a laugh. "Come on. What's going on? Just give me the CliffsNotes and we'll get you home."

"Home?" I let a little bitterness through. It's better than losing my shit in a McDonald's parking lot someplace in... Where am I? Northern Virginia? "Where's home?"

"You can always stay with me."

"I'm not squatting in your living room, Geege."

"Whatever. It'll be like college. My bed's big enough for—"

"I lost my phone."

"What?"

"It's in his truck. Well, not his. His friend's truck. This big, buff white guy, a little older and kind of solid. A painter or something, maybe? His jeans were dirty. Liev...something."

"Shreiber or King?"

"King."

"You're shitting me."

"What?"

"Liev *King?* The sculptor? The one who..." She's still driving, her sunglass-covered eyes facing the road—I hope —but her hand's doing an explicit up and down.

"What are you doing? What is that?"

"He's the artist who did the obelisk? The new one? On the mall in DC? You're the one who lives—"

"Lived."

She ignores my interruption, as usual. "In DC, for god's sake. Didn't you see it? And, you know, all those sex agony pieces that were all over the place a couple months ago. The New Yorker, the Post, TikTok? Remember?"

"Ohhhh, right." The sculptures come back to me: piles of people writhing in an almost feral ecstasy. "He's really good."

"What's he like?"

"Nice?" I shrug, fiddling with my computer. "Fine?"

"You're hopeless. You know the guy's a recluse, right? Like mega famous and nobody ever sees photos of him. I'd love to meet..." She peers at me as I open apps on my computer. "What are you doing now?"

"Tracking down my phone."

"Any luck?"

I click on the location and lean in to stare at the map that pops up on my screen.

The address is 2349 Old Camp Road in a place called Blackwood, Virginia. That's it. That's the place. "It's at camp."

"What?"

"They said they were going to camp. And that's where it is."

"Grown men? O-kay..."

"It's Liev's place. On Old Camp Road. South of here. Hang on. I'm googling the address." There's not much to see. A few photos with fall foliage and mountains. "Looks pretty. Way out in the country. Wait. Let me try... Liev... King..." I type his name and the address.

The results are not what I expected.

"What the hell?" Every hit seems to be referring to something called Camp Haven. "Okay. This is not what I expected."

"What? What? What is it?"

I click on the official Camp Haven link, confirm that I'm over 18 and enter a site dedicated entirely to the BDSM lifestyle. In great, vivid detail.

"Holy shit." What am I seeing here? What is this?

"Put me out of my misery and tell me what's going on."

"I think..." All the emotion I've been fighting dries up as I take in this totally unexpected new development. "It's a sex camp. Zion's gone to a kinky sex camp."

"Hang on, stop. Stop talking. I'm pulling over."

By the time Gigi's pulled into a fast-food lot of her own, I'm knee deep in the type of uber personal images that no one in their right mind should be sharing on the internet. The heaviness in my chest is gone, replaced by surprise and curiosity and, if I'm being honest, more than a touch of excitement. The anger inside me shifts, simmering harder, sending all the hurt back up to the surface. "This is it, Gigi. This is where he goes."

"Website."

I send her the link and keep scrolling and scrolling, my stomach tense, while other parts of me, parts farther south, grow heavy and hot.

I can't help it.

"You're into this shit," Gigi says, knowing me all too well. "This is like the *thing* for you. This, right here. The chains and the torture and the—"

"Hey! I told you that when I was drunk. You're not supposed to bring it up."

"You're into the..." She lowers her voice as if someone else will hear. "Forced sex fantasy thing."

My heart's going wild, my insides are a mess. I want to deny it, but I can't. Not to Gigi. She's the one person who knows.

"Wait. Wasn't there a guy... Oh my god. There was!" I know what she's going to say before she opens her mouth. "That white guy with all the piercings. What was his name? The batting you about the face with his—"

"Don't say it!"

"You know? The one who—"

"Please, Gigi. Come on. That was—"

"The batting you about the face with his cock guy," she finishes. So darned stubborn. "The man who got away."

"What? He didn't get away. I broke up with him."

"Because..."

"He was weird."

"It wasn't because he smacked your face with his penis?"

I stifle a laugh. "You *know* that isn't why I broke up with him. It was the other stuff. Remember the weird food hangups? Remember? And the—"

"Fish! Oh my god, that was Fish Guy."

"Yep. I broke up with him because of the fish."

She watches me, eyes big, mouth shut. I know what she's thinking. We've been friends for that long.

And what she's thinking is that the man in question, Eric Witmer, was odd in many ways, but I stayed with him for longer than I should have because of my very specific sexual proclivities.

I'd never explored them until him.

She smiles. "You *reallllly* liked getting slapped with his penis."

My "shut up" has no oomph, because she's so totally right. I loved it.

"You were also into the spanking, the getting tied up, and the trash-talking, slut-calling stuff." She shakes herself. "Not for me, thanks."

She doesn't see me roll my eyes.

"Oh, and you loooooooved when he shoved his—"

"I'm done here."

"Wait. You should go to the camp."

"What? No way."

"Yes."

"Why?"

"Because the SMA is there."

"I wish you wouldn't call him that."

"What Sexiest Man Alive? But he is."

"Not really," I lie.

"Are you saying it doesn't get your goat that the man who convinced you to marry him—"

"You're the one who convinced me."

"Potato, potahto. The fact is, he promised you a gold

mine and then literally destroyed every single thing you've worked for in—"

"Literally *everything*?"

"Your entire career's down the drain. People are saying the worst shit."

"Whoa, whoa. Wait, Gigi. Hold on." I straighten in my seat. "It's not *that* bad. Is it?"

A pause, during which every terrible feeling comes rolling back in.

"It's bad."

"Really?" I whisper. "Like, on a scale of one to ten and ten is—"

"Bad." She sighs. "Just don't check social. Honestly, don't check anything."

I glance up when a car pulls in beside me, and frantically turn my computer so the family innocently heading out for kiddie meals doesn't get permanently scarred by what's on my screen.

My stomach's a roiling mess of emotions. "So, I'm just supposed to...take it? Is this it? The end? The moment I accept that my career's over and I'm homeless, sitting in a rental car that smells like weird crayons..."

"Wasn't someone supposed to get you to a hotel?"

"I couldn't deal with the security detail. Glorified babysitters." I think of the way Zion fobbed me off on them, like he couldn't wait to get rid of me, so he could go freaking play in a sex camp. And then, god, then, I remember the thing that happened earlier this week when I woke up in front of the TV and we... I shut my eyes hard on the memory. "When did it happen, do you know?"

"What, you mean the..."

"Sex tape. Yeah. When was it made?"

"Um, he met her at some art opening, I think? That's what she's claiming, which, you know, I could—"

"It's true." Suddenly, I'm numb. Three nights ago, he and I had what I'll allow myself to think of as a near-miss —thank god—and apparently the very next night, while I read for a casting director, he went out and did...the *thing*, with that woman.

While I was channeling a young, hard-nosed Prosecuting Attorney, fighting for justice, he was out doing dirty things with someone else.

I doubt I'll get the part now.

Eyes unfocused, I watch the family head inside before dragging the computer back so I can see the full screen, whips, chains, and all. "Why did he do it? Why offer the marriage thing if he was just going to go and mess it all up?"

"Just couldn't help it, I guess."

"Fine. Fine, if he couldn't help himself. I wouldn't care about that if it didn't involve me, you know?" My voice is getting higher, louder. "We've all heard the rumors. This just confirms them, right?"

I'm too worked up to hear her reply. "This'll be a blip for him. Just another wild boy getting his rocks off. But, no, he had to go and marry me and drag me into it. Gah! Selfish prick!"

I'm yelling now, my voice shrill, raw. My eyes filled

with tears that I will absolutely not, ever, no way, not for one single second shed over the guy who just turned my life into a nightmare. No way will I let him get to me. No way.

A message pops up on my screen. It's from my PR person, Candace: *Whatever you do, don't get online. DO NOT.*

I blink at it, then force my gaze back to Gigi, every cell in my body blazing. "Tell me, Geege. Tell me now. What are people saying?"

"It's a shitstorm. Don't even look. Throw that computer away if you have to. Just..." Her expression is as serious as I've ever seen it. "Promise you'll stay offline."

"Tell me."

"I mean... You know. He's a stud." Eye roll. "And you're...all the bad woman things."

I can imagine it perfectly. Every single slur I've ever received, times a million—about my size, my origins, my skin color, my looks, lack of talent, and on and on. I've seen it all before. Except now...

"So, that's it for me? Might as well retire? Become a preschool teacher?"

"Or a phlebotomist."

"You don't even know what that means," I say, with a grudging half-smile. Inside, though, all the emotion's coiling tighter, tighter... "Fucker," I say, sitting back in my seat. "He's there, right now, having wild, kinky sex with whoever the hell he wants, and I'm hanging here, like a...a...a..."

"Chad?"

I'm too pissed to acknowledge her attempt at humor. "I'm sitting in a literal parking lot, lost and... Shit."

"What's wrong?"

"I should have told him."

"Should have told him what?"

"That he's a jerk. That I hate how badly he's fucked me over, while he comes out of the whole thing scot-free."

"Amen."

"That he's not the only one who needs to get his rocks off occasionally. That if he was going to run around getting filmed having dirty sex he damn well shouldn't have dragged me into it." I think back to the cab of the pickup truck and how I sat there, quiet, my mind racing, too uncomfortable in the silence between him and his friend to have it out with him.

"It's not okay, dammit."

"Sure isn't."

"And he was so...cold. Emotionless about the whole thing. Like, how could he stand there like some...some... icicle, while he literally blew up my career, my entire life." I swallow back the hurt working its way through me. This isn't about hurt. It's about the rest of it. The lack of consequences or acknowledgement or any recognition at all. "He asked for the marriage, Gigi. It was him."

"Yes it was."

"So why am I the one losing a career? Why am I the one taking a hit on social and in the tabloids? Huh?"

She inhales, watching me with sad eyes. "We both know why."

I nod. Yeah. We do. Because it's a shitty system,

rigged against women from the start. Because I fell into the trap of thinking that I could use the system to my advantage. What fucking hubris, right? Well, I've learned my lesson. I have. I just wish it wasn't so one-sided. "He's come out of this looking like a god." Gigi doesn't say a word. "He gets to just slam the door, say goodbye, and go whistling off to this sex camp, like the whole thing was just a minor inconvenience."

"A bump in the road."

"Not even! Not even a blip." The pain's back in full force, but it's intertwined with something else now, something sharp-edged and strong. "Was this the plan all along? Did he always intend to take me down? Is that the kind of toxic person he is? I mean, he's at a sex camp this very minute. Like he couldn't wait a single second, couldn't take a moment out of his day to help deal with the aftermath. He was always going to go ahead and just live the life he wanted, wasn't he? God, he's made such a fool of me."

And to top it off, he'll face absolutely no consequences. That doesn't seem fair at all, given the nightmare my life's bound to become.

Gigi's silence speaks volumes.

In the next instant, everything goes hard. Solid. Cold. "I'm going."

"Where?"

"To the kink camp. To Camp Haven."

"Uh, no. Not a good idea, TeeTee, you've still got a career, you've got to—"

"I've got to nothing. Nothing, okay? What I'm

supposed to be doing is auditioning and working. But that's not happening right now, is it?"

"Probably not," she concedes. "I'm dealing mostly with media."

All that anger's hardening inside me into this dead certainty. The fizzle of hurt's disappeared. I can't explain it, but it feels good. It's something to hold on to. I've gone from being the weak victim here to powerful, unbreakable. "I'm doing this. I'm going."

"Why's that, again?"

I scroll through the pages, scanning confidentiality agreements and registration forms and consent rules and all kinds of legal stuff.

The hard thing inside me is growing, getting stronger. "I'm confronting him."

"Didn't you do that today?"

"Not really. Not the way I should have. This is different."

"How?"

"I'll figure it out." I bend forward, enunciating each word. "But that asshole destroyed my life and took off for his next orgy without blinking an eye and I'm not okay with that."

"Fucker."

"I'll come up with a plan when I get there."

"I wish I could come with."

"I know, Gigi."

She breathes out a long, audible breath. "Just don't make things worse for yourself, okay?"

"I won't. This isn't about revenge."

"You sure?"

"This is for *me*. I need to confront him, that's all. I need resolution."

Now, she's tilting her head back and forth, considering. "Okay. Okay. I get that."

"I just want one *real*, honest conversation, you know? One face to face. One chance for him to...to...to get how *badly* he's fucked me over. You know?"

"I do. I know, Tee. Okay. Let me book you a hotel." Louder now, she says, "Give me a minute and I'll find you a store, too."

"A store?"

"Do you happen to have kink-friendly clothing in your suitcase?"

I look at the seat beside me. "I don't even have my suitcase."

"Girl." She pulls her laptop up, opens it, and types away. "Okay, I've got your location. Now...we can get you a Hilton...Um, ha. Just kidding. Days Inn."

"Whatever."

"Ooooh, check out The Secret Box, two towns over. Featuring sex toys and clothing and..." She ignores my groan. "You've got a Target, too. You'll want some regular clothes. Shoes. Sex shoes and I don't know, flip-flops for showering? Are the showers communal? Sneakers, for when you're not, you know, kinking it up."

"I'm not staying there. I just need an outfit. One."

"Ooooooh, yeah. A really good outfit." She bites her lip, typing like a demon. "A *you-screwed-me-so-I'm-*

gonna-make-you-regret-it-forever outfit. The outfit he will forever remember you in."

"Listen..."

"Links are sent. I'll call the sex shop in the morning and brief them on what you need. And I'll place a Target order for pick-up. You need body wash and razors and underwear. Oh, and condoms, in case—"

"I'm not going there to get my rocks off. Just because he ignored the stipulations in our contract doesn't mean I plan to. You know what, Gigi, I'll figure it out."

"Have you done this before? Purchased a sex-camp appropriate wardrobe?"

"No, but you've got better things to do than—"

"Not really. Besides, I'm not doing it just for you. I'm doing it for all of womankind."

"That doesn't make sense."

"Are you pissed?"

I breathe deep, letting the anger sear the inside of my lungs. "Yes. Yes, I am."

"Enraged?"

"Like fire." It's burning my stomach, lava, hot and thick enough to choke on.

"Good. Good. Now, I want you to go there and I want you to show the Shittiest Man Alive that he doesn't get to have his filthy little sex cake and eat it, too."

"Ew. I draw the line at cake-sitting."

"Agreed. It's a waste of perfectly good cake." She giggles and I join her, totally wiped out, but not nearly as alone as I was an hour ago.

Anger, it turns out, feels way better than self-pity.

"You good?"

"I don't know. I kind of feel like you're sending me into Mordor right now."

"Omg, is that one of your Lord of the Rings references? Please don't ever say anything like that to the media. Or at sex camp. Or to your husband."

"Don't call him my husband."

"The man to whom you are legally wed. Wedded? Wed."

"The man you advised me to legally—"

"Potato, potah—"

"Will you come?"

"You know I would." And she would, if she weren't scrambling to save what she can of my career. "Now go."

"Yes, ma'am." I reach for the ignition, picturing myself showing up at this sordid sex place Zion apparently goes to every summer, planting myself in front of him, his expression when he sees me... Beyond that, I have no idea.

6

———

Zion

Probably most people wouldn't get it. But to me, Camp Haven is home. Liev's amazing house doesn't hurt and his woman greeting me at the door with a beer and a hug doesn't either, but it's more than that.

I know what it means to pretend. I do it constantly. Everywhere but here. Hell, it's easy being on set and saying someone else's lines when I've gotta improv the rest of the time.

Liev's partner, Grace, meets us at the door in her usual summer outfit: a hacked-up band T-shirt, cut-off jean shorts, and flip-flops, with miles of pale skin, featuring tattoos of her own design.

"I'm so glad you made it," she says, not quite letting go of our hug as she draws me inside.

Liev's eyes follow the movement, but there's not an ounce of jealousy there, not a second's hesitation. Grace is his, so totally, so fully his that he doesn't have to worry.

He never will. The two of them are solid. I envy their closeness, even if I know that life isn't for me.

"You still lettin' him chase you through the woods?" I give her an extra squeeze before letting go.

"You know it." She flashes me a smile, shaking her head when I refuse her offer of a bottle opener and tap the cap off on the edge of the counter instead.

I take a long pull on the beer, let my arm drop and look up to catch them both watching me, their expressions half wary, half amused.

"What happened?" Grace asks, looking from me to Liev. "Am I allowed to ask?"

I shrug. "Ah, sugar. You know I'll tell you anythin'." I lean in. "Especially if it'll get you riled up enough to let me—"

Liev hip-checks me out of his way. "I'll call the paparazzi here myself if you don't lay off Grace, you asshole."

I wink her way, grin at her eye-roll, and let her fill my hands with bowls of chips and dip before following them both out to the dark, quiet porch.

I fucking love it here—right here. This house on the hill above Camp Haven. I love the night sounds and the star-filled sky and the smell of summer. I love the thump of music from below, the faint splashes from the pool, the occasional howl of pleasure or pain or probably both.

Liev—and now Grace's—place is one of those big, wide brick houses that looks low-slung, but has weirdly high ceilings. I've never hit my head on a single doorframe here. I like the sturdy pillars on the front and back porches, the thick walls and tall windows. According to Liev, it's a craftsman bungalow, whatever the hell that means. I like it, though, and I like the way Grace has worked with Liev to redecorate. Everything about it is warmer than the pristine finish of the significantly older, fancier, and more expensive Georgetown house I share—shared—with Twyla.

"You okay?" Liev asks, watching me in that quiet way of his that sees everything.

"Good." Ignoring the twinge in my chest, I sink into the old-fashioned rocking chair, suddenly not looking forward to telling the whole story of how I got here. "Fuckin' glad to be home."

The front gate squeaks. Out of habit, I lower my head, hiding my face in the shadows, although it occurs to me for the first time that it might not matter anymore if my fellow kinksters—the folks I consider to be my people, after all—recognize me.

Shouldn't have bothered. The voice that sails over the boxwoods is instantly familiar. Lamé. The only other person who knows my secret.

"He here yet? I swear to goddess if you are hoarding *the* Zion Mason up in here, just keeping him all to your-selves, you two, I will—" Lamé's tall form sweeps around the bushes, all floating dress, swishing hair, and swinging bag, and comes to a dead stop the moment they see me. Their pale ochre skin glows warm in the light of the candles, their eyes wide and bright and excited. "Oh my god, honey. You made it." Lamé starts up again, picking up speed.

I stand and, by the time they're on the porch, I've got my arms open and, I'll tell you, Lamé knows how to hug. There's a fierceness to the embrace that makes me feel... well, loved, I guess. Embraced in every sense.

I sigh, long and deep, breathe in this summer's new perfume, and hug them tighter.

They finally step back with a sniff and flick a long-nailed hand into the air. "I'll take a mai tai, Boss."

Liev, who's started to stand up from the seat he's sharing with his girlfriend, sinks back down when Lamé snorts. "Kidding." They drop the sparkly rainbow bag from their shoulder and hold it open. "Brought my own." From the tote, our very own Mary Poppins pulls out a ton of shit, only instead of a lamp and so on, there's a massive cocktail shaker, four martini glasses, a jar of ice and then —Christ, I swear there's magic involved—they produce a tray of those little pigs in blankets that in my other life are called canapés.

Once our glasses are all filled and the food's served— somehow still hot—and Lamé's settled into a deep, wicker armchair, they lean forward and give me a stern look. The kind that brooks no argument.

"Now, what fresh hell did you go and get yourself into, young man?" Lamé's seven years younger than me, but whatever. "And what, pray tell, have you done"—they look over one shoulder, then the other—"with your lovely spouse, 'cause I know you didn't leave her to fend off the paps on her own."

Half to piss them off and half because I need it, I slug back the whole fucking mai-tai in a single gulp and let my head fall against the chair, with a long, drawn-out, exhausted, "Fuck."

"You left her," Lamé says, voice flat.

"She's safe."

"Safe? Where? There's no safer place than camp."

"Twyla's not like us, Lamé. She'd hate it here."

"Yeah?" Lamé's thick, perfectly-shaped eyebrows lift above eyes that are currently tinted purple. "If she hates what we have, then she doesn't deserve you."

"It's a *fake* marriage. How many times do I have to tell you? We were not...together." Liev sniffs and I turn to him. "What? You saw how it was in the truck. She hates me." A sick feeling rises up inside me at the way I left things with her. No, it wasn't a real relationship. But I fucked her over and I know for a fact I didn't do enough to fix it.

I will, though. Somehow, I'll make it up to her.

"No comment." A smile plays at Liev's lips. That happens a lot these days, which is good to see, generally. What I don't like is the knowing expression he's wearing. Like somehow I'm not seeing what's really happening here and it's my life, dammit. *Mine.* They have no idea what it's like being me right now.

"I've got a comment," Grace says, so casually I know she's about to set fire to this whole conversation. "If you're not into your wife, Zion, then why'd you go and fuck someone who—"

Liev clears his throat, catching Grace's eye with a quick head shake. I see it all, obviously. How could I not?

"Someone who what?" I ask, though I'm pretty sure I don't want to hear what she was about to say.

"Never mind." Grace shoots a look at Liev. "So, how is she, do you think? Pissed?"

"Twyla?" That nasty thing squirms inside me again. It feels like guilt or shame or a toxic mixture of the two. "Yeah, she's pissed. She'll be fine, though." I hope. Shit, why'd I leave her to fend for herself like that? What kind of selfish prick does that?

"You know what would be funny?" Lamé jumps up and pours me another drink. "Imagine if your gorgeous little hotty of a fake wife turned out to be, I don't know, kinky or something? Wouldn't that be fun?"

"What?" My head's starting to hurt. "No!"

Lamé rears back, looking almost hurt. "Have you not even wondered if she's kinky?"

"No." I pause. "Yes. But, she's not."

"You of all people know you can't tell by just looking at someone."

"No, but, she and I..."

I shut my mouth.

Lamé's head tilts to one side as their attention narrows and focuses. "You what?"

"Nothing," I say, fast and a little frantic. I can't dwell on the things I feel when it comes to Twyla. I fucked up. And it's over. That's my focus. Fix and forget.

"Was it worth it?" Liev's voice cuts right through me.

"Huh?" I blink.

"The woman." All three pairs of eyes watch me closely. "The video."

Not in a million years. The worst goddamn decision I ever made. "Fuck, no," I spit out, harsher than I intended. I swallow back half the drink, hoping it obliterates everything in its path.

My friends agree in silence.

7

———

Twyla

Early in my career, I learned that if I wanted to be taken seriously, I needed to play the part from the second I walked into a casting call or an agent meeting. I'd dress for the role I wanted and act like the person I'd be portraying...and then I'd stick to it. It's not method acting exactly. I didn't talk to the crew of *A Midsummer Night's Dream* as Titania or anything annoying like that. But I definitely held myself straighter when I played that part. It helped to channel her unerring self-confidence.

I do the same thing the next evening as I open the door to the kink camp dungeon and step into the hot, loud, crowded space. Except I'm not Titania here.

I'm a seductress.

And I look the part, too, although I can't say the confidence has fully set in quite yet, despite Gigi's multiple pep talks.

I wish she were here, holding in giggles and strutting her stuff beside me so I didn't feel like such an outsider.

No. No, I belong here. I can do this, I decide, throwing my shoulders back, letting my vinyl-clad breasts lead the way.

The space is a massive barn, converted into what looks like a permanent play area—or rather, areas. The door slams closed behind me, forcing my eyes to adjust to the dimmer light and I'm assailed with new sights and smells and sounds. At first, it could almost be a club in here, or a big party, with music and laughter, low over-head lights hanging from a cathedral ceiling. But then specific noises pop out of the morass—flesh slapping flesh, moaning that's too long and loud and low to be anything but sex. Or pain.

I shiver and look around. Most everyone's in dark, sexy clothes, or few clothes, or none. Some wear nothing but a collar, some are in full, head to toe vinyl, even their faces covered.

I send up a quick prayer to Gigi for ordering my outfit, take another deep, nervous breath, and forge farther inside.

My high-necked bodysuit, while blessedly full-coverage, is the most blatantly sexual thing I've ever worn. It zips from the top of its mock turtleneck, down my front, under my body and then back up to the top of my butt on the other side. My body's like a suitcase waiting to be opened. I added a flippy faux-leather miniskirt, which at least makes me feel dressed, and went for mid-sized heels instead of the massive spikes Gigi ordered. Up top, I've got on a sort of Cat Woman mask with a zipper at the mouth. Only my eyes are visible.

A huge, mostly naked, very, very hairy person bumps into me on their way out the door. I automatically tense up, ready for some kind of clash.

"Oops. So sorry," the person says, smiling under their mask. "Need some air."

"Oh. I'm sorry." I jump out of the way of the door, feeling foolish and awkward.

What am I doing here?

I consider turning around and leaving, but I'd regret that. So, I grab ahold of the jitters, try to pretend it's just stage fright, and walk deeper into the big space.

Carefully, I look at the few faces I see close to the entrance. There's a tiny white woman dressed as a sexy fairy.

Okay. Not Zion.

A big, Black man brushes past me, wearing nothing but a sort of sack around his sex, attached to a belt at his waist.

Definitely not Zion.

Deep inhale...even through the mask, I can smell sweat and other human odors. Okay. It's okay. Another inhale and a slow pan right, where a large-bellied, elderly Asian man is getting a lap dance from a very slender, tall, white person, fully dressed in a suit and tie, with buffed leather shoes on.

Not Zion. My eyes linger for a few seconds anyway before skipping forward to the next play area, where—oh, god, I think that person's getting fisted. No. Nope. I can't look at that. Not yet, at least. It's all too soon, too much. I feel raw here, scared and also wide open.

I'm shaking, just a little.

The barn is long and narrow, the ceiling high over-head. The middle of the space is filled with a line of cages and structures—all currently occupied. The exterior walls are lined with individual play spaces that look like stalls, open to observers, and separated by short wooden dividers.

I head right.

I have no idea what I'll do when I see Zion. *If* I see him. What if he's not in the dungeon? What if he's in one of the many other play areas the camp brochure lists? The club house? The pool? The Sex-o-drome? The Hangar? I can't remember the others. There are so many places he could be. Are they all as crowded as this?

I'm moving slowly forward, zombie-like. In the next stall there's a writhing pile of bodies, the parts indistin-guishable from each other. Are they... Oh yep. Okay. They sure are.

Buzzing with surprise, feeling caught out, like I'm seeing things I shouldn't, I turn and look anywhere—at the scuffed concrete floor, the bars of a cage, an empty swing hanging from the ceiling. I guess I wasn't quite as ready for this as I'd thought.

As the initial shock fizzles, I register excitement, adrenaline, curiosity. And here's the thing: I really want to see what they're doing.

So I turn back.

After a few seconds' staring, the writhing flesh separates into body parts and finally humans of all shapes, genders, colors, sizes.

From the bottom of the pile, a woman—I think—looks up, tilts her head fully back onto the shoulder of a person she's lying on, her mouth wide open. A man edges over on his knees and...holy shit, my entire core clenches as he shoves his erection straight into her mouth. Within seconds, he's thrusting, hard.

My body moves closer of its own volition. My eyes are glued to the scene, between my legs I'm throbbing when I realize that the woman's sandwiched between two other men and they both appear to be penetrating her—one from below, one from above. She grunts, the sound muffled by the cock in her mouth.

Mid-moan, I realize I'm staring, which I read last night isn't necessarily polite. Although, here, out in the open, maybe they want that. It's a fine line between voyeuristic and intrusive.

I'm already walking, but I glance back just in time to catch the man on top of her as he yells and sinks deep, then holds.

He's coming inside of her.

One of my hands flies to cover my mouth.

I want to see and I want to know how it feels to—

No. No, I'm not here to do any of this. Confront Zion and go. Make him understand what he's done. That's something, right?

I'm breathing hard and it's not just the edginess I've been fighting all evening. It's excitement, plain and simple. What these people are doing is sex like I've never experienced it: brutal and fierce and totally free of shame.

I don't intend to get sucked in, but I'm already caught in its glow. Tonight, in this sultry second skin, I'm not Twyla Hernandez or Tina, the name I registered under. I'm Twilight, the camp name I chose at the gate.

It says so on the bracelet I'm wearing. Right beside where it says She/Her. Next to it is a band that shows that I'm cishet and another that shows people this is my first camp, then a bright yellow one telling the camp photographer that they may absolutely not snap pictures of me. I sure hope they obey that rule.

I tear myself away from the scene that's got me completely turned on, and move up to the next space and the next.

A slow, sultry electronic song is playing, the bass vibrating to my core. It carries me further into the human fray.

There are people doing things *everywhere*. To my left, I draw even with what looks like a mini paddock, filled with people dressed as ponies, complete with tails and saddles and...

I peer closer at one of the long, fluffy tails, which looks like it's—

Okay. Okay, that is a butt plug.

The sex shop woman tried to sell me one—with a bright blue jewel on the end, which she claimed would look beautiful against my skin.

I thought that was when I stepped through the looking glass.

Now, I realize I was wrong. It's here. This is it. The tornado's hit and I've landed smack dab in the middle of the bright, technicolor mayhem of Oz.

It's equal parts scary and fascinating.

Half of me wants to run away as fast as I can.

This other half, though...the half I've kept under lock and key for so long? Well, it's just getting warmed up.

Maybe, I consider from the anonymous safety of my mask, I could just find someone here to put me out of my sexual misery.

A few steps along, a crowd has gathered around a person hanging in a leather harness. It's not until I draw close that I realize the crowd is actually tickling them. The sounds they're making are unlike anything I've heard—high-pitched squeals that are perfectly balanced pain and hilarity. I can't help but smile.

Everything, everyone is in pursuit of one thing—pleasure. Even the people in the cages are enjoying it. They asked for this. They want it.

I move on to see someone getting spanked in the next stall, their entire body vibrating with every smack of the paddle.

My nipples harden with each dull *thwack* of wood to flesh.

I'm squirming at the sight, my thighs going tight in search of friction, which it's definitely not getting in this stretchy vinyl number. Another smack jiggles her butt. My mouth falls open as I get closer.

Wow. Just wow.

The two men spanking her are blocking my view. I

want to see badly enough to step up just a few feet behind them and push up to my tiptoes.

I can see the woman fully, now. She's bent over some kind of bench, her legs strapped apart. Her butt cheeks are red, what I can see of her face is in complete ecstasy, and her entire sex is visible.

The taller man says something and moves closer to her, lifts a paddle, and brings it down with a thud.

I'm so totally focused on her that I pay him no attention. He's big. Tall and broad enough to block my view from his new position.

I scoot to the side and crane around for a closer look. I'm almost inside the stall now, less than six feet from her, just a couple from the spanker. I can see how wet she is, how badly she wants it, how good it must feel. The man hits her again—hard—and I jolt.

Another smack and I gasp, as if I'm the one being forced to open up and spread out and take the pain. More solid hits, each one speeding up my pulse, drawing me closer—too close, probably. My body's hypnotized, my brain's flying, caught up in the net of a hundred grunting, groaning voices, the smell of bodies and pleasure.

"Harder," she screams.

Yes. Do it. I shut my eyes, letting myself imagine how it would feel to be up there. I could ask. I move in another foot. Now, I'm close enough I could reach out and beg one of them to take me into a dark corner.

The man spanking her chuckles low.

Recognition stands every hair on my body up straight.

Slowly, like swimming through molasses, I force my head to the side, my gaze sliding over perfectly-fitted dark pants, a broad, muscled, lightly-furred, pale-skinned chest, topped with—

I take a startled step back, blink, and realize he's wearing a mask. It's creepy. Smooth steel, devoid of detail, pulled straight from a horror film. Something about it shocks me to my core. This isn't Zion. Not the one I knew. Or thought I knew. This is another person, a hard, blank-faced stranger.

"Go ahead," says the other man. "She asked for it."

My body clenches up at the words. What would Zion have done if I'd asked him to hit me, back in that cold DC house? I flush hot at the idea.

"If you say so, bro. She's your sub."

His voice, so familiar, has a hard, cutting edge to it that I've never heard.

I'm frozen in place, close enough to touch him. So close he could touch me, hit me with that paddle. I'm excited by the idea, my body so turned on I can feel how swollen I am, how sensitive and needy. How ready.

Both men laugh, low and mean and my skin prickles. The woman cranes her neck to give them a smile. "Please. Please, Zed. Don't stop."

Zed? The name jars me out of my fevered thoughts, leaving me caught here in this dark place, staring at the vacant mask, unable to move or make a sound or possibly breathe.

As if I didn't know it already, I wake up to the certainty that it's him.

I've found my husband. I've found Zion. But now that I'm here, all I feel is lost and confused and more than a little turned on. I've got no idea what to do.

"You gonna fuck her?" the other man asks, jolting me from the spot I've been glued to. "She wants it, man."

No. I can't watch this, can't even listen to him say it. Frantic with the need to get away as far and fast as I can, I turn and run.

8

———

ZION

The hairs on the back of my neck stand up, making me pause, paddle poised.

Slowly, I turn and look behind me, take a step outside the play area and look first up one side of the dungeon, which is crowded with onlookers, then down the other. In the thick of it, I catch a flash of light on vinyl, there and gone. A few seconds later, one of the exterior doors opens, someone scoots out and it slams shut.

"You okay, man?"

Dully, I nod, shoving back the conviction that I should go figure out who that was and why my body wants to race after them.

"Yeah. Sorry. Thought I…"

There's a smell on the air that I can't quite put my finger on. A perfume, maybe? Something flowery, elusive. I shake my head, hard, and turn back to look at Sadie Jo.

Her ass is flushed, her back arched in welcome, her cunt all wet and warm-looking. And yet...

"So, do you?"

"What?"

"Want to fuck her?" Godric asks.

Normally, I'd suit up and sink right in—especially my first full day back. Somehow, though, today...

"Nah, I'm takin' it easy tonight, man." I glance down at where he's tenting his kilt. "You raw doggin'?"

"You wanna watch?"

"Fuck, yeah." My cock's finally starting to stiffen, thank god. I hand him the paddle, which he uses to give his wife's ass one last smack before setting it on her back like she's nothing more than a table.

Her eyes roll back into her head. She always loved being used.

"Still got a breeding kink?" Godric asks.

I manage a quick nod, though my eyes are now firmly fixed on where he's holding his dick, ready to plant it inside that juicy cunt.

Yeah, I'm into the breeding thing.

"You know I'd let you in there bare, if you wanted."

My erection goes rock-hard at the idea of sliding in without a condom. "Rather watch," I lie. Or not exactly a lie, but I've never fucked without a condom and I don't plan to start now.

When it comes to sex, I've got exactly three hard limits: no shit, no bareback, and no kissing—ever.

There's other stuff I avoid—like certain bodily excretions, electric play, and extreme degradation, which I'm really not into, but my hard limits are non-negotiable.

I don't do shit. It's just never been my thing.

No going raw because the risks are too high.

And the kissing thing...is complicated. I've gone through enough therapy to get that my childhood left me with scars I'll never erase. I was loved once. I remember it. Kind of.

Enough to remember the pain when it was taken away. Enough to know that it's not a risk worth taking.

So, I've never kissed outside of work. Period. And I don't plan on starting now.

The exit slams again behind me and I force myself not to turn back to look.

Instead, I watch this big man fuck his wife without a condom on. It's usually a huge turn on for me, but tonight... Dammit, there's something wrong with my body. It's like the bullshit from my real life is messing with my libido.

My cock stays at half-mast while Godric drills Sadie Jo. The creampie—the part I'm usually wild for—gives me no more than a minimal thrill and, by the time he pulls out and I head off, I'm half terrified.

If I can't get it up for a spanking or a breeding, what the hell am I gonna do?

And damn my brain for choosing this very moment to supply me with an image of my wife as she was driven away last night—her eyes big and wide and angry, her face as pale as I've ever seen it.

In sudden need of air, I shove open the side door and

head out into the cool night, wishing I could wipe my mind clear of Twyla's painfully beautiful face.

Twyla

I'm racing down a hill in these heels, wishing for a drink or a change of clothes or some idea of what to do next.

I don't even know where I'm heading. Toward the parking lot, probably, though I haven't accomplished what I set out to.

At the bottom of the hill, I stop and look around, pull my mask up over my mouth and drag in big lungfuls of fresh, pine-scented air. It's cooler out here, though still warm and humid. I'm a hot, sticky mess inside the vinyl. Above me, the sky is clear, cloudless, and there are so many stars, twinkling down on this place. It's been a while since I saw stars or noticed the moon or heard the scraping song of night creatures.

My breathing slows. I take a long look around.

There, a few feet ahead is a quaint wooden sign pointing every which way.

I stumble up and squint at it. To the right is the pool and the clubhouse.

Straight ahead is a darker, wooded area, with a group of tents. Beyond that is the lake, apparently, and the Hangar. Lord knows what happens in there.

Why did I even come here? I need to go. Where's the parking lot?

I turn, stare back up toward the dungeon I've just left. It's that way.

I can just trudge back up and get in the car and drive to... Where? The Days Inn again?

Or should I hop a flight to LA and face what's left of my dumpster fire of a life?

I do a 360, look up the hill, and exhale, long and slow.

No. No way. I'm not done with this place. I haven't even accomplished what I came to do.

Wait, what did I come for, again?

To talk to Zion. To confront him. And I couldn't exactly interrupt the spanking, could I?

You gonna fuck her? The man's words come back to me. *She wants it, man.*

Is that what he's doing up there right this second?

Yes. Obviously.

Jealousy, the poisonous little ingredient I've been ignoring since I first saw that video, shoots straight to my stomach and twists. It's a sharp, long blade and it hurts. God, it hurts. More than the anger. More, even, than the betrayal. Not only have I been made the fool, I've done it to myself.

Because, if there's a time or a place to be honest about these things, it's here and it's now, and I wanted to be the woman in that video.

Is that why I came?

Not to confront him, but to...

I wind an arm around the signpost. It's the only thing holding me up.

Seriously? What was I thinking? That I'd *seduce* him? Win him back somehow?

Back? It's not like I ever had him anyway.

Because despite being a rational, intelligent woman on the cusp of a decent career, I, along with everyone else, fell for the ridiculous Prince Charming thing. I did.

And, oh, this is so pathetic, but I can admit, here in the dark, surrounded by people fully owning their secret, inner lives, that for one second this week, before he went and got filmed with that woman, a tiny part of me foolishly thought that Zion, despite the fake setup of our marriage, might somehow choose me for *real*.

As if what we were making was a life. I mean, a few fake dates and stay-at-home dinners and a single, confusing movie night do not a couple make. The fact that it felt so right just makes it all the more pitiful.

It's exactly like the time I got up the courage to ask Andy Burke to the prom after tutoring him in Spanish all senior year. Every Thursday after school, I'd gone to his place. And every Thursday, I'd sensed a connection between us—moments that felt so real, so meaningful. The night I asked him, he looked at me like I'd just spoken to him in Klingon or, you know, told him I ate koalas in my free time.

I can't believe I'm here: little Tina Hernandez, thinking she can bag a ten when society's decided she's nowhere near that.

Someone moans loudly from one of the tents. Another voice giggles in response.

I force out a slow, calming breath, straighten, and let go of the sign.

No, I'm not admitting defeat yet. I've not been entirely truthful with myself, but that's okay. It's been a messed up couple of days. A girl can be forgiven a delusion or two, right?

You know what? I need a drink.

To the bar, then.

I slip off my shoes and take off at a fast walk, my feet so sensitive on the paved path that I move over to the grass. It's chilly and damp and feels so damn good I could lie down and do a grass angel.

The idea makes me smile.

Okay, so cocktail first. Then, maybe I'll have the courage to return to the dungeon and confront Zion. Or maybe I'll do something completely different. Something wild, something kinky. Something that in no way involves Zion Mason.

Something that is just for me.

9

———

Twyla

After making my way through the crowd, I settle on the last empty barstool, happy to get this chance to sit and just take a minute.

Standing behind the bar is the small, white, short-haired pixie of a woman who checked me in earlier at the front gate. She'd explained the bracelets to me and given me the rundown on the camp's stringent consent and privacy rules. At the gate, I'd immediately checked her bracelets and seen her pronouns.

"Hey," she says as she makes her way over to me now. Behind her cat-eye glasses, her eyes dip to look at my bracelets. "Oh, nice to see you again, Twilight! You registered with me!" She waves. "I'm Max."

"Yeah. Nice to see you again, too." It *is* a relief to see a familiar face, even if I only met her today. She was nice. And if she recognized me at check-in, she made no mention of it.

"Must be hot in that thing." She points at my mask.

"It's awful." I laugh, looking at the people dancing and flirting and fucking in the space behind me. "Especially in here."

"Imagine how they feel." She indicates a person a couple stools down, in head to toe latex.

"Ouch."

"Right?" She smiles and plants her elbows on the bar. "You having fun so far?"

I shrug and immediately her eyes sharpen. "Need a drink?"

"Please," I moan.

"That bad, huh?"

"I'm fine," I say, though I'm not entirely convinced it's true. "I could use something strong."

"Of the human or alcoholic variety?" she asks with a toothy grin and a head tilt toward the massively muscular human to my left.

"Booze...for now," I breathe, smiling. This is good. This person's familiar. A bar is a place I know how to negotiate. I can do this. "Surprise me."

"What do you like? Soda? Juice?"

"Something frilly."

"You're speaking my language."

I hold up my wrist and she scans the barcode on one of the bracelets, charging the drink straight to my account.

I watch her expert movements, mesmerized as she adds booze and mixers into a shaker with easy, fluid motions. "Tada!" When she finally puts the glass in front of me, dripping with fruit, topped with an umbrella, and finished off with a stirrer shaped like a penis, I burst out laughing.

"This is amazing. What is it?"

"It's called a Glory. In honor of tonight's activity."

"Oh yeah?" I lean forward and take a big sip through my mask's mouth-hole. It's a weird feeling. "Ohhhhhh." My eyes close of their own volition, taste buds absolutely screaming from the tart, fruity citrus, with berries and gin.

"You like?"

I nod, my mouth still full. After a couple more sips, I sink back, my shoulders finally relaxing. "It's delicious."

"Good. Okay. You are aware of the two-drink max, right?"

"Oh, yes. Right." I read that in the brochure, along with the other camp rules, like the safe words and various details about consent and behavior and what it would take to be asked to leave. I take another sip under the bartender's benevolent eye, and sigh.

"Want to be added to the list?"

"The list?"

Max points at a door to one side of the bar. "Old Glory. The Gloryhole." She leans forward and puts both elbows on the bar, cradling her chin in her cupped hands. "Or, as I like to call it, Seven Minutes in Heaven, adult-style."

"What, um..." I clear a surge of excitement from my throat. "What happens in there?"

Max's eyes are sharp behind those glasses. "Whatever you'd like. Literally, anything."

"Oh." I grab my glass and suck back a whole lot more of my delicious cocktail—barely tasting it. "How...how do you tell the person what you want?"

"Here." She pushes a clipboard at me. I scan the page and look up.

"This is like signing up to sing at karaoke."

Max throws her head back and cackles. "Oh my friend, it really is. Except it's so much more fun."

My vision's a little blurred when I look down again, although I'm not sure if it's the buzz from the alcohol or from the options I'm being presented with.

There's a blank for my camp name, then a line of text stating that by checking the options below, I'm giving consent, which I may withdraw at any time simply by stating the camp safe word, which is followed by a space where I'm supposed to write the safe word, and sign.

Easy peasy. I can do this. I *want* to do this. Maybe.

I look up. "Excuse me, Max?"

She wanders over.

"Uh, with this... um..." I can't bring myself to say Glory Hole. It seems too dirty, somehow, which is ridiculous given that I'm thinking about doing it. My body's humming at the possibility. "*Event.* This is weird, but, how do I know I'll be attracted to the person? Is that...is that awful?"

"Nope. I get it. You don't want to go in there with, like, a deep thirst for hefty thighs and find out you're barely getting a handful, right? I'm a Switch, which gives me lots of options, but I've got friends here who would never, in a million years, top, others who'd never bottom. Shove two hard-core tops in a dark room together and it'd be like cats fighting for dominance. Which would suck. Unless that's their thing." She grins.

I can't help but laugh. "So, it's dark in there? How does it work?"

"Well, there are the traditional glory holes. Booths with holes at strategic levels. We call those Old Glories. Then we've got the Black Hole."

"What's that?"

"A bigger, two-person booth. Total darkness. Anonymous. No speaking, unless you're safe wording or need to get out. No actual holes, but all the benefits of pure anonymity. You'll never know who you just did terrible, wonderful things with."

My breath's gone all shaky with excitement and nerves. "What if someone comes in and I'm, I don't know, not attracted to them? Not into it or scared or weirded out? Is that awful? I don't want anyone to feel bad, you know, but if—"

"Safe word. Just safe word. No excuse needed. No hard feelings." She points something out on the paper. "Look. Here, you just give details of soft and hard limits, wants, specific physical stuff. Whatever you're into, curious about, desperately seeking. Honestly. It's anonymous. You get assigned a number and you're matched up."

"*We* met in the hole," says a voice to my left. I turn to see a small, round woman holding the end of a leash that's attached to a hairy, tatted-up biker in nothing but a leather thong and a collar.

He's got his arms around her. "Luckiest day of my life," he says, looking down at her like she just hung the sun

"Oh. Wow. That's amazing. Congratulations," I tell them.

"Listen. No pressure, okay?" Max's tone is suddenly serious. "If you're curious, just fill it out. You can change your mind anytime."

Curious? That's one way of putting it. I'm half-terrified.

It's the other half that pushes me to grip the now sweat-slicked pen. The half that's already fully caught up in this sex-filled underworld. The half that definitely gets why Zion comes here in his off-time.

Even now, I grind into the stool, thinking of that woman's ass and the paddle, that sick blend of excitement and jealousy.

Would I like that? The spanking? Would I like the way Zion and that other man stood there, objectifying her, talking about the woman like she wasn't even there?

From the way my insides clench up, I'd say yes. Yes, I'd like that very much.

It takes concentration to focus on the words dancing on the page in front of me. Words like Penetration and Anal. Impact, Force, Oral, Pain. Top, Bottom, orientation, special requirements, specific desires.

What if I did it, just this once? One time, one experience, and then I leave. Back to life, back to the shitstorm.

I could make this whole ordeal about me instead of us or him.

I inhale, long and slow, shut my eyes, and picture the video—Zion doing things to that woman's body, her moans, every muscle tensing up.

I want that pure, unadulterated pleasure. Just once. One time and I'll go.

Maybe that's all the confrontation I need.

"Think I could have that second drink?" I ask Max, fully decided.

"You're on."

After a while, I put down the pen and push it toward her, along with the form.

"Alrighty then." She scans the sheet, her face expressionless. "You're all set. I'll send this in to Benji and he'll assign you a partner."

A few minutes later, just as I'm slurping the last of my drink, she looks over. "Oh. I think it's your turn."

I don't know that I've ever been this nervous—and I've walked onto a lot of stages in my life.

I stand, careful not to appear as buzzed as I feel, push the barstool in, thank Max, and walk slowly to the door wondering, with every single step, what it is I think I'm doing.

Zion

Penetration: check

Oral: check

Silence: check

Lights out: check

Physical requirements: tall and muscular. Not too big.

Whatever that means.

"You'll like her," says Benji, who's monitoring. He's a tall, calm guy I have a deep respect for. The kind of person you'd want on your team no matter where you're headed or what you're doing. I've seen him defuse a fight that seemed inevitable, in seconds. And he's pretty handy with a pair of safety scissors. "Max was gushing."

"Why didn't Max partner with her?"

Benji smirks. "Max isn't her type."

I glance at the page again and read the section on likes and wants. I can do whatever I fucking feel like to this woman, apparently. Aside from anal.

Perfect. No faces, no voices. We'll use each other to get off and never be the wiser.

No harm, no foul if I happen to think about someone else the whole time.

Finally, at that, my cock comes to life.

"Which room?"

"Five. You in?"

At my nod, he puts the form in the outbox and lets me into the pitch-black anteroom, where we both allow our eyes to adjust, then leads me to door five. "You know my limits, right?"

"No shit, no bareback, no kissing." He smirks. "I'll make sure she knows."

I go inside and wait. A minute later, Benji lets the other person in in total darkness.

I've always loved this moment. The calm before the storm, or whatever you want to call it. It's the indrawn breath, the quiet before the movie, the moment before a jump. Right now, we can turn back or do it.

It's the Schrodinger's Cat moment when anything is possible. The woman who just walked in could be anyone.

I take my time, inhaling through my nose, and smell... Oh, that's... What is that? Why's it familiar? Why's my cock suddenly standing at full fucking attention? I exhale, let her hear me. Inhale again, anticipating that scent, which... Is it what I got a hint of earlier, in the dungeon? Flowers and... I don't know. Springtime? Sunshine? Fuck, it's frustrating. Whatever it is, it's shooting straight to my balls.

I've got to hold my breath for a second just to think straight. And, when I do, I hear her. She's breathing hard and fast. Quick inhales that tell me she's nervous. Even from this distance, the exhales heat my chest. Is she working extra hard to get oxygen through a mask, like me?

There's also a sound of friction. Cloth to wood? Is she pressed to the wall? Hiding? Scared?

My stomach tightens. I want to talk, dammit. I want to tell her she'd better be fucking scared. I want to hear that nervous gasp move into moan territory. I want to know what she sounds like when I slide my cock down her throat and tell her how good she is.

Is she good?

I take a step. Her breathing stops.

Another step, this time, with me reaching for my fly. I make a production of unbuttoning, slide the zipper down with a slow, terrible precision. If we were out there, where I could look at her, I'd make her come to me, just to watch the fight in her eyes. But here, my senses are all occupied with the sound of her and that too-elusive scent.

Finally, I'm close enough to feel her body heat. It's a warm shadow in front of me.

I could lean down and kiss her, if that were the sort of thing I did. I could reach out and wrap my fingers around her skull. I could turn her around, bend her over and take her, deep and hard, then pull out and leave her frustrated. Make her wait for the orgasm. Make her work for it.

I don't, of course. Making people come is one of life's greatest pleasures and I want it, now.

Instead of doing any of those things, I shove my pants down around my hips, pull my cock out, and let it bob forward against her while I give it a good, hard stroke.

My knuckles rub against a plasticky material. Vinyl, maybe latex. I rub her with my crown, smearing a fresh bead of pre-come against her tit. She's small, I can tell. It's perfect.

She still makes no sound. Which is fine. We're not here to get to know each other, are we? We're here to get each other off and leave. Wham bam.

Just as I'm about to reach for her, something touches my cock. It's her hand—tentative, light. Not something I'm used to at camp. I shudder at the sensation, breathe her in, like a drug, and let my head hang back.

Oh, fuck. This is going to be good. Whatever happens, I'm already feeling more myself than I have in...since...

That strong little hand finally gets up the guts to tighten around my tip and, fuck me, it's good. A little hesitant, which I apparently like. Who knew?

I lean in. She smells more potent here—like a...a... My brain's giving me yellow flowers, and musk, sex. She's turned on, maybe a little sweaty in the vinyl. I want to get my face in there, want to sink my nose into her skin and breathe in every primitive scent her body puts out.

Waiting is better, though. Waiting means this will last.

Her hand's joined by a second, the two of them stroking up, circling my head, stroking down. I shift closer, wanting to feel her weigh my balls and, like magic, like the type of communication that only happens with a long-time play partner, she does it. One soft hand cradling them, mapping them out.

With a suddenness that hits me hard in the solar plexus, I want more. I want tight holes and nasty grunts, force and ferocity.

Before I've thought it through, I reach out to where I think her head must be, wrap my hand around her throat and clasp her, tight. Her gasp is a fucking gift.

In response, I tighten further and push her back a couple steps, letting my hand explore what my eyes can't.

She grunts when her body connects with the wall, and I don't give her time to do more. I investigate. A zipper. I drag it down, down. Something gets in the way at about her hips and, though I want to yank it all the way open, I can't wait to get a hold of her tits, to feel the warm skin, to call up goose bumps, to bite and wet her with my mouth, mark her up a bit.

My hand slides inside, over a soft belly, lower, stopped by...a skirt.

I shove that down, just to where the waistband traps her thighs, keeping her here. My prisoner.

I take another foray under the latex, this time with both hands, one either side of her center, stroking up and up to those big, soft tits.

"Fuck, yes," I whisper, without any sound, weighing and squeezing until her breathing's absolutely haywire. "Look at these." My words are pure consonant.

I can't see her. Of course not. But I fucking want to. Are the nipples brown, the way I picture them? Thick and brown and getting longer while I tweak them. Fuck. I pinch them both, hard, and hold her up straight when she tries to crumple.

I grunt, feeling so close to the fantasy I'm holding in my brain I think I might need to punch myself.

The low groan she lets out shoots straight down my spine to grip my balls.

I pluck at her nipples now, one after the other, stretching, tugging so hard it's got to hurt. She fucking loves it, her body's writhing against me. I lean in and give her weight just to keep her up.

And then, fuck I've got to find out why she smells so good. Right this second. Right now.

Compelled by this need that feels like hunger, I drop to my knees, give my aching cock a hard tug with one hand, shove her skirt to the floor, and unzip her the rest of the way with the other.

Then I lean in, barely aware of the hot little whimpers filling the small room, put my nose to her, and inhale.

This. This is it. What I needed.

I don't ask for permission before ripping off my mask and burying my face in her hot, wet pussy.

10

———

Twyla

Oh, god, god, god, god, god, god.

I'm flat against the wall, my arms spread for balance, my legs as wide as my skirt will allow, with a man between my legs.

A man who's absolutely devouring me, his lips and teeth and tongue, his rough, animalistic growls, too low and incoherent to get a bead on, but somehow just what I need to fly me up, up, up.

This stranger's relentless, coarse, scary—god, *so* scary —and hungrier than anyone I've ever been with. The men I've known don't dive in and consume. Even... what was his name? Even he sort of skirted his way around my parts.

This man—whoever he is—is melding with my body, using me so totally that it feels, I don't know, symbiotic. Is that the right word?

I grunt when his teeth take my lip between them and tug.

I want it. Oh, god, do I want it. I want his tongue... right...there. Where it's lashing back and forth. And, just when the empty ache inside's getting too harsh to bear, I want something else, anything, whatever he'll give me— and he does.

One thick finger slides inside me, parting me, making me feel full and taken and—

I gasp when he crams another in beside the first, twists them both around—his tongue now working fast, its rhythm relentless—one hand pressed flat to my belly, while he uses those other fingers inside me in a come-hither motion and presses...presses...

"Oh, no," I have time to whisper before the pressure shoots me up and out of my skin, turns my eyes back in my head, tightens my hands into fists. And I'm pounding, pounding the wall, my hips thrusting at his face, one hand reaches for his head, my fingers spear into his hair, grip hard and twist, pulling him tight into me—so tight. The gruff, involuntary grunt he makes ricochets through me.

And this man, this faceless stranger, just keeps going, keeps pressing for more, biting and twisting at me like he's trying to get the last bit of juice from a fruit, and like *that*—holy shit—he urges just that extra drop of pleasure from me. And it's pleasure I've never felt before. It's plea-sure I didn't know I had. Pleasure torn from way, way down, a place I've never dared examine, a place so primeval and deep and unexplored that I know it's bound to scar.

In absolute silence, muscles taut, mind numb, I experience the kind of climax I've never truly believed existed.

I'm shaking when he gives me a last, luxuriant lick, rubs the entire side of his face through my wetness, as if to mark himself, and backs away, catching my pussy lip between his teeth and pulling for a few beats before finally letting go.

I can't move, can barely think in this place where nothing's real, life's suspended, and a dark stranger brings me to orgasm almost without trying.

Or, no. No, that's wrong, because as he pushes up to standing, I hear the way he's breathing and it's not an easy in and out. It's a labored thing, an effort. This was work for him. But he liked it, I think. Liked my taste and my smell, liked the feel of my soft flesh against him. He's slow as he rises, takes his time, strokes his face against every bit of me he can reach and then—oh, those rough hands are back. One's on my breast, kneading and then tugging so hard at my nipples that it should hurt.

It *does*. It hurts. But it's like a taut thread, attached directly to my core and every time he drags at that hard bead, he's pulling straight at my clit and, no. There's no way I'll come again. I can't. I've never done that, not this soon.

I get a flash of Zion shoving his fingers into that woman's mouth. It's a hot and cold thing running through me—attraction and repulsion, jealousy, shame, want,

want, want. I wanted to *be* her when I saw the video. I wanted him to do those things to me.

It's different here, though, shame. It's a feature, not a bug. It's still bad, but it's a pleasurable bad. The bad is the point. It's the kind of bad that makes me fight that rough hand tightening around my neck. The sort of bad that makes me think I like that nipple pain more than I like the tentative kitten licks my past partners gave me. How maybe I'd like something rougher, too.

He's breathing hard. The sound's choppy. It makes me weirdly proud of myself. I'm the one who's done this. Who's made this big, hulking, shadow of a stranger breathe like an excited teenager.

I did that.

When he nudges my thighs wider with his knee, I'm in no way prepared for the quick slap of his palm against my sex.

The sound I make is high and strange and unlike any sound I've ever made.

Almost before it's left my mouth, I'm whimpering for more.

"Again," I whisper and, oh, yes, he complies, although it's not me calling the shots. He makes sure I understand this by tightening his hold on my throat. Just a little. But enough.

"Oh. Oh," I whisper.

He's slapping me again. Again. Every time, it's an electric shock to my clit, to my conscience. To that horny little part of me that's been clawing itself out all day, week...whatever.

I'm not the sedate, sometimes-sexual person I thought I was. I'm not. I'm a big, swirling mass of want and filth and need and and and…

My mouth drops open on a silent scream as his assault on my pussy picks up its pace and now he's spanking me the way he licked me—without respite, without mercy. Using my own body against me.

I'm going to come again. I'm going to, even though it's too much and the possibility's almost frightening. The way his hold on my airways is frightening and also just right.

He goes tighter, his fingers clamping my flesh hard enough that I'll see bruises in the mirror tomorrow. I want that. I want those prints. They might be the only thing I have left from this experience. The only tangible thing at least, since orgasms are fleeting.

This one's barreling toward me, as scary and inevitable as a freight train and, with the way he's holding me up with that hand beneath my jaw, I'm seeing stars, but they're beautiful. It's beautiful.

This whole… sordid… adventure… is… beautif—

I'm gone, bursting open. My body just a bright, impossible light. My clit, my nipples, my useless knees, the hand I've wrapped around his at my neck, the other that's twisting my own nipple—it's all gone. It's all nothing.

I'm nothing.

I don't know how long I float here—a while, I think. Long enough for him to open a condom and somehow roll it on one-handed, then drag my hand over it, to show me that he's wearing it. Long enough for him to turn me and push me face down on a bench I hadn't even known was here. Long enough for his strong hands to pull my ass apart before, with a groan, he dips down to lick that, too—not for lubrication, I hope, since I didn't check that particular box. Also, I'm soaking, so I don't think lube is needed. I'm slippery enough for anything we might want to do.

He's licking me there because he *wants* to, I understand, when he does it again with a hungry sound, before getting up. As if he has all the time in the world, he runs his hands over my ass, up my sides and down, where he pries me roughly apart again. Then, oh god, then with a quick exhale, he puts the tip of his erection to my opening.

"Now," he whispers, his voice low and gruff, but no longer a whisper. "Take this cock like a good girl."

Shock fizzles through me at those words, that voice, the command, straight from the video. Recognition is somehow both ice cold and electric.

Zion.

God, oh god, I don't move. I can't. I can't do anything. I can't breathe or think or make the tiniest of sounds. All I can do is take whatever this man wants to give.

This man. *My husband.*

This man whose voice I'd know anywhere.

This man who definitely—after everything that's happened—should not be about to fuck me.

He sinks in the tiniest bit and just that first inch is huge, too tight. Perfectly, terribly wrong.

It's just the tip and already it's too much.

Zion

This whole thing feels good. Better than any sex I've experienced in my life. And it's just the fucking tip.

I open my mouth and almost say Twyla's name.

No. No, I'm hallucinating. Fantasizing too hard, wishing it to be her I'm on the cusp of sinking into.

This can't be real. My tight, aching balls have somehow wished her into existence. No way is this the woman whose life I've just destroyed with my bad decisions. My wife.

But, fuck, I want that. I want it so bad. Instead of plunging in the way I normally would, I edge us both, by keeping my hips perfectly still and running a hand slowly from her hip over her ass and the slope of her spine and back.

Fuck, I've got to make this fever dream last.

It's almost not even a surprise when the woman the tip of my cock's barely wedged inside says my name—and not my camp name, Zed, but the real thing. "Zion."

One moment, I'm about to have sex with a stranger.

The next moment, everything shifts, reality takes a back seat, and it almost seems like I'm fucking my wife. My *fake* wife, but still.

"Fuck," I whisper, seeing Twyla's face in my mind. The way her teeth scrape over that bottom lip, the way her little tongue peeks out. "Say that again."

"Zion," she whimpers.

This can't be Twyla. It can't. But I want it so bad I don't care that someone here knows my real name. I don't care. I want the fantasy.

I know for a fact she's not here—at camp, wearing a mask and a tight vinyl bodysuit, smelling like my exact brand of sin. And she absolutely isn't in this pitch-black room, ass in the air, soft cunt begging to be pounded.

My system's backfiring, wires crossed, fact and fantasy inhabiting the exact same space in my body. All I can do is wait, my crown wedged inside her in this painful limbo.

She doesn't move. Another handful of seconds. Still nothing.

I don't pull out. If anything, I nudge my tip in a little farther, tighten my hold.

I close my eyes and pretend, diving deeper into the dream world. Pure wish fulfillment.

Yeah. Yeah, that was her plump little hand cradling my balls just the way I needed, that sweet, tight pussy I plunged my finger into, her whimpering—fuck, that voice—it was so close to Twyla's that it sent shivers up my spine. It sure felt just right when I sank my face between her legs and ate like a man finally allowed the one thing he's always wanted.

"Zion... It's me. It's Twyla."

I blink, stunned, mouth dry. *It's her?*

I go hot and then cold, my eyeballs weird and tight as if my vision's gone, which it probably has. Can't tell in the dark.

My system's glitching. I can't loosen my grip on her hips or pull the head of my weeping cock from where it's notched just inside her.

"No," I whisper, keeping my hips still. Not sinking, not moving, when I want—*need*—to take her. "Twyla." Her pussy's non-negotiable at this point. I'm keeping it. It's mine. All I want. *Everything.* I'd sell my soul to stay here.

Hell, maybe I already have. Maybe that's why she's appeared in the dark, brought here as if by the devil himself.

"Red," she whispers. "Red. Please, Zion. Red. *Red.*"

I pull back, my reaction to the safe word automatic, though every part of me wants to hold on to her.

"You okay?" I force the words out, backing up a step to give her space. "What do you need?"

A zipper sounds in the dark, followed by a pained exclamation, scuffling. She moves toward me. "Open the door." Her words send goose bumps up my back. "Please."

My chest goes tight, a dull *whomp-whomp* starts up in my temples, my skin tingles like it's been flogged for an hour.

The fantasy haze starts to clear, leaving behind a terrible reality.

"What are you..." No. No, this just isn't possible. "You shouldn't be here."

She scrabbles around at the wall beside me.

"Where is it? Where's the door?" Her whispers pick

up in volume. "I need to go. Let me out. Let me out, let me out. Oh, god."

I've got no motor function, no control over anything.

Finally, my throat forces out a raw, *"Twyla?"* though my brain still hasn't caught up with whatever the fuck's happening here.

Her whispered, "I'm sorry," settles low and hard in my belly. "I'm so sorry. I didn't mean to..." The door opens, washing her in the faintest red light as she hesitates for a split second—still just an amorphous shape—then slips out. I can't move as her silhouette crosses quickly to the main door. It opens, letting in light that's dazzling after the dark.

My head drops, my eyes squeeze shut. That weird thing in my skull gets louder, faster, making my eyes tight and my neck hurt.

When I look up again, she's gone.

I feel nothing for maybe ten seconds. Then, just as suddenly as the surprise and numbness took me, I blink back to reality.

Get her back, my brain shouts. *Get her, now.*

My first step sends me barreling into Benji, who looks at me and says, "Put the mask on, man."

It says a lot that the mask's the first thing he mentions —not my unzipped pants or my stiff, condom-covered cock. And there's no shock on his face, at all.

"You know who I am?" I pull off the condom, and throw it in the disposal bin. Fuck me, but I'm still aching.

For the woman.

For her.

For...*Twyla.*

Twyla?

My brain's a scrambled mess of questions and regrets and—*fuck*—need. Need that's pounding and aching and telling me to go out there and find her—now.

"Sure, man." Benji half-shrugs, slow and friendly, and I don't care how easygoing he is, I want him to hurry up and finish his sentence so I can move. He glances back and lowers his voice. "You're kinda famous."

My muttered "goddamn it" only makes him laugh.

"We all love you, bro. I mean, I get why you're incognito. Nobody talks about you outside of camp." His grin's huge. "You're our best kept secret."

Great. Just great. Not only have I been deluding myself all these years, but apparently now, my goddamn *wife* comes to camp? My very vanilla wife.

"The woman," I say, straightening my clothes, rushed and frantic and nothing like myself. "You seen her before? You know her?"

"Don't know her."

"Where's she staying?"

He shakes his head. "We don't disclose that, man. The Hole's anonymous. You know that."

I know it. I fucking do, but she's my wife. My *wife.*

"You're right. I've got to, uh..." When I turn around for my mask, my foot nudges something. It's a shoe. Just one.

I bend and grab it, which Benji clearly notices. He doesn't comment.

"All right, man." I slide my mask on, doing my best to sound calm and not totally frenzied. "I'll see you around."

"Count on it," says Benji, smirking at the shoe. "Prince Charming."

I flip him off on my way out, which only makes him laugh louder.

At the bar, I flag down Max. "Hey. That woman?" I try to keep the tension from my voice. "The one in room 5."

"Yeah?"

"Who is she?"

"You serious?" Max shakes her head. "Come on, Zed. Not happening."

I scan the room, eyes hopping nervously from one person to the next. Not her. Not her. Not my fucking wife. "Okay. Okay. But I... You see her? She still here?"

Max shakes her head. "She took off. Fast."

"Goddamn it!"

Max shifts, looking wary for the first time since I've known her.

"I need to..." I look down at the shoe in my hand. "She left her..." I hold up the shoe, feeling like a total dick. What am I gonna do? Chase her down and see if the thing fits? "I need to find her," I finally say to Max with way too much desperation.

"Want to leave that with me? In case she comes back for it?"

"No. No. I've got it."

I take off, do a quick circuit of the room and finally rush out into the night, where I literally run smack into

Bart, this middle-aged white guy who's been coming to camp solo for years.

"Whoa, you okay, Zed?"

"You seen a woman wearing one of these?"

He looks at the sandal and up at me, grinning. "Is this a new game? 'Cause I'm in."

"Have you seen her?" I sound frantic. I hear myself. I just can't fucking control it. "Full mask, vinyl outfit. Little…" I motion to my waist. "Skirt."

At his totally unapologetic *Sorry*, I turn and scan my surroundings, the need to find her clawing at my guts. Locate her and make her leave. She can't stay here. She can't be here, or I'll…

No. I can't think about that. The way she felt, the way she smelled, the sounds she made. The things that I'd do to her if she stayed. I can't. That's not her. This place isn't her, dammit. There's no way I've read her that wrong all this time. No. No way is Twyla Hernandez like me. She's not of this world. And she does not fucking belong here.

I've got to find her and make her leave.

Now.

Before something happens that we both regret.

With her shoe held tight in my hand and her scent all over my face, I set off for the dungeon at a jog, not once letting myself wonder what sweet, serious Twyla was even doing in The Hole.

11

Twyla

"Coast is clear." Max pats my shoulder and puts out a hand for me to stand up from where I've been crouched behind the bar.

I grab it and stand, lopsided on my one shoe. "Thank you."

"Yep," she says, as if this kind of thing happens all the time. "He didn't hurt you or—"

"No. No, it's...complicated."

"Is it related to the fact that you two are..." She looks right and left, then comes in close and whispers into my ear, "Married?"

With a jolt of shock, I open my mouth to deny it and then shut it, deflated. "So you did recognize me. At check-in?"

"Well, sure." She grins. "I've got a friend who's a huge fan. We just binge watched everything you've ever done, including a bootleg version of Threepenny from your college days."

I groan. "Seriously?"

Her expression goes serious. "You okay?"

"I...I don't know."

"All right. Where are you staying? You in a tent? Someone can walk you to—"

"I'm not staying. I mean, I...I didn't plan to."

"Well, you can't drive like this."

"I don't know what to do." Panic makes my voice high.

Her narrowed eyes search my face and then, some decision apparently made, she sighs. "Have a seat. I need a few minutes." When I don't immediately move, she points at the lone empty bar stool and says, "Sit."

It's a relief to have someone tell me what to do. After what happened in that room tonight, I've lost my moorings completely.

I collapse onto the stool and accept water from Max, along with a bag of chips, which I gobble down so fast, she hands me a second. A while later, someone shows up to take her place behind the bar and we head outside together.

When she immediately turns right instead of left, I pull up to a stop. "Where are we going?"

"To a friend's."

"I'm sorry. I didn't mean to turn this into a big deal. I just need to go to my car and change and—"

"Listen for a sec, okay? First of all, is there any chance tonight was your first experience with kink?"

"Well, no. I had a boyfriend once who... One. So, kind of, I guess."

"You've never attended a party or a munch or anything?"

I shake my head.

"That's a big deal. Was it maybe also your first time having sex in a dark room with a stranger?"

"Definitely."

"One night stand?"

"That's never been my thing."

"How about, I don't know, having accidental sex with your superstar spouse?"

"We've never even had sex. We're not a real—" I meet Max's wide-eyed look and go still.

What am I doing? And why'd I just divulge that to a stranger? I'm not thinking straight. Not thinking at all. I sag against the side of the building like an old balloon. "This is bad."

A few people come up to the door, yelling out hellos to Max, who gives them a quick smile, and nudges me away from the entrance. "You need aftercare, Twilight. It exists for a reason. Beyond that, you need to process what you did in there. Listen, I'm a therapist in my other life. And I really don't want you to go anywhere after two drinks and an experience like the one you just had. Okay? Will you trust me on this?"

"I feel... I just really don't want to..." I wave my hands, finding it hard to communicate with my stomach all twisted up and my mind in such a tailspin. I want Zion. I do. I can admit it, though I feel like a fool. *You shouldn't be here.* His words were a bucket of ice water, a painful wake-up call. I shouldn't be here. He's right, and yet... "I didn't know it was him. I had no idea and I'm..."

A mess. A huge, hurt, confused wreck. Part of me wants to run away and hide or turn back time.

But mostly, I want to do it all over again. What kind of person does that make me?

"I know. I'm sorry Benji partnered you two. I didn't realize Zed was even here. At camp."

"It was..." The orgasms that he gave me come swooping back into my brain and my head thunks back against the clubhouse's rough wood siding. "It was so...*good*, Max."

"I know," she says, with a grimace. A kind grimace, but an admission all the same.

Heat washes through me—and not in a good way. "You... Oh. Right. So, you and he have..."

She nods, looking a little sheepish. "We've played. A few times. Never in the Hole, but...I'm sorry. I thought you should know, given... Hell. I don't know. The nature of your relationship, or something. Do you want me to—"

This is good. A dose of reality. Or two different realities: my life versus Zion's. "Has he played with everyone here?"

She shrugs, head tilted, features scrunched up. "Well, not *everyone*, but..."

"Oh my god." I shut my eyes and blow out a long breath, working hard to shove back the stomach curdling jealousy that's trying to take over. Jealousy I have no right to feel. No claim at all.

I have to face it. It's a fact. Every summer, Zion comes here and has sex with—I don't know—dozens of people? Hundreds? Thousands?

The last thing he needs is his fake wife hanging out while he sows his wild oats.

"Twilight."

I startle.

"I'm taking you to a place where you can cool off and process this, okay?"

I stare at her blankly for a few seconds, then focus. "A place...here?"

"It's on camp grounds, but it's a private home. Off-limits to campers." She smiles. "The safest place I can think of. Truly. You can have whatever kind of meltdown you need to there. Or not. You can sleep it off and... Well, you'll see. This is the right choice. Promise."

I give her a long, careful look. She seems earnest. And trustworthy. Also, my knees have now turned to jelly. I look down. And I'm only wearing one shoe. "Is it close?" I ask, staring at my own feet like they don't belong to me. "I don't think I can walk far."

"I've got you. Come on," she says, offering me her arm and setting off into the darkness. "You're gonna love Lamé."

Zion

Twyla's gone.

I've searched every single space I can think of,

including doubling back to the Black Hole—again—which made me horny and frustrated and pissed off.

Why was she here? Why the fuck would she do that? Why would she...

I shove my way out of the dungeon and walk right into a swarm of gnats. How the fuck will I even recognize her in that outfit? Every third person here tonight seems to be wearing a vinyl body suit with a little skirt and a mask.

Twyla.

Her cunt...I can still smell her, still taste her. My dick's still hard.

My insides are still in knots. I bend at the waist, put my hands to my knees, breathe deep.

My head's fuzzy, weird. I'm a mess.

Maybe I can run this thing off, catch some sleep. Tomorrow, I'll feel clearer.

My body's already moving

After a few steps, I kick off my flip-flops, leaving them wherever they land, and take off, her sparkly sandal still held tight in my hand.

It feels good to run, to let my body work hard and my mind shut down for a while. It's funny—I guess—how I'm the one usually doling out the pain here, not craving it. Right now, it's all I want. The burn, the effort. I'm pushing myself harder than I should, sprinting for longer than my muscles are used to, sticking to the lit paths, since it's dark as hell out and my feet are bare and the last thing I need is to trip and fall and break a leg or something.

People I know fly past me, their bodies and faces a blur. Their hellos just background noise to this thing eating me up from the inside.

Fifteen minutes later, I yank off my mask with relief as I push through Liev's front gate and walk up the stone path, surprised to see the light on in the massive studio behind his house. As I get closer, the sounds of Rage Against the Machine get louder. The screaming, the anger, the noise all hit the right chord inside of me. I shove open the giant metal door and spot him up at the top of a massive scaffolding, working on another obelisk—this one unflinchingly explicit and clearly not meant for the same audience as his last one.

I head straight to the fridge, pull out a beer, and at Liev's nod, grab a second.

I don't shut off the music like I usually would, partly to annoy him and partly so we can talk.

Tonight, I don't want to fucking talk. I want to—

Twyla.

Her name hits me like a blow from Liev's hammer.

I want to... I want to... Fuck, I want to talk to *her.* Make sure she's okay, then send her away. Once I do that, I'll be good. That's all this is. I'm worried about her. Concern for a fellow human being.

Relief floods me at the realization. I can fix this. We can talk and laugh over the mistake we made.

Best mistake of my life.

Groaning, I sink onto Liev's saggy sofa.

The music shuts off. "You look like shit."

"Thanks. Got a phone I can use?" I stand.

With an eyebrow lift, he points at the landline plugged into the kitchen area.

"Seriously, Liev? A landline?"

He grabs the beer I opened for him and shakes his head with a smirk.

"What?" I ask him. "Why are you looking at me like that?"

"You know why."

"No. Why don't you tell me?"

"You got her number memorized?"

I huff out a breath. "No."

Another head shake from him sends me back to the old sofa, where I flop down, exhausted and boneless, feeling foolish. I finish off my beer and, as if by magic, he's got another one out and open and in my hand.

"She's here. Was here. Is here? I don't know."

Liev's dust-coated eyebrows fly up almost to his hairline. "At camp?"

"Yeah." I shut my eyes. "Why was she here?"

"She gone?"

"I don't fucking know. She ran away."

"What happened?"

I give him the short version. Or the long version. A version. By the time I'm done, he's pulled out the half-full case of beer and plunked it on the table in front of me, then sunk into an armchair.

"It was good." It's more a statement than a question, but I answer anyway.

"Fucking spectacular."

"You usually do the Black Hole?"

I shake my head with a low, pained laugh. "No. No, man, never. I just wanted to..." I can't finish the sentence. Some things I'm not quite ready to admit, even to Liev. "I'm so fucked."

"Eh." Liev grimaces. The big metal door opens. "Won't kill you."

"Who's getting killed?" Grace walks in and grabs a can of her own, watching us with those dark, smiling eyes.

"We're discussing his chances of surviving tonight's accidental glory hole session with the fake wife."

Grace's mouth drops open. "You're what with who?"

Liev grins. "Maybe you and I should try the Hole sometime, babe. You up for it?" He grabs her thigh and hauls her onto his lap.

I look away from all the tickling and giggling. "I need to call her."

"Nope! Wait. Hang on, Liev. Ow! Stop it." She smacks his hands, still laughing, but clearly flighting it. "No, you can't do that. You can't call."

"Uh, why not?"

Liev finally lets her go and she leans forward, pulling a phone from her back pocket. I immediately recognize the ornate teal and white modern art painting on the case. It's Twyla's. No doubt about it.

"It was on the floor of the truck. Found it on my trip to town this evening." She sets it on the table. "I turned it off so it wouldn't run out of juice."

"How am I supposed to get in touch with her now? Through our fuckin' publicists?"

Grace lifts one tattooed arm in an elegant half-shrug. "Try the Hole again tomorrow?"

"You could always make another one of those viral videos." Liev's wearing his annoying smirk. "Seems to have gotten her attention."

Grace snorts. "No way can he find another Twyla doppelgänger."

"Doppelgänger?"

Liev snorts. "You kidding me, boy?"

"Boy?"

"Act like a little shit and I'll treat you like—"

"Stop it." Grace lightly smacks Liev's arm. "He's being serious."

"Z. Bro, come on. You're not usually this..." He glances at his woman, as if for help. She replies with a wide-eyed shrug. "Dense."

"What are you talking about?"

"The video... The woman?" Grace is watching me wide-eyed, obviously waiting for me to catch up. "She's a perfect replica of Twyla Hernandez."

That dull, rhythmic thing starts up in my skull again, a loud, throbbing pulse in my brain.

"Mmmm." Liev seesaws a hand in the air. "An okay copy."

"She was cute."

"I met Twyla last night, babe, and that woman is a whole lot more than cute."

"What the fuck? No, she... This..." I stand up, not sure where I'm going. The head thing's squeezing my eyeballs now, making everything flicker. "*What?*"

"Here, give me that." Grace pulls the crushed empty from my grip.

Behind her, Liev gets up, all humor gone from his face.

Somehow, they tag team me back onto the sofa, this time one of them on either side of me. Liev's got his arm around my shoulders and Grace is turned to face me, both hands holding mine.

I'm looking down at her fingers. They're long and thin and strong. Artist's hands, like Liev's, although not nearly as chewed up as his are. And she's got ink winding down into her palm—an invitation to follow.

Twyla's got tiny hands. Nothing like these. They're soft and sort of...plump. They're busy little hands with short, neat nails and tiny wrists. Pin-up hands.

I had those hands on my cock tonight and they felt like absolute paradise.

Everything about her was Goldilocks perfect. Just right.

I shut my eyes and let my head fall back onto Liev's arm. He tightens his hold on me and somehow that show of support, casual though it is, makes me realize what an ass I've been.

"You're both right. *Fuck.* She looked so much like her. Why didn't I see it?"

Grace grimaces. Liev grunts.

"She was at this art opening I went to. Saw her the second I walked in. For like a minute, I thought it was actually Twyla. And, you know how it is, she dropped hints. Flirted. It was her smile, maybe, the way she watched me—like she had a secret. Reminded me so much of... Couldn't resist."

"Fifteen years you've been living like this and you've never once fucked up." Liev shifts and I lift my head. "Then you decide to go and get married—for reasons no one quite gets, even now—"

"Oh, *I* get it," Grace cuts in, looking pleased with herself.

"And then came the video."

"I mean, Zion." She looks from Liev to me, wide-eyed. "It's *so* obvious."

I wipe my hand down my face, remembering the moment she approached me at that event. "Even sounded like her, you know? Got my dick so fuckin' hard." I blow out a long, exhausted breath. "I don't...do this. I don't do..." I can't say it. I mean, how the fuck can I *do* a thing if I can't even say it, right? Relationships, love, vanilla sex. Take your fucking pick. None of it's for me.

"I know," Grace says, patting my shoulder with a smile. "You'll get over it."

Will I?

I suck in the smell of beer and dust and summer in Virginia. Smells of home. Not where I grew up, definitely, but where I became the person I am now. I exhale and look around the familiar space. A lot of shit has gone down in this place. Not just out there at camp, but right here, in Liev's studio. On this sofa.

I'll never forget walking in a few months after Liev's wife died to find him on the floor, pale and still and waxy-looking, an empty bottle of bourbon beside him. I was sure we'd lost him, that time. And we damn well would have if Lamé and I hadn't stuck around to spoon feed and wean him off the booze and pills.

I've never been so scared.

My next inhale's full of other things—Liev's sweat, Grace's shampoo or something. I smell Twyla on me, too, but it's not as strong, not as potent.

"Yeah." I'll get over it. I can. I will. I sit up tall. "You're right." As usual. Grace is good like that. She sees people and really *gets* them. She got Liev pretty fast. Hell, she saw right the hell through me. I swallow, nodding. "Whole thing's just a blip." Turning, I give Liev a light smack on the shoulder. "Probably just tired after the shit hit the fan." Ignoring the look on his face, I stand and stretch. I'll get over it. I already am. "I like Twyla, you know? But I..." Shaking my head, I give the two of them a rueful grin. It's not easy, but I get it out and by the time a couple seconds have passed, it feels natural. Almost real. "I fucked up marrying her. You know, we had that red carpet thing and the PR people went wild and, with the rumors about my..." I manage a low laugh. "I'll have to reach out to them tomorrow. See what I can do to fix the shitstorm out there. Anyway. I'd better hit the sack. Got a couple play partners set up for tomorrow." This is a lie, but I'll remedy that first thing in the morning. The best way to handle this whole thing is to find someone to scene with and work this out of my system.

The idea sits heavy in my stomach, but I'll get over it.

I walk over to the door, forcing a spring to my step.

"Hell, if y'all see my wife around, tell her I said hey, would ya?"

Ignoring their twin looks of skepticism, I push the door open and head outside.

Hours later, I'm in their house, in bed, still awake, when Grace's words come back to me: *"You'll get over it."* I took that to mean I'd get over Twyla. Like this whole episode is just a snag. Easily repaired. Quickly forgotten.

Except in the dark, after hours of running over it and over it in my head, it occurs to me that Grace might have meant it differently. As in maybe it's not Twyla she thinks I'll get over, but the other thing, the thing that keeps me from entering into any relationship, ever.

I don't like this, at all. Which is why, first thing tomorrow, I'll make sure Twyla's long gone. And if she's not, I'll just have to convince her to leave.

12

Twyla

The screen door to the sweetest little log cabin swings open and a tall, lean silhouette appears in the rectangle of light. From inside comes low, smooth music, Chet Baker singing about his funny valentine.

"They're playing it cool," Max says under her breath.

"They?" I whisper in response.

"Lamé's pronouns are they/them. And, since your last movie came out—the one with you and Zion—they're a little obsessed."

"Obsessed with wha—"

"You're here! You're actually *here!*" We've made it about halfway across the garden when Lamé, clad in bold reds and blues, swoops down the steps toward us. "Oh my goddess, I can't believe you came. In the flesh. You must be burning up in the mask. Can you take off the mask? Get up in here and let me look at you." I'm half-carried up the steps and inside and my mask's somehow unzipped and pulled off me and I'm suddenly draped in the arms of this tall, gorgeous person, clad in scarlet and peacock blue and smelling like expensive perfume and coffee. Mid-hug, I'm abruptly released and left to wobble on my own against the screen door. "Oh no. I'm so sorry." They take a step back, hands to their face, which is wrinkled up in dismay, morphing into outright horror. "I can't believe...I've never done that. I mean what the hell happened to safe, sane, and consensual, right? One glimpse of you and every last brain cell just fled! I am so sorry. Please forgive me, Twy— Ms. Hernandez. It'll never—"

"It's Twyla." I put a hand on their arm. "I'm fine. It's okay. I appreciate the welcome." Calmer now myself, somehow in direct opposition to them, I follow them into the most colorful, plush, cozy space I've ever seen. "Wow."

"Look... Don't tell Zion, okay?"

I blink. "What?"

"If he finds out I jumped you like that, I'll never hear the end of it. He'll *never* let me live this down."

"I won't tell him." I offer a wobbly smile and a quiet, "Trust me."

"Promise?"

"*Definitely.* Look. I...I should just go."

"Is it my fault?" They swoop close again and back off, finally stopping when Max puts an arm around them. "Don't go on my account. I mean, Zion's going to be so glad when he finds out you're here and—"

I meet Max's wide-eyed look and then everything that's happened sort of bursts open inside me. Max grins and a second later, I'm laughing uncontrollably.

After what feels like forever, I gasp out an apology and let Lamé maneuver me toward the sofa. I flop down and sink into the soft cushions, wiping tears of laughter from my face. When I gather myself enough to meet their gazes, they're watching me with expressions of concern.

"Sorry," I manage through hiccuping breaths. "I totally lost it."

"It's okay, honey," Lamé says. "We've all been there."

"Oh, yeah?" The hysteria rises back up. "You've accidentally fucked your fake husbands in the glory hole?"

"Well, no," says Lamé.

"But our own versions."

"I was just trying to..." I blink. What was my plan again, coming here? What did I think I'd accomplish?

Lamé's big brown eyes slide Max's way before returning to me. "Would you like a cup of tea?"

"Am I allowed something stronger?"

"As long as you don't play anymore tonight."

With a groan, I lean forward and drop my face in my hands. "I'm never playing again."

"Okay. You take off your...um." Lamé looks at my filthy bare feet. "Just get comfy." They pull a blanket out from an enormous basket and set it on the sofa beside me. "I'll get you that drink, shall I?"

Max follows them out of the room and, though I didn't plan on it, something about this place and its wild array of colors makes me want to sink back into the pillows and pull the thick, cable knit blanket over me. I do both, leaving just my feet hanging off the edge, and try not to think about what Zion said.

You shouldn't be here.

So much for not thinking about it, right?

Shoving back a fresh dose of hurt, I look around. The room is overstuffed with furniture and decorations, but it works. Plush fabrics, tons and tons of books, candles and lamps, an elaborate, multi-colored, handblown glass chandelier hanging from the ceiling.

It feels...safe, enveloping, cozy.

Lamé comes in bearing a round, rattan tray with drinks and snacks, looking like they've stepped out of a Rita Hayworth movie. They're tall and slender, with sleek almost-black hair and burnished bronze skin, their features as long and slim as their body. Their peignoir swishes and flows around them. The whole effect is absolutely mesmerizing.

Everything in this place is beautiful, including the drinks, which are tall and frosty, topped with mint and some kind of edible flower. They hand me mine and take a seat, while Max does the same.

"Here's to fresh starts and wider horizons and...I hope, new friendships?" says Lamé, lifting their glass for a toast.

I suck in a nervous breath and tap my glass to theirs. A shiver runs through me.

"You feel that?" asks Lamé, watching me closely. "You felt it, didn't you?"

Max shakes her head, but I don't say a word, because,

yeah, I felt something. That shiver, though brief and easily ignored, was real. A physical manifestation of awareness. Nothing bad. More like one of those *your life's about to change* moments that you don't usually recognize until long after a thing has happened. Which is kind of apt for today, considering the night's many life-changing events.

Lamé smiles, finally looking away. "So. You and Zion played—finally. My goddess, you two took long enough to—"

Max clears her throat and I blink down at the glass in my hand.

"Okay." Lamé puts down their drink, the wide glass straw clinking loudly against the side, while Etta James eases into a song about how her lover's changed. "What'd Zion do this time?"

"He didn't..." Shaking my head, I take a huge sip of mojito. Anything to push back the moment of actually having to think about what I did in that pitch-black room. "Holy crap, this is good."

Lamé smiles.

After another fortifying dose of what's possibly the best cocktail I've ever had, I talk. "The glory thing. It's all my fault."

"Debatable," mutters Max.

I sip some more, at a total loss as to how to explain what's actually happened in the last two days, and then it just emerges. "Why did he marry me? You know? Why, out of the blue would the world's biggest star ask me to—"

Shit. Nobody knows about the marriage being fake. We signed NDAs. I can't go talking about it like this.

"The marriage of convenience thing?" Lamé sighs. "I love it so much."

So much for the NDA. "You...knew about that?"

"We're pretty close."

I blow out a hard breath. "Does...does everyone know?"

"*I* didn't know," says Max, her thin brows lifted in surprise, her mouth pursed around the straw, through which she's quickly emptying her beverage. "This is *amazing*."

"Crap. I hope you'll—"

Max waves. "Oh, cone of silence, honey. We don't out our own people."

"Or anyone," adds Lamé.

"That's...good." Feeling a little messy and a little loose, I take another long sip and lean back with a sigh.

"Well, whatever bad decisions brought you here." Lamé offers up a plate of what look like freshly-baked scones. "In my mind you've always been kinky."

I take one and bite in. "Oh, I'm not... Holy shit, this is good." Looking up, I catch them both watching me, their expressions pointed. "Why did you think I was kinky?" Wait...*am* I kinky? Is that how you'd define it?

"Are you?"

"You know what I think," Max says to Lamé.

"Max believes that everyone's got a kink in there somewhere. Hidden or not."

"I've seen hundreds of therapy patients, okay?" Max

grabs a little sandwich and gesticulates with it. "Trust me. We've *all* got something." She smiles at me. "Glory holes, for example, are a very specific—"

I need to make sure these two never meet Gigi or it'll turn into a circus. A really fun circus, but still. Especially if she tells them about the ex-boyfriend. And the ravishment thing. And every little filthy fantasy I've had since I was a teenager. "Shit." I slurp the remainder of my drink.

"Knew it." Lamé leans in to refill my mojito from a crystal pitcher.

"How?" I ask, bewildered as to how a total stranger has this kind of insight into my inner workings.

"He owes me," they say to Max.

I'm so lost. "Who?"

"Zion. I bet him you were a deviant. Just to bug him, really." Their eyes slide toward Max. "And, you know, like Max says, We're all something."

Max nods sagely.

"Anyway," Lamé goes on. "He insisted it wasn't possible. 'Zero percent chance,' is how he put it." The words are said in a decent imitation of Zion's accent. "Twyla's a good girl."

I sit still for a few seconds, in a weird limbo of shock and hurt and annoyance. Just who does Zion Mason think he is to write me off like that? I'm shaking my head, huffing out angry little noises as I picture the dead certainty on his handsome, arrogant face. The number of times I've been written off or typecast or pigeonholed is astounding and that Zion would do it?

Well, I guess I shouldn't be surprised.

"A good girl," I finally mutter. "Well, if by good girl, he means that I fantasize about letting men do very dirty things to me, then I guess he's right."

"Woooooooooo!" says Max.

Lamé's dark eyes stay focused on me, their expression more curious than anything.

"But I am far from the repressed, vanilla person he apparently assumed. And, frankly, I resent that he wrote me off like that."

"So, you've always been like this?"

I take another sip as I consider Lamé's question, letting the booze warm me, loosen me up, open my mind to something fresh and new and sort of light in a way I've never looked at it before. I feel better now, though my irritation at Zion still simmers close to the surface.

Maybe it's how casual these people are about their desires and sexuality. Or maybe it was the *rightness* I felt in the glory hole, before recognition kicked in. And maybe even a little bit afterward. Whatever it is, it's important. A self-discovery.

"Yeah." I nod, almost surprised at my own answer. "Yeah, I guess I have."

"Have you considered delving deeper into that side of yourself?" Max asks, sounding like a therapist, but looking like an extra on the set of some post-apocalyptic film.

"Not really. It's pretty incompatible with the life I'm trying to build." Or *was* building, before Zion "Wrecking Ball" Mason shoe-horned himself in and blew it all wide open.

"Well, you're here now," says Lamé, almost casually.

I am, aren't I? I'm here, my professional life's probably a write-off and there's truly nowhere else I need to be.

"Can't think of a better place to dip a toe into the lifestyle."

The lifestyle. It sounds almost wholesome put that way. But also big, all-consuming. A lot more than trying out a sexual fantasy or two.

And then I think of Zion, who'd assumed he knew me, scoffing as he wrote off a whole facet of who I am. Unexplored, maybe, but still, a part of me. *Twyla's a good girl.*

This time, his words don't irritate or hurt, they feel like a challenge. *Am* I good girl? Is that it? Sweet, innocent, boring Twyla, studying hard and following the rules and never giving in to the baser urges and *nonetheless*, getting shafted in the process?

"You know what? Yeah, maybe I'll do that." I'm all bravado now. Fuck Zion for assuming he knows the first thing about me and then for dismissing me. "Maybe I'll dip a toe."

"I knew it. The Black Hole worked its magic on you."

"Broke on through to the other side." Max laughs, turning to look at Lamé. "That place *is* magic."

"Remember Tara and Clive, after the breakup?"

"That's right. Meeting in the Hole every night."

"I heard they had no idea until she waited around to see who left."

"It's pure fantasy, you know? Head into the Hole, close your eyes, you could be fucking anyone."

"Beyoncé!" Max squeals.

"Idris for me. Always and forever." Lamé closes their eyes with a wicked smile. "I'd picture those huge brown eyes, looking up at me. Begging."

"Oooooh, I'd do that freckled British actor."

"Eddie Redmayne?" I offer.

"No, no. The one with the scary eyes. Peaky Blinders."

I yell, "Cillian Murphy!" enjoying the game.

"I'm picturing him next time," says Max, mouth full of scone.

"What about you, Twyla?" Lamé watches me. "You get in there, close your eyes and picture, I don't know, Zion Mason?"

"I'll bet he pictured Twyla Hernandez," Max says with an impish smile.

I go still, my insides buzzing. Why? Why would he picture *me*, of all people? Vanilla good girl that he assumes I am.

No way. He thinks I'm a prude. And he told me I shouldn't be here. So, no. He didn't, for one second, imagine me in that closet.

But then my mind slides back to the first moment in the darkness, when he was nothing but a shape, a presence. Did I picture Zion when the stranger first touched me? Was that part of the appeal? I want to say no, but I'd be lying, wouldn't I?

When I look up, they're both watching me. Rather

than face their open curiosity and whatever questions they're about to throw my way, I swallow and say the first thing that springs to mind. "Cillian Murphy's Irish."

They exchange a look.

"Even better," says Max "The man is humpable."

"Total top energy, alas." Lamé sighs with regret.

"Yeah." Max's sigh contains anything but regret.

"I met him recently," I break in. "I mean, just a hand-shake, but... Oh, crap. You know what? He kissed me on the cheek."

Max and Lamé are leaning in, identical expressions of awe on their faces.

"Seriously? How was it?"

"Okay, so..." I think back to the cocktail party where I'd been a total fish out of water. "He put his hand on my shoulder and got kind of close and..." I gasp, my eyes wide at the memory.

Max says, "Total top," into her drink.

Lamé, however, is watching me closely. "Was *he* there?"

I know exactly who they're asking about. Zion. "Yeah."

"Who?" Max is a half step behind.

"He didn't like it, did he?"

"Come on, who?" Max repeats, louder.

I shake my head, biting my lip at the memory. "He, um..."

Lamé's watching me like a hawk now, like they know, they *know* exactly what happened, what Zion did that night.

My nipples go hard at the memory.

"He put his hand on me."

"Cillian Murphy?" Max's face is all scrunched up.

"Zion," Lamé and I tell her together.

I reach up under my hair. "My nape. Right here."

"*Fuuuuuuuuuuuck*," Max says. "That is hot."

Zion's fingers had wrapped around my neck, long enough to curl over both sides. Hot and possessive. I remember exactly how it felt. Like I was his, somehow, which I knew wasn't real. All an act.

"I can guess who he pictured in the Hole tonight," Lamé proclaims, looking smug, as if they've already rested their case.

Max snorts. "Absolutely. Shoulda seen him come out, Lamé, holding one sparkly shoe, looking exactly like a boy who'd just lost his favorite new toy. And wow did he lose his absolute shit when I told him said toy went racing outside!"

"He has my shoe?"

"Yes, Cinderella, he does."

"Oh, glory, glory hallelujah." Hands steepled under their chin, Lamé smiles, their eyes focused sharply on me. "All righty, then." They stretch theatrically. "That's enough action for one night. Let's get you to bed."

I look down. "My clothes are in the car."

"I've got you covered, honey. Shower, nightie, new toothbrush. Everything you could need. On your freshly-made bed. I'll get you water."

I'm about to refuse their hospitality when my body

betrays me by forcing a long, jaw-cracking yawn from my mouth.

Lamé stands and holds out their hand. "Now, how about you get some shut-eye and let your fairy kinkperson take care of everything?"

13

Zion

I'm fucked. And not in a good way. I'm fucked in a can't-get-my-fake-wife-out-of-my-head-and-get-back-to-life kind of way.

Which is absolutely, definitely fucked.

Because the only thing that's ever mattered—aside from my career and the few friends here who make up my chosen family—is playing.

Except now, I can't do it.

I mean, yeah, I can run the flogger over Ponyboy Todd's pale, freckled back. I can slap his muscular ass with it and appreciate the slight jiggle when he gasps. I can even nudge his buttplug tail with my foot, but the thrill I'd usually get just isn't there. At all.

And I can't figure out what to do about it.

It's not like Todd's changed from last year, when the way he swayed and bucked and squealed made my cock hard and ready. I'd flogged him and toyed with his tail last year and then pulled the thing out, put a condom on, and fucked his ass until he came in his wife Kim's mouth.

Today, my cock's nonresponsive.

It's not just my cock, though. And it's not just with Ponyboy and Kim. This morning's scene with Aretha—one of my most dependable long-time play-partners—left me absolutely cold in a way I can't get around. Aretha's Ace. Our scenes aren't even sexual, dammit. They're pure, platonic bondage. Easy. A little rope play, suspension, a little degradation thrown in for her nonsexual pleasure. I generally enjoy all of it, but this morning, I went through the motions like a goddamn cyborg while my brain ran itself ragged, wondering where Twyla was and what she was doing and who the hell with.

"Sorry," I tell Ponyboy, backing up a step.

"It's all right, man," he replies, craning his neck to look at me.

"We're good, Zed." Kim walks up beside me with a smile. "Happens to everyone."

I fake a laugh and make some excuse, quickly escaping the big, open hangar space, all the while thinking that *No. No, this shit doesn't happen to everyone. Not to me. Not ever. Not once in my life have I left a scene unfinished.*

Outside, I barely see the people wandering by or sitting in the grass or playing soccer in way too little protective gear. All I can think about is Twyla.

Is she back in the Hole? Or is she gone? Did she leave camp? Is she with a lawyer, right this second, telling stories about what I get up to here and what a deviant I am and planning to take me for everything? No. That's not something Twyla would do. Not in a million years.

Then again, I'm pretty sure she didn't think I'd go out and ruin the marriage thing within two weeks. Hell, even I didn't think I'd do that. More than anything, I wish I hadn't. I wish—

"Zed!" says one of a pair of men riding by on a tandem bike, clad in nothing but metallic body paint.

"You're here!" finishes the other. The Perkins, we call them, sort of like a unit. Two men who prefer, at camp, to be seen and spoken to as one single entity. They're partners who are two parts of a whole. God only knows what'll happen the day they break up.

"Let's play tonight!" yells the light-skinned Perkins as they pedal by, not waiting for a reply. In the distance behind them, I catch a glimpse of a shape I know well, the movements familiar even while she's wearing a mask.

Every nerve, every damn cell in my body comes alive, so fast it burns.

"Twyla!" I yell, anonymity forgotten. Goddamn it. She doesn't hear me.

I set off at a run.

Twyla

I've had a whirlwind of a morning.

From the moment I got up, I've been fed and pampered, spoiled and fawned over. After the most restful night's sleep I can remember having in years,

Lamé served breakfast and told me to take a bubble bath if I wanted. Which I did.

"Aren't you sick of me yet?" I asked them, feeling like I'd already started to outstay my welcome.

"No. I like having you here," they said, settling across the kitchen table from me with coffee and a slice of toast. "You're distracting me from my issues."

My brows flew up at this mention of Lamé's personal life. Up until that moment, I was the focus of things. "Well, I'm glad to provide distraction," I told them. "And if you need to talk about it, I'd be happy to—"

"Oh, honey." They buttered their toast and sighed, shaking their head. "Just...family crap. I've got a brother who's just popped back into my life after a decade of pretending I didn't exist and, you know, it's a lot."

"Do you want him back?"

They set down their toast and stared at something over my shoulder. "I wish he had done this, like ten years ago." A glance my way and then a tight smile. "But you know. No point wishing for the impossible." Their one-shouldered shrug was overly casual and it made me want to reach out and hug them. I kept myself still instead, and listened. "Anyway, one of my partners is also driving me up the wall right now with his requests to move in together. He wants..." They crunched into their toast, chomping hard. "He wants what he calls *more*. And I frankly don't know that I'm there yet."

I nodded and thought about how Zion's the closest I'd ever come to living with a partner. "So, is it a deal breaker for him? The not moving in together?"

"I hope not." Their smile was bittersweet. "I like him a lot."

"But you like your space, too."

"I really do."

"Hello?" Max called from the front of the house. "I come bearing gifts!"

Lamé reached out and squeezed me hand. "Come see me play tonight. He's the blond."

"Okay."

"Look!" Max tromped in, holding my purse and a big bag from Target. "I'll stick this in your room. Car key, too?"

"Yes! Thank you!"

I started to get up, but she shooed me back down. "Finish your breakfast. I've got to head over to the front gate for a shift." She turned to Lamé. "Did you know the Primals are doing a movie?"

"Yep. The board voted on it. Gave them permission."

I straightened up, instantly alert. "Are they filming here?"

"Yeah, but it's very restricted. Just the Primal group." Lamé shook their head. "We've had a documentary crew before. We review all footage. Just make sure you wear the yellow bracelet so the camp photographer knows you're off-limits."

"That still seems risky, right? With all the folks who don't want to be in pictures?"

"She's been doing it forever. I personally look over everything, with a small committee. We've never had a leak."

I gave a slow nod, not entirely convinced that the system could be failproof.

"I've gotta run!" Max waved goodbye and took off, leaving us to finish breakfast and get dressed for my first day at camp.

So, instead of all the things I should have been doing —like conferring with a divorce attorney or phoning my publicist to figure out next steps—I spent an hour bathing and shaving and, with the help of Lamé, picking out the perfect outfit.

We settled on a fluorescent yellow bikini, layered with a gorgeous, short, brightly-colored floral robe from Lamé's overstuffed closet.

As we walk out and across the wide field now, past a massive hangar and down a slight hill, the raw silk rubs, soft and coarse against my already sensitized skin, reminding me of Zion's stubble last night, against my thighs, my breasts. My already aching nipples prick out hard and I swear I hear him calling my name and—

"Well, what do you know," says Lamé, an edge of glee in their voice. "Looks like you've been spotted, honey. Want me to—"

"*Twyla.*" Okay, so that *was* his voice, not some phantom echo from last night. It's stern and hard and hits me right in the pelvis.

I suck in a breath and turn. "Yes?"

"Are you kiddin' me?" His accent's harsher than usual as he jogs toward us. "How'd you two hook up?

"It was fate," sings Lamé.

"Yeah?" He's breathing hard, his body a little sweaty,

his eyes a little wild, looking so good it hurts my stomach. "Well, you shouldn't be here, Twy."

I go still. "Here?"

"At camp."

Those words shatter the heaviness between my legs, turning it to anger. "Is that so?"

Beside me, Lamé makes a low *Oh, no he didn't* sound under their breath.

"Come on. This isn't your thing."

"My thing? And just what is that, in your expert opinion?"

Clearly frustrated, he sighs, running a hand through his already messy hair. "You should be—"

"Should? *I should?* Oh, no you don't. You don't know the first thing about me. And you know why?" He opens his mouth, but I bowl through. "Because you never asked. You don't get to tell me where I should and shouldn't be. Fuck this." I step around him and my robe falls fully open, revealing my body in its full, bikini-clad glory—fat rolls and all. Fuck it. If there's one place on earth I can feel good about showing off my big, beautiful self, it's here, dammit.

Zion moves to block me. Behind his leather half-mask, his eyes slide down my body. Below the mask, his mouth drops open, whatever he was about to say apparently forgotten.

At his sides, his hands tighten into fists and that move, more than any of it, gives me the confidence to just stand here. To let him look.

To show him what he's missing.

"I believe you have my shoe, Zed. I'd like it back. And here at camp, you can call me Twilight," I tell him, high on this unexpected surge of power at his reaction. And anger that he thinks he knows where the hell I belong. "Like everyone else. Now, excuse me. I'm running late."

"Late?" He snarls. "Late to what? You meetin' someone? You playin'?"

Beside me, Lamé snorts.

I ignore it, along with the people slowing to watch the exchange, the game behind Zion coming to a literal stop while the players gawk. Instead, I let this new blend of hard confidence lift my chin and straighten my spine. "I'm heading to a workshop, *Zed*." His camp name is a line drawn in the sand between us. Here, we are nothing. "As if that's any of your business."

There's whispering and shuffling and maybe a shocked laugh or two. All of it makes this feel more like an act than reality. The bathing suit's a costume. I can do this. I can play the uncaring woman who takes no shit. I force a hard smile to my lips, pretend my heart's not thumping out of control, and step around him, as if I've got the slightest idea where I'm going.

"What workshop?" He's keeping pace on one side. Lamé's on the other.

"Spanking," I say, lightly.

His frowns and his Adam's apple pops like he's swallowed something big and I swear he looks like he's about to pass out when he rasps out, "Why?"

It's my turn to snort. "Because I'm interested. Obviously."

"Oh, look at that! I'm late for my shift," Lamé says giddily. "Would you mind walking her to the learning tent, Zed? Behind Sex-o-rama?" I glare at them, the traitor, as they take off skipping, roller skates tied over their shoulder, hair flying out behind them.

Why do I feel like I've been set up here?

"I'll find it myself," I tell Zion.

"Nah, it's okay." He puts out a hand to indicate the way. "Madame." As soon as I set off, he falls in beside and slightly behind me, not touching, but sort of surrounding me. He's big and imposing and definitely sending some kind of signal to the other campers, most of whom have dispersed. "Maybe I'll learn somethin' new."

Yeah, right. I'll bet he could teach the damn class.

I pick up the pace, wishing I'd closed the robe now that it's just the two of us. Although it's not just the two of us, is it? There are people everywhere. And either I'm imagining it, or they're paying us special attention. All the wide-eyed looks and whispering can't possibly be the way they do things here normally.

"Is everyone looking at us strangely?"

"What?" I swear people straighten up and act casual the second Zion turns toward them. "Course not."

"Hm." Skeptical, I glance around. All the whispering's stopped, all the looks quelled. I guess I imagined it. With a deep inhale, I gather that strong, ice queen character again, throw back my shoulders, and do my best to glide down the slight slope beside the clubhouse, past the pool where kinksters are splashing and playing and probably having all kinds of sex. I don't look. I can't. This character wouldn't notice things like other people. She'd forge straight through to her objective, single-minded and driven, and she absolutely wouldn't let some muscular, six-foot-five Adonis keep her from it.

I keep it up past the sign I floundered beside last night, up into a forest, by a fenced-in area filled with an assortment of people playing together as animals, and then a large, white, airy-looking tent, divided into rooms with sofas and benches and—

Whoa. Okay, a very sensual blow job happening right now. I can't help the way that tightens my core. Especially with Zion hovering over me, so big and angry and hard.

My character would get off on it anyway, I decide. The way she'd get off on Zion's irritation or frustration or whatever the hell it is he's doing.

I round the corner of the big tent and come to a stop at another, smaller tent. This one's got maybe two dozen people seated on the grass or folding chairs. At the front, a thin white person is laid out, face down over a leather bench, their limbs on adjustable arm and leg rests, while their naked ass is in the air. Behind them is the woman—according to her pronoun bracelet —who I'm assuming is the instructor, holding up a little leather riding crop thing, with cute sparkly tassels at one end. They thwack it lightly against the other person's ass.

Their only reaction is to blink.

"Okay. Next we have the cane."

I look around and find an empty spot on a big poof,

close to the front, but off to one side. Head low, I scoot in, smiling at the people who make way for me, and sit.

Good. Maybe Zion will leave. Or not. Maybe he won't.

Why does that idea appeal so much?

"Welcome," says the instructor, with a smile toward me. She's holding what is apparently a synthetic cane. "Come on in, Zed. We can make room for you."

"I'm good here," he says from right behind and above me, voice solid, final. Great. Now, he's acting like my bodyguard. Or prison guard.

The presenter—a beautiful, tall, fat, pink-haired Black woman in a matching, skin-tight minidress—looks briefly at me, her brows high, then back to Zion. "Okay, then." She looks down at the person on the bench. "All right, Bentley. Now, a birch." She lifts a tied bundle of fine twigs, tickles the other person's ass with it and then gives it a thwack. "We're lucky here at camp to have an endless supply of these," she says with an evil grin, going on to tell us that she's holding back because she doesn't want Bentley bleeding at this point." She talks about the advantages of each implement—including a hairbrush, which is apparently perfect for a nice lap spanking. People titter.

She picks up what looks like a big, black night stick. "The club."

"Good for *so* many things," says someone from the audience, which gets everyone laughing.

The teacher makes a ring with her fingers and thumb and grasps the club in a much more suggestive way, running her hand up and down the length. "That's right. There's potential everywhere."

Another easy laugh from the group.

"You okay?" asks the woman beside me. "Got enough room?"

"I'm good," I say with a smile, noting how the woman glances over her shoulder, I'm guessing at Zion, then smirks at me.

"Your bodyguard's intense."

"Yeah?"

She eyes him, her smirk deepening.

Curiosity wins out. "What's he doing?"

"Just watching you. Surprised you can't feel that stare."

"Now that you mention it, I do feel a little irritation between my shoulder blades."

They snicker. "He your Dom?"

I snort. "He wishes."

"Oooooooh." They look up at him with a delighted grin now. I'll bet he hates it.

I get the sudden urge to blow him a raspberry or something equally childish and, you know what? Fuck it. I twist, look up at him, and stick out my tongue.

Around us, a murmur goes up.

"Oh, you've riled him now," my neighbor tells me with a wink.

A burst of satisfaction runs through me.

"Here." They pull out a sheaf of papers and hand me the top one. "You might be into this."

I look down and read.

Kidnapping, Hostage Party, Big Hunt, oh my!

Hunting season is officially open!

Want to be taken? Mauled? Made to do things you've only ever imagined in the darkest recesses of your kinky little brain? Our kidnappers have been hard at work plotting, planning, and preparing absolute mayhem for your pleasure. Sign up now to experience Camp Haven's very own fantasy kidnapping experience.

Orientation* 3pm. Clubhouse.

***MANDATORY FOR KIDNAPPINGS / HOSTAGE PARTY / BIG HUNT**

Every word smacks me like the implements the teacher's talking us through at the front of the tent. Kidnapping? My body's response is visceral. Taken? Mauled? *Made* to do things?

What things? I'm dying to know.

The teacher's voice goes on, people yell reactions that I'm sure are funny or sexy or any number of things, but I hear none of it. I've got this rushing in my ears, my brain.

After a few minutes, I notice the prickling at the back of my neck and straighten up, concentrate, stop reading the words over and over. He's still back there, still watching me. I don't need to turn to be sure.

That attention feels right, somehow, infuriating but... satisfying. What's that about? Does pissing him off feel good? Is that what this is? Like the more riled up he gets, the more pleased it makes me?

We get more spankings and I barely hear a word, though I focus back in whenever I catch myself wandering. Somehow, not paying attention to Zion seems like just the thing to rankle him.

And, god, I want to do that. I want to poke him, provoke him, piss him off, and wait with baited breath to see what he'll do next. He's like a lion in a cage—prickly and dangerous and close to blowing up—and I want to see it when it happens.

Never mind the consequences.

Maybe half an hour goes by like this, with discussion of spanking methods and tools and experiences. I'm itching to move, to turn, to poke the lion again. I don't, though. I practice patience and wait, through interruptions, with questions and comments. If *he* weren't back there, glowering, I'd actually enjoy the easy, open, frank talk amongst this remarkably heterogeneous cross-selection of the population. It's not at all what I expected. There's none of the taboo, overly-sexualized element I'd imagined coming in. Instead, it's a thoughtful, friendly discussion of a subject that some of these people clearly know a lot about.

Too bad I can't relax and just enjoy it.

Although, this squirmy, giddy feeling? It's good. Like really, really good. I could get addicted to being this naughty and gleeful and ripe for... I don't know what, but it's there, here, hanging over me, inside me. *This, this, this* is what I feel right now. Like I've landed right on some target, but I don't yet see the big picture.

"All right," says Morgana, the teacher. "Any takers?"

I stiffen in my seat, my back straight, my nape tingling harder.

People shuffle, a big, hairy man in strappy leather stands up. "Me, me, me!" he shrieks, jumping up and down, which has everyone laughing and teasing.

After a quick wipe-off, he takes the other person's place on the bench. She looks around, asking if anyone's up for spanking or if she should do the honors herself.

Someone gets up—a small, muscular woman in a sports bra, gym shorts, and sneakers. "I got this." She cracks her knuckles, to the delight of the crowd, she chooses a small leather strap and, after a quick discussion on specific limits and consent, sets to work on the man. The spanking itself is fun and theatrical, with a few pointers from Morgana making it feel like a learning experience. The wildest course I've ever taken.

She asks for more volunteers, gets a new couple, then another. All the while, I'm thinking...I could do it. I could. The idea builds inside me and builds, the rushing in my head with it, the tingling, the squirmy, excited feeling that I'm on the cusp of something big and meaningful and right. I want this. Not just an idea now, but an imperative. I need to get up there and bend over that bench, desperately. Now. Now. And then, Morgana's asking for a volunteer and I stand before she's finished her sentence.

"I'll do it," I say. "I'll get spanked."

"Great!"

I move quickly to the front, before I can talk myself out of it. "Should I..." I indicate the bench Morgana just wiped off.

"Might want to take off the robe."

"Oh, right." I pull at the sash.

"Any spankers present?"

Someone starts to get up. "Sure. I'll—"

"The hell you will." Zion's voice slices through the levity like the sharp tip of a whip. Shock ricochets through me

Everything goes quiet.

My robe, forgotten now, drops from my shoulders with a slick slide. I barely notice it. All I can see is the hungry way he watches me, the danger lurking in those eyes. A shiver runs through me, drawing goose bumps to the surface of my skin and I can't for the life of me figure out if I'm unnerved or excited or some other thing entirely.

With effort, I tear my gaze from his, working hard to appear indifferent. When I do, I could swear that a low, threatening growl rises up from his vicinity. It takes everything I have not to react.

I guess the lion's out of its cage.

14

———

"Bend over," I say into the silence.

At the front of the tent, my wife's in nothing but that bright yellow bikini, her eyes wide, her mouth a tight little O.

"You okay with this?" Morgana asks.

Twyla doesn't take her eyes off me, though her expression morphs from surprise into a squinty-eyed annoyance that I feel in my gut. Good. She should be irritated, dammit. She's the one who busted into my life here, breached walls she had no fucking right to. If the little brat's gonna traipse around *my* world half naked, then she'll get exactly what she's got coming to her.

Lips tight, eyes slitted, she nods. "Yep. Fine."

Morgana watches us. "Want the switch or a pad—?"

"Bare-handed," I cut through, cracking my knuckles for effect. "You good with that?" Her easy nod only chafes me. "Limits?"

Twyla's nostrils flare. "Nope."

"Okay, then, sweetheart. Bend...over."

Barely hearing the gasps and whispers behind me, I watch, riveted, as my wife lowers her top half to the leather bench, glaring over her shoulder, and presents me with the finest ass I've ever laid eyes on. Fuck me. Look at that. It's round and wide and dimpled and it does something to me—turns me wild and raw. Makes me want to hurt and plunder and take, take, take.

Before I know what I'm doing, I'm stepping in, canting my body to the side. I rear back my hand and stop.

"Fuck, baby," I mutter as my hand drifts down to cup one plump cheek. "Look at you." I pull her swimsuit up and settle it in her buttcrack, then do the same on the other side, the backs of my fingers rubbing her skin as I go.

She's so fucking soft.

I've got to explore. My hands tighten, dig into her flesh, knead it just a little. Hell, if this is my one and only chance, then I'd better learn her here and now or that'll be it and, no.

Hell, no.

Her back rises and falls faster. I reach out to soothe her, to tell her it'll only hurt for a minute, but the rush is so good she'll never want me to stop.

Someone behind us coughs. I blink back to the setting —outside, daytime, small white tent, packed full of more people than it should hold. My wife—my goddamn bratty-ass *wife*—volunteering to get her first official spanking, as if just anyone here would do.

"You want this, baby?" I ask, ignoring the shuffling behind us. "You sure? I'll stop if you—"

"Just do it!" Her harsh whisper comes with a glare that turns my warm, heavy cock solid in seconds.

"When I'm ready," I force out, not letting her see how much topping from the bottom apparently turns me on. Or is it the brat thing? How'd I never notice the brat thing? And why's it so fucking hot?

With a final, painfully slow stroke, I raise my hand and, in a single motion, bring it back down in a stinging slap.

Her ass shakes, her whole body jolts, and she lets out a little squeak that'll be forever enshrined in my permanent spank bank.

My cock's rock hard, already leaking pre-come, more ready than it's ever been.

Hell, look at these curves. All this fucking *bounty* that she hides behind her boring, everyday clothes. I'm half annoyed that I almost never got a look at this body and half relieved, though I hate everyone else looking at her right now. Seeing this, her, us. But damn, if she'd spent our time together walking around in bathing suits all day, I'd never have gotten any work done. Neither of us would have.

Every time I caught sight of her, I'd have felt the need to unload on her, inside her. Fill her up so she knew exactly who she belonged to.

Reality and fantasy blend as my hands explore the

width of her hips, run up the outside of her suit and slide under it, gathering it up and twisting high on her hips until both sides are tightly coiled rope.

She wiggles, probably working to get friction on that sweet little clit, that juicy cunt I ate last night, with its thick lips and the snug hole my cock barely got a taste of. Fuck, I want in there. And I don't want it in the dark, without names or faces or voices. I want it out in the open, in front of everyone, so they know who all this belongs to. I want it, masks off, so I can see her expression, so I can eat it up, while I lap at her, nibble her, bite every inch of this skin, mark her with my—

"Hey, Zed. You gonna spank her or put her to sleep up there?" barks Morgana, with her friendly brand of snark.

There's laughter. I force my mouth into a smile, relieved that they can't see my entire face behind this mask, because for once, I've got no control over my expression. Hell, I've barely got my body in hand. It's like my brain's shut off and the rest of me's gone rogue.

"Need help up there, bro? I could—"

"No!" I snarl over my shoulder. "I've got this."

But do I?

Yes. I'm the king of fucking control. Everyone here knows that. I never lose it. Never give it away.

I inhale, eyes closed, working hard to expel the chaos.

"Spread," I tell her, my body thrumming with a fresh surge of satisfaction when she obeys immediately. "Good girl. So good."

She wiggles a little, lifts her ass, her legs wide apart. I

step aside, my body remembering how this works, though my mind's not entirely online, and smack the other cheek, then the first, harder.

She gasps.

I shake out my stinging palm. Yeah, I want her gasping. I want her moaning. I want that plump little body writhing with pain and need and the frustration I'm dealing with just watching her. Waiting. Wanting.

Another smack, this one low and close to that little patch of yellow that's gone darker than the rest. Part of me can't comprehend that it's real—Twyla, wanting this, getting off on this. Taking this, from me. Who is this woman?

I want to know so bad it hurts.

"You wet, baby?" I lean in, get a good look. "Christ, look at that. You like it, don't you? Like gettin' punished?"

With her suit twisted up, cutting into all that flesh like a thick, yellow cord, she's equal parts lovely and obscene, a sacrificial virgin from an old B-movie. Until you catch sight of that little wet patch, and then she's pure filth. I think of pulling the offending fabric aside and running my knuckles through all that plump slickness and then, fuck, my body's not obeying anymore, because I shouldn't do this—not here, not in front of the crowd without explicit consent.

But she said no limits. And she's got her safe word and...

I drag the scrap of cloth to one side, let my knuckles skim her lips, lean in. "Want me to stop?" I ask, shielding her from the others with my body.

She shakes her head.

"Say it, so it's clear."

"N-n-no. Don't stop."

I lower my voice. "In front of all these people?"

"Yes. Yes, please." God, I love that word on her mouth. *Please.* Her teeth dig into that pouty lower lip. Her eyes turn to look at me. "I don't want you to stop," she says, louder, projecting like a good little stage actress.

Fuck, just that image ramps me up for a second. The idea of taking her on a stage, not just in front of this group, but a fucking horde of people. A Broadway production.

"Good girl." I lean back, step away, and angle my body so every one of these fuckers can see what's mine. Then I brace myself and look down at what I've felt and tasted, but never seen.

My vision goes dark at the sight of plump, glistening, freshly-shaved flesh, pink and brown. I reach out—her cunt's pure heat, her wetness cold on my fingers. "You shave today? Is this for me?"

When she doesn't reply, I lean in, tap her ass and pull the cheek wide, focus on the little brown hole above.

My balls go tight and high, my belly knots up. Fuck, fuck, I'm gonna come. The urge is uncontrollable, almost painful. I want to do it inside her. I want to make her take it, show her she's mine. Show all these people. Lay claim and—

She whimpers, arches up, opening herself to me.

My hand's about to pull out my cock when someone in the audience whistles, low. The sound unblocks something in my brain and, suddenly, I hear the hum of people around us again—a lot of them.

"Nice," says Morgana. "You just about done?"

I turn and see not just the original tent full of workshop participants, but dozens more. There's gotta be a hundred people out there, watching and whispering, while I come close to disobeying every one of my own rules and raw dogging my wife in public.

After just a spanking. Not *even* a spanking. A half a damn spanking.

What'd I get in? Like three slaps? Four? Her ass is barely pink. I want it a dark, angry red. The kind of red she'll feel for days when she sits. A pain she'll embrace because it'll be something I gave her. Shared pain. I want to make her hurt so bad her body digs deep and finds pleasure.

"Just a sec," I mutter, honing in on the arch of Twyla's back, the elegant line of her shoulder, the spill of hair covering her neck and half her back. I picture a glint of silver under that hair, a hint of leather at her neck, a thick ring at her throat.

With a possessiveness I've never once felt in my entire goddamn life, my eyes trail down, down, along the deep central divot of her spine, to that ass and that perfect little cunt, just begging for me to—

"Okay," Morgana cuts in. I don't know whether to be pissed or relieved. "That's all the time we've got. Thank you, Master Zed. And your, ah, partner."

"My wife." Once the words are out, I know I

shouldn't have said them, but I can't drum up an ounce of regret.

Morgana's face morphs to surprise. "Right. Okay. Your wife."

On the bench, Twyla shimmies around to glare at me. For some reason, that look makes me brighter inside. Happier. It makes no fucking sense how good I feel. None at all, considering all the shit that I've done.

Behind me, people are moving, laughing and talking in excited, hushed voices. I ignore it all, reach out to straighten Twyla's bathing suit, itching for whatever contact I can get, but she's already scooting off the bench, away from me.

She accepts her robe from Morgana and nods at whatever the other woman tells her, then turns back to me.

"Thanks." Her voice is high and light, casual. Is she acting right now or is this real? "That was fun," she says, then waves her fingers and takes off.

Fun? I watch her, stunned. That's it?

No, it can't be.

I go after her, working hard to sound casual, though I feel anything but. "Where you headed?"

"Oh, um..." She pulls a folded sheet of paper from her pocket. "Where's Tent C?"

"C Tent? That's..." I focus in on the flyer, trying to make out the words. "Why? What's at C Tent? Wait. What's that?"

She keeps walking, though clearly she's got no idea which direction. "Orientation."

"Orientation? Wait. Hang on. What orientation?" There's only one orientation I know of happening today and it's Kidnapping. *Kidnapping?* "No," I say like a fucking fool.

"Whatever." The look she gives me confirms it.

But fuck, fuck, no. No way can I just sit back and let her do this shit. "Are you doing this on purpose?"

She pauses, halfway up the hill to the craft fair. "Doing what?"

"Antagonizin' me."

Her head tilts. "Is *that* what I'm doing?"

"Goddamnit, Twyla, you *know*."

"It's Twilight, thank you. And what is it I know, exactly, *Zed*?" Her face is placid, but the quick rise and fall of her half-naked chest tells me there's more going on. What is she? Turned on? Pissed? Upset? All of the above?

And doesn't she get to be all of that? an annoying inner voice chimes in. Yes. Yes, she does. But I don't have to like it.

I force myself to calm down, make my voice measured and even. Hell, I even get my mouth to curve up a little on one side. "You sure that's what you want?"

"No." The answer surprises the hell outta me. "No, Zed. I don't know what I want. But why shouldn't I explore my options?" She watches me closely, her expression dead serious. "No reason I can't."

What can I say? I can't stop her from doing anything she chooses. Does she choose this? Is this really her, or... Shit, I don't know. I wrack my brain for a moment in our public lives when she showed this side of herself. I was convinced she couldn't relate to me, to this.

What if she can? What if the way I saw her before is flawed?

Half of me thinks she's doing this to make some kind of point. That half wants to pick her up, throw her over my shoulder, and lock her up someplace safe and quiet and as far from camp as possible.

But it's not my goddamn choice, is it?

She's not mine, despite what my cock seems to think.

Which is for the best.

I move aside, but only half a step. "Why'd you come here? To camp?"

Her face changes again, the lines going sharper, more thoughtful, a little curious. "Why do you think?"

For a second, a feeling rises up inside me, unfamiliar and raw. I've experienced something like it before, once or twice.

The time I went home to my dad's place after landing my first big film role. I felt something like it. A swelling bubble in my chest. I didn't know what to call it then and I don't now.

But I remember how that trip wound up—with Dad glancing at my newly-bought clothes and my gifts and shooing me off, telling me to stop wasting time, he had shit to do. Shit which I know involved beer and his shows and, if he was lucky, whatever Clive Seal had dropped off from his latest hunt.

Hurt and deflated, I'd turned and stared at the TV, where a commercial for dish detergent played, showing a happy TV family with their white, white teeth, their clean house, that cheery, too-bright world that had to be more than just a dream. Sunlight and music and people holding goddamn hands.

Why do I *think* she came to camp? To harass me? To make me feel worse than I already do? The other question, the one I'm much too terrified to explore, is why I *want* her to have come. But thinking about that right now is a terrible idea. The idea, just a sprout of a notion, that this feeling I have could be real, that she could reciprocate and understand and be a part of this world. Of both worlds?

It's too much, too strong, so close to hope that I can't quite look it in the face. Instead, I deflect, hard. "I don't know, Twy. Why'd you come?"

Her eyes—those big, deep, unfathomable wells—look down for a split second before rising to meet mine again. "To find out what I'm missing," she says with a smile as fake as any I've seen in Hollywood. She's an expert. A real pro. A magnificent actress, which is only part of what caught my eye the first time I saw her. "Now." The smile deepens, goes slicker. "Which way to this?" She shakes the flyer again and I go cold.

15

───────

Twyla

"You serious about the Kidnapping?" Zion asks, his jaw hard and mean, a wild look in his eyes.

"Maybe. Or the Hunt, or the hostage thing." Once I find out exactly what they are, obviously. Not that he needs to know how ignorant I am. "I'm interested."

"In *that*?"

I pause and look right at him, shoving all shame and embarrassment aside, along with a good dose of the lust running through my body since that spanking. He's not ashamed of what he does here, after all. He's not denying his kinks. Why should I?

"Are you seriously shaming me right now, Mister? Are you judging me? I was under the impression that this was a judgment free zone. I'm just exploring my options here, digging down and learning more about who I really am. Got a problem with that?"

His lips compress, like he's got things to say, but he's holding them in.

Wow, he looks worked up. His brow's crinkled, the lines carved deep. I fight the urge to smooth them with my fingers, which I'd then run through his hair, maybe grab a big handful. Maybe I'd give it a yank. Would he like that? A little pain from me? A little retaliation? Would it bring something besides irritation to those perfect features? I'd like that. A lot. Which is odd, because giving pain has never been my thing. Suddenly, though, I want to run through the gamut of what my body can take—and give. And, despite the plethora of beautiful men around me, and this deep curiosity regarding all things kinky, I want Zion. And only Zion.

My body and my mind, both, are so wrapped up in him, how can I look at anyone else?

That face, those freaking eyes, somehow lazy and piercing at once. He's got this long nose, straight and perfect, except for this little bump I want to test with my finger. And his lips, pressed flat right now, are usually just the right amount of plump for the cameras. And for other things.

God, he's beautiful. And it's not just the aquatic transparency of his eyes or the flawless line of his jaw, glinting with a fine layer of growth beneath his mask, or the somehow sexual heft of his shoulders, or the sprinkling of hair on that chest. Nor is it the ridiculous amount of talent he walks around with every single day, embodying each role without apparent effort, although that's a part of it, I guess. What I know about Zion now that we've spent a bit of time together, is that he doesn't just embody the roles, he understands them. Naturally gets the characters, inhabits them, makes them a part of him and vice-versa. And that's not just talent, it's empathy, pure and simple.

Which, in a way, makes what he did to me so much worse. He knows how it feels to be in someone else's skin. He knows how it feels to hurt.

And, yes, the issue is my career, but it's more than that, dammit. Way more. I can see that now. I can admit it. No, he didn't promise love or anything close to it. The fact that I started to develop feelings, well, that's on me.

I blink up at him, then let my attention slide down to the words on the paper:

Kidnapping, Hostage Party, Big Hunt.

A shiver makes its way up my spine. A little fear, a little curiosity, a lot of anticipation. What did he ask? If I'm truly interested in those scenarios?

I am. Almost as much as they scare me.

With a firm, "yes," I turn a full circle, look back down, and finally squint out toward the faint glimmer of the pool. "The clubhouse is that way, isn't it? Pretty sure C Tent's by the Clubhouse." I set off without awaiting his reply.

After a few seconds, he appears beside me. "You don't want to do those. Any of them."

All the lingering heat whooshes from my body and, without looking his way, I hiss, "Don't you *fucking* tell me what I want, Zed." I feel him stiffen at my coarse language. He's not used to it, obviously. Probably doesn't like it, either.

Yeah? Well welcome to your new reality, motherfucker.

That little sign of shock makes me want to push him harder, to get a rise out of him, to see what he does when he's really upset. "You think a little marriage license lets you decide where I go, what I do, who I damn well do it with?"

He doesn't reply, which is a wise choice, given how much rage is washing through me. It's pricking my nipples up, hard and aching, it's coiling tight and low in my belly, turning everything inside out. "You think you know me at all? You think what we were doing was real? It was a goddamn business deal, you asshole. A deal you went and broke within two *fucking* weeks of the wedding."

He opens his mouth, but I plow on, quickening my pace down the grassy hill toward the paved path to the pool and the clubhouse and, beyond it, C Tent.

"Thank you, though, for giving me this." I force a lightness to my tone that I don't feel in the slightest. "I mean, where else can a person get their freak on without shame? Without fear of getting caught? God, if I'd known this was here, I'd have—"

"You'd have *nothing*. You don't belong here. You're not doing this because you want to, you're doing it to piss me—"

"Oh, shut up," I say, my voice hard and loud enough

that a few faces turn our way. "You know nothing about what I want...clearly."

"Nothing?" He steps closer, edges me to the side, away from the path. "That's bullshit."

Suddenly, I'm pressed against a tree, the bark rough through the thin silk of the robe. I look up and...oh wow, look at him. Tight and hard and furious. And big. Huge. With his bulk, he could overpower me in a second. Without effort.

My back arches, my shoulders pushing harder against the wood, my aching chest seeking more contact with his body. More pressure. More pain, more pleasure.

Our movements come in quick, hushed bursts. I twist to get out, his fist catches my wrists, traps them above me, his other hand circles my throat, pinning me in place.

I still move, though, I still struggle. Hell, the struggle's half the fun. It's a game of chess, where every move I make forces him to counter, move, counter. I thrash, he boxes me in. My knee lifts, fully prepared to kick him where it hurts, but he knocks it aside with his, grinds his pelvis against mine.

His erection's stiff, massive. I remember that. The size of him, from last night. The way his tip barely breached me and the stretch almost hurt.

Almost. Less than spanking. Although, if he'd thrust in, I'd have gotten a bite of that pain I can't seem to get enough of.

"You want this, you little brat?" he whispers close to my ear, then hunches lower, takes the lobe between his lips, and bites me.

The shock's immediate, electric, thrilling.

I pull away just so he'll bite harder and, goddamn him, he does. He does. It's a struggle, a fight, a battle, and I want this so badly, I'll do anything for it to last.

Anything at all.

"Get off," I mutter, my voice a raw, angry bark.

"You safe wording?"

I open my mouth and close it again.

Zion, the bastard, just laughs, sounding nothing like himself and, at the same time, like the purest, most elemental version.

"Get the fuck off me, you—"

Teeth bared, he lowers his head and tears my bikini to one side, scraping my skin as he bares my breast to the world. Without support, it hangs heavy, but I don't care. Not in this place. Not in this moment, with this man. Everything my body does is right, meant to be, somehow. I feel this when he tears the other cup off and digs his face between my breasts and growls like a rabid beast and then goes wild on me, all snarling, snapping, biting the thickest part of me, then moving and doing it again, again, to my nipple.

Oh, god, that hurts. Another bite. More pain, but it's blissful, pulling at my center, my pelvis, which I'm tilting forward, trying to get the friction back from his lower half. I want that. I want his mouth, his cock. No. Not want. I *need* it. More than air, I need to be taken, covered, filled. Pounded to oblivion.

He sways back—the opposite of what I'm begging for —his eyes flicking over all the parts of me he's splayed wide open, reaches out and slaps my breast, right where he's just tortured it with his teeth. I groan, head falling forward, my whole body boneless. I'd be on the ground if he wasn't holding me up. I stare at the indentations his teeth have left in my skin. I want to touch them, but I can't.

"You're a little fuckin' brat, Twy." He reaches down. I follow the movements, dully, almost from outside, an observer, watching, wanting. Taking, taking, taking. He leans in. My face turns toward him. Of course it does. It always will. "You're my little fuckin' brat. *Mine.*"

That word's said with more steel than I've ever heard from him. On screen or off.

"This." He cups me between the legs, his shoulder now pinning me to the tree, his body weight so easily holding mine. "This is mine."

My bathing suit's shoved aside again—this time not for show or whatever that was back there, but for him. Purely him. There's something selfish about the way he does it. Something impatient and mean and, god, why do I love being used like this?

"Nobody touches this but me, got it?" His fingers slide up my wet slit and back down, spreading me open, wide. "And this." Faster than I can keep track of in my zoned-out state, he reaches up and smacks my tit again, makes it jiggle, makes it ache. With a pained groan, he bends over and sucks my nipple into his mouth, then more and more of my breast, like he'll consume every bit of me he can take. I swear he almost chokes on me before drawing back and then—

Then—oh, this isn't me to want this, to ache for this, to love it as much as I do—he *spits* on my breast, as if my body's not wet enough already.

"Look at this bratty little cunt." He leans back and I know—I *feel*—how I look. Completely debauched. Destroyed. Bite marks on my skin, my nipples swollen and bruised, shining wet and dripping with spit.

I don't have time to worry about the people walking by, watching, and reacting—some with approving laughter, some with comments I can't hear. Some are blank-faced, wide-eyed. None of it matters with his hand between my legs again, rough and bossy, spreading me, flicking my clit, as if it's an afterthought—or a punishment—and then, oh god, this is what I need.

"Yes, yes, yes yes yes." It's a guttural chant, forced from my lungs the way his finger's forcing its way inside.

Not that it's hard work, given how soaking and ready I am, but still it's an intrusion.

He fucks me like this for a few beats—or forever. Not long enough—withdraws and paints my other nipple with my wetness. When he bends and licks it off, his eyes are on me—no, not on me, in me, digging deep, pinning me in place like something sharp and glinting and now I'm dangling here, caught like a fish on a hook. I am ravished and raw and so fucking turned on, I'll come if he touches me again. I want to. I want that.

I want him to fuck me with his finger and his cock, I want him to tear me apart a little at a time, consume me like something wild.

When his hand disappears from view again, the last

thing I expect is for him to separate my labia, to stretch me open. "Give me your hands," he orders.

I do it. Of course I do. Anything he wants in this moment is his.

He places my hands at my crotch, makes me hold myself open, as if it's beneath him, somehow, and oh my god, I'll do it if it pleases him. I'll splay myself and flay myself and lay myself at his feet.

I'm not ready for him to sink to his knees, bend his head and cover my entire pussy with his mouth. I'm not ready for his tongue on my clit and then his teeth and then, like the violent flick of a whip, his hand spanking me there.

I'm not ready to fly, fly, fly above him and us and the camp and everything I ever thought mattered in this world.

But I do. And it's fucking beautiful.

16
———

So much of my life's been about control. Keeping it. Never letting it go.

Liev's a man whose entire sex life revolves around losing control and letting his inner animal take over.

Not me. I'm the man holding the reins. I'm the man who decides. I pick and choose and stay level-headed throughout everything that comes at me.

When Twyla's eyes roll back into her head, her sweet little pussy clenched around my finger, her lush, round body limp in my arms, something happens.

I don't lose it, so much as I make new choices. Choices I'd normally take the time to think through first, to figure out, to ensure mesh with my lifestyle, long and short term. Choices I know for a fact will have no bearing on anything I do—at camp or away.

But when my wife's orgasm gives its final gasp and she looks at me in that satisfied, bedroom way I'd never once thought to see on her face, my brain goes off-line or something. Hell, maybe it melts. Maybe it's her smile that shuts me down and fucks with my head. Or maybe it's the way she slowly leans in, wraps her arms around me, and sighs, the sound the happiest thing I've ever heard, right against my cheek. "Zion," she whispers, her lips a hot caress on my jaw, my neck, up, up, over my chin, toward my mouth—

"Stop." The word's harsh, shocking in the hot, sweet, lazy aftermath.

"You safe wording me?" Twyla whispers as she brings her nose in line with mine, our lips not quite touching. Not quite, but almost, so close I feel the heat of them, the brush, the almost-friction of moving air. "You saying Red? Yellow to slow down?"

I shut my eyes and don't move an inch.

"I know, I heard," she singsongs in that low, lulling voice. "Zion Mason doesn't kiss." Her nose slides along mine, our masks catch, fabric to fabric, as she eases over, to the other side, the move slow and sensual and intimate enough to hurt. "Oh, I mean *Zed*. Sorry. No kissing for Zed. And I respect that. We all have our limits, right?" Another unhurried slide of skin, another near-miss between our mouths. Her breathing's as shaky as mine. "I won't kiss you, Zed. At least not..." She taps a finger to my lips. "Here."

She tilts her head and trails her mouth to the side of mine, down, under, and back up the other side. It's such a long, leisurely path, I almost don't notice she's just traced the outline of my lips with hers. We're a hair's breadth from it happening; so close, I could turn my head and just let that part of us fuse, the way we did on that red carpet all those weeks ago, when I told myself it was the right thing to do. Not a role, but a duty. And, if it felt good, then so be it, it wasn't real, it was for the cameras.

"Can I kiss you down there?" Her whisper's so low I can barely hear it. "Can I suck you?"

The words jolt me out of it. My eyes snap open. I catch her watching me, her expression still soft enough that I wonder if I heard right. Is this disappointment? No. I huff out something like disbelief. No fucking way.

"Let me suck you, Z."

Definitely heard right. And my dick's on board, even if the rest of me's caught in a different spell.

"That what you want, baby?"

She nods, the teeth digging into her lower lip a siren's call to my balls. Before I know what I'm doing, I stand and pull myself out of my shorts, giving my cock a few rough strokes, though it's more for show than necessity. I'm not sure I've ever been this hard.

"Look," I tell her, as she drops to her knees, the robe getting in the way, her breasts loose and heavy and covered in my bites, her body on display. "Look at what you do to me, you little brat, with those tits and that pussy." With my thumb, I gather the pre-come beading at my head and slide it over that plump lip, releasing it from her teeth. "And this mouth." I push my thumb between her lips, hook her bottom teeth and pull down. "This fucking mouth, telling those people you wanted a spanking, giving permission to do whatever." I pull my thumb out and suck it. "Limits?"

"Nope," she says, all provocative defiance.

"It's hard to concentrate with these out here, displayed for the world." I bend slightly and pinch a nipple, hard, then tug until her tit stretches toward me. The image is pure filth and when she arches back, either easing the pain or giving me more, it's fucking beautiful. "And this goddamn face. I hate that you cover it here, hate that they can't see how fucking gorgeous you are."

"So take it off," she taunts.

I want to so bad that my fingers grab the bottom edge of the leather and lace thing she's wearing. I pause. "You brat. You trying to push me?"

"I just felt like sucking cock, Z." Her glance takes in the people meandering around us, close enough to see, but not hear. "If you're not up for it, I'm sure someone else can—"

Possessiveness, pure and fierce takes over and I'm nothing but a beast, all rage and want.

I grasp her face, tighten my hold until her mouth pops open, and ease my cock inside.

She starts to fall and I grab her by the back of her head, my cock a good two inches in her mouth, and pause, so close to going against every rule I live by—consent, first and foremost. Safe, sane, consensual, dammit. Why do I keep forgetting that with her? "You know how to tap out if you can't talk?"

She starts to shake her head, apparently recalls the rules, and nods.

"Show me."

Her body finds its balance, she stretches up onto her knees and grasps my thighs, then taps them both, three times.

"Good. One hand's enough. You can't get to my thigh, touch me anywhere. Do anything three times and I'll stop. You understand? Hell, you have my permission to knee me three times if that's what it takes." Her smile, stretched around my throbbing dick, is pure poetry. This whole exchange is surreal and perfect.

"Now," I say, gathering up all that long, luscious hair and sliding slowly out until she's got just the tip of me on her tongue. "You gonna be a good girl and take what I give you, Twy?"

She blinks, her eyes so dark behind the mask it's hard to gauge just what she's thinking. But, I'm a monster, and in this moment, I decide it doesn't matter what she thinks. She's given me permission, so we're safe. Definitely consensual. Sane? Not so sure.

And I don't fucking care. I push in, slowly, slowly, wanting this first feel of her mouth on my cock to last as long as it can. Bending my knees, I wind my right hand in her hair until it's a rope in my fist, pull her head back enough to look at her face and bare her neck and slide my left hand on her throat.

I'd planned to take my time sinking deeper into her mouth, but Twyla—my eager little brat—impales herself on me.

Twyla

My eyes water. For a second, I want to reach up and wipe the tears, but then I let them go as I fuck my own face on his massive cock, practically choking myself.

Once I've started, I don't for a second ask myself why I'm doing this. But once the idea's there, I ask why it feels so good. Why?

Why is the discomfort so much better than any one too-intimate fumbling I've had in my life? The back of my throat's not an erogenous zone, after all.

He grasps my hair, cutting off my train of thought, and watches me expectantly, as if waiting for a sign that I want him to stop. I don't. I can't. God, how *could* I when what starts as pain at my scalp shoots pure, unadulterated pleasure to my pussy?

The grind of dirt under my knees, the obscenely wide stretch of my mouth, the way he pulls, too hard, at my nipples. It's all awful. Terrible. The exact opposite of pretty. The most painful thing I've chosen to do of my own accord, and yet, I've never wanted anything more.

With a grunt, he thrusts—hard.

I gag, lose my breath, my train of thought, a handful of brain cells.

"Fuck, look at you, taking my cock like a queen."

Between my legs, I gush moisture. From the sound of his voice? The feel of him inside me? I've got no idea.

"You wet, baby? I want you wet and ready. Got to taste you again, get you all over me. I want to fuck every part of you, make you..." He groans the words out. A torrent of filth that sounds as out of control as he looks and it pushes me higher, twists me tighter. I want more of this—him, his body, his words.

Oh, god. Oh my god. How can I be this wild after that brain-destroying orgasm?

I'm moaning—a low, constant hum that sounds bestial in a way I've never seen myself. It's not *my* noise. Not of my choosing. It's been wrung from me. Taken.

"That's it. Take it. Take this cock. It's yours. Fuck, look at you. Such a good girl. So fucking good."

A shimmer of pleasure runs through me at those words.

Another thrust and I'm leaking fluids everywhere. My eyes are streaming, my mouth's trailing saliva. My nose is probably dripping, too, but it doesn't matter. I don't care. I don't.

I don't care about a fucking thing except this. And it's glorious.

I strain to look up, wanting to know if he's as destroyed as I am or if he's still that easy, sly, pristine creature I thought I knew before everything blew up. He doesn't appear angry or mean, the way I half-expect, but something else.

Concentrated. *Fascinated.* There's a look... What is that? A sort of *I did that* expression on his face as he pumps into my mouth again, slow and deep. Something close to pride that's somehow absurd and also very, very appealing.

Wonder.

That's it.

"Oh, you don't fucking know how often I've..."

What? He's what?

I pull back and lick the musky salt at the tip of him. It's a flavor I've been craving all my life, I just didn't know it.

Zion looks amazed. Like a boy who's opened a gift at Christmas and it's a million times better than what he expected. Or wanted.

"Fuck, Twy..." His growled words betray the slow, measured, deep strokes he's clearly straining to maintain. "So goddamn good."

I get another happy rush from the compliment and pick up my pace.

"Such a good little brat."

Brat.

Shivering as those words echo through me, I give him another slow lick, then pull him out to stroke his stiff length against my face, leaving another wet mark on my cheek. I can't look away, don't want to break this connection between us.

"You're beautiful," he says. Maybe. I think. I don't know. "Beautiful brat. Takin' me so good."

I shiver from those words and go deeper, try harder. *Brat. Good girl.* Something like pride's running through me at the idea that I'm taking him well and pushing his buttons and, just that makes me want to try harder, do better, open wider for whatever he gives me.

Why is it this way? Why does this man make me feel hungry and aching and empty and also such raw tenderness that it scares me?

And all this from a blow job.

He presses deep and I relax my throat and take him, the rest of my body pure fire. Inside, though, something shifts. It's tiny, but momentous.

It scares the crap out of me.

"Oh, fuck, that's it, Twyla baby," he growls, low and mean, the words hitting every nerve ending in my body. "That's it. Suck it. You like sucking me, little brat?"

I love it, I want to say, though words are clearly impossible. I love it so much I'm afraid what will happen when it ends.

17

Twyla looks up, tries to nod—not easy caught in my hands like this, with my dick nudging her throat.

She gags and I pull out all the way, release her throat long enough to take myself in hand and paint her lips with another gush of pre-come and then, since she likes spankings, slap her on the face with it.

With a groan that sounds like pure, distilled pleasure, her body goes loose, her weight pulling at where I've got her by the hair. It's got to hurt, but that only makes her jolt and stretch and shove those titties at me, like an offering to some fucked up god. "These are mine." I slap one, then the other, ignoring the way her mouth follows the movements of my dick. "Fuck, you're wild for this, aren't you?" Another slap of my dick to her face, which isn't as satisfying as it'd be without the damn mask, but her reaction's just as electric. My baby likes to get her face slapped. How hard and with what is just something we'll have to explore.

But not now. Now, I'm starving for more of that wet, soft tongue, that blank, open-mouthed gaze, those little gaspy whimpers I'd record if I could. "I'm gonna fuck your face now," I warn her. "Safe word if you need to." I look down at where she's touching herself. "Put a hand on my leg, baby, so you can tell me to stop."

She shakes her head and whatever she's trying to say comes out garbled and wet as I slide back inside, but she obeys and that's all the permission I need before I let myself lose it.

"Oh, fuck, yes," I mutter, watching her open wide, watching myself sink in, pink lips, stretched wide around me. I pull out, my cock slick with all that spit. She tries to suck me, but I'm beyond that.

A long slide out, another slow intrusion, deep, deep, until I hit her throat. She gags, I let her hair go, back out again and then clench my ass and thrust, harder, faster, deeper, my balls slapping her chin. I want more. What, I don't know, but it's not enough, doing this.

What the fuck more could I want? I look down and she looks up and that mask is pissing me off and I want it gone. Swept aside like the bikini that's half off her tits.

No. No way can I risk her showing her face. Not even at camp. Not even if the only thing I need right now is to get a good look at the tears gathering in her eyes and sliding down to mingle with her spit and, after that, my come. I want it so bad and now there's more than want mixed in with what I'm feeling and it's fucked—totally fucked—that I can't just enjoy a goddamn phenomenal face fuck out here in nature without *feeling* all this shit.

Want and need and hunger for more, more *more*, despite the way I'm slamming myself inside her and she's taking it, pushing back when she needs to breathe, but otherwise moaning and grunting and whimpering and not once telling me to stop and, goddamn it, I'm dying here, dying from this other thing that's clawing at my chest—not from outside, but within—at my throat, my guts, my balls.

"What are you doing to me? Huh?" I ask her, planting both hands on the tree trunk above her, using it as leverage and pumping, pumping, pumping into her until she gags and gasps for breath. I back up to give her space and she reaches for me again.

I groan, my balls going tight.

"I'm close, Twy. So fucking close. You gonna swallow my come like a good brat?"

She nods, as best she can, her hold tightening on my leg. One hand lifting up to her face.

I don't know what she's planning, but my eyes are wide as I take her in. She could do anything right now and I'd want that thing. That one thing. Fuck, she could kiss me. I'd let her. I'd take it from her.

Instead, she grabs the leather mask and slides it up, over her head, where she gives up when it gets caught in her hair, making her look even more ruined, which only feeds the monster. I want her ruined. By me. I want her so fucking destroyed there'll be no doubt who the hell she belongs to.

And those eyes. "Fuck you're so beautiful." My voice is a song, a dirge. "Your eyes are like..." What am I saying? I've got to shut up. I've got to hold on to myself, not give these parts away. "Your soul, Twyla. It's so perfect."

I sink inside her, reach down to grab my balls as they go almost too tight to stand, and take the base of my cock in my other hand, pull out almost all the way and jack off in her mouth as the come boils up. "Fuck, Twyla," I gasp out, sounding not half as tortured as I feel as the first spurt hits the back of her throat. "The fuck you doing to me?"

But it's not enough, is it? It'll never be. So I pull out and let the second jet paint her lips, marking them to spite my hard limits. And Twyla—god bless the filthy little brat who's been hiding inside my queen—sticks her little pink tongue out and laps it up.

With a grunt, I stumble back far enough to stripe her tits with my come and then, because I'm a dirty mother-fucker who gets off on all things filth, I feed my still-hard, pulsing length into that mouth again and make her lick me clean.

Which she does with the sweetest little smile.

My brain comes back online slowly, my body still buzzing with endorphins. I watch her get up, help her slide her bathing suit back into place, not at all unhappy when my knuckles graze a nipple on the way.

"Wow," I tell her, once she's got the mask out of her

hair and most everything back in order. "You look...debauched."

She snorts and glances around. "Think anyone'll mind?"

I smile, picturing her walk of shame with those swollen lips and tear-stained eyes and come-stained bathing suit. "No. No one here'll mind. But I'll walk you. Where you stayin'?"

She gives me a half-annoyed look, which doesn't bother me in the slightest.

"I'm doing Kidnapping Orientation? Remember?" She slides into one sandal, then the other, looking around, completely oblivious to the storm rising inside me. "You probably made me late and—"

"*You're not going.*" My voice is too harsh, too angry, but I'm firm on this. It's a bad idea. "You shouldn't be here at all."

In the next moment, she completely transforms from looking happily well-used into a furious hell-queen. "You know what you are, Zion?" she whispers so low I have to lean in.

"What am I, Twyla?" I hold my breath, waiting. Wanting.

"Never mind. Forget it." She backs up a step, blinking hard and fast, her expression almost betrayed. "Get out of my way. I'm late for my kidnapping."

She stomps off, that silky robe billowing out behind her and all I can do is stand here and stare, one hand on my chest, all the air knocked out of me. I'd thought...

Hell, I don't know. That she'd stay and battle it out, I guess. That this thing we're doing—whatever the fuck it is—might be more important than attending orientation for an event she has no business taking part in.

But, shit, does it hurt.

18

Twyla

"Jesus, Teetee. Can't leave you alone for a minute." Gigi's voice sounds tinny and faraway through my computer's speaker. "Okay. Then what happened?"

"I went to orientation. He was there, of course, the whole time. Hovering over me like a sexy...*malevolent* shadow or something."

Lamé cackles where they're making a snack in the kitchen.

"Did he, like, take you again, up against a tree? In a bush? On a mat?"

"In a box with a bat?" Lamé chimes in.

I shake my head, working hard to hold back a smile.

Gigi, who's loving every second of this, laughs so hard I'm afraid she'll crash.

"I'm not telling you more until you pull over."

She sighs. "Fine. Give me a sec." After a moment, she asks, "You gonna do it?"

"What?"

"The kidnapping."

I shrug. "I signed up for it, but—"

"Seriously? You little—"

"Please don't crash! I'm hanging up, this isn't safe."

"You're such a buzzkill. There. Okay. I'm safe. Stopped." Her camera flips to show me a generic parking lot. "Now, what happened after?"

"I went to suspensions. Another workshop."

"Getting all tied up and stuff?"

I nod. "And then anal."

"No!"

"Yeah." I give a one-shouldered shrug. "I'm definitely into anal, but I mostly stayed to annoy Zion."

She gasps. "He was there?"

"The whole time."

"Girl, be careful."

"What?"

"He likes you," she says in a singsongy voice. "TeeTee and Zion hanging in a tree..."

"Literally!" yells Lamé from the kitchen.

"K-I-S-S-I-N-G."

"Or *not*," I say.

Suddenly it's too much. My face scrunches and I lean back into the soft cushions of Lamé's sofa, clean after a long, hot shower, but still a total mess after the day I've had. "Ugh! Why didn't I safe word? Why'd I let him..." I don't want to think about the moment when he came all over me, the look in his eyes, feral and possessive, as he rubbed it all into me.

"You regret it?" asks Gigi, watching me through the screen.

I blink back into the room, half turned on, close to crying. "Which part? The spanking? The public orgasm or the..." I wave vaguely at my freshly-showered, terry-cloth robe covered body.

"You know which part." She sounds giddy.

"No."

"Come on. You know which part I mean. You know it. Say it. Say the words. Did he or did he not—"

"Cut it out, Geege."

"Bat you about your face with his—"

"Come on."

"Was it good? Better than—"

"So much better."

Her mouth's still open, since she clearly didn't expect my easy capitulation.

"Better than anything." I let the truth out. "Like another universe. Another...*me*. You know?"

"But it happened. For real, right?" Gigi is obviously loving this. "First, you had literal *intercourse* with your superstar husband, and then—"

"Just the tip!" shouts Lamé from the kitchen. It's a good thing I've got nothing to hide.

I roll my eyes as Gigi breaks into a fresh bout of hysterical laughter.

"Yeah, yeah. Just the tip," I yell back. "Doesn't count."

"Can I meet Lamé?" asks Gigi. "Just for a sec?"

"Coming!" Lamé emerges from the kitchen bearing a

tray full of food and drinks. "Here you go, honey. Need to get your energy up."

"My energy?"

Gigi gasps from my computer. "Hold on. Can you hold me up, T? I want to see what Lamé's got on. Oh my god, you're gorgeous."

"You should see the shoes." I turn the computer so she can ogle the skin-tight rainbow sequin jumpsuit Lamé's sporting this afternoon.

Not that Gigi will hear. She and Lamé have dived into conversation, chatting, just the two of them. I'm clearly not needed here. I pass the laptop to Lamé. "Go ahead. You two talk. I'm starving. Thank you. You're the best, Lamé," I yell, sitting up to examine the tray, which is an absolute cornucopia of delights. Dates and figs and cheeses and fruits and sliced meats and all kinds of things I haven't eaten in ages—if ever.

My stomach rumbles as I grab a cracker covered in some kind of cheese and pickle and maybe a sliver of date?

"Wait, what?" I vaguely hear Gigi react to something. "She *didn't* like it at all?" And then louder. "I thought you'd love suspension, Teetee? Isn't getting tied up one of your things?"

Lamé holds the computer to show me stuffing my face. "Mmmm." I lick some kind of cream off my fingers and wipe them on the tiny, tasseled cloth napkin they've provided. "It was okay. I thought I'd like the tying up part, too, but..."

"Who'd you play with?" Lamé asks, eyes narrowed.

"Burn."

"Ohhhhh. He's sexy, isn't he? And really knows his way around a rope."

I consider. "Yeeees."

"Buuuut?" I look up to see both Lamé and Gigi waiting.

"It was awkward? Weird? I don't know." I shrug, swallowing before going on. "Zion was there, like a feral guard dog, staring at anyone who came near me or even like looked my way. He pulled Burn aside and had a quiet word before he'd let him string me up."

"Oh my goddess." Lamé's watching me wide-eyed. "What'd he say?"

"I don't know." I lower my voice to as close to Zion's bass as I can get. "It was a Dom thing, clearly."

"He's totally possessive with you," says Lamé, nodding.

That sends a current of feelings through me, turned on, and hurt and confused, the way I've felt most of the time since I got here. I recall Zion's face when I stepped into that last session, the singular fury, the burn in his eyes. "I had to leave the anal workshop."

"Bummer," says Gigi, making Lamé crack up and drawing a smile from me.

"Well, maybe one day. You know, with the right partner..." I grab another cracker from the coffee table and sit back again. At the total silence, I look up at Lamé, who's seated, knees primly pressed together, in what I've come to discover is their favorite chair. My best friend's face is front and center on the screen in their lap, the two expectant, pursed-lipped expressions eerily similar.

"What?" I say, my mouth half full.

"Right partner?" Lamé says.

"Like maybe," Gigi puts her index finger to her pursed lips. "I don't know. What's his name again?"

"Zion?" they finish in unison and descend into laughter.

My heart does something weird in my chest.

I roll my eyes and shove another hunk of cheese into my mouth, hoping that will keep them from pressing.

"She told you about the spanking workshop?" Lamé asks, cutting me out entirely.

"Oh my god, yes. Did he really say that?"

"*The hell you will*," Lamé imitates in a deep, southern accent, giving an extra syllable to the word hell so that it almost sounds like hey y'all.

"Wait. Did I tell you that?" I ask Lamé.

"It's all over camp, honey."

"How could it not be?" Gigi agrees, as if she and Lamé are already besties.

"Hot, right?"

"Listen." The cheese thickens in my mouth. "Listen to me!"

They give me twin innocent looks. "What?"

"It's..." I take a sip of tea and swallow back the cheese, set down the plate, let myself feel the weight of this whole bizarre situation. "He was *not* happy to see me."

"Are you sure?" Lamé asks.

"Yes, seriously. I promise. He says I'm antagonizing him."

"This is so fun," Gigi says. "We *never* get to have fun since your career took off."

"Your career's going gangbusters," I tell her. "And you have fun all the time."

"I do," she agrees. "I have so much fun. But you don't. Not anymore."

"I have fun at work?"

Gigi snorts. "Doesn't count."

"You know, Zion doesn't have much fun anymore either," says Lamé, drawing a definite evil eye from me.

"Spare me," I reply. "He literally goes to a camp for adults every year."

"Yeah, but he's coasting."

"Coasting?"

"He's bored." Lamé sounds more serious than I've ever seen them. "Zion's been bored for ages. Years."

"That's almost insulting. I work my ass off to get where I am and he's just coasting? Great. I might as well—"

"I meant here. He's bored *here*, Twyla." They shake their head. "Work is work. As long as he's challenged, he's happy."

I sit back, mollified. That does sound like him. Although, bored? Here?

"The way he looked at you out there today..." Lamé's eyes narrow on me.

I watch them, waiting for more.

"Not bored?" Gigi prompts.

"Most assuredly not."

"I knew it!" says Gigi. "Oh, crap. I've got a zoom in a few minutes. Will you call me, Lamé?" My best friend ignores me entirely. "When something happens?"

Lamé stands, turns the computer to face them and wanders toward the kitchen, the two sharing contact info.

When something happens? It already *has* happened. Done and done. I've gotten as intimate with Zion as I'll ever get.

Which is fine.

It was... God, it was so good.

I zone out, my gaze caught up in the glass lighting fixture, my brain back at that tent. The spanking. Pulling my suit aside and giving every single person there a look. It felt dirty and uncomfortable and also perfect.

How was it that the fifteen minutes I spent getting strung up by the extremely handsome Burn had been like torture, while that spanking and everything that ensued was so painfully good?

I lie back and hide my face in the cushion, the way I'd hidden during that session. The mortified pleasure of all that attention on me—his, the others'—and Zion's single-minded focus. He'd been so *angry*. As if I'd done something to hurt him just by being there. Or being me. Or wearing that swimsuit. Or getting it wet.

My legs cross, my thighs tight, trying to squeeze every ounce of pleasure from the memory. And the blow job was beyond good. It was transcendental. Like last night, only...well, I knew it was him. The taste of him, the smell, the sounds he made.

And he knew it was me.

So, he wants me, right?

I mean, I could argue that he volunteered to spank me to keep me safe, like out of some random person's clutches or something, but pulling my bathing suit aside and baring me to literally everyone's gaze was not about keeping me safe and out of trouble.

And what we did against that tree? Why'd he do that? Is Lamé right? Am I somehow messing with him? Is my very existence throwing him into such turmoil that... Hang on.

Abruptly, I stand and head into the kitchen, where Gigi and Lamé are still talking over Facetime.

"That's a kink," Lamé says, pulling a huge container of flour from a high cupboard.

"Seriously? How?"

"It sounds like you're a service bottom."

Gigi scoffs. "I am *not* a bottom. Nobody tells me what to do."

I watch their easy back and forth, totally unsurprised that they've hit it off.

"Okay, then. Not a bottom. I'm a Dominant, myself, so I get it. You know what you are, then?"

"What?" Gigi sounds half-scared, half-excited.

"You're a service top. You know what? You should get your ass to camp. You'd love it here."

"Hey, Gigi." Lamé turns at the sound of my voice. "I have a question."

She stops talking and the computer gets turned my way. "Yeah?"

"Why did Zion's people reach out?"

"I'm the one who—"

"No. No, in the beginning. The very first time. For the setup? The PR marriage angle? What did they tell you?"

"Ratings."

"Ratings," I repeat. "What ratings? We weren't on TV. He's not on TV. What...what the hell did that mean?"

She considers. "It was about his image. You gave him gravitas."

"Right. So, I was there to make him look like a serious actor instead of a big action star. Which would have worked out if we hadn't..."

I look up to see their faces both totally focused on me. "Hadn't...?" Lamé urges.

"Wait. Was this the thing? When you..."

"We made out."

Lamé smiles, then abruptly frowns. "Made out how?"

"Movie night. Popcorn. A rom com for me followed by a horror for him."

"Figures," Lamé says.

"I fell asleep and woke up and he was...we were..."

"What? What, seriously. What?"

"He was hard, behind me. Just spooning me, you know? And I turned and sort of...ran my hands over him and he did the same and then I leaned in and tried to..." I touch my lips, blushing, hard. "He stopped it. Like, quickly shut it down."

"Prick!" Gigi's pissed.

"Hey!" Lamé lowers their face to the computer camera. "I get to call him that. You don't."

"I stand corrected."

"The poor prick." Lamé sighs.

Gigi cackles

"What?" I ask, feeling the emotion in Lamé's voice.

"Did you two actually kiss?"

I shake my head and then stop. "Almost? Kind of?"

"Tell me."

"I kissed him. Like, on his neck and…" I move my hand from my neck up my jaw to my cheek, my forehead. "We were close. Noses rubbing, lips touching."

"And?"

Total quiet from Gigi.

"We'd kissed before, you know? The premiere that changed everything?" At Lamé's nod, I go on. "We were kind of rubbing noses and, I don't know…" I glance at them both, going hot at the memory. "Dry humping."

"Like teenagers," sighs Lamé.

"Just like that." I flush. "We kissed everywhere but our mouths. And when I tried, he sort of…" Why does it feel wrong to talk about this? Like I'm giving up a piece of him? Of us? "Look, I can't—"

"You tried to kiss him and he stopped it," Lamé supplies and I concede, although it's nowhere near as momentous as the whole thing felt.

"Right. Like that." He'd groaned when he pulled away, as if it hurt, as if he didn't want to stop, but he had to. Without looking at me at all, he'd gotten up and mumbled that he was sorry and gone to his room, leaving me alone on that big, soft, white couch. The credits had long since stopped rolling and the network was trying to convince me to watch a pseudo-documentary about a serial killer.

I remember feeling like I'd done something very, very wrong. A terrible blend of shame and embarrassment and maybe guilt, too. Like I'd pushed our working relationship in an inappropriate direction and he'd clearly not wanted that. When I'd tried to talk to him the next day, he'd already headed out someplace.

The worst part, though, was the rejection. The *he doesn't want me* part. The part where I was somehow not good enough or fit enough or attractive enough for the likes of him, despite the closeness I felt.

I turned the TV off and went to bed and didn't see Zion until after his sex video came out, two days later.

Just thinking of it now makes me feel awful.

"I kept thinking... Did I somehow coerce him into making out with me?"

Lamé shakes their head. "No, honey."

"Then what? Why'd he go and do that the next night? The video."

"The *very* next night?" Lamé's wide eyes narrow.

"Yep." Gigi's thinking. "That's wild."

"Curiouser and curiouser." Lamé's still watching me.

"I know, right?"

"What? What's curious?" I look from one to the other.

Gigi says, "He almost kissed you..."

"That's a hard limit for him. He never kisses." Lamé

leans in. "Ever."

"Why, though? Why won't he kiss?" I throw up my hands, exasperated. "He'll do literally anything else, right? And he kisses on set."

"That's work. And you know the boy's good at compartmentalizing." Lamé examines their long, deep red nails and then looks at me. "I don't know why he doesn't kiss. I have an idea, but it's not mine to tell. And I've found conjecture about what happens in other people's heads to be an exercise in futility. Also, potentially destructive."

I sigh. They're right. It's no one's story but his. And there is a story there. Even without Lamé's confirmation, I knew that. "How can a person live two such separate lives?" I'm unable to keep the sadness from my voice. "Can't be easy."

"He's had a lot of practice. Been doing it his whole adult life." Lamé shrugs. "Sex here. Work out there."

"Except for that one time," Gigi yells from her perch on the table. "With a woman who looks a hell of a lot like you, TT."

"In the video?" I squint at Gigi. "She looked nothing like me."

"You're like twins." Lamé nods.

"Identical."

"Shit," I say, sinking into a ridiculously comfortable kitchen chair.

From out front comes knocking.

"What's that?" asks Gigi, trapped in the computer. "Crap, I'm gonna be late for my meeting."

"Door. Be right back." Lamé disappears and quickly reappears, eyes wide.

I look behind them just as a woman walks in. She's striking, with long black hair and the kind of lean, tragic good looks that would make her perfect for a period film. An intricate tattoo of what looks like a thorny rose stem curves from her shoulder down to her hand, the dark ink a sharp contrast to her pale, nearly transparent-looking skin. Her fingers, I notice, are stained and work worn.

"Hi, Twyla. I'm Grace." With one of those secret Mona Lisa smiles, she sits down beside me. "I'm *so* excited to meet you. Oh. Here. This is yours." Leaning forward, she grabs something from the back pocket of her jeans and sets what looks a lot like my phone on the thick, battered wood of Lamé's kitchen farm table.

"What's that? What is it?" Gigi's voice blares through the speakers.

Lamé stage whispers, "It's Twyla's phone."

"Ohhhhhhhhh. And who's the new woman? I love that tattoo, by the way."

"Thanks," says Grace.

"Liev's partner," comes Lamé's reply. "Tattoo artist. Primal. She's good people."

Grace's smile deepens as she watches Lamé.

"Dammit, I have to go," Gigi says from the confines of her computer prison. "You'll call me with updates, Lamé?"

"Yep." They smile, looking around the room, as if they've arranged this themselves. "Or you could just get your ass to camp."

19

———

Zion

"Heard you had quite a day." Liev says from his front porch swing as I step outside, letting the screen door slam behind me. I'm freshly showered, dressed in clean clothes, ready to head out for the night.

At least I look okay. My insides are another story.

"I've got to get her to leave."

His eyebrows flick up. "Twyla?"

"She's signed up for a kidnapping. Two assailants. Very few limits."

"Guess she's enjoying herself."

"*Enjoying* herself? She's doing it to torture me."

"Fuck, man." A low laugh rumbles deep in Liev's chest. "You starting to fall for the Hollywood bullshit?"

"What are you talking about?"

"I mean, you sound like all the other bigwig pricks who think the sun shines out of their asses."

My jaw goes tight.

"Fact is, she's here, Zion. According to Grace, she likes it."

"*Grace* knows her now?"

"Lamé, Max, Grace. They all love her, man. Hell, *I* like having her here."

"*What?* You don't even know her. Twenty minutes in your truck doesn't count."

"I don't need to know her to enjoy this." He squints up at the darkening treetops. "Easygoing Zion. Everything rolls right off you, nothing ever gets to you. Except this." Liev wipes the sweat off his brow with the back of his thick forearm and meets my glare with a smirk. "Look at you, all worked up, angry. This shit's fun. Better than TV."

"Great. Thanks. Pissed off. That's what you want? I can get pissed off, Liev. Trust me."

"Yeah? Go on. Show me." He leans back on his porch swing, challenging me, like he wouldn't mind if I lost it right here. I won't, though. I don't do that shit. I don't yell or hit in anger. Hell, I don't get angry. I'll act angry for a part. But that's different. It's a choice, whereas the real thing...

Why the hell does my mind choose this moment to think of Twyla in that little yellow, come-stained bikini, skipping across the grass on her way to one workshop after another, racking up interest as she went. Thank god she left that goddamn anal class or I'd have broken something.

"Fuck, Z. You look like you're gonna lose it."

I stop pacing long enough to glance down at my body.

It's hot as hell out tonight, so I'm in clothes I can sweat in —shirtless, board shorts, with a mesh mask in my hand and a sports bag over one shoulder.

I'm playing tonight. With anyone. *Everyone.* "What?"

"Have you eaten today? Anything?"

"Sure." The lie is easier than admitting I've been running around all day, distracted by Twyla. It didn't occur to me once to put food in my mouth.

"Bullshit."

Yes, so, he's right though I'm not prepared to admit it aloud. Admitting I haven't eaten—me, the *my body is a temple* guy. The man whose good looks were all he left home with and all that ever mattered—would be like waving a red flag in front of Liev right now. Or maybe a white one.

"I'm good. Listen, I'm heading down to—"

"Hold on a sec." Liev stands and disappears into his house.

I wait more than a goddamn second. It's been closer to two minutes when he comes back out holding a white paper bag. "Here."

"What's that?" I don't move.

"Your dinner. Now shut up and eat it."

My head's already shaking side to side. "Man, you've got to stop trying to—"

"No, I won't stop." He steps forward, shoving the bag into my chest and letting me feel just a hint of his substantial strength. Liev's a big guy. Shorter than me, but wide. Powerful. He hammers stone for a living, dammit. I prance around pretending to be other people.

"Eat your goddamn dinner, Zion. Or lunch." He pushes harder, probably smashing whatever's in the bag. "And then think long and hard about why you're so pissed right now. After that, I want you to consider that maybe being pissed isn't always a bad thing. A whole lot better than feeling nothing, right?" I don't move. "Maybe pissed is the other side of some coin you've only just picked up. And maybe, if you throw that fucking coin away without turning it over, you'll regret it." Another shove and I smell him—sweat and dust and the iced tea he's just downed. Salami, too, maybe. And something else. Something elemental and basic that I've noticed on him recently, but haven't paid attention to.

I inhale just to be sure and there it is again. "You smell like Grace," I tell him.

"Asshole," he says, forcing the bag into my hands and stepping back. "Don't talk about my woman's smell."

"Hey!" I look at him, his blue eyes in partial shadow, his face craggier than it looks in full daylight. He could be one of his own sculptures, right now. Pure stone, made mobile and alive by the hands of a true artist. "I don't mean it like that. Sexually."

His brows lift. It turns his sockets into bigger, deeper holes. Makes him intimidating. My best friend, barely recognizable. "How do you mean it?"

"I mean..." I huff out a laugh, feeling ridiculous. "I mean you *always* smell like her now. And, you know, vice versa."

His eyes narrow, their glint shifting. "Okay."

"And it's..." I shake my head, thinking of wolf packs.

Of belonging. Of family. Home. I think of the day Ms. Tucker, Language Arts teacher, wrinkled her nose and said I smelled like an ashtray. I was nine. I felt the shame in my bones.

I think of the time I spilled Dad's beer and he made me wipe it up with my sweatshirt. The only one that fit. The one I wore to school every day, two winters in a row. I think about how I must have smelled to the other kids, to the teachers. Like home, like my dad, sure, but for some of us, home's not all it's cracked up to be. "I don't know. I don't know what it means. Or why I said it. I just... *Fuck.* I've got to go."

"Eat your sandwich."

My hand tightens into a fist, balling up part of the bag before I force it to loosen again. "Whatever, Dad."

Snorting, Liev reaches out and lightly smacks the back of my head, although it's more stroke than strike. There's no pain inflicted. Only affection. "Don't do anything you'll regret."

"I don't do regret," I lie, heading down the steps.

"Hey." I turn to see him standing up on his porch like a fucking gargoyle. "I mean it, Z. This whole thing with you and her? What you decide to do next? It matters."

I open my mouth to tell him to mind his own business, but the wrong words come out. "I know."

"*You* matter."

I snort. It hides my choppy breathing. "Jesus, bro," I say, already heading down the garden path, through the squeaky gate, and between the two rows of vendors selling candles and leather and sex toys and blades.

Pretty much anything you can get at a medieval festival or a sex shop or a saddlery. They're packing up for the evening, probably heading out to eat and shower and dress up for a night in the dungeon or the hangar or the big Sex-o-drome tent. Maybe a queer orgy in someone's cabin or a poker game.

I'll do the same. But first, I need to assign faux Kidnappers to Victims, the way I do every year. We'll go over the forms our self-proclaimed victims have handed in and figure out times and places and assailants, make up scripts. The works. It's pretty fun, actually. I'm hoping it'll distract me until dungeon time.

I pull out the sandwich. Salami. But also probably a half a pound of other meats, lettuce, cheese, peppers, onions, tomato. An Italian sub. My favorite. Clearly purchased from an actual deli. Probably at lunchtime. Probably by Grace when she went into town to do whatever she does when she's not wielding a tattoo gun or running through the woods, trying to get Liev to tackle her. Making him happy, after so many years of shit.

I bite into the sandwich and sigh with pleasure. Even a couple hours old, it tastes fucking amazing. It's gone in five bites, but there's more in the bag. I reach in and grab the peanut butter cookie I figured I'd find in the bottom. Also my favorite.

Those jerks know me so damn well it hurts.

Ten minutes later, I come out into the field, walk by the pool without bothering to glance at the late afternoon sunbathers and swimmers, go into the now-empty club-house bar—was it only last night that everything fell apart here?—through a side door and up the stairs to the meeting room. There's already a big group of longtime campers gathered, looking over forms filled out by potential kidnapping victims.

The atmosphere's light and easy, the laughter flowing as it always does here. A low voice mumbles something and Jeanette—a fifty-something woman with a penchant for fisting, responds with a tried and true, "That's what she said," which turns the giggling up a notch.

The door behind me falls shut with a bang and everyone turns. The laughter stops so suddenly it's got to be me.

Great. What's happening now?

"Somebody die?" I ask, expecting at least a grin or two.

Instead, people I've known for well over a decade look down, scuff their feet, clear their throats.

"Aw, shit, y'all. Come on. Whatever it is, you can tell me."

"He's on the committee," says Chatte Noire, a Domme I've known for ages. "Every committee member sees every request. It's in the rules. We know that. We can either show him now or drag this out forever. Outcome's the same."

My pulse kicks up. Silently, I look around the group.

"Pretty sure you're not gonna like this," says Burn, a rigger I've always liked, but who I came close to maiming today when he offered to vertically suspend my wife. We had words, though, and he clearly understood the parameters because the suspension was a prime example of how to respect boundaries and keep a scene as nonsexual as possible.

Dammit. I inhale, though it doesn't do shit to calm me. "What'd my wife do?"

"Here." Chatte holds out a sheet of paper. "We'll let her tell it in her own words."

20

Twyla

Getting ready for an evening at kink camp feels like a countdown to the ultimate girls' night out.

Except even better than that.

Camp Haven does that. It makes you feel like you can be anyone, do anything. It makes you feel gorgeous and absolutely free. There are no limits here. No expectations or judgments. Nothing you can't be or do, no matter your gender, body type, skin-color, sexual orientation. None of it matters here.

It's especially freeing after spending the last few weeks in Zion's spotlight.

This freedom? It's what brings Zion back every year. No doubt about it.

So, if Lamé and Max and Grace insist that I can get away with silver stretch bootie shorts that leave little to the imagination and a crystal tassel fringe halter that plays peekaboo with my nipples, then that's what I'll wear to tonight's Share-n-Try at the Hangar.

The top, along with my crystal-studded medical mask, were purchased earlier from one of the craftspeople selling wares up at the top of the hill, near what I was told is Liev and Grace's house.

It's big and beautiful and mysterious, sort of like Grace and Liev themselves, and it sends a bittersweet envy through me that I try hard to ignore.

It's just getting dark out by the time Max and Grace and I leave Lamé's, arm in arm.

We're heading for the massive, open-sided hangar which, for tonight only, is filled with experienced kinksters offering to share their expertise with others. Lamé is apparently amongst them.

"What's Lamé showcasing, exactly?" I ask as we skirt the lake in the direction of the big corrugated roofed structure.

"You'll see," Max says.

Grace smiles.

Up ahead, people dance around a bonfire, drumming and singing and howling to the moon.

"Primals!" says Max, grinning the way she does whenever discussing kink. I love her evil grin with that sharp little tooth of hers that peeks out to dig at her bottom lip. "Why aren't you and Liev there, Gracie?"

Grace snorts, bending forward to glare at Max, who I found out has been her best friend literally forever. The two of them grew up together south of here. "Have we met?" she asks, rolling her eyes. "First off, they're filming.

Look." She points out a small film crew, documenting something that looks like some kind of ritual. "Nobody films me. Ever."

"Grace is not the most demonstrative person." Max kicks her chin back toward the fire-breathing, screaming revelers, and giggles. "Liev's not either, so it works."

"We're Primals," Grace informs me. "You know, I like the bestial side of things. Getting chased down, hunted, taken." She flicks long fingers toward the group, which is now literally howling at a nearly full moon. "I'm not really into the drumming and chanting shit. Although I get why people like it. I do. It's just not for me."

"She prefers a quiet stalking in the woods."

I'm sure I'm wide-eyed when I look back at Grace. "So, like the Big Hunt?"

"Absolutely."

"I was thinking about doing that," I tell them.

"Yeah?" Grace considers me. "You into that idea?"

My shaky inhale is audible enough to make them both laugh.

"Guess so," says Max.

"Nervous, but excited?" Grace asks.

"And scared," I confirm. "But in a good way." I shrug. "Mostly."

Grace's nod is easy, calm. "I know the feeling." She squeezes my arm into her side and shortens her long stride. "It's like nothing else in the world."

"Evening, friends," says a man, walking by with two people on his arms. "Have a lovely night."

I smile and Max replies and we continue down the

path, passing people who wave and smile and greet us easily. "Oh my god, you all are stunning," says a person I met earlier today. Kevan? Kiernan? I don't remember.

And it's true. We do look pretty amazing. My overtly sexual, bejeweled outfit's definitely eye-catching, even in the near dark, while Grace is rough and gorgeous in an entirely different way. She's got on a ripped, ancient-looking Metallica T-shirt, cropped and tied at her waist, baring a flat belly, complete with a piercing and a good amount of ink. Below that, she's wearing cut-off denim shorts that show miles of leg—and more tattoos—with scuffed black flip-flops on her feet.

Max's look, which during the daytime is a tough, kick-ass, post-apocalyptic steampunk, has turned sultry. She's in a sturdy, brown leather corset with a bunch of straps and buckles. Makes me think of tankards of mead or Vikings or something. She's paired the corset with a short suede skirt, wide-gauge fishnets, and thick-soled combat boots.

"I love this so much," I tell her, nudging the bustier with the arm I've wound through hers. "You're like a warrior princess."

"Nikki makes these. Didn't you see her stall?"

"No!" I sigh. "But I'm gonna need a whole lot more income for the full kink wardrobe of my dreams."

Grace makes a coughing sound. "Zed can afford it."

"I'm not taking his money."

"You should," Max says, with a smile. "Not like he has any use for it."

It's true, now that I think about it. Zion's not one of

those spendy stars you hear about, splashing out on absurd, flashy, ridiculous purchases. From what I've seen, he's pretty frugal, considering he's one of the richest actors in the country.

"Gives most of it away," says Grace, something like admiration in her voice.

"Really?"

"He funds hundreds of memberships here every year."

Grace is nodding. "Yep. Does nonprofits, too."

"Doesn't he have a freaking foundation?" asks Max.

"Seriously?" I'm stunned. "I had no idea." Not that Zion would help people, but that he's done it so secretly, without splashing it all around the media, like so many people in the spotlight.

"Yep. Helps LGBTQ youth. Runaways. Survivors." She casts me a look. "He's not all bad."

"I never thought he was." I stop, forcing them to, as well. "I..." I pull my arms from theirs and face them. "I *liked* Zion, you know? I respected him."

"That still past tense?" Grace asks, her voice light.

It takes me a second while I try to parse out the complicated ball of feelings I've got for him. "I don't *want* to like him."

Max grins. "Can't help it, though, can you?"

"No," I say, feeling a little raw at the admission.

"The asshole's damn likable."

"Definitely."

"Come on." They slide their arms through mine

again. "Let's go see what Lamé's got up their sleeve for tonight."

"And maybe see what Zed's up to while we're at it."

"After today, he'll probably do everything he can to avoid me." For some silly reason, the thought hurts my feelings.

Grace eyes my top through narrowed eyes and gives one of those secretive, tight-lipped smirks. "Oh, I doubt that."

We continue on our way, between two little tent villages, past a big cabin, which is blaring vintage rock. A pair of men stumble out the door, wearing nothing but leather straps and body hair. One of them shoves the other against the wall and sinks to his knees. I look away, my own knee-bruising experience from earlier swamping me with a sudden, almost debilitating rush.

"Queer leather night," says Max, knowingly.

We pass a couple doing naked cartwheels and then a campsite with maybe five retirement-age folks sitting around having a beer, fully clothed. Funny how they're the odd ones out.

"This place is magical," I say, accepting a condom from a sparkly, winged fairy and sliding it into the tight, high pocket in my shorts.

"I know," Max sighs. "I love it here.

Grace just smiles.

We're almost level with the Hangar when a deep voice rumbles from the dark. "Evening."

The man is tall, Black, and well-built, shorter than Zion, but just as cleanly-muscled, his skin a dark pattern under a black fishnet top, his bottom half clad in wide-legged linen pants, his feet bare. He's gorgeous.

"Blade!" Max jumps into his arms for a prolonged hug and a big smack on the lips, before dropping back to the ground.

"Grace." He nods. Grace, who I'm not pegging as much of a hugger nods back.

Then his attention focuses on me. "You, stranger, are beautiful." He blinks hard, as if to underscore what he's saying. "I can't keep my eyes off you." He sticks out his hand. "I'm Blade. I apologize for being weird, but..."

"Well, you are weird," says Max, amiably.

"There is that." He grins and...whoa. Yep. The man is stunning. The kind of beauty I'd like to capture on film. He should be a star, dammit. People need to see this charisma, that smile, the heat in his eyes.

I reach out and he clasps my hand and his is warm, but dry, and his handshake is the right amount of tight—not trying to impress, but somehow respectful. He's attractive. Wildly so. And clearly interested.

And I feel absolutely nothing. No excitement—aside from the sudden desire to catch him on film and see if he's got the on-screen allure to go with his amazing good looks.

Not a hint of that visceral buzzing I get whenever Zion's near.

"Hey," I say, in total admiration, but beyond annoyed at my own body.

"You going in?"

I nod.

"I'm doing a flogging demo. Maybe you could stop by. Try me out." His hand releases me. "So what's your name?"

"Oh, sorry." My face goes hot.

"This is Twilight," Max cuts in.

And then he changes.

The smile drops, his easy closeness shifts to sudden distance, the flirtatious glow in his eyes hardens. His mouth loses its sultry smirk. "Shit." He shakes his head, hands up in front of him. "Sorry. My mistake."

"Why? What's going on?" I'm totally confused.

"You're Zed's."

"I'm *what?*"

"You're mine," says another voice from the dark. Only this time—of course—it's Zion's.

I turn, ready for a fight.

Zion

"Excuse me?" says a very irate Twyla Hernandez, so beautiful I want to pamper her or put her on a pedestal or pick her up, throw her over my shoulder and take her back to my goddamn cave.

"You're my wife," I grate out, fully aware that I'm digging my own grave, but unable to stop.

What can I say? My rational brain's been on hiatus since she showed up here. And who can blame me when she looks like every teenage fantasy I ever had, on a platter. Most of my adult fantasies, too.

The little top she's got on doesn't count as actual clothing, since it covers literally nothing. Not her shoulders, back or belly or tits, and definitely not the bite-sized brown nipples that threaten to poke out every time the slithery strings of diamonds shift. Which is every second, because she's a living, breathing dream. I can't function while she stands there in that top. And I definitely can't trust my mouth to make sense.

I'm not even letting myself look at the bottom half again. I'd die right here.

I thought I wanted her before camp, before the marriage, hell, before we even met, but this is pure fire.

"I don't know what you think you're doing, but we're getting a divorce. This farce is over."

My eyes shift up to her face. "I don't want that."

"No? Well, maybe you should have thought about that before embarrassing me in front of the *whole entire world*, Zed."

"I know. I'm sorry." And then, because there's clearly something wrong with me, I open my mouth again.

"You signed up to be kidnapped."

"*Yeah?*" Her eyes are twin razors slicing straight from my solar plexus to my balls.

"Maybe we should, uh..." Grace takes a step back, Max with her. Blade is long gone.

"Listen to me. That woman? The one from the video? I thought—"

"Do we really need to do this right now?" She turns, looking for her friends, who wait a few feet closer to the dungeon door, giving us space, but unwilling to desert her entirely. The fucking sparkly necklace shirt flies around her like iridescent snakes, giving me the full bounce of breasts I now know the taste of. Breasts I need to taste again, soon.

Focus, asshole. This is important.

"I thought she was you," I say, desperate for her to know the truth.

Her brows lift high. Otherwise, she doesn't move at all, just waits, impatient or annoyed. The hell-top twinkles at me like it's laughing.

"For maybe a minute, I thought you'd gotten out of your meeting and shown up at the gallery." Everything's weirdly quiet out here, as if not just Twyla's listening, but the entire world, hushed and waiting, breath held. Even the noises from the hangar are somehow muted, waiting. "And I was so damn happy." I feel a leftover scrap of that moment even now and I hate how weak it makes me. "But it was her and she must have known about this." I put my hands out to show the camp around us, and then bring them back in, rub my face to clear out my brain.

"Why didn't you just go home?"

"I wish I had."

"Yeah, but *why didn't you?*"

"Because I was... *Dammit.*" I lean in and hiss into her ear. "What we did in front of the TV? The night before? It scared the shit out of me. I never did that before."

"What?"

"You know, vanilla stuff. Just..." I will her to understand so I can stop pouring this shit out into the night air.

"Just messin' around because you *like* a person? No scene, no pain, no *rules*."

Her "Wow" is so quiet, it's just a shape on her lips. "You could have stopped, though. At any time." She doesn't mean our make-out session. She means the video woman.

"I thought it would get you out from under my skin. You were a *thorn*. A constant itch or ache or something and she was a..."

"Distraction?"

"A painkiller."

She blinks.

"I wasn't myself that night. I was a zombie." I hold her gaze. "When it came time to do the deed, I shut my eyes and pretended it was you."

Shock takes over her features, making her mouth tiny and her eyes huge. In any other circumstances, I'd take pleasure in that expression, hell, I'd chase it.

"I'm so sorry, Twyla. I've never regretted anything this much. If I could..." I shut my eyes, unwilling to spout some bullshit about turning back time or taking it all back, because if I could do that, my entire fucking life would be a do-over, from when I lost my mom, hell, even before then.

"I don't know what to say to you, Zion. You bring this up now?"

I nod. She's right. It's a terrible time to bring it up, but fuck, everything's bubbling under the surface. I'm a volcano, so close to blowing I'm not sure how to keep it down any more.

"Don't do the kidnapping. It's a terrible idea."

"I told you I'm a big girl. I can take care of myself."

"I saw your kidnapping intake form." My voice is harsh. "You're askin' for trouble."

Those lips tilt up at the corners. I stare at them, picturing the things I want to do to that mouth. The things I'll never stop wanting.

She moves closer to me again and every part of me sings. "What makes you think..." I see the moment she gets control of herself again. "The thing is, *Zed*," she says, all the emphasis on my camp name. "It turns out you're not the only one who takes their fun with a side of trouble."

"Yeah." I work hard to come up with a smirk. "Just a friendly warning."

"Between colleagues? Kinksters? Fellow campers?"

The smirk drops off my face like a ton of bricks. We're not just colleagues or fellow campers and she damn well knows it. She feels this thing between us as solidly as I do. She has to. "Between spouses," I say to remind her that what's between us is something else.

"Whatever." She sighs and rolls her eyes and every single cell in my body wants to pick her up and take her somewhere private and show her... Fuck, I don't know. Show her who she belongs to, I guess.

"I don't need your approval, Zed. For anything."

"I know," I admit through gritted teeth. "So long as you're sure."

"I am." Her brows lift high. Otherwise, she doesn't move at all, just waits.

"Kidnapping it is, then." I force another smile to my face, this one as slow and mean as I can make it.

"Yes."

I nod. "All righty then."

"Okay." She half turns to where her friends wait, her eyes flicking back to me. "I'll just…"

"Yep. Go ahead." I give her a salute. "I'll see you in there."

"Wait, are you… Never mind. I'll just…" She points a thumb over her shoulder and does an awkward shuffle and she's so goddamn beautiful I have to fight the unfamiliar urge to lean down and hug her.

"Yep. I've got work to do." My attention focuses over her shoulder at where Max and Grace are milling around, pretending not to listen. "Glad you're in good hands. Hey!" I project. "Thank y'all for showing my wife around. Don't let her get into too much trouble, will you? Least not until I get back."

Max shakes her head, hiding a smile and Grace waves me off with an eye roll. Right. Message received. I get it and they get it, though Twyla might not. *She matters*, the message says, loud and clear. *Keep her safe.*

Just as she casts me one last frown and heads over to them, a thought occurs to me. "Where you stayin'? You in a cabin or something?"

She hesitates. Probably figures I'll get the information one way or another, and gives in. "Lamé's."

"Of course. Have fun." And then, because I really like messing with her, I say, "I'll head back over when I get done."

"No need. I've got company." With one last glare, she heads into the hangar, arms linked with her new friends'.

I watch, trying hard to feel nothing.

To remember that I may want her, but I don't *need* her.

I'm not like Liev. I'm not part of a pack. I don't get to have a partner and I definitely don't need a family. I've known that all my life. Since the first time I saw a mom lean down and pick up her little boy and kiss him on the cheek, as if that's just what people do. Not my people. But people.

This place is as close to a family as I've ever gotten and, even here, I'm just skimming the surface. The families, networks, relationships of all kinds—I'm just coasting on all the love they feel for each other.

None of it's for me, though.

And that's fine. I'm solid. Not made of stone, like Liev, but something flexible. I'm strong as a wire, twisting, bending, but never breaking.

I watch her go and the moment she gets swallowed up by the crowd, it's like everything comes back—the smells of sweat and summer, the sound of screams and thumping music. It hits me with a painful blast, every note a spike to my head, unbearable until I catch one last shimmer of that fucking top, and then—*what the hell's happening to me?*—the near-silence is so much worse.

In the silence, there's no ignoring the voice telling me to go after her. To get her. To make her mine, no matter what it takes. No matter how much it hurts. It's chanting *mine, mine, mine*, although it might as well be saying *home, home, home*, and that's pure fucking delusion.

I blink down at the rough ground, shoulders heavy, vision out of focus, and I understand, in this moment, beyond a shadow of a doubt, that I'm broken. Beyond repair.

Heavy with that knowledge, I cast one longing look inside the hangar before setting off, back to the clubhouse.

I've got work to do, dammit. No time to sit around trying to think my way through this clusterfuck I've created.

A kidnapping's not an easy thing to plan, after all. And this one's got to be just right.

21

Twyla

I let Grace loop her arm through mine and lead me into the enormous, open-sided structure, past play areas set up like booths in a craft fair. I barely notice the kinksters calling for volunteers or discussing the benefits of specific tools or structures or... Wow. Okay. Electric components. Not something I've seen before.

"You okay?" Grace leans in to ask.

"Dandy," I reply, though it's not the whole truth. I mean, yes. Yes, I'm good. I'm here and it's wild and I'm loving this place.

But I came here to confront Zion and I've miserably failed at my task. What was it I wanted, originally? Through the haze of everything that's happened, I can barely recall. What I do know is that he hasn't suffered any repercussions at all.

The thing is, now that I'm here, in this transformative place with its wonderful people and accepting vibe, I don't want to battle it out with him anymore. The realization is freeing. I'm making friends here and living a life I'd never have experienced without this whole crisis.

But, my god, could Zion just be...I don't know. Simpler?

I press a fist to the aching spot on my chest and try not to think about his words: *I shut my eyes and pretended it was you.*

What does that even mean? That he wanted me, but for some reason known only to him decided he couldn't have me? "He pretended she was *me*," I say to my new friends. "He just told me that."

They stop walking and huddle around me.

"Wow," says Max.

Laughter erupts in one of the stalls. There's a different feeling to the scenes here tonight. It's more casual than the dungeon last night. Friendly, easy-going. I'm too stunned to be able to enjoy it.

Grace nods slowly, seeming unsurprised. "From Zed, that's a lot."

"I know. I just don't know what to *do* with it right now."

"Nothing?" suggests Max.

"Yeah.

Which won't be easy, because with that confrontation outside, Zion did two things. And, god, did he do them well.

First of all, he reminded me of this damn marriage hanging over our heads. We've got to take care of it. The sooner, the better. Hell, with just two weeks under the belt, maybe we can get an annulment or something.

I swallow, absolutely hating the sound of that.

He thought of *me*?

Why is he the most confusing, infuriating man in the world?

And the second thing he's done is gone and made me worry about the kidnapping I signed up for. I mean, does the idea appeal to me? God, yes. Does it scare me, too? Absolutely.

But I really, really want to do it. The fact that my brain's put Zion in the main role is only slightly vexing.

"So, you signed up for a kidnapping, huh?" Grace reads my mind as she starts to lead us deeper into the massive space.

"Yeah, I didn't..." I sigh. "I did it more to annoy him than anything else."

Max leans. "You going through with it?"

"I kind of have to, don't I?"

"No!" Says Max, always earnest. "You've got a choice. Cancel if you—"

"Do you want to do it?" interrupts Grace, who's now watching me with a pointed, narrow-eyed attention.

I sigh. "Yeah." We're shouting now to be heard above the music and talking and yelling and all the other camp sounds. "And no?"

"Oh, do I know that feeling." Grace is wearing that secret smile. "You can always safe word out."

"I know. Everyone says that. It just seems kind of, I

don't know, rude or something? Like these people came for a scene and—"

"Happens all the time," says Max. "It's literally the point of everything we do here. Choice. Consent. Fantasy coming to life if and how you want. Or not."

"True." Grace grins now, full-out. "Remind me to tell you about my first hunt."

I shiver. "Okay."

"It was good. Scary as hell, but..." Her inhale is deep and happy. "No regrets."

"There'll be security there. Hell, depending on when it is, I might be on."

Grace watches me. "You turned in a brief, right?" It sounds so official.

"Yeah." I think of the details I wrote down. Things I've only really thought about in the dark safety of my bed are suddenly out there, written black on white. I nod. "Yeah. I want to try it."

"Yes!" Max raises her hand for a high five.

"Next you'll be out there doing the hunt with me."

"Hostage parties!" Max's voice is low and ominous. "Now that shit is hard core."

I shiver. "Really?"

"Oh, yeah. Now, I love the Big Hunt. But the hostage thing?" Grace fake shudders. "Not for me. I don't do well with that many people on me at once."

Oh my god.

She gives me a wide-eyed look. "I'd hold off on that one."

"Roger that."

Rubbing her hands together, Max looks around. "Okay. Now what's on the menu tonight? Grace?"

"Observer." She quirks a brow at me. "Chaperone. You?"

"I'm playing with Taylor later."

"I thought you two were over?" Grace pulls us to a stop again. "You said they're a shitty communicator."

"They are." Max shrugs. "But they're so good with the rope."

Grace laughingly shakes her head. "All right, well. You know I'm here if you want to talk. I feel like I've barely seen you this season."

For the first time since we first met, Max looks almost shy. "Sorry."

"Have you been avoiding me?"

"Not avoiding, but you know. You and Liev are so...together."

Grace straightens. "I thought you liked us together?"

"I fucking love it, Grace." Max wraps her arm around her friend and holds her tight for a few seconds. I look away, feeling like a third wheel, and focus on a person laid out on a platform, getting wrapped up in clingfilm by a group of kinksters. They're all laughing, including the one being mummified in plastic.

I move farther away to give Max and Grace a moment's privacy, scanning the booths. In the first, a couple of people appear to be discussing the merits of two different cages. Beyond that, a few people watch someone climb up on what is possibly a chair made for sex. It's an attractive, sculptural piece, covered in shiny leather or vinyl.

My attention slides a little farther on to a set up with two people trapped in a wooden device that looks like those old-fashioned stocks. Stockades? The device has been set up perpendicular to where I stand, so that I can see their heads and hands on one side and their naked asses on the other.

I look up, surprised to see none other than Lamé, in a glittery, low-cut wrestling singlet, fishnets, and rainbow roller skates, swooping up and back, slapping their bare asses with a crop one way and then the other.

Lamé's movements are languid and graceful, their hair flowing out in a silky wave behind them, in contrast to the sharp, quick flick of the crop. With each hit, the men twitch and grunt or moan or shriek. It's kind of sexy and kind of silly and quite the spectacle.

I watch, fascinated by this window into Lamé's world. They've been so kind and helpful with me, full of advice and opinions, but not particularly forthcoming about how they spend their time at camp.

I guess I'm not all that surprised to see that Lamé is dominant and charismatic and more than a little theatrical in the way they play out their scenes.

Max and Grace come up beside me.

"Aren't they amazing?" asks Grace.

I nod, entranced as the two prisoners squirm and shift against their bonds, their responses so different it's like watching two different scenes at once. With every pass, Lamé hits a different part of them and, with every pass, they seem to like it more. The groans turn to grunts, one of them goes silent. The blond. A partner of Lamé's, I remember them saying.

At one point, he stiffens and curls in on himself, the pleasure so blatant that I've got to look away.

"Whoa," I say, breathing a little harder now.

"Hot, right?" Max wiggles her eyebrows. "Lamé's so fun to watch. Such good flow."

Lamé glances up, catches sight of us, and gives us a wink and a bow before bending to stroke the face of their person. The move is tender and unexpected. There's a mastery to their movements. A confidence that speaks of experience and the deep joy they find here, as well as obvious affection. The connection between Lamé and their play partners is obvious, even from a distance.

"Twy?" Grace nudges me with her elbow, drawing my eye from Lamé's scene. "See anything you want to try?"

"Tonight's the night," says Max.

"You two good?" I look from Max to Grace and back. "I understand if you want to hang just the two of you. Please don't feel like you need to babysit me or anything."

"Nope. We're good. Just needed to catch up." They look at each other and smile with such complicity that I gulp back a sharp pang of missing Gigi. It's like homesickness when I don't see her for so long.

"Come on," Max takes my arm again. "It's fun showing you around. What'll it be?"

I shrug. "I'll know when I see it, I guess."

"So, I have a theory. If you want to hear it."

"This'll be good," says Grace. "Max's theories are gold."

"About what?"

"Zed."

My breath leaves me in a whoosh and I slow down. "All right. Go ahead."

"I think there might be a little bit of a Madonna-whore complex happening."

"Whore. God, I hate that word," Grace grumbles.

I say, "Me, too."

"Yep. Love slut though." Max puts on a fake British accent. "*Why is thy lord so sluttish, I thee pray?*"

"What is that?"

"Chaucer," she says, with an impish smile. "Anyway, I think what we're talking about is more a Vanilla/Kinky thing. Zed's thing with you, I mean."

"Yeah, 'cause he doesn't do Vanilla," says Grace. "Like, at all."

"By choice, though, right?" There's irritation in my voice. "I mean, we did sorta, kinda almost make out before everything blew up. He's the one who stopped it."

"The problem is that the man seems to actually like you."

I roll my eyes. "Whatever."

We stroll by booths where people try out various types of rope and wax and needles and anything else you can possibly imagine, including what appears to be an entire hardware store.

One setup catches my eye, along with the man inside it. "There's Blade."

"Yep," says Max. "Looks like he's flogging tonight."

We walk over to where Blade's running a series of quick slaps over someone's butt and back. In motion, Blade's body is mesmerizing, each movement complex and graceful. I get the feeling that not one of his strikes is off target.

"That's a St. Andrews cross, right?"

"Yep. Also called an x-cross or an x-frame." Max looks at me. "Want to try?"

"To flog or be flogged?" Grace looks at me. "That is the question."

"Be flogged," I say, without hesitation. The only person I can imagine hitting right now is Zion. And not in a sexy way.

A woman stands beside Blade watching, arms crossed. After a few minutes, she says something. He nods and sets his flogger down. The two go and untie the other person from the cross. They collapse, giggling, into the woman's arms before the two of them take off together.

Blade sets to work spraying and cleaning the structure, then looks up, sees me, and stops. "Hey."

"Can I have a turn?"

"Flogging?"

"On the cross."

He sighs, glances over my shoulder and shakes his head. "Not a good idea."

"Just a flogging. Please. I've never done it before."

"Asking for trouble." He makes a face, sticks the

flogger he just used into a basket and pulls another from a case. "Shit. Go on then."

"We'll be right over here," Grace says, pointing to a spot in the corner.

I step up to the cross, and wait. It smells slightly orangey, like a natural cleaning product. When I lean against it, the cushioned, bright red leather is cool against the skin of my midsection. It's been set up perpendicular to the Hangar's interior, which means I can either look at the people passing by on my right, or focus at the hangar's rough wooden exterior half wall and posts to my left. Beyond that, there's nothing but dark forest. I concentrate on that.

"Cuffs?" I jump at Blade's voice.

"Um, sure."

I hear the sound of chains, metal scraping metal, then with gentle, quick, efficient movements, he wraps something around my ankles, followed by my wrists.

My stance is wide and easy now, my arms supported by the soft leather cuffs, my midsection leaning into the center of the X, with my head and shoulders and chest above.

"You know who you remind me of up there in that outfit?" Grace asks. "Princess Leia. Empire Strikes Back. Is that the one?"

I strain to see her. "Return of the Jedi."

"Oh, so you know." One side of her mouth quirks up into a dry little smile.

"That scene was a recurring theme in my youthful

fantasies," I admit. "Being tied up and taken advantage of."

"Origin story." Blade's voice rumbles from behind me. "We've all got one."

"Yeah?" I twist to watch him organize his toys like the evil sadist in a torture scene.

"Yep." He nods, giving my body a slow up and down. "Hope Zed knows how lucky he is." I blush and smile at this easy, open appreciation. After a few seconds of eye contact, he looks at his array of tools. "So. You ready for this?"

I nod, my pulse skipping all over the place.

"Can I hear you say it, please, Twilight?"

"Yes. I'm ready."

"All right. And you know the camp safe word?"

"Red."

"You said you're new to this?" At my nod, he says, "Look at this, please."

The instrument he shows me reminds me of a horse's tail, with a black handle and bright red leather or suede fringe. It's thick and evil-looking, the strips of leather wider than the others on the table. "I'll start soft. Just your butt."

I nod again, shut my eyes hard, and wait.

I hear the swish of leather before it touches me. When it does, there's none of the pain I expected. Just a light, smooth, back and forth swish. It's not unpleasant.

"You good?" Blade leans in so I can see him.

"Yeah. Yes. It's fine."

"Fine?" He chuckles. "Geez. Kill me with compliments, why don't you?"

I smile and shift, wondering if I'm supposed to do anything, like maybe stick my ass out or, I don't know, react more? Act, maybe, like I'm on stage? "What, um, should I be doing?"

Blade lifts one thick black brow. "Seriously?"

My face goes hot with embarrassment. "Total newbie here."

"Right." He moves in, his smell a nice citrussy musk that does absolutely nothing for me, although this close, the fine lines around his eyes give him a touch of seriousness that I like. And then there's his rich, deep voice, which he uses to amazing affect by telling me to "Just lie there and take it. That's your only job. Enjoy it. Or not. Let me know when you've had enough."

"That's it?"

"You know what, darling? You and your Dom might want to have a talk."

Your Dom. At those words, my nerves do an involuntary shimmy, which I immediately tamp down. "I don't have a Dom."

With a sexy low chuckle, he flicks his wrist, doing a quick figure eight in the air.

"Anywhere you don't want me to touch?"

I shake my head.

"Go on, let me hear it."

"No. Will it hurt?"

"You want it to?"

People slow and stop, watching, with varying degrees

of interest. Being on the receiving end of all that attention is equal parts nerve-wracking and exciting.

I squeeze my eyes shut against their stares and reply, "I'm not sure." I breathe deep, let the nerves fill me, then shove them out until there's only excitement. It's not sexual, exactly. But there's definitely titillation. "Yeah."

"I'll start light." He turns and walks a couple steps away, a bit of showmanship for the crowd, then swishes the leather straps against my shorts-clad ass. It tickles. I stifle a giggle. Behind me, Grace laughs low. "Maybe I'll make Liev do this one day," Grace says. "Never really saw the appeal, but it's kind of...flirty, isn't it?"

"Exactly," says Max. "It can be flirty and fun and low-key. You can pretend it's his tail or something."

Grace snorts.

Giving them a grin, Blade swipes the fringe in a languorous figure eight that covers my ass and part of my thighs, never hitting my back. "You good?" he asks.

"Yeah," I smile, let my gaze glaze over a little, and ignore the people gathering by the booth.

I don't know how long he goes on, warming me up rather than hurting me. Although I know absolutely nothing about flogging, it's apparent that Blade does, because the transition from that easy, almost lazy, painless cadence to a light sting is so smooth, I almost don't notice that it hurts.

But it does. And I like it.

No, not like. I...respond to it. Nothing overt and, again, I'm not particularly aroused. But there's a little strain when the strips of leather nip at my ass. My back arches, my butt wants more.

"Nice," Blade says, satisfaction in his voice. "Good," he says, matter-of-factly, never once changing the cadence.

Somewhere along the way, I sink into the pain, the regularity, the very slight changes in pace and power, I lose my inhibitions a little and close my eyes, not quite as self-conscious about our audience.

And then, as if a switch has been flipped, everything changes.

I go stiff with tension and open my eyes, wide, feeling...

Watched.

Which is ridiculous, right?

Until I spot him, right there toward the back of the crowd. It's Zion. No doubt about it. And he's seen me.

I swear, it's not his presence that pricked my awareness so much as his stare.

Because it's fierce. Angry, intense. Mean, almost.

And now, oh, now, my body responds with pleasure. And it's not the scratching of an itch of these past few minutes, it's pure carnality, from deep, deep inside me. Rolling out in waves, turning me lush and wet and open and...wanting.

The play session that felt casual and easy and not the least bit sexual a moment ago is now fully charged, my body gone from relaxed to galvanized in a split second.

The halter top that seemed risqué, but kind of fun and flirty, is suddenly inflammatory, turning my nipples into hard, aching points that I push, push, push against the cross. Tension coils low and hot in my middle and every single thing he and I have done over the past two days comes flying in to pelt my skin like a million little floggers.

The way he's watching me, his eyes burning a path straight to my wet, throbbing, achingly empty core? Nothing in this world could tear my eyes from the man steadily forging his way through the crowd like a lion through a herd of gazelle. It's the hottest thing I've ever seen, felt, lived through.

I want him. I *need* him. However I can get him.

Except, no. Seriously. Fuck that.

Without taking my eyes from Zion's approach—as if I could—I say to Blade, "Do it harder. Make it hurt."

Zion

I push through the crowd to Twyla.

The faces are a blur, the people an unidentifiable mass, if anyone talks to me, I don't even hear it. All I see is her, strung up on an x-cross like an offering to the gods.

To me.

Every precise hit from Blade's flogger ramps up the tension in my muscles, tightens my jaw, reduces my vision to nothing but a tunnel. A link from me to her. I feel her responses from the base of my spine to the top of my head. I feel it. Want it. Because it's mine.

Mine, mine, mine. The word's a heartbeat, a pulse

driving my soul, keeping me going until I'm in the booth with them. Max and Grace's twin expressions of surprise nothing but a blip.

Blade steps back to where I'm standing. His voice sounds like an echo from someplace far away. "Your sub's sweet, man."

"She's more than sweet," I tell him, without looking his way. "But she's not my..." I stop, breathe, watch her writhe while Blade teases her with the flogger, Twyla's gaze never once leaving mine. Not once.

What if?

"Want to take over?"

I stare at the flogger in his hand, meet his eyes, see something there, as basic and animal as the monster twisting in my guts. Understanding.

"No." I watch her fists grapple with the chains and tighten around them, watch her head strain to the side so she can keep me in her sights, allow my gaze to sink deep into her eyes. "Don't stop."

Mine.

My feet take me to her side, just out of Blade's reach.

After a moment's hesitation—and another look from me—he steps back and to her left, hooks the flogger between two fingers and takes up where he left off. It's an easy, rhythmic slap of wide leather that falls to the stretchy material covering her ass. The sound's not as satisfying as it would be without the cloth. I make the mistake of picturing the light jiggle of her golden-skinned ass without a barrier and work hard to tamp down the possessiveness lashing at my insides.

My wife, god bless her, doesn't shift her focus for one millisecond. It's intense, constant. The heat between us is nuclear. Too dangerous this close.

I don't give a shit.

I'll take whatever she gives me. Everything.

Her expression's edging from pain to pleasure, lingering in the liminal place between them as I move closer. "That feel good, baby? The way he's hurting you?"

Her nod's loose. That lush, wide mouth drops open, releasing a wheezing gasp.

"Yeah?" I lean close, breathe her in, and feel that inner monster pounding its chest. *Mine, mine, mine.*

Her yes is a hiss through slack lips.

I want to touch them.

Mine, mine, mine.

Swallowing hard, I shift away, my monster snarling in triumph when Twyla strains to follow.

"Don't go," she whispers. "Stay."

The writhing in my chest stops short, like something gone dormant.

"Not goin' anywhere." I reach up, catch a lock of that long, dark hair, and give it a tiny tug. Her eyes roll back and close. I make my way around to her front, which is fucking breathtaking.

It takes everything I've got not to uncuff her right now, take her in my arms, soothe the pain that asshole's causing. Or maybe cause her more. Fuck, I don't know. I just want to be in charge.

The flogger connects and she jumps, her eyes meet

mine—wide and surprised and full of dark, deep pleasure —and that inner voice turns greedy, selfish.

"You like it?"

Her expression's a question.

"The pain. The way it hurts."

"I..." Her groan is low and throaty and just about the sexiest thing I've ever heard.

"You look so good like this. You know that, baby? My cock's so goddamn hard watching you. You like it? You like the pain?"

"A little." She shakes her head, gasps at the next strike, and leans forward so our foreheads are so close to touching, we share heat. "I like you watching." Her next gasp, bright with shock, trails into rich pleasure, deep enough to resonate in my bones. "It's better with you." Her smile's half wild.

With you.

I go still at the intimacy in those two words, in our stare.

It feels off in my stomach. Uncomfortable.

I push a thin smile to my lips. "Yeah? Well, pain looks good on you."

She smirks, flinches through the next strike, and stares me dead in the eyes. "Being an asshole looks good on you, Zion."

I bark out a laugh and she grins, breaks into a whimper. Her head drops forward, severing our connection.

Before I know it, my hand's in her hair, fisting it, dragging her head up and back.

"Don't you take your eyes off me."

Her gaze centers on mine, though her nod's laborious, her head heavy. I wrap my other hand in her hair and hold her up, make her look at me.

"You're such a fuckin' brat, Twyla. You know that?"

Like the good brat she is, she shakes her head. Or tries to. My grip's too tight to allow much motion. All she can do is watch me while I carry the weight of her head and soak up every startled gasp, every pained jolt.

They're mine now. Mine.

Over her shoulder, Blade catches my eye. He motions and mouths something. I nod.

He shifts position, swings in that easy, effortless way and catches her right between the legs and there... There's the sound. A higher whine, close to a sob. I've heard it before. Last night. Today. It means she's close. Close, but not there.

"Pull down her shorts," I say, watching her closely for a reaction. There's a full-body shimmy, a brief struggle against her cuffs. Her face tightens up, as if she'll say *No. Red. Stop.*

Instead, she lets out a long, low *Oooooh, fuck*, spreads her legs just a fraction wider, tilts her ass up...and smiles.

Fucking beautiful.

It's all the consent Blade needs. Within seconds, he's got her shorts down and both legs cuffed again.

"It'll hurt more. You want that?"

"Yes." Her gaze is direct, if clouded. She nudges her mask aside with her shoulder. It doesn't occur to me to slide it back in place. "I want that."

I nod at Blade, watch the lazy rotation of a couple

dozen tails just before they connect with her naked skin, then focus in on her eyes as they roll back. Another strike, low to high, another on the left cheek. He goes on like this for a while, his rhythm steady and smooth, his muscles barely shifting with the effort.

Between my hands, Twyla's heavy head occasionally jolts, her eyes stay fixed on mine, her mouth opens. The sounds she makes...fuck, this is my favorite new soundtrack. Straight from her lungs to my dick.

"Harder," I tell Blade. He complies and immediately, she's deeper into subspace, her body tightening and going lax with every strike. And then, "Her cunt."

Without breaking his stride, he shifts, lowers his arm and...

"Fuck, baby, there it is."

Another strike. Her eyes roll back. I shift, cradle her skull, keep her head upright. "Watch me. Watch me, Twyla."

Her gaze is bleary, her mouth hangs open. Her cheeks are a dark, angry pink.

I want her. So badly it hurts.

I bend, put my mouth to her temple, sensitive lips to wild pulse. Slide down to her cheek, soak in the jolt of pain, the sigh of pleasure.

"You gonna come for me, baby? You gonna do that?" Her nod rubs our cheeks together—soft skin rasps against stubble. "I'm fucking you tonight, Twy," I tell her—a threat? A promise. "I'll slide deep inside that tight little cunt. You want that?" Another nod brings my nose to the angle of her jaw, just below her ear. My lips press there, hot skin to hot skin. "I'm gonna pound you so hard. Gonna stretch you wide, gonna make you feel every fucking inch of me."

A strike, a moan, a twist of skin to skin, dragging my sensitive lips lower, to her throat. "You're so hot. Right here," I mutter, spreading words like kisses. "And here." Over her throat. She swallows. I lick sweat, the sweet taste of her.

Another strike. Another jolt. I twist, she turns. Up, up... My lips and hers.

Almost a kiss. Almost. Just mouths touching. Doesn't mean a thing.

Sobbing, she explodes.

22

Twyla

Oh, god. Oh, wow.

I didn't...I don't...

I open my eyes and shut them again.

Whoa. Okay. I try to slow my breathing, try to find my footing. Not easy. Not pretty.

I'm clenched and wide open, full of pleasure and pain and something more elemental. More basic. Essential.

At some point, I manage to open my eyes as wide as they'll go and watch Zion watch me. A feedback loop of pleasure and pain with no beginning or end. So mixed up. All of it. Me, him. This place.

It's too much. I shut my eyes. The world spins and I open them again.

"Come on." Zion pulls up my shorts.

"Okay."

He talks to someone, while undoing my legs. "Need you for a scene tomorrow. You free in the evening?"

A scene? What scene?

"Sure, man," replies Blade. "Happy to help out."

While Blade undoes one of my hands, I smile at him and thank him for the flogging. "Any time, darling."

"Come on, Twy. Let's get you home." My other hand comes undone. I'm a limp, loose noodle and I'd be on the floor without the arms that wrap around me. Zion. Holding me against his chest. Like a baby. Carrying me.

"Where's Max?"

"There."

I strain and catch sight of my new friend on the other side of the partition. She looks at me, offering a thumbs-up and thumbs-down, her expression questioning.

With a smile, I nod and give her a thumbs-up of my own. With that, she takes off.

"Put me down."

He slows. Leans in. "Why? You want to walk?"

"Hurt your back."

He huffs out a laugh, hefts me higher so I can wrap my arms around his neck, and starts moving through the crowd.

"Where are we going?" I ask, not really caring.

"Home."

I picture the Georgetown house and the Malibu beach cottage I've never seen. Neither one appeals. The idea of leaving this camp right now scares me.

Just thinking of the outside world turns my sweat cold.

"Lamé's cottage, right?" He looks over his shoulder at the kinksters who've dispersed since our grand finale, and leans close. "I'm takin' care of you."

"Oh." I suddenly get it. "Aftercare." Not the urgent coupling I'd pictured. As if I could manage anything close to an urgent coupling right now. I swear that lashing and orgasm was the most exhausting thing I've ever lived through—and I didn't have to actually do anything.

He frowns and keeps walking.

The air out here's slightly cooler than in the hangar, and fresher. It clears my head. "I can walk," I tell him.

"I know."

"So, put me down."

"Would you just..." He glances at my face, then forward again. "Let me do this?"

Oh. Okay. Rather than answer, I slide my head back into the crook between his jaw and his shoulder, and snuggle in tight. Slowly, I relax. Close my eyes. Listen to the night noises—cicadas and music and voices. Laughter, moaning, the crack of a whip.

I'm floating. Warm. Cocooned. Held and... "I love it here."

His step hitches slightly before moving on with a grunt. "You mean camp."

"I love the people. They're so...happy. Free. Real. So *nice*."

His steps are steady, but the heartbeat under my hand's picking up speed. Or it's my imagination. He's probably tired from carrying me. I open my mouth to tell him to put me down when he responds.

"It's a good place."

A dozen more steps, slightly uphill. The swish of grass. A door slams close by.

"I know you don't want me here," I whisper, shocked to feel tears spring to my eyes. He stops moving. "I know it's special to you and I've blasted in like a—"

"Stay." The word hovers in the air between us. He starts walking again. "You should stay."

I smile against his throat, burrow deeper, and then nip him.

He stumbles, with a muttered, "Fuck," and clamps one hand tighter around me. "Don't do that again."

For a moment, I feel chastised. Why are my instincts so wrong? Why am I always messing up and making him... Under my hand, his chest expands, his breathing faster than before. I turn, nuzzle his pulse point, lick him, concentrate on his heartbeat. He likes it, I realize. Likes the teasing, the contact.

Slowly, I pull my lips back and scrape my teeth there —more than a tease now. A threat. "Or what?"

A growl rises up from deep inside his rib cage. It's a call my body responds to before I've recognized it for what it is.

"Or I'll make you stop."

Oh, wow. That did it.

Turned my resting nerves way up, taking my pulse from its languorous, post climactic meandering to a racing thump that he probably feels through the bottom of his feet.

"How?"

"Baby, you don't want to know," he says.

Foolish, foolish man. It's like he hasn't even met me.

"I think I do," I tell him.

In the next moment, he shifts my weight, throws me over his shoulder, and forges up a set of porch steps to a log cabin.

Without hesitation, he throws open a door marked Private and stomps inside before kicking it closed again.

We're in total darkness.

"This isn't Lamé's place." My voice sounds quiet in the dark.

"No. It's mine."

23

ZION

The first few seconds inside are a complete blank. All I see, all I feel or hear or smell is that moment in the Glory Hole when I realized it was her.

This is a fork in the road. A choice. A big one.

I know it. Denying it right now would be lying to myself. To her.

To every person I know and respect here.

She wiggles in my arms and, rather than release her the way she wants, I take two long steps. As soon as my shin connects with the bed frame, I drop her on the mattress.

She lets out an *ouf*, bounces once, and goes still.

"You gonna lie down and rest like a good girl?"

She snorts. "That doesn't sound like fun."

"It sounds smart."

I hear her roll over the comforter. "Nothing I've done since I met you was smart, Zion. Why start now?"

"What are we doing here?" I ask, just to be clear. "What are you consenting to?"

For a few seconds, she breathes, probably thinking. "Anything. Everything."

"You sure that's wise?"

"I'm sure it's not. And I don't care."

"I have rules," I tell her. A low, rough voice in the dark.

Her "*Okay*" is not nearly as compliant as I'd like, but I go on anyway.

"One: No scat."

"Scat?" She asks, shifting.

"Shit."

"Oh." More movement puts her farther up, against the headboard. The light from the big glass door to the back plays over the crystals in her tasseled top, reminding me of something slithery and scaled. Dangerous. "Yeah, I'm good with that. Do people really—"

"Two: no bareback."

Her breathing's audible, suddenly. Quick, excited. We're doing this, it says. This is happening. "Agreed."

"Three..." I swallow, scrub a hand over my face. The rasp is loud in the silence. "No kissing. On the lips."

"I know that."

"Yeah, well you almost..." *made me do it.*

"What? What did I do, Zion?" She sounds hazy, still. In need of aftercare. Not a hard fucking. But a little irate, too, a little annoyed. A little snide. Her whole attitude's an aphrodisiac made just for me.

"I don't do brats." It's not a lie, exactly, since brats aren't usually my thing. Not that I have anything against them, they just annoy me, usually.

Usually. When sex and kink are straightforward and easy. Rules, consent, desires. It's all set out, decided, lines drawn.

Right here, right now, with her, though...

"Geez, wow." The jangling of crystals as she moves to the edge of the bed. "Great aftercare, Zion. Seriously. You're a freaking genius at this. A little constructive criticism, though? You might want to—"

"You're such a goddamn brat." I go to the bedside table and switch on the light, blinding us both. Before I know what I'm doing, I'm on her, over her. She's trapped and, still, she doesn't look cowed. Not intimidated. Not for a fucking second.

I slide my fingers into her hair, grip it tight, hold her still, and let my eyes roam this fucking *face*.

"*Usually*," I bite out, my breath skating over her ear, her cheek, her nose, lower. "Play partners let me take care of them after a session." I dig my hips in, let her feel how hard I am, how desperate. "So. What you need to do now, Twyla." I tighten my grip until it's got to sting her scalp, but she doesn't care. Doesn't notice. Her eyes are hot and steady on mine. "Is tell me what you need." My breath's ragged. "Are you thirsty, you little brat?"

"No."

"Need a shower? Massage?" I lean back enough to brush the evil jewel top aside and bare a soft breast, paler than the rest of her. "Bath? I've got a hot tub in the back." I skim my knuckles over the painfully soft curve, lean in and bite her nipple, then counter the lift of her hips with my own.

Oh, fuck. *Fuck.* I dip and tighten again, the pressure of my erection to her mound almost enough to send me rocketing right here.

But that's not what this is. I'm not coming in my pants while she lays here. "You hungry, baby?" I ask with another slide, then another. She shakes her head, which only serves to annoy me farther. "Warm enough?" Another thrust, another. Nodding, she bends her knees and pushes up, meeting every dip of my lower half. We're dry-humping like teenagers—the most vanilla thing I've done since I found out what sex was—and I swear I'm about to come in my pants.

"Too hot?"

The long, slow slides turn into quick thrusts bringing my hard dick right into the crotch of those fucking shorts. I reach down between us and rub the seam. Wet. Of course.

"Not hot," she breathes. "Just right."

How the fuck does she sound so in control when I'm about to blow in my goddamn shorts? How? And when did this bullshit behavior start turning me on?

Frantic, I reach down and knead the same tit, pull at her nipple, then move to the other and, unable to stop, bend to take the dark tip into my mouth. I suck, hard.

She arches and squeals and I pound her little pussy through way too many layers. Caught up in some sort of frenzy, I reach into my shorts and pull myself out, shoving the waistband down as far as it'll go without too much effort.

She gasps, looks down. Her mouth drops open.

"You ready, you fucking brat?"

She nods, quick and eager, but I've always been a words man and I need to hear it. "Tell me."

"I want you in me."

"Yeah? How?"

Her eyes flicker up to mine, clouded for a few seconds before understanding dawns. "Hard. Fast. Deep." Her gaze stays fixed on where I'm stroking my cock. "Fuck me," she whispers. "Now. Now."

"Get those shorts off."

She can't with my weight on her, but it doesn't stop her from trying. Her scrambling struggle tugs harder at my balls, makes me want her more. And then, because there's this *thing* between us that I just can't understand, I grab her face in one hand and squeeze it, puffing her lips up into a look that's almost comical.

Except it's not funny at all. Nothing about her is. She's deadly serious, even with that evil spark in her eye.

This woman will end me.

The thought comes and goes so fast I barely recognize it. Leaving in its wake something dark and mean. "Peel. The fuckin'. Shorts off. Twyla," I say, sounding so much like my old man that it scares me. And then, unable, to stop—a bad, bad thing in the world I inhabit—I move the hand from her face to her throat.

It's a control thing, the choking. I don't love breath

play, unless a partner's into it, and even then, it's not an envelope I'm too willing to push. But control, I enjoy. Although crave might be the right word.

Twyla, it seems, likes it too, judging from the way she's squirming under me, the way her hips thrust up to meet mine, the hard curve of her back as she arches to get parts of her closer while others try to get away.

That struggle, more than anything, unleashes me. Or shuts my brain down or, hell, destroys it once and for all because, in the next second, I've ripped the fucking shorts off. Her throat's a hot, living thing against the palm of one hand while her pussy pulses against the other.

And my cock's the aching, throbbing monster between them.

"Don't want to listen to me?" I tighten both hands. "Doesn't matter, baby. I can make you." I bend so my face is close to hers. Under my fingers, her cunt spreads like butter. I ignore the way she squirms, trying to get more friction, more pleasure. "You want that?"

Her face goes tight and stubborn, while her whole body shudders. Like she can't get the two on the same page.

My thumb runs up and back through her juices, separating her lips, opening her up, getting her ready. Although, as swollen and soaked as she is, I'd slide right in. Another up and down and I let my middle finger dip inside, plunging it deep and curving high to hit her G-spot. Her body stiffens, her pussy goes tight.

"Shit, baby. You thinkin' 'bout coming right now?

That what you're doin'?" I shake my head. "No. No coming 'til I get in there."

"You're..." I tweak that spongy little spot and she twitches. "You're inside me."

"This?" Another pull, another uncontrollable reaction from her greedy little body. "Not what I'm talking about and you know it." My hand twists, pulls out. Her hips chase it, giving me the satisfaction of shoving her back against the mattress. Adding a second finger to the first is the kind of torture I love. None of the possessive, jealousy bullshit I've been dealing with since she pranced up in here. This—complete, calm control—is my wheelhouse.

"Better." The third finger's a squeeze. Her pulse races faster under my other palm. She's got a hand on mine at her throat, the other one wrapped around my wrist below. We're a loop like this, a closed circuit. I should be relaxing, finding my flow, but those dark, knowing eyes won't let me. Only, it's not the challenge that stops me this time. Not the brat working to piss me off.

Fuck. If she were fighting or angry or annoyed, it would be easier. Anything would be easier than the shit she's showing me. The softness. The understanding. The goddamn *affection.*

It's the affection that's killing me.

It's the affection that drags my fingers from her hot core. Affection that forces me to scrabble around in my bedside table for a condom that's not there.

Why would I have a condom next to my bed when beds are made for sleeping, not fucking? And certainly not whatever this is we're about to do.

For a split second, relief flows through me. No condom. No sex.

And then she says the four most excruciating words in the English language.

Twyla

"I've got an IUD." I reach for my shorts pocket. "Oh. And a condom."

Zion sits back on the bed and goes completely still. He watches me with a look that's both predatory and lost, somehow. A cornered beast. The only movement in the room is the ticking of a muscle in his cheek.

"We can use the condom, but I've...also got the other thing. And I get that it's a hard rule for you. I respect that."

His mouth opens and closes. His eyes flick from one of mine to the other.

"Have you done it before?"

"Unprotected sex?" I ask.

He nods.

"No. I got the IUD because I could. But I've never done it. You?"

He shakes his head, his eyes huge as his gaze travels down my body.

I talk, filling his continued silence. "Anyway, I get your rule. It's about safety. Pregnancy, STDs. And, probably, you don't want to risk it, given who you are and—"

"Not just that."

I wait.

His gaze shifts down, slow and heavy as a caress, over my chest, my stomach, to my toes and back to the empty, aching places between my legs. "It's a fetish."

My brows go up. I don't speak.

"Breeding. Come... A kind of ownership thing."

Something long-dormant curls to life inside me. Not quite in my sex, not as high up as my heart. Someplace in between. Someplace secret and private.

My eyes flick to the side and down, to where his thick, heavily-veined erection strains up. Hungry.

That's how he looks. Ravenous and ready and very, very dangerous.

It sends a fresh thrill through me, this one shimmering out to every nerve in my body.

"I'm, uh, not good at..." He clears his throat and looks toward the wide French doors on the back wall. "I need control."

My head tilts as I try to figure out exactly where this is going. "You want to control me, you mean?"

"Well, yeah." He throws me an ironic, humored look, though it's nowhere near a smile. "Not what I'm saying, though. I need control to make this..." His hands are big, tight fists in his lap. "Work."

"This?"

"All of it. My life. The balance."

Slowly, realization sets in. "And if you lost it, you're afraid you'd... What? Lose everything you've built? Your career? Reputation?"

"More than that."

"Okay." I search his face for some clue as to where this is going. Come up empty. "I don't get it, Zion."

"This. Here."

"Camp?"

"My people. They're like..."

"Family." In that moment everything clicks into place. "You're afraid of losing them. If you're, what? Real? Yourself? If you show them..." I screw up my face. "Isn't this the whole point of coming here, though? Being yourself? A few weeks a year, you get to—"

"Two. Two weeks a year."

My mouth drops open. "That's it? Seriously? And the rest of the time you're, what? Faking it?"

His eyes meet mine. "Mostly." He looks bleak, alone. I want to hug him.

"I still don't get it. You're afraid of losing control? With these people? Your family? Why would..." And then I see. And it splits me down the middle. Crushes my heart. "You're faking with them, too."

"I don't..." He stands, runs his fingers through all that wavy beach hair, and paces, his body too big and intense for the space. I look away from his ass, ignore that he's somehow still half-hard, despite the sharp turn our conversation's taken. He may look like a sex god, but right now, he's just alone. So alone.

I stand, half naked and awkward, knees wobbly, butt aching where it's been flogged, and walk to him, the fringe on my top swishing noisily. I wish I hadn't worn this ridiculous thing.

"Come here," I say, undoing the tie at my neck and letting the halter fall in a puddle at my feet.

His eyes skip down to my breasts, then back up.

I move closer.

He watches me. Another step puts me in his space.

I reach out my arms.

I don't know what he thinks I'm planning, but the hug surprises him. I can tell from the way his body jolts, his sharp gasp.

"Come here," I say again, running my hands around his hefty ribs, wrapping his big back, pressing forward into that strong, strong chest. Between us, he's getting harder.

I ignore it, tighten my arms, pull him in, cram my face into his torso so hard it'll probably bruise.

But what's a little physical pain in the face of all this hurt? What's a bruise when your soul's at stake?

"I lost control with you, Twyla. That night back in DC."

My smaller, softer body cradles his big, hard one. Giving him safety, affection. Everything I have to give.

"I lost control and almost..."

He almost kissed me. Almost felt something. I get that part of him now, though I still don't know the why.

"I'm so sorry. I didn't want to hurt you, I wanted her to be you."

I stiffen for a half second and then pull him closer, so close I feel the beating of his heart against my cheek.

"I've got you." I give him every ounce of strength I have, every drop of affection, all the compassion and—though it hurts—the love I have in me. "I've got you, Zion."

It takes a minute. Maybe two, but at some point, he just...gives in, I guess. His body loses a little of its tension, goes slack, then clamps up again, though this time it's around me. "This isn't what I wanted," he says.

"I know," I tell him, nuzzling his chest hair. My lips skim over a taut, pink nipple and he shivers. "I know."

"Hurting you. You know?"

I nod, explore more of him with my lips, my tongue, let my hands drag up and down the sleek muscles of his back.

"I'm fine. It's fine."

"Your career."

"I'll figure something out."

"*We* will." He shifts his arms higher, wraps them tighter. "Together."

"Yeah." I nod, though I'm not entirely sure there's a solution.

"The world needs more Twyla Hernandez movies."

I snort.

"Seriously. You're fucking mesmerizing. You deserve to be a star. And I know it's why you agreed to the marriage."

I untwine myself from him and step back. "Partly."

That evil Zion grin makes a brief appearance. "And partly cause you wanted to get into my pants?"

"What pants?"

We both look down to where his cock's at full mast between us, the tip, wet with pre-come, bobbing against my midsection.

I lose my breath, look back up to see his eyes glinting darkly at half-mast, his mouth firm, decisive.

"I get tested regularly," he says. "No STDs."

My pulse picks up. Are we doing this? Taking this step and exploring this kink of his—ours—together?

"Same." I bite my lip to keep from showing him my excitement. "All negative."

The backs of his knuckles drag over my shoulder, the side of my breast, my waist. He bends his knees, grips my hip, stares at his hand as it runs lightly to my center. Gently, so gently, he skims my sex, then uses those thick fingers to open me up. "Get on the bed," he whispers.

I don't hesitate.

"On your back, legs wide. Let me see it. Let me see."

Nervous now, I splay myself open. I feel objectified in a way I've never been before. Exposed and vulnerable.

I want more.

He doesn't make me wait, though, and even that's like a gift, because the way he comes over and hovers over me is so eager and uncalculating, there's no doubt in my mind that I'm wanted.

If anything, he's desperate.

For me.

That desperation makes him sloppy. The body that seemed incapable of so much as fumbling a minute ago is suddenly tripping over itself to get to me.

"Fuck, fuck, I want you."

"You've got me," I tell him, sensitive and tender and exposed.

"Baby." He covers me, his body competent despite the emotion or excitement or whatever it is making him clumsy. "Twyla."

He shifts to one side, runs his hand over me and then hitches my leg up high, rolls between my thighs and, before I'm mentally ready for it, presses in.

"Oh, fuck," he says, barely breaching me. "Fuck, Twyla, it's so... you're so... Fuck."

I'd giggle at his inability to speak, but I'm feeling pretty much the same. "Yeah," I manage, encouraging him with a hand on his back, another tight on his ass. "So good."

"I'm bare."

"Yeah."

His cock forges in another inch. Another. God, how did I not equate just how big he is? The fit's tight. He has to work to get inside me. It doesn't hurt, exactly, but the stretch isn't comfortable either.

"So goddamn hot."

He draws out a little. My hands spasm, tighten, drag him back.

His answering laugh turns immediately into a grimace when he plunges in another inch, another, drawing a groan from me before bottoming out.

For a handful of inhalations, he stays there, lets me adjust. Maybe he's adjusting, too, given the newness of it all.

"I've never…" I pause while he draws out, brings his tip almost to my entrance, and then plunges back in, hard and swift.

"Never what?" He asks, lifting up on stiff arms, looking down between us, admiring our bodies together.

When I don't immediately reply, he pauses and looks up.

"Never done it like this either."

"Raw?"

I nod.

Raw. That's exactly it. And not just my body, but my feelings. My being. I'm open. I feel fragile and new and tender. So exposed, anything he does or says is sure to hurt me.

At the same time, his next thrust feels so good. So right. The pleasure closer to the surface than it's ever been. Raw, I guess, isn't just about pain. It's about all the things. About being open and ready and willing. About taking, but also giving.

No walls to breach. No visible limits.

"Harder," I tell him, not entirely sure I want that, but needing something to keep me from crying. "Fuck me harder."

"You sure?" His gaze meets mine, snaps to my mouth, then back up, his face an open book. Eager, wanting, excited.

He's gorgeous, yes. Strong and sexy and all those

things that the world admires in him, but what I see now is better than any of that. It's not his strength that he shows me. It's his vulnerability, his pain. It's the lonely little boy inside him.

And that's a million times more beautiful.

24

ZION

"I'm gonna come inside you," I warn. Or threaten. Doesn't matter. I'm fucking into her, faster and harder than I should. Every cell in my body's wound up tight, screaming out with pleasure and excitement and all the pent-up want from years and years of fantasies. Finally. God, finally, I feel the warm friction of skin to skin, the intimate slide, the knowledge that it's just us. And then...

"I'm gonna fill you up with it," I warn her, as much for my sake as for hers.

"Oh, god, Zion," groans Twyla. And hearing my name on her lips—talking about *this*, of all things— ratchets everything up even more, makes me plunge deeper, push harder, luxuriating in the naked, taboo thrill of being bare inside her. "Do it, fill me up."

"Got to unload soon, baby. Can't take much more of this. Not like this." Not with you.

I could never have done this with another person,

never found someone I trusted the way I trust her. This woman, smart and real and honest to a fault, has torn me open and ripped through her own quiet composure to give me this...this...this...dream.

Breath shaking, I pull back and look down at where my cock disappears inside her, then slowly pull out, letting the light catch her wetness on my skin.

"Goddamn it." I push her bent leg higher, open her up so I can see and feel everything. So I'll never forget this. Never lose the feeling of wonder. How has she done this? Torn me open, given me my own soft insides in a way no one else ever has? It's kindness and torture, wrapped up in one. The way she's complex and real, strong and giving. The way when she takes on a role, she lights everything up—not with a bright, glaring spotlight, but with the kind of warm glow that lasts for eons. Forever.

Her nails dig into my back and I welcome the pain, I need it. It centers me. Keeps me here, instead of flying up and out of my body, because the way we are together sends me way up there, above it all.

"Fuck. I can't just...I gotta see, baby." Quickly, I shift and settle back onto my ass, cross-legged. I pull her up to sitting and help her drape her legs over my thighs.

"This isn't—"

"Give me your weight. Come on. I can take it."

Looking uncertain, she wraps her legs around me and, before she can worry for another second, I grab my dick and sink back inside with a moan.

"This is good," I gasp, grabbing her ass, tight.

Her head falls back, her hair cascading behind her. It's beautiful, *she's* beautiful, but I want her eyes on me. I need to watch her when I unload deep inside.

"Look at me." I punctuate the order with a quick slap to her ass.

"Can't," she hisses.

I bend, nuzzle a breast and then bite, feeling wild and ravenous and out of control.

See? taunts a voice inside me. *Knew this would happen.*

"Zion, I'm close."

I snap back into my body, straight into the pleasure and the feel of her bucking and moaning on top of me, her thighs thick and solid on my lap, her dancing tits begging for another bite.

I bend and sink my teeth in, fight the pull of her cunt. Another bite, she clenches tight. I grasp her hair, pull her head up to make her look at me—see me, dammit—and when she does—

"Let me suck you."

What? She scrambles back and I blink at the way she bends, her ass in the air, and pulls my cock into her mouth, licking and sucking in the kind of shared frenzy I've never experienced before.

Another lick, a deep suck, and...

"I'm gonna come. Stop it."

"Come," she begs. "I want it."

Those words go straight to my balls, drawing them high and tight and ready to explode.

"Where," I choke out, wrapping my hand in her hair

again as if I'm controlling a single damn thing happening here right now.

She looks up, wide-eyed, her face a bright, hot red.

"In me. On me. Everywhere. I want it everywhere."

"Fuck. It's coming." I drag my cock from her hand and shove her back as the first jet of come splashes out. It hits her tit, drips off. I release the next spurt and, frantic, I fall on top of her and manage to line my dick up with her hole just as the next rush comes, surges up, up, up, and...

"Filling you up," I choke out. "Breeding you."

Her moans turn to gasps as she comes all over my cock and the feeling is is is...

Putting a hand on her soft belly, I give her more just inside, pump the next jet deeper, my balls caught between us as they empty every last drop I've got.

"*Zion.*" My name's a chant, a hiss, sacred and profane.

I go still. Pull out, barely, stare hard at the white spunk on the crown of my still-stiff, still-pulsing prick, and slide it back inside her. Easily.

Another long slide out, another deep pump inside my wife's hot, wet, welcoming pussy.

"God, Zion."

I lift my head and shake it, work hard to focus on her face. How long have I been sprawled on top of her like this, boneless and heavy?

"Shit. Shit, are you okay?" I start to move away, but she holds on.

"Yes. I'm great."

My cock, though only half-hard now, is still inside her. "I should—"

"Don't." Her hold gets tighter. "Stay."

Not wanting to suffocate her, I roll to the side.

A little at a time, I let myself feel things. The sweat cooling between our tightly-pressed bodies, the slow rise and fall of her chest against my ribs, the smell of sex, without latex, our scents mingling in a way they haven't before.

My cock, which definitely likes the smells and the feel and the weight of her, starts to raise its head again. Who knew how simple things could be when you don't have to pull out, drag a condom down, tie it off, and throw it in the trash. When a quick tightening of the glutes is all it takes to get started again, when the woman beside you lifts a warm thigh over your waist and shimmies closer and now you're having sex in a bed, face to face, sharing breath and sounds, seeing feelings so obvious in her eyes there's no way to deny them.

And maybe some part of you doesn't want to deny them as you tighten your arms and your ass and sink into her welcoming heat, all slick from your first release—and hers—and wish you had the guts to dip down and take her lips in a kiss.

But you can't.

I can't.

Because fucking's one thing. Kissing is a whole other level.

25

Twyla

I've never had so much sex in one two-day period. It's intense and physical, and I'll probably feel it tomorrow, but right now, I'm in such a floaty, high, dream world that I don't care.

It's worth it. I know this, beyond a doubt. I think it as he slowly, slowly presses into me and comes a second time, then shifts back, his gaze skimming over my body with admiration and maybe something else. Maybe something deeper. Something meaningful. He squeezes his hand between our bodies, gets his thumb right up against my clit and rubs quick circles until I climax again. And so does he.

He doesn't pull out. I don't ask him to. I don't want him to. I want to keep him inside me—his cock, his semen. These feelings, too. The fresh, raw power of them.

This is real, they're saying. This is real.

He twists and turns off the lamp behind him, plunging us into near darkness. I don't say a word. He doesn't either. I get it. All this emotion's left me open and unguarded. Real. Me. I'm afraid of what I'll say if I speak right now.

Before settling back, he pulls out from me, his spend drips down between my legs.

"I should use the restroom," I whisper, hating to break our shell, but knowing what'll happen if I don't.

He switches the light back on and points at a wooden door halfway up the opposite wall.

For the first time, I look at the place. It's small. A one-room cabin, made for sleeping more than anything else. Like a hotel room.

Except it's his. More truly Zion's than the Georgetown rental or anything I've seen in a magazine spread or anyplace else.

It's dark wood, simple, and sparsely furnished. The furniture's big, solid, rough-hewn, high-quality. I'd bet everything in here's handmade. Hardwoods, raw fabrics, all massive, all straightforward stuff. Comfortable.

I slip into the restroom, turn the light on and look around, doing my best to avoid the big, wood-framed mirror above a dark granite counter and its deep, utilitarian sink.

Plush, blue towels hang on a bar, neatly-folded.

Unused. Everything here looks brand new. As if this place were a hotel, not a home.

I use the toilet and clean up and, finally, unavoidably, face myself in the big mirror, wincing at the makeup streaking my eyes, my cheeks. I've taken raccoon eyes to new heights.

I scrub it off as best I can. Okay, so I look like crap. But I was flogged tonight. And then, I made the unwisest decision of my life and allowed the man who's already torn everything apart, literally, into my body.

I meet my own eyes. Stare.

And smile.

What the hell, Hernandez? I mouth, still smiling.

And then, given that there's no denying the power of good sex, amazing sex, the best sex of my entire life, I stick out my tongue.

Back in the room, Zion's sitting up in bed. I hesitate, consider what all of this means and then, because I'm me and he's him and we're here, together, I take a running jump and flop right on top of him, giggling my ass off. This quickly turns to mutual tickling, rolling around, wrestling until I'm face down in the bed and he's over me and his erection's there, again, between my legs and, though I'm sore and feel more well-used than I've ever been in my life, I lift my ass and he slides in and we're fucking again.

Except it doesn't feel like fucking to me. It feels like more. I know this. I recognize it, admit it, take the knowledge and wrap it up tight, stow it somewhere deep inside me.

And I arch and strain, twist and moan, gasp and whimper until the difference between sex and love is as meaningless as the sounds we make. Just sounds. Just syllables, muttered loud, sung low. Do I love him? Yes. God, yes.

The thought curls me into myself. He follows, wraps around me, still deep inside, telling me I'm beautiful, taking his cock like this. I'm his now, with his come filling me up, his body and mine so fully intertwined there's no beginning or end, just a circle. Just connection.

I love you, I think, just aware enough to know how those words could backfire. I love you. I love you.

"You're mine," he mutters, pummeling my body with his for a dozen quick strokes, his arms going tight, then loose, like a boy worried he'll crush a baby bird in his hand. "Mine, mine, mine," and I believe it. I do. How could I not, when we're this close? This hot? This fierce and possessive.

But I feel it too, that ferocity. That desire not to just give, but to take. To share, to belong and to have. So, rather than lie here and let him use me, the way my libido demands, I twist and turn and work my way over him, above him, wrap his wrists in my hands, held high on the mangled pillows, and I get right into his face—so close we could kiss. We should. We *have* to. I don't, though. I'll respect his rules as long as he does—and echo his words.

"I'm yours?"

"Yes," he growls. "Now, get down here and—"

"Well, you're mine."

He stills.

"Mine," I whisper, right up beside his ear. "Mine," against his cheek. "Mine," close to his lips, but not on them. Not on them. Mine, with a twist of my hips that sends his eyes rolling back in his head. Mine, mine, mine.

It's a chant, a dance, a proclamation. A claiming. At least for me.

By the time the words fade into nonsensical sounds of lust and animal excitement, we're back to being just bodies. It's a shock to feel myself building again, reaching and reaching for the climax and then sliding right over it, keening as he pulls out to watch himself spill on my mound—using me, fetishizing me, which, god, is the horniest I've ever felt—before shoving that huge thing right back inside me, filling me, filling me up, giving me every little bit of himself. Every drop.

And then, then the man leaves my body, settles back on his knees, and pushes my legs apart. I look down to find him staring at my wide-open sex, intense and hungry and...proud, maybe?

"Fuck, baby, this is..." His gaze slides up to meet mine before going inexorably back to stare at where his come's dripping out of me. "This is so fucking beautiful." With a big finger, he nudges me. It takes me a second to realize he's slicking his finger through his semen and then pressing it back inside me and then, because that's not enough kink for one night, he bends low and licks it up.

"Zion, I don't—"

"No, no, you've got to let me. Please. Fuck, it's so good."

I release a shaky breath and examine my own feelings. Do I like this?

His tongue runs up between my labia, glances my clit, which makes me jolt and, when that happens, he reaches up and digs his fingers into my hip, holding me in place. He's ravenous, I can tell. The sounds, the way he's eating at me, consuming me, like a starved man. Like a man who's always wanted this and never had it.

The tiniest shred of doubt ekes its way through my brain right at this very moment. I know he desires me. It's clear. The way I know he didn't want to or he was afraid to or, maybe Max was right and he thought this wouldn't be my thing. I know he wants. That's not it.

So, what is it? Part of me worries at that little shard, while the rest of me moans through Zion's wild ministrations. Why does this feel good and bad? Bad like it'll end? Bad like I'm something he'll want and cherish, but never love. Not to keep?

His tongue spears me and the questions fritter up and fly away, leaving my brain this empty shell of a thing that once worked, but is now capable of the barest bodily functions.

A low groan tears itself from my lungs when he grabs my thighs and pushes them up and open and licks my ass like a man who hasn't been fucking for hours and hours.

And keeps on fucking me, using me, giving me every bit of himself until I fall asleep, still clasping his body in mine, which is what I want. It's enough.

It will be. It has to be.

Zion

The floodgates have opened. I knew they would. I knew I'd be like this.

A beast. A brute. A brainless monster who wants one thing and one thing only—her. I feel dangerous, on edge. Exhausted, but unable to let go and sleep, because what if...

Fuck. I loosen my hold on her waist, though I can't force myself to let go entirely, and breathe. The air smells like her, us, and I never want to leave.

What if this is it? What if one night's all she'll give me?

The thought makes me tighten my hold and pull her sleeping body in closer.

She hums and half-giggles, sounding cute and sweet and dead tired.

I need to control myself. I will. I just... I lean in and nuzzle her cheek, hover above her mouth...and pull back.

The fuck is wrong with you, boy?

My father's words. Clear as a bell. Like yesterday.

The fuck is wrong? Nothing. Absolutely nothing.

And that scares the shit out of me.

"Zion?" she whispers. Is she awake or just mumbling in her sleep?

"Yeah?"

"Remember the first time we met?"

I pause, thinking hard. Not that I don't remember. "I do."

"You said...you were glad to *finally* meet me. Remember that? Before the red carpet boob fiasco and the..." She waves a hand in the dark, apparently not willing to use the word kiss. "What did that mean?"

For a handful of seconds, I'm trapped. Admitting truths to others isn't easy when you can barely own up to them yourself. "Saw you on screen first. On my phone, actually."

"Really?" She sounds stunned.

I remember it like yesterday. She was filtered, separated from me by time and space and actual distance. I couldn't look away. Not for a breath, not a single goddamn heartbeat. Then, like now, she was mesmerizing.

What if?

What if the woman from that screen test were mine? Not just sex. And not just a fake marriage, set up for fake reasons, so I could... Fuck, I don't know. I don't know what I was doing. But now, I want it for real. The life we made people think we had.

"Your *Angels* audition. Remember that?"

"Of course. It was a big deal for me. You saw that?"

Her reading for the part of a young, Mexican-American mother who'd lost her child was gut-wrenching. Soul-destroying. She was beautiful, yeah, but that wasn't what did it for me, ultimately. It was her self-containment. The other actresses poured everything out into the world, but Twyla kept it balled up, tight, not letting it out, like if a drop of emotion escaped, she'd lose the last of her sanity.

"I was hypnotized," I admit, the words gruff and too honest.

Exactly how I felt in the hangar, with her gaze holding mine hostage, pure defiance making her features hard and hot, on edge, a volcano about to blow. Dangerous as hell and beyond compelling. And that wasn't for a casting call. It was for me.

Even here, in the dark, without eye contact, half asleep, I feel the pull of her. I'm enthralled.

"You were so fucking good. So *real*."

"I was acting."

"Didn't look like it. Or feel like it."

"Thanks." She sniffs. "You're not so shabby yourself." I hear the smile in her voice.

"Ach, I'm not in your league."

"Shut up." She shuffles back enough to smack my shoulder, tired and playful.

"Seriously. I'm decent. I just don't have that deep thing. I'm a shallow actor. All surface."

It's not until she opens her mouth that I realize she's truly pissed. "Bullshit. You're as good as anyone. Jonny Devine was... Oh, I *loved* that character."

"It was good writing," I concede. "The source material's—"

"Oh my god, you're kidding me, Zion."

"What?"

"You think you've gotten where you are because of strong scripts and luck?"

"Partly. Mostly. Yeah."

Her laugh's low and scratchy, her voice well-used. "No. No, that's your trick. That's how you fool them all."

"What?"

"You seem so simple."

"Wow, thanks."

"That's not what I mean." She pokes me and I trap her hand against my shoulder and keep it there, caressing her palm with my thumb. "I mean you've got that easy, slow, southern thing. Like, I don't know, Matthew McConaughey or something." I go still, outwardly calm, while something simmers beneath the surface. I feel an edge approaching. A sharp cliff. "I've seen you arrive on set, all lazy, like 'Hey! How's it hangin'?' Looking like you never have to try all that hard." Something's dawning as she leans in close, her breath heating my face, her focus intense, like she's searching for something and got it just on the tip of her tongue. I can't tell if it's relief that I'm feeling or something entirely different. "You pretend you don't, but I've seen you work your ass off for every role. I've seen it."

"I have to work hard. I'm dyslexic."

"Oh." She pauses. "I didn't know that."

"A few people know, but I don't really advertise it."

"Last minute script changes must be a nightmare."

She's right. I dread it when a scriptwriter's right there reworking lines 'til the last second. "My memory's good, thank god. And I've got tricks." I flick her a quick look. "I'll ask the director for a line reading and go with that."

"You must hate it."

I shrug.

She moves in and hugs me, her head rubbing as she nods against my chest. "I think you're amazing." Another tight hug. "I could help you. Only if you want." The proposal's careful, her voice light.

So light, I could pretend it's not a big deal what she's asking. But the subtext is there, loud and clear.

Will you let me in? it asks. *Will you let me see your weaknesses? The real you?*

And that's just the thing, isn't it? After all the time I've spent doing this balancing act between one existence and the other—the entirety of my adult life—I can't honestly say I know who the real me is. My life's like those people who've suffered an accident that severs the two sides of their brain. Connections lost. Or maybe they were never there. I'm one thing here, another thing entirely out there in the world. What if I'm neither? Not worth getting to know at all?

I could tell her how it feels to live in a world where my compartments are made of stone or steel or something more solid than that. All it would take is opening my mouth and letting the words out.

It would be such a goddamn relief. To share the truth, to open up and be...what? Who? I'm good with easy-going Zion and filthy, hard-edged Zed. But that third person? The one I've stifled all these years? I can't let him out of his box. He was raised by wolves. Or might as well have been. A feral child whose only experience with love died with his mama when he was five.

I picture Twyla's reaction to that kid: incomprehension, shock, pity? I can't do it. I'm a coward, I guess, because all I say is "Sure, I'd like that," not once looking her way.

She makes a happy sleep noise and I let out a breath I've been holding and close my eyes, though I didn't realize they were that wide open.

I think of this marriage and feel guilt and shame and the sense that I'm lying by omission. But there's not a chance in hell she'll want anything to do with whoever poor little Zion Mason grew up to be.

Twyla snuggles close, our bodies probably too hot to stay like this 'til morning, but I don't care. I want this. Her. Whatever I can get, for however long I can keep myself secret. Though my brain's telling me otherwise, my body craves the closeness and, in this moment, it feels so right, I let it go.

She shifts and gasps. "Crap."

"What. What is it? Are you okay? Did I hurt you? Dammit, I knew I was going overboard. I knew I shouldn't—"

Her hand lands on my mouth. "Stop that, Zion." I hear the friction of her hair against the pillow. "I need to get something straight, okay?"

I nod.

"I'm just as..." She goes quiet for a moment. "As, I don't know, dirty or kinky or perverted as you are, okay? I am. I just haven't had the opportunity to practice what I've fantasized for most of my life."

My pulse quickens. I breathe through it.

"I like the...the come thing. A lot. Okay? I like feeling used. Taken. Forced. I like a little pain, although it didn't feel nearly as good before you were there." She snorts. "I'll admit that was you, okay? And me. And this chemistry we've got. I mean, I didn't hate the flogging before you came around, but the second I saw you, it went from kind of pleasant to holy shit, I'm burning up. So, it's you and it's the attention you gave and your... your...your..."

"Jealous glare?"

"Possessiveness."

I stay silent.

"The possessiveness is very appealing. And the kidnapping thing, well, I like the idea."

My body clenches up and, at her next words, loosens again.

"Will you do the kidnapping?"

"Guess you'll just have to see," I say, working hard to keep the happiness from my voice. The possessiveness that seemed messed up and wrong a second ago settles in a new way that feels right.

"Okay." She sounds happy and I feel...fuck, I feel amazing. "And you?"

"I what?"

"You'd be okay with, you know, what I asked for? A second person?" She swallows audibly. "I mean, I made a big stink about the...video. Seems a little hypocritical for me to fantasize another person in a scene."

"Not the same thing at all," I say, my gut churning with the mix of excitement and jealousy her words stir up. "I...I shouldn't have done that. It was cheating. This is a scene. It's consensual, planned out. Agreed to by all parties. The other guy and I will have limits, too, you know? We can safe word."

She seems to consider. "Okay. But you're truly okay with it?"

"It's complicated, okay? The way I feel about you is..." I blow out a long breath, my feelings all over the place. "As long as I'm in charge and it's clear that you're mine and... I get off on it, too, you know? Like the jealousy thing, the fact that they can touch you, if I let them, but you're mine."

"Yeah," she whispers, sounding almost amazed. "Yours."

"The brat thing, too. It feels right with you, you know? Just pushes it up a notch. Makes it more dangerous. Makes you and me and our scenes feel edgier," I say. "Where'd that come from? You born a brat?"

I hear the smile in her voice. "I don't know. It's just... the way I am." A pause. "With you."

With you. Her words run through me like alcohol. Oxygen. "I like it."

"Yeah?"

"I mean," I huff out a laugh. "It drives me wild. Makes me want to break shit. But also." My hips press forward, showing her how hard I've gotten, just thinking about her natural kinkiness and brattiness. "Also, I've never been hotter. And I've played with a lot of brats. Usually, they just annoy me."

"Okay."

"You're right, though. About the chemistry. We've got that."

"We do."

I blow out a breath. "I'll admit that it, um, freaks me out a little."

"And yet you married me."

"Yeah. That was…"

She waits. I consider, then finally shrug as I let the truth out. "I wanted you to be mine. Even if it wasn't real."

Her body stiffens. "Wow." After a second, she inhales and goes on. "Why? I still don't get it."

Oh, here it is. The precipice. The danger zone. Alarm bells and flashing red lights and the calm, radio voice countdown, such a contrast to the alien invasion or approaching bomb or whatever's about to wreak its destruction in this scene.

What's worse? If I tell her the truth or brush her off?

The way I feel right now, open and raw and pared down to something more basic than I've been in decades, there is no choice.

"What you said about my acting, that I'm all surface?"

"I didn't say that."

"Easy. Or lazy or—"

She stiffens. "That's not what I mean. You work hard and you're talented and—"

I'm so full of gratitude for this woman who's literally defending me from myself that I tighten my hold and close my eyes and smile against her skin and try again. "What I mean is, say I'm one thing, like warm sunshine and quick smiles. Well, you're the opposite. You're those still waters that run deep."

"Okay." She sounds skeptical. "Go on."

"I wanted that. The depth. The stillness. Even if it was only for...pretend."

"Fine, but couldn't you have, I don't know, asked me out on an actual date instead of setting up a PR stunt through your manager?"

"That whole life's a PR stunt, Twyla. That version of me. It's not real. It's a role."

Through the next few seconds of silence, I've got no idea what she's thinking and then she says, "So, we started playing house and then..." She sucks in a deep breath, like she's getting ready to do something hard. "What you said? Outside the hangar? About our not-quite-make out session?"

"Yeah?"

"So, you like me."

The snuffling sound that escapes me is not a laugh or a groan, but a weird combination of the two. "God, baby, I like you. So much. And I hate what I did to you. If I could—"

"I know."

"I'd tear a limb off."

"Please don't." After a second. "You called her a painkiller. That's kind of awful."

"I know. I'm sorry for her, too. I regret every second of it."

"You hurt me, Zion."

"I'd rather die than do it again, Twyla. I don't know how to show you that."

"I don't...I don't know either."

It hurts that she says this, and I let it.

I shut my eyes and tighten my arms, understanding for the first time what a precious thing it is to hold another person like this. "My therapist calls it compartmentalizing. The way I live my life. She says it's a response to childhood trauma. She calls them my walls. Says I should take them down." I smile. "Like Berlin." I chuckle low and push straight on, needing to scrub myself clean, to start over, to give her this new, half-born version of me, no matter how stunted it is. "My mom died when I was five and... *Fuck*, the kissing thing is linked to that. I get that now. Edna—my therapist—told me it's obvious, but... Mama was...I don't remember much, but she was so warm and affectionate, and she loved me *so much*." The last two words come out high and tight and weird, all balled up with the pain of telling it. I forge on or it'll never come out. "When she was gone, my dad became a ghost and I turned...*hard*."

Her tragic little *Zion*, floats into the air above us.

"It's okay. I'm okay." I force myself to go on. "You're the first person who's ever crossed those walls, I guess, and... Shit, this is hard to say."

She sniffs. "You don't have to."

"No, I... You've broken through. Maybe even before, I think? Over the last few weeks, you didn't bust through them, you sort of nudged the bricks aside and made a little hole or something." Shit, don't let me cry. I don't want to, but the prickle's turning to a burn in my sinuses. "I thought it would hurt if the walls came down, but it doesn't? It's like..." A tear escapes and I drop my head and press my mouth to her hair and just breathe her in. "Scary as shit, but also freeing."

She nods and tries to move, but I hold her still, keeping her close so I don't have to see her face and acknowledge what a clusterfuck my life's been. I don't want to see tragedy there. Or pity or any of it. "I was wrong to pretend we didn't have something. I was wrong to betray you. I'll never do it again, Twyla. I promise. On my life." And then, because I'm being this honest, I might as well go for the gold, I tell her, "I just didn't think you'd want this version of me."

"And now?" Is that hope in her voice? "What do you think?"

The silence is suddenly so thick around us, it's like a third presence in the room. Solid, waiting.

"You're mine," I grate out, though it goes against every self-protective instinct I've got. It's a leap and it's scary as hell, but I'll take it. For Twyla, I'll be this naked, skinless, and flayed wide-open. "I want this. I want you. I want what we're doing to be real."

"I want that, too, Zion. I want that, too."

I suck in a breath like it's my first and feel something that might very well be joy. I don't know. It's light and bright and more hopeful than anything I've ever known.

I nod, wondering if she's waiting for me to kiss her. Wishing I knew how. But all my kisses are caught up in a net of memories so dark and confused and full of pain that it's as opaque as trying to look into a nightmare. My mom probably kissed me when I was a kid, though I don't remember it too well. I remember the feeling of being taken care of, being loved. I had five years of it before colon cancer took her away and left me with an angry, apathetic shell of a father.

That's how it was when she died, just there one day and gone the next. Before and after. Love and...nothing. Or, no, other things. With dad, there was anger, pain, guilt, and eventually, with other people, I felt lust. A shit ton of lust.

"Goodnight, Zion." Twyla twists into a new position, apparently as happy to ignore the hard cock pressed against her side as I am. Taking my insistent desire in stride. "I..." She sniffs. "Thank you. For telling me. For sharing and opening up. For everything."

I wrap around her, feeling lighter and heavier all at once. "Goodnight, Twyla. Thank you for being you."

Her sigh feels like pure light. "Sweet dreams."

"Okay," I say, sounding like a total fool. I want to kiss her, to lean in and show her my feelings with that one little move.

It's just skin to skin, right? Just friction, nothing more. Not the moment Mama died and left me alone in this world. A stubborn little five-year-old boy living in a shack with nothing left but the responsibility to keep his dad alive. I think of the time when, as a teen—filthy and feral and mean as a snake—I somehow convinced twenty-two-year-old Donnie Rae Minton, who must have been hella hard up while her husband was locked up for armed robbery, to get frisky on her unmade bed in her trashy doublewide. I know now that it was statutory rape and should never have happened, but at the time, it was the most exciting thing in the world.

She let me squeeze her tits and touch her every which way, but when she leaned in and put her tongue in my mouth, I froze up.

It felt all wrong. Too close and intimate and not at all what I wanted.

I shoved her off me, told her to stay the hell away from my mouth.

It was a sign of Donnie Rae's low self-esteem—or just the luck she'd had in life, I guess—that she didn't blink before telling me to chill the hell out and fuck her.

I spanked her that first time. And every time after. We didn't have a safe word or anything of the sort, but Donnie liked it rough and I liked it rougher. Right from the beginning, I needed the edgy stuff. I was hardwired that way from the start.

By the time her husband got out, I'd learned pretty much everything there was to know about sex and pain and pleasure. Today, I get that it should never have happened. That I was too young and unable to consent to any of it.

But it was defining, I guess.

From that moment on, there's always been a clear divide between sex and love in my life. Love is about friendship and support. About being there for those who matter. Love was Liev taking me under his wing when I first showed up on the kink scene and Lamé seeing through my bullshit and accepting me the way I was. Love was the bottom falling out of my life when I thought we'd lost Liev after his wife died. Love was holding him in my arms while he shook through night after night after night.

I learned to disassociate when I kiss on screen. It's easy to feel nothing when I'm playing a character.

But Twyla, well, she was a spoke in my wheel from the start. Just looking at her feels intimate. The way she looks back, her eyes burning straight through, seeing a whole lot more than I've ever wanted to share.

Until now.

I ease slightly away from her and listen as she passes out fast, her breathing deep and slow and, though I should get some sleep, I take the time to enjoy every second of this.

So many firsts for me tonight. My first time being told to have sweet dreams—that I can remember, at least. My first time sleeping with another person. My first time agreeing to a relationship.

My first time wanting romance or intimacy or maybe love with a partner.

"I'd like to kiss you, sometime," I whisper, half-hoping she's not awake to hear it.

With a tired hum, she says, "I'd like that." And then, "Whenever you're ready."

"That's... Yeah. When I'm ready."

I think back on the time I kissed Twyla to help her out on the red carpet, the way I justified it to myself by saying it was for her benefit and it wasn't real anyway.

Red carpets are basically improv performances, complete with cameras and costumes.

Those were lies, I realize now. Just bullshit I told myself when my brain was too shocked for honesty.

I need to tell her all this. And I will. I want her to understand why I'm like this, even if I don't always get it myself.

She's definitely under when I scrape up the nerve to lean in and press my mouth to hers—just to see. Just to know how broken I really am.

But maybe she knows or feels it in her sleep or dreams it or something, because though it barely lasts a second, I swear her lips turn up into a smile.

It's a little gift, just for me. And I'll never, ever forget it.

26

Twyla

The first thing I notice when I wake up is how much my body hurts. A good pain. A stretch out the kinks (ha!) and take a long hot shower and maybe do the whole thing all over again pain. Between my legs, on my ass, in my calves, which I really don't understand.

The second thing I notice is that I'm alone.

All of my happy, stretchy, enjoying the ache energy disappears and I'm up, untangling myself from the top sheet, and out of bed in five seconds flat.

Wrapping the sheet around me, I race to the bathroom, this time managing to ignore my reflection entirely, clean up as best I can, and then return to the main room and hesitate.

Is Zion outside, through those French doors, maybe?

It's late. I can tell from the bright, hot sun slanting through the window. Outside, someone shouts a heads-up, people squeal as I'm guessing a ball lands in their vicinity. It sounds like a full-fledged company picnic happening outside and, though I know I won't be judged, I can't stand the idea of leaving in last night's clothes, which are currently balled up by my feet.

I need something to put on.

I spin, eye the bed again and realize that the top sheet I'm wearing—the sheet Zion spread over me while I slept—is my only choice. A toga it is. Once I'm draped to my satisfaction, I peek out the French doors at a tree-shaded porch, overlooking nothing but forest. It's beautiful, I recognize, though the fact that Zion's not out there waiting for me has something balling up in the pit of my stomach.

It was too much last night. Too soon.

Or maybe not soon. Maybe just not meant to be more. That's what he's telling me, right? By leaving? An easy goodbye. He's changed his mind after our conversation.

And it was heavy. Everything we shared was pretty major.

I need to get out of here, get back to Lamé's and regroup. Maybe I'll...I don't know. Leave? I mean, I love camp and I love Zion and I...

Shit. No. No, I can't do that right now. Not when I'm feeling sore and weak and somehow almost hungover from everything we did and said to each other.

Running from something now, I yank open the front door and rush out into the unbearably hot, bright day.

Immediately, I get smiles, of the knowing, commiserating kind. I get a few thumbs up, too. Some surprised looks, which, coming from the man wearing a literal cage over his testicles, is almost odd. Whatever. Holding my head up, I march on.

The smell of chlorine hits me and, right behind it, the sweet pull of fresh coffee and, rather than race back to Lamé's cottage and hide, the way I'd planned, I think maybe that's the key to everything. Caffeine will make it better. I let the scent draw me to the coffee shop, where I pull open the door, and slam right into a big, hot body.

"Whoa, whoa, there baby. Hold on, sweetheart." It's Zion. Of course it is. He shuffles whatever's filling his arms to one side and puts his other hand on my waist. "Twyla, baby." He leans in and puts his nose to the crook of my neck and, I'm pretty sure, smells me, before placing a gentle kiss right there.

When he pulls back, I'm stunned speechless. "Um..." I squint up into his face and let myself look at all that glorious, golden skin before tearing my gaze away. It's not easy. He's in nothing but those board shorts and flipflops and, despite having been up against it all just last night—who am I kidding? This morning— his chest looks somehow better, wider, with that perfect, shimmering sprinkle of hair over muscle-packed skin. His thighs scissor with impatience—my god, were they always this thick or did he put on mass for that upcoming movie he's supposed to start on in September? I swallow and force my eyes shut. "I'm sorry."

"What?"

"I probably stayed in your cabin too long and you needed space and I was there and you—"

"Got us coffee. Breakfast." He holds out a greasy, brown paper bag and whatever's inside smells so heavenly, my stomach growls, which puts a lopsided grin on Zion's face, bringing out those deadly dimples and... Where was I going again? Where am I? What's my name?

This big, sweet, beautiful man was getting me breakfast?

Affection and, yes, love, god, love, I can admit it, rushes me so hard and fast that it's like a pain and a weight lifted and, despite the stuff in his hands, I wrap my arms around him in the biggest, most heartfelt hug I've ever given.

"Oh, hey. Hey, baby. What's this for?"

I step back, shoving all this excessive emotion as far aside as I can, because this is a man who doesn't kiss, for god's sake, how will he react to getting attack-hugged at whatever time it is in the morning.

"You good?" He watches me closely, his eyes warm and sweet.

I nod just as behind me, the door opens. He glances up then looks back to me.

"Come on. You want to go or stay here? You look hungry."

I do? Wow. I am, actually. Starving. "You're right."

"Let's sit down and get this in you now, then." He scoops that same arm around me and drags me to an empty table against the back wall of the coffee shop, which is bustling with mid-morning business, Lamé at the helm. They steam milk and brew espresso and sling muffins onto plates and the scents make my mouth water so hard I could drool. Bill Withers oozes from hidden speakers, telling us he wants to be used up and, for the first time in my life, I completely understand the senti-ment. Hell, I *am* the sentiment.

"Oooooooooh, now would you look at what the lion dragged in?" Lamé stops mid-steam, skates to the end of the bar, and breaks into a teary slow clap. "You two look like you've been up to...things. Did you consummate your marriage? In the old-fashioned sense, I mean? Can I get out the word and put everyone out of their misery? There's a lot of money riding on the when and how, so I need details and—"

Setting his cups and bag on a table, Zion casts a quick look around before focusing in on Lamé. "Would you quit it? Please?"

"Oh. Oh, sorry." Lamé meets his gaze, their eyes wide, their expression theatrically innocent. People are milling around, over-stirring their coffees, and pretending not to hear, while almost literally bending their ears to listen. "It's just that between *your* obvious coffee order and your wife wearing a sheet I know is from a bed you've never shared with another person, and the fact that you're both usually incognito, but today you're just out here, faces naked, owning your IRL selves, I figured—"

"Oh, shit."

Like two marionettes controlled by the same puppet

master—aka Lamé—our hands fly to our faces as one, confirming that we both did, indeed, forget to put on masks when we left the cabin this morning. Zion for whatever reason and I because I was absolutely flipping out about everything that happened—and my perceived desertion by Zion.

Nervous, I glance up at him, meet his stare, which is steady, and then watch him look at the people standing around, barely hiding their smiles. "Y'all knew already, didn't ya?"

For a second or two, nobody answers, then, as one, the kinksters burst out with *Yeahs* and *Obviously, mans* and outright laughter. The ambiance goes from a low simmer to a happy boil, and something bursts in my chest as I watch Zion take in the obvious affection with which his crew acknowledges him.

Has he always felt apart from this, then? Or at least since he hit some level of stardom? Or was it earlier? Before he got famous? Has fame been an excuse to deepen the division?

And why the hell does this idea break my heart?

I sink into a seat and open the bag Zion's left on the table, grab the coffee I'm assuming is mine, and watch him adjust to the idea that literally everyone here knows exactly who he is and that, beyond that, they've kept his secret for years. It's a testament to their affection for him, I think. Or maybe it's just a sign of how very private these people are about their lives. There's a definite here and out there mentality. There's Camp and there's Real Life and, while people will share details if they wish, nobody asks. It's a rule that is deeply respected. Photos are only put on the site of people who've agreed to it. Others, like me and Zion and probably half the people here wearing bright yellow bands, have something to lose if the outside world finds out about us.

Us. Not them. Am I part of this now?

Yeah. Yeah, I guess I am.

When Zion finally sits in the seat beside me, he's half smiling, a little flushed.

"You okay?"

"Guess so." He shrugs, the movement of skin over thick muscle and bone attracts my gaze, and I'm brought right back to that first moment he laid atop me last night. The moment he penetrated me, skin to skin. The pure intensity in his gaze, his frown, even his body, so tight and ready for anything. I want more of that. "Got plans for today?"

I blink. "Sorry?"

He grins, his mouth curving up slow and lazy and totally confident of his sexiness.

"Stop that." My skin flushes under his stare.

"Stop what?" He's close, his voice quiet, intimate. My gaze hops from his eyes to his mouth, then skims over his beard-dusted chin, his Adam's apple, that dip at the base of his neck, which I can't remember tasting last night and, dammit, I want to taste it now. I want to sniff it, feel it with my cheek, my fingers.

"Baby." I look up to find him biting that plump bottom lip, his focus as acute as last night. "Don't make me bend you over this table right here and fuck you in front of everyone here, baby." He leans in. "Show them exactly who you belong to."

I swallow.

"Come so hard and deep inside you, you'll feel it drippin' out all day." He grins full out. "Lamé won't like that. Some health and safety bullshit."

I'm breathing hard and fast and, while I hear his words telling me it's not the best idea, my body's perfectly on board with that public over-the-table bending thing. Like, big time. Like now.

"Do it," I say, half out of my chair, when, out of the blue, a tall, gold-clad figure whooshes between us.

"Absolutely not." Lamé slams both hands on the table, jolting us out of what was surely the most frantic sexual desire I've ever had. I can't speak for Zion, obviously, but a glance at his crotch says he'd have had no problem following through on his threat. "No sex in the café." They point up at a big yellow sign, with blue lettering, hung askew right over the exit. "Even if I know people would vastly enjoy watching you."

Okay, now I'm probably glowing red. No doubt about it. My face is a furnace.

Zion leans back in his chair and stares at me. I bury my head in my coffee—which is absolutely delicious, by the way. Vanilla syrup and whole milk and foam and... ugh, why is everything so perfect right now?

"Oh no. The famous Zion Mason glare." Lamé's eyes go wide and faux frightened. "I've seen all the movies, honey. You don't scare me."

He snorts. I bleat out a surprised sound when Zion's

warm foot overlaps mine. "Guess we'll have to resort to playing footsie under the table."

"There you go. Least he's a quick learner." Lamé looks at me. "You both are. Anyway. The cottage is open." They start to skate to where the line at the bar's now ten deep, and swing back, pointing a long-nailed finger at us. "No sex there either."

"Got it," I reply.

"My wife's moving into my cabin," Zion says with a certainty that raises my hackles, even while the meaning sends a thrill through me.

"Excuse me?"

"You belong in my bed, Twyla."

"I belong where I want, *Zion.*"

"We settled this last night," he says, voice resonating deep and final. "You're mine."

Every muscle in my body tightens up, ready for a fight.

"Oooooooh, she has *released the Kraken!*" Lamé announces melodramatically, skating a gleeful circle out and back to our table. "We need thoughts and prayers, everybody. 'Cause hell hath no fury like a possessive Dom." They skate off again, yelling to the room at large, "And this Dom's finally met his match."

I stand up to go, turn back for my coffee, and stop when he rises, his body towering over me. "I need sleep, Zion. This has been..." I look up at him, breathe deep, and will myself down from the unbelievable high of every interaction we have: angry or affectionate, loud or quiet, soft, painful, emotional. "A lot. Okay? In a short time."

After a few long moments, he sniffs, nods, backs up a half step. "Good idea. You need rest."

"Don't you?"

"Nah." His smile's way too slow to be trusted. "I've got work to do."

27

Twyla

I wake up after hours spent sleeping at Lamé's, feeling pasty-mouthed, but otherwise well-rested. Beside the bed, my phone vibrates. I pick it up, see the number of notifications, and set it down again. No. No, I'm definitely not ready to face the outside world.

Like a ton of bricks, the past couple of days come back to me. For the first time since I got here, I take a minute and let it soak in. Reality, as I knew it, has changed.

Am I okay?

I think of the many faces of Zion, his possessiveness, his demands. My body squirms, stretches, my thighs tighten. Okay. Okay, yeah. I like that side of him. A lot.

Really, though? Do I really want that? A man who's perfectly happy to make demands of me, but unwilling to even give me a kiss.

One after another, memories fly through my brain—

Zion kissing my shoulder, my neck, my pussy. My forehead, my cheek.

My lips, on the red carpet.

But that wasn't real. This is.

Is it, though? Will we be together when camp's over? Will this last?

I want it to, I admit, with an almost embarrassing rush of emotion. Right behind it is the certainty that this will go nowhere. It can't.

How, for example, will we ever get over the video, in the public eye, at least? I mean, I'm over it, mostly. Or I'm pretending it didn't happen, I guess.

I don't know. I don't want to think about it.

Except I do. I think about him and that woman in that hotel room. I think about her tied up on the bed, her arms and legs stretched out like mine were on the flogger last night, and I imagine him doing the things to her that I want him to do to me. Under the sheet, my hand slides down my body, dips between my legs. I'm wet. Of course. When have I not been since he came into my life?

Wait, really? No. No, that's not true. Just at camp.

Except there's the time on the sofa, back in our rental. And the night before. And when we worked on the film together and I caught him watching me. Crap, I fantasized about him even back then, didn't I? But I figured everyone did it. I figured...

I'm rubbing my clit now, fast and hard, thinking about how it felt when he picked me up last night and took me back to his place. The caveman thing really does it for me.

The breeding thing. The come. That's something I've thought about before, too. It's bringing the orgasm closer very, very fast now. My clit's so swollen and sensitive, I back off, thinking about the way he stared down there, with his come dripping out. And his words.

Goddamn it. Got to unload soon, baby. Can't take much more of this. Not like this.

I groan. I mean, what the hell is wrong with me that his crass language turns me into a writhing mass of nerve endings, when the sweetest, poetic words from past boyfriends left me totally cold?

I rub harder, faster, fuck myself with my left hand, imagine it's him, fucking me, taking me, making me, which... oh, god, why do I want that? Why?

A few more strokes and I'm coming, hard, high, my pussy contracting around my fingers, my mind swirling in the morass of all the stuff we've done. The good, the bad, the absolutely filthy.

It takes a minute to come down. I concentrate on the feel of my pulse in my clit and stretch out, languid, hot, light...happy.

Happy.

And, when I dig deeper, I understand that I am truly happy for the first time in forever. Here, amongst the Owners and Pets and Bigs and Littles and Doms and subs and Sadists and Masochists. I mean, gosh, aren't they all *happy*? Isn't that what this is about? Being true to your beautiful, messed-up inner self, no matter how flawed it is?

When I think back to the night I got here... What was

that, five days ago? Four? I thought I knew about kink, but I had no freaking idea.

I didn't know, for example, what sounding was, or blood play or wax play. I had no idea that kink and sex didn't always go hand in hand. I'd never accidentally walked in on an orgy or watched someone get their testicles abused or suffer through a chastity belt or a penis cage. They want it. All of it. The pain, the humiliation, the blood, sweat, piss, tears. They want the make-believe and the real. I want it, too, and it's...beautiful.

Someone knocks on the bedroom door and I pull my arms under the blanket, embarrassed to be caught almost masturbating. "Twy? You okay? It's Max."

"Oh. Oh, hey! Yeah, I'm good."

"I, um, I've been sent to get you ready."

Ready? Ready for what? "Do I have plans?"

She gives a low, evil laugh. "I think you do."

"I do?"

"I believe you signed up for a certain scene..."

"Oh my god." I cover my eyes and groan. "I totally forgot about the kidnapping. I don't know, Max. I'm not sure I should..."

"Can I open this door? Nothing will shock me."

"Yeah. Sorry."

She comes inside and I scoot over to make room for her on the bed.

"So," she sits and then lies beside me, which is one of those easy, casual Max moves that makes me already love her so much. And reminds me of Gigi, who'd be practically spooning me by now. "What's holding you back?"

I consider. "Honestly? Zion."

"Mm hm." She nods, slowly. "Because you think he'll be jealous bringing a third into the mix or..."

"We got emotional last night. Both of us." I get weak just thinking about it. "What if...I don't know. What if he doesn't want to do the scene? Or, even worse, what if he does the scene, but acts like last night never happened? What if..." I huff out a harsh breath.

"Okay. There are dangers, right? To scening the way you're planning to scene tonight. Big, tough things. I honestly wouldn't recommend this kind of play for everyone. But if you want to go through with it..."

I picture Zion, the way he was last night. At the flogging, in his cabin. This morning at the coffee shop. "I want to do the scene if he's there."

"Mm hm." She nods. "Well, I'm not at liberty to divulge specifics. But..." She rolls to standing. "I'm your security detail." Evil eyebrow wiggle. "And I think you're gonna like it. So, if you still want to do this, now might be a good time to get dressed. Oh. Here." She goes back into the hall and grabs a massive package from a big department store. "This came for you." Another evil grin. "Open it and see if there's anything kidnapping appropriate inside." She looks like she wants to open it herself.

"You do it." Excitement swirling inside me, I watch her tear into the bag with glee and paw through what looks like thousands of dollars worth of clothes, finally pulling out a sweet little red dress with white polka dots and a prim collar. "Oh, I love that."

"Put it on." She scrabbles around in the pile of fabric.

"With this. And this." She throws me a demure, old-fashioned-looking white bra and cotton panty set.

I get up, pushing past my remaining prudish tendencies the way I would backstage during a quick change, and put the outfit on.

Max disappears and comes back with another package. This one shoes. After a minute, she opens up the pair Gigi clearly meant for me to wear with the dress. They're cute little round-toed pumps, totally impractical for an outdoor camp environment, but seeing as how that hasn't stopped anyone here yet, I don't worry about it. I slide them on, move to the room's full-length mirror, and grin.

"He's gonna love that."

My heart skips around in my chest. "Wow. I guess I'm doing it."

Max wraps her arm around my waist and leans into me, watching me in the mirror. "You sure?"

"It's Zion, right? He's doing it?"

She gives a tiny nod.

"All right. I need makeup."

"You're beautiful without it."

I make a *tsking* sound. "Come on Max, you know how much he'll like smearing it."

"True."

"And if I cry... Raccoon eyes."

"Oh, yeah. Sadists dig that. Big time."

Half an hour later, makeup done and fed—which I make a mental note to pay Lamé for—we head out.

"Nervous?" Max asks.

I take a last look around, notice my phone, with its

approximately five million notifications. It can wait. Probably. Definitely. "Yes."

"Good." She tightens her hold on my arm. "You should be."

Zion

There's an art to good role play. Good kink in general, but this kind of setup in particular. In a scene like this one, we're digging deep and pulling out some real nasty shit.

Easier for some of us than for others.

I picked Blade tonight for a couple reasons:

First off, he gets the deal with me and Twyla. He knows the limits, gets that I'm calling the shots. He's nothing but a tool for us—actually, for her. I'm the boss, using what's available to me and, the way I've set this up, Blade's nothing but a glorified sex toy. Another cock, another mouth, another pair of hands. And the goal isn't to get either of us off, although I figure it'll happen. This is for Twyla. All for her.

From the moment we leave the clubhouse, we've taken on our specific roles. I feel him beside me, pumping himself up, getting mean, getting angry. The perfect side-kick to the sternly seething persona I've taken on.

We are pure aggression as we walk through camp side by side, sticking to the shadows. The few people who see us steer well clear.

Second, Blade is as experienced at this sort of scene

as I am—if not more. He's done many kidnappings, many hostage parties. And, since his divorce a few years ago, he's been a loner, not remotely interested in attachments. An ideal wingman. Kind of how I used to be until Twyla came along.

We near the spot we've selected for the pickup and adrenaline rushes up and through me. It's the pine smells, maybe, along with the quiet, which, together give the impression of being way out in the middle of nowhere. Someplace where she can scream, but not a goddamn soul will hear her.

A shiver runs through me—part anticipation, part fear.

The fear's essential. It's the part that understands the risks we're taking here, both physical and emotional. A scene like this can be cathartic and profound and painful—for any one of us. It can be blissful, too. Magic.

But I worry. And the fact that it's Twyla just ramps it all up. The excitement and the other shit.

At the same time, the worry adds to it, makes it sharper, more intense.

She wants this. And it's that desire that pumps through me right now—hers, mine, Blade's. My dick's hard and ready, pounding between my legs like a third presence.

Yeah, I know you want her, boy. Me, too. Me fucking too.

"That her?" Blade squints at a bright red form visible through the trees.

I nod and force my breathing to deepen, force my guts to simmer the hell down and my limbs to relax.

Does she know with absolute certainty that I'm the one coming to get her? I'll bet there's a shadow of doubt in her mind. The idea that she'd allow some random person to do this sends jealousy writhing through me like an uncontrollable monster.

Shit. I stop, close my eyes, inhale. Beside me, Blade waits. Finally, when I've gotten back at least a little of my normal calm, I look at him. "It's her."

How do I know?

She's my wife. I'd recognize her anywhere. Her smell, her taste, the sounds she makes when she comes.

Her shape's clear now, in that cute as fuck red dress. She's little and round, with tiny ankles and knees and wrists and big tits and an ass that I want to spread apart and press my face into. Tits that I'm dying to play with again, even though I had them in my mouth just this morning.

"It's fuckin' her."

We watch as she bends down to pick a flower.

"Shit," I breathe.

"She's so cute, man."

"She's mine," I growl, as if he didn't already know. She makes me wild like this, sends me over the top, turns me into a creature I don't even recognize. "Fucking mine."

"Lucky man," he whispers. We're so close now, I don't need to imagine the bruises or the dimples or the sharp curve of her back. It's all right there, perched on two tiny little red heels, just begging to be plucked and stolen away.

A few feet to one side, Max sits on a little stone bench, pretending not to see us. The second the scene starts, she'll throw on her security sash. She'll keep an eye on things while we're outside and make sure other campers don't stumble into us.

We've got very clear rules in place: Half hour check-ins. With Twyla, with Max, who will relay with the other security people. Well-marked "Abduction in progress" signs every step of the way. A whole goddamn choreography, which we've run through five times, start to finish. We don't take this shit lightly at camp, as a general rule. And this is Twyla. I'm leaving nothing up to fate.

Except for her reactions, of course. And I can't fucking wait for those.

"Let's go," I mutter.

We cover the last few feet quickly and quietly, moving up behind her. Blade right, me left. He's swung the hood up and over her head before she knows we're there and I've got her wrists cuffed behind her back in seconds.

Twyla yelps, struggles.

Max walks up, and says, "Safe word?" loud and clear.

Twyla goes still. "Um, um, red. Red."

"And if you can't talk?"

She stomps one foot three times.

"Good. Need to safe word now?"

She shakes her head inside the hood.

"Need to hear you say it, Twyla."

"No. No safe word." She sounds out of breath. "I'm in."

"Sure?"

"Yes."

"Got it. Safe word any time. For any reason. Three of anything." She steps closer, puts a tiny bell in Twyla's hand, closes her fingers into a fist around it. "Worst case scenario, you drop the bell. They stop. Check in. Pick up from there or end the scene. Got it?"

"Yes," Twyla gasps. "Yes. Yes."

"All right. Enjoy." Max moves a couple steps back, grinning wide, and nods at me and Blade. "She's all yours, boys."

"Boys?" Twyla whimpers.

"Shut up." My voice comes out sounding mean as shit, and nothing like myself. I doubt she recognizes me. "Don't talk, don't fucking move. Or you get hurt."

She fights us, my sweet little brat. Of course she fucking does. She twists when I grab her, she turns and shakes her head and tries to scratch me with her empty hand.

That's my girl. I'd expect nothing less.

This is gonna be so much fun.

28

Twyla

There's a difference between expecting something, having imagined it, and actually experiencing it.

My fantasies seemed dirty, but they weren't. This is dirty. They were safe, this is pure danger. This is stark reality. Or as close as I want to come to it.

And pure, pure fear. Shit. Why didn't it occur to me that it would be this terrifying?

I heard them a second before the black bag went over my head and the world got shut down to nothing but sensation, sounds, and the smell of freshly-laundered fabric.

I answered the safety questions with my mind in a million places. Images, not solid thoughts.

The hood smells good, freshly washed. *Thank you, thank you, thank you.*

It would be filthy if this were real.

Not real, not real, not real. Real would smell bad. Dirty.

I jump. Who's that? Behind me?

Where's Zion? Shit. Zion's not here. Is he?

"Zion?"

"Shut up," someone says. Is that him? No. Can't be. Too hard, gruff.

"Tell me you're here. *Please.*" My voice comes out shrill and scared. "I need you to be here."

"Such a fuckin' brat."

It's him. Relief floods through me, followed a second later by more of the fear thing. The nerves, the edgy thrill.

The cuffs hurt my wrists. For real, not just pretend.

Something—someone—knocks my legs out from behind. I slam onto my knees with a loud, pained *oof.*

Ow, shit, shit. I'm already scraped. Bruised. Do I want this?

A flash of my knees, tomorrow. When it's all over. Will it be over tomorrow?

It can be over now, if I want.

Red, I mouth. *Red, red, red.*

Something slips down around my neck, goes tight.

Oh my god. It's real.

I twist. There's pain, fast/slow movements, my back arches, my arms tight behind me, my shoulders already strained.

I take a breath to scream and wobble, then fly, weightless for an incomprehensible few seconds. I'm a sack of potatoes, thrown over a shoulder. An arm between my legs, wrapped tight around my thigh, squeezing. Fingers digging into my flesh.

We move. Bounce. He's running, I think.

I struggle. I don't mean to, it's not something I can help. Like my brain's on a different plane. Or maybe that's my body. I don't know.

I don't *know*.

I hear crunching. Forest. Branches snapping. Leaves rustling.

Birds, cicadas. Is that thunder, far off?

I don't know.

The air's hot, humid, but I'm cold. I shiver, my body limp and heavy and then taut, twisting in the grip that's got me between the thighs, my arms pinned against my back. It's not secure. Not safe. I'll fall. I will.

The grip tightens. A hand grabs my shoulder, fixes me in place. Someone else. Definitely two people.

I knew that. I heard the steps. More than two?

A shiver races up and through me. I'm whining, low, the sound like humming, except there's nothing musical about it.

I shift, squeal when my weight tilts back again for a second, and then settle on the wide shoulders, that stabilizing hand going tighter.

I try to say words. You'd think it would be easy, right? —none come out. Nothing but a high-pitched hum.

"Shut the fuck up," The arm between my legs eases up and slaps me, close to my ass. The other hand—the one holding up my lower shoulder—tightens. Something hits my face. Oh my god. Are they slapping me? I'd never pictured that. Not my face.

"You stay quiet, this'll be easy. Make noise, we can't control what happens."

It's Zion. I know that voice. And yet, maybe not? Maybe someone else entirely?

My stomach flips, clenches. Oh, god, please don't let me throw up. No. No, that's nerves. Fear. It's a lot of stuff, but Max was right about the light lunch. Salad and crackers. That's it. Bless her.

Something changes. The air? The ground? I can't tell. It feels different now. Maybe their pace? The sounds? Smells?

I've got to calm down. Focus. Breathe.

Okay. Okay. I want to be *here* for this, right? I don't want to miss my own abduction. Mindful and present. That's what I need.

A laugh pops up from out of nowhere, in my belly, my throat, out my mouth. Like a shout.

"Fuck. She's too loud," one says.

"Dammit." A pause. We stop moving, I feel the heavy breathing of the one carrying me. Zion? I don't know. Maybe. *Yes?* Maybe. "Show her."

"Got it."

The hand under me shifts away, my balance is thrown off. I kick my legs, trying to...I don't know. Get away? Why, though? I want this. I notice in a far-off way that I'm barefoot.

The realization hits me as my legs are wrenched

wide, my dress dragged up. "Fuck, man. You see this?" A rough hand grabs a butt cheek, squeezes like kneading dough, then slaps, fast and painful.

I grunt.

"Shut up." That stern voice sends another shiver through me. This one's cold and hot and ends right at my pussy. With my next heartbeat, my cute, pristine, white cotton undies are yanked down to bare my ass.

Even under the hood, I squeeze my eyes shut, hold my breath. My bottom's pried apart. Something cold rubbed on my ass. No. No, what are they doing? It's slick, slippery. Wet.

Someone spits there. Right on me. I feel it drip, hot and humiliating.

"No!" I yell as a rough finger rubs against my most private place. Outside, in the open. Are there people watching? Oh my god, what are they doing?

That finger, thick, warm, prods at my tight asshole, rubs, again, then pushes in. In. Oh my god. This is how they're doing it? Like this? Me, flung over a back, outside, unable to see, to understand? I'm lost. Caught up in it, questioning everything, full of doubt and excitement and —god, yes—a pulsing thrill of desire. I'm a mess of nerves and pain and questions and, oh, god, want. I want this.

I do.

How?

I don't know.

The finger presses in, quick and deep. It's not an easy invasion, it's brutal and aggressive.

It's a message. To shut me up.

He pulls out. I gasp, half relief, half disappointment and, oh no, something different presses in—cold and hard and slick with whatever they spread over me.

With a quick slap, it's lodged inside me. "That'll shut her up," says one voice.

The shoulders beneath me shake so I feel the evil laugh more than hear it. "For now."

Another slap, right over what has to be a butt plug. Butt plug? That's right. I asked for Double Penetration, didn't I? I've never done it. Hardly ever done anal at all, aside from some unsatisfying explorations with my ex.

I've thought about it, though. Like, a lot.

But that was almost a dream. Something I'd fantasized and pretended and lived out in my head for years. I even wrote it on the form, but those were just words. Words, ink on paper. That's it.

Not this...this...this flesh and blood thing. Not this dirt on my knees and scrapes I'll feel for days. Not this humiliating ignoring of everything I want, ask for, need.

But I asked for this. I wanted it.

Do I still want it?

The walking starts up again, the hand between my legs possessive and cruel, so deadly certain that it owns me. The shoulders so solid, inflexible. The pace quick, stern.

And in my ass, an intrusion. Just as I think it, someone pulls my falling dress back up and hits me, right on the buttplug.

The groan I let out is the most bestial, basic sound

I've ever made. It's pleasure and pain at an anatomical level.

For a few bright seconds, that's all I've got room for in my brain.

Nothing else.

Nothing else.

Zion

I used to wonder, after those sessions in the trailer with Donnie Rae, if I'd like sex as much without the spanking and the other shit we did.

The next time I tried it, I'd just turned eighteen and finished high school. It was a couple months before a modeling scout spotted me working construction and changed my life.

A neighbor used to come and check on me when I was a kid and still brought the occasional casserole when Dad was on a bender. Which was pretty much always. I wasn't close to her family, but she was better than most.

The summer I graduated, the woman's niece came to visit. Molly Pratt. She was this skinny, white college girl with a certain look in her eye. I'd gotten to the point in life where I knew what that look meant, and I knew that it made my dick hard.

Molly arrived one night with food from my neighbor —Mac and cheese, with roast vegetables snuck in it. It was good, though the vegetables colored my opinion.

Molly dropped the dish in the kitchen, asked if my

dad was around. When I said no, she turned over, swiped all the random shit off the kitchen table, pulled up her skirt, and bent over it, showing me her naked, white ass. I fucked her—she provided the condom. I provided the very quick ending. And when I was done, I looked down, and obeyed some ingrained instinct to give her ass a smack—like I'd done with Donnie Rae—and came again when she squeezed tight around me.

Cause and effect. I smacked, she clenched. I kept fucking her. Came three times. Smacked the shit out of her ass. When we were done, she licked my cock clean, grabbed ahold of my balls, and told me never to talk about it again or else, then walked out, leaving me standing there with an overflowing condom still held tight in my hand and the knowledge that I needed to do that again— all of it—very, very soon. I just knew that I needed it. Didn't matter with who.

And it didn't.

Until now.

Now, it's for Twyla. All of it. The pain, the pleasure, agony, ecstasy. Every drop I've got is for this woman. And this woman alone. Every time Blade smacks that sweet little diamond-studded butt plug I bought, specifically for her. Every time she gasps and moans. Every step bringing us closer to a scene I know I'll cherish to the end of my days. All of it's for her.

I'm hers.

Which, looking at any of this as an outsider would probably make no goddamn sense at all. I get it though. I get that sharing my woman is a symbol. It means, above all, that she's mine to share.

Mine.

It's my one word mantra.

"Let's move," I order, needing to get this scene to the space before I drop her to her knees right here and force my cock in her throat just so I can see her face. Which isn't part of the plan. I mean, it's a decent idea, but the trick in these role-playing situations is that the person in charge needs to keep his whole fucking head and not lose it, the way I would if I started improvising.

We've planned this every step of the way, including shoving that butt plug into her tight little asshole, right here, at the edge of the woods.

Now, I heft her higher, glad that Blade's spotting her, given that we've bound her arms behind her back, making it impossible to hold her safely in a fireman's carry. It was a choice. All of this is a choice. The type of carry, the cuffs, the hood. Even the goddamn butt plug, which is a size Small. We've got a Medium in the space, a Large, and an XL, to get her good and stretched out for the big event.

If we get that far.

I feel her breathing against me—her chest and stomach heaving, her mouth gulping air like she can't get enough. I look over at Max, still moving steadily, and urge her over with a tilt of my head. "Check in," I say, low. "Breathing."

We stop.

"Hey, Twy," Max says in her calm, matter of fact

way. "You still good with this? You're breathing kind of fast. I want to make sure you're okay. Can you talk for me?"

"Yes," Twyla puffs out, her voice high and tight. "Fine." Panting. "Good. I'm good."

"Sure?"

"Yes."

"Okay." Max meets my gaze, nods, then turns and nods at Blade. We carry on, across a clearing filled with picnic tables, some occupied by campers. Conversations pause, people turn and stare, whispering, giggling. Clapping breaks out at one table and the rest join in.

Twyla struggles to get down, probably embarrassed. Probably filled with some level of shame. Blade, the sadistic bastard, reaches over to pull her skirt up again, opens her butt cheeks wide so our audience gets a good look at what we shoved inside her, and gives it another smack, the sound not nearly as satisfying as the slap of palm to butt cheek. Twyla's gasp/groan is pretty wonderful, though. God, I love making her scream.

"Nothing to see here," Blade hams it up, while Max holds up the "Abduction in progress sign." As if it weren't fucking obvious.

"Let's go," I say in the low, angry voice I've taken on naturally since the start of this thing.

This thing. Fuck, this is so much more than a *thing*. It's... I don't know. Not just a scene or an experience. It's...a beginning, maybe? Is that it?

I squeeze her squirming thigh, let my hand slide up,

up to where her pussy's pressed to my shoulder, and twist to cup her and find…

"Fuck. Brat's soaking wet for us."

"Knew it," says Blade, his tone gruff. "Little slut's been begging for this. For days."

I grunt. "She'll regret it," I warn. "Gonna destroy this pussy."

"Both holes. If she can take it." He laughs. "Think we'll fit?"

"I know we will." My cock pulses at the way she twists, working to get some friction on that pussy. "We'll give her no fuckin' choice."

Up ahead, the shack's ready and waiting, prepped with every toy, rope, and torture device we'll need over the next few hours. Hidden behind a partition, there's a kitchen with food and drinks, and a bathroom. Nothing else. No windows, no decor. Just a big bed, an x-cross against a wall, a bench. It's the perfect sordid little space for what we've got planned.

My booted feet hit the porch steps, the sound satisfyingly ominous. Her body stops fighting, goes still. I can feel her listening.

I turn sideways and wait for Blade to open the door before going in. Max gives a final thumbs up and sits on a chair out on the porch, settling in for a long wait.

"Where…where are we? What is this?" Twyla sounds truly scared. I have to work to push back the part of me that wants to coddle her, take care of her. That guy—who's more dominant than I'd ever imagined—doesn't want to put her through this, despite it being exactly what she asked for. That guy wants to wrap her up in velvet and silk, hand her a glass of wine, and draw her a bath full of bubbles. He wants to buy her shit and watch her revel in it. He's the guy who wanted to marry her in the first place—not as a plan hatched by some PR team, as we told her, but as a caretaker.

"Shut up," I force through my throat. Because, alongside that sweet, caring man is a total asshole. And the asshole's been invited—by Twyla herself—to come out and play. So here he fucking is.

And he's a real piece of work.

"On the floor," I tell Blade, though he already knows this.

The floor's bumpy. We'll only leave her there for a minute or two, but I want her to get a feel for how crude this place is, how rough. I want her to picture the filth—though it's been thoroughly cleaned.

It's the idea that matters.

I lean and drop her—gently—onto her knees. I don't want to hurt her. She whimpers, fights against her cuffs, tries to scuffle away, and comes up short against Blade's jeans-covered legs.

"I love it when they fight, man. Don't you?" asks Blade.

I squat, grab her by the chain loosely knotted around her neck, and draw her head close. "You know why he wants you to fight? Huh?" When she doesn't reply, I go on. "'Cause he's just dyin' to teach you a lesson."

She moans, twists. I tighten my hold, forcing her to push up higher on her knees. Her tits almost spill out of the cute little dress. I want to rip it open, but manage to hold off.

"Now," I put my head against hers, holding her tight, almost hugging her. "You gonna be a good girl and let us do what we've got to do or are you gonna fight us every step of the way?"

29

Twyla

"Be good. I want to be good," I tell Kidnapper #1. The one who carried me. The one who sounds like Zion.

He tightens his hold on me—a quick hug—and pulls away. "Good. Very good." Something tugs at my neckline. "How about you start with a little act of good faith, huh? Come here."

My whole dress is ripped open—top to bottom. Buttons fly everywhere. I'm in nothing but a bra, a hood, and a buttplug, which feels huge in my ass.

"Fuck, man," the second voice says. Do I recognize him? I don't know. "These tits... You see the nipples? They're fucking huge."

One of my bra cups is yanked down, my breast manhandled, weighed, like an object being evaluated. It hits the bull's eye of my deepest, darkest fantasy and my pussy clenches, hard, around nothing.

"Yeah." Another hand grabs my other breast, rough and efficient. "Nice, right?"

My pussy's aching and empty and I'm so very thankful for the buttplug's sweet pressure that I let out a high, needy sound.

"Shit." A quick slap to one breast makes me gasp. The first man did it, I think. Maybe? I don't know. I can't tell. I don't know.

"Check out her pussy." Okay, that's definitely Zion. "Bet she's soaking."

I hold my breath. Someone rubs me, quick, businesslike. This isn't for my pleasure. It's for them.

It's awful. Wonderful. So scary I want to stop it, but I need what they're giving me too badly to do anything but take it, hungrily. After a second, they pull away and I hear the wet slurp of what has to be someone sucking me from their finger.

Oh my god, they're filthy. I mean, I knew it. Most folks here are sexually open in a way I've never experienced, but this...this...do they have limits? Do I? Did I give limits on my form?

I can't remember. I don't know.

I don't *know*.

"Fuck, she tastes good. Little slut's so goddamn horny for it, bro. Think two of us are enough?"

I whimper.

They both laugh, the sound so mean it feels real. Real. Is it real? I don't know.

"Come on. Show of good faith, we said." A slap to my

breast makes me flinch. Whatever's keeping the hood around my neck disappears.

I'm so excited at the prospect of seeing my attackers that I feel light and grateful. I'm smiling when the hood's lifted.

Too soon, though.

"See? She likes it."

My eyes remain hidden. Only my mouth's free. It feels good to breathe fresh air. New smells assail me—cleaning products and wood and cologne. Something else. Plastic or rubber, maybe.

"See how she likes this."

Within seconds, someone's got my head in their grip, the other person shoves something cold in my mouth and now I can't close it. A gag. They attach it behind my head, leaving me with a metal ring in my mouth, my lips forced wide open. I...don't like it.

I want to see them. I want to undo my arms and...I want to...

As they pull me higher from where I've settled back on my haunches, the bell I'm holding in my hand falls, tinkling quietly onto the wood floor. I don't do it on purpose, but still, in the split second that follows, relief washes through me.

The next second, everything changes. The gag's off, the hood's pulled up. Zion—oh my god, Zion—squats and holds my face while the other person undoes the cuffs. "Baby." Zion talks to me, quick and urgent, his voice gentle. "Baby, you okay? We hurt you? We'll stop. Right this second. Come 'ere." I'm up and on his lap, my arms around his neck. He's holding me tight, so tight against his chest and the world is warm and soft and, no I don't want to stop the scene, but I also need this. I need it like air.

"You good?" Max calls from outside.

"Yes," replies Zion. "Taking a break."

I squeeze harder and snuggle in deep. The sides of my dress flap open, covering me, but leaving my front to press naked against Zion. Footsteps move away, giving us space or privacy. I hear water running, footsteps again.

"Thanks. Here, baby. Twy. Here. Drink this."

I don't want to move, but I force myself back, look up and accept the glass of water he's offering. Drinking it down feels amazing and, before I know it, I've finished the whole thing.

"More?"

I shake my head and snuggle back in to his body.

"Tell me what you need, sweetheart, okay?" He shifts, lowers himself farther to the floor, and gathers more of me in so I'm latched onto him like a monkey on a branch.

"Want me to go?" The other voice asks.

"Yeah, man, I think—"

"No," I say, loud, sure. I swallow and turn to look at Blade, whose voice I guess some unconscious part of me recognized. "Stay."

"You sure?"

I nod and give him a once-over. He looks good in jeans and a slim cut white T-shirt that sets off the deep, gorgeous brown of his skin. His arms are huge, his hands rough-looking. I've felt those hands, the calluses, the scars.

"I don't want it to end."

Beneath my head, Zion's chest stops moving. After a few seconds, he lets out a long breath. "You sure?"

I nod again, a smile blooming on my face. Blade sits on the floor close beside Zion, trapping my leg between the two of them. "Maybe no more of the kidnapping stuff, though. For tonight. I might...want to try that again later? But like, a little at a time, you know?"

"Yeah. Okay." They exchange a glance. Zion leans in and kisses the top of my head. I don't let myself think about his mouth and kissing. I don't let myself wish he'd press his lips to mine. "You want to just cuddle with us for tonight? Would that be good, baby?"

"After."

Blade's eyebrows lift. "After what?"

"After we finish." They stir, maybe unsure of the new rules. Maybe excited.

I turn and see the gag on the floor. "I want to try that."

"The O-ring?"

"Yeah."

Zion's voice goes low. "You know what we use that for, don't you, sweetheart?"

I nod, enjoying the slightly condescending tone he's put on for me. My nipples go hard and tight.

"No more cuffs. I didn't like that, behind my back."

"Noted," says Blade. "What else?"

"Um...I really liked when you..." I hide my face in

Zion's chest again, a little squeamish or shy of discussing these things out loud, but also so, so glad we're doing it. "Sort of...*tried out* my breasts? You know, like..." I shrug, at a loss for a way to describe the way that made me feel.

"Treated you like an object."

"Yes. Exactly."

"Something to be weighed and measured, judged?"

Shame washes through me, along with a fresh dose of lust, thick and heavy and ticklish in my belly. "Yeah. *Used*," I finally whisper, hiding my blushing face against Zion again.

"What else?" Zion asks.

I squirm. "The plug is good."

"Yeah?" Slowly, Zion runs a hand down my side, under my dress, over my hip, my ass, and right there to where the thing's poking out of me. Very gently, he toys with it and it feels... *uuuuuuuuuuh.* "Figured you would."

Just that nudge of fingers to metal pushes a sigh of pure pleasure from me. My hips rock just the tiniest bit.

Zion feels it, of course. He amplifies the movement of the plug, pulls it out a little and presses it back in again. "Okay. You want a bigger one?"

"Really? It feels massive."

"Grab a size up, man."

Blade gets a bigger plug and comes back with that and a bottle of lube. "We back on?"

"Hold on a sec." He looks at me. "Tell me more of what you want, Twyla."

My body wants to move, to take, my brain wants...

more. "Um. I want to keep going. Without the hood," I rush to add. "I want to see you both."

"Okay." Zion slides his fingers into my hair, his thumb rubbing circles on my temple, my cheek. His gaze takes in my whole face, my eyes, my mouth, my eyes again. "What else?"

"I like feeling used." That sounded wrong, so I consider for a moment. "No. Not *like* exactly, but the idea turns me on, you know?"

"Okay. Yeah. I know that feelin'. You want to be objectified?"

"Yes. You decide what happens, I have to...take it. Accept it. And I want to push things. With you. I mean, I want you to push them. Farther than I'd..." I swallow. "Than I'd maybe be comfortable with. With anyone else."

His eyes flare briefly. "Okay, so, we make you do things you'd never get caught dead doin' in real life?"

My pulse quickens. "Yes. Yes, that."

"A little degradation? What about the name callin'? Too much?"

I glance down, weirdly shy, and then back up. "I liked slut. A lot." It had felt dirty when Blade said it. Wrong and a little humiliating, but not hurtful in a deep, real way. "Not bitch, though. I don't think that would work for me."

"Got it. What else?"

"I think I'll need breaks."

"Yep." His gaze doesn't leave mine and, this close, I can make out the individual crystals of his eyes. They look otherworldly, almost lit up from within. I want to kiss his eyelids. I want to kiss him.

"And…" I stare at his mouth. No. No, I can't ask for that. He's already ripped right through one of his Very Important Hard Limits with me, I can't ask him to ignore a second.

"Yeah?" Is he eyeing my mouth with hunger, too? Or is that just wishful thinking on my part?

Voice shaky, I say, "I like being your brat."

"You do?"

I nod. "And I trust you. With all of it."

"Good thing," he says, trying to push it off as a joke.

I won't let him, though. "Seriously. I *trust* you, Zion. I do."

His expression goes stern as he nods. "Thank you."

"Now." I turn to Blade. "Are you gonna give him the plug or what?"

"Oh, no, my little brat, that's not how it works," says Zion, his expression as cold as the blue of his eyes. "We give the orders around here. You just lie there and take what you're given like a good little slut."

At that, my entire body flushes hot.

Zion

I nod to Blade. He goes to the door and explains what we're doing to Max, who checks in with Twyla. After a quick chat, she goes back out. None of the check ins or discussion affects my libido one bit. It's all just part of rough play, part of the deal, and, in a way, setting out the rules, the wants, the limits, just makes it better.

Once Blade's back, I settle into this new role she's written for me—softer, in a way, but firm as hell, a caretaker, but also a user.

I harden my jaw and nudge her slightly away, give her a slow, ugly up-and-down, and adjust my hard-on in my jeans—as explicit a move as I can make it.

"Got that plug, man?"

"Sure do."

"Good. We've got a tight little asshole to destroy tonight."

Blade's eyes glow with the same excitement I'm feeling. He likes this sleazy scenario more than the kidnapping thing. Me, too. "Yeah. Got to get it ready."

"That's right. We're gonna fuck it so hard she won't be able to walk tomorrow."

She whimpers and squirms and I give her a fake, narrow-eyed smile, putting out a hand to weigh one of her tits while I say, "Don't worry. You'll like it. You'll fuckin' beg for it."

"Can I..." Blade looks up from where he was watching my hand on her, and holds up the plug. "Want me to lube it up?"

I nod, lean back against the wall like a goddamn king on his throne, and say, "Actually, we should get her on the bed. Do this properly." I grab her tit again, play with it like it's nothing more consequential that a set of worry beads or a fruit I'm checking for ripeness, and say, "Go ahead and put her up there."

All of this is done without direct eye contact with Twyla. The more I ignore her and treat her like an object, the more she wiggles and shimmies on my lap, trying to put pressure on that wet little pussy.

Blade reaches for her, as matter of fact about the whole thing as I'm trying to be. He grabs her under the arms and hauls her up, ignoring her gasp when her hands and knees land on the mattress.

"Legs apart," I order getting up on my knees to join him behind her. "We need to see."

"This shit's in the way." I pull the dress off, brusque, but careful not to hurt her. I can't help but smooth a hand over her back, her ass. "This is nice."

"Looks good." Blade looks at me, expectantly. It takes me a moment to understand that things have shifted between us, too. Right now, he's asking for permission. Because we've veered from the script and because she's mine.

"Look at her tits."

He leans back to look below her at where they're only half-held by the sweet little white bra she chose for today. "Go ahead, man. You can touch. I don't mind."

She whimpers and arches her back. Blade's hand's almost shaking when he reaches down to pluck at her round nipple, which sets her off on a low, guttural hum that I can feel in my balls. "Fuck, she's such a little slut."

"Such nice tits," he says, playing with one and then the other, then looks up. "You ever fuck 'em?"

"Not yet." And now it's all I want. All I can think of. Until she twists her body and I catch sight of the sparkling diamond at her asshole, and suddenly there's nothing I want more than to play with it. I move close and caress her ass cheeks. "You ever seen an ass like this?"

"Not often."

I give her cheek a quick slap, which works her up. "It's gonna feel good."

"You gonna let me in there, man?"

"I don't know yet," I shrug, though it's hard to maintain any degree of nonchalance when it comes to sharing this woman's body with another. Because, yeah, I've planned it and set it up and, yeah, it's hot to watch him touch her, but beneath it all, that mantra of mine's just chugging along like a never ending heartbeat. Every time his hand gets near her, every time I think about his cock inside her, the Mine gets louder, angrier, ready to punch and kick and throw him the hell off.

Breath shaking, I work the little plug from her ass and immediately fill her with my thumb, soaking up every pleasured sound she gives us. And then, because she is mine, because she trusts me, I look up at Blade and say, "Hardly needs any lube, man. Check it out." I hold her ass open. "Go on, feel her cunt. This little brat's dying to get her holes filled."

His evil chuckle cuts off abruptly the second his fingers touch my wife's sweet pussy. "Fuck," he mutters, the awe in his voice gratifying. "Fuck, man."

"Right?" I pick up the other plug. "Here."

He grabs it and lubes it up, while I bend over and spit on her asshole, working my finger in and out, enjoying every tiny reaction she gives us like a gift. When he nods,

I pull out and work the wider gauge plug in and she tries to get away and I fucking keep her right there with a fist in her hair.

That move—the attempt to flee, the hair restraint—ramps things up again, from calm and calculating into something more feverish.

"Like that, don't you, brat?"

"Fuck, look how she takes it." Blade twists the plug and smacks it for good measure, then looks at me, waiting for what's next.

"Let's break her mouth in," I say, keeping my voice as calm and sensible as I can, though my whole fucking body's screaming with want.

"Fuck, yeah." He grabs the O-ring gag and we move up to her head. Slowly strap it on her, giving her the opportunity to stop things if she wants.

When it's on, I grab her chin and force her face my way. "Fuck, man, look at that hole." I run a finger around the metal O, inside her lips, press it to her tongue, feel her teeth. Just testing the goods. "This'll do." I'm all business now. "Just to take the edge off."

"Makes sense."

"On your knees," I tell her, with a hard slap to the ass. She scrambles to obey while Blade and I stand. I unzip my jeans and pull out my cock, nod to Blade to do the same, and watch her for a reaction. If there's too much hesitation, we stop.

There's none, though. Not from my sweet little wife. The woman I thought would never, in a million years, understand the lifestyle I live. God, how fucking wrong I was. Because my baby's between us on the bed, her spread knees giving us a clear look at her soaking pussy and, if I lean just right, the rather impressive item in her ass and, if that weren't clear enough already, her sweet little hands are plucking and pulling at her nipples like a little pain is just the thing she needs to get off.

"Fuck, look at that," Blade whispers, full of awe.

I know how he feels.

"All right. It's your first gag, right baby?"

Her gaze meets mine. It's out of focus, her pupils blown wide open. She nods.

"So, we'll ease into it. You know how to stop if you need to?"

She slaps the mattress three times and I pat her head with a patronizing smile. "Good girl. Now take what we give you."

I grab my cock and give it a slow, menacing stroke, eyes on the wide-open hole of her mouth, before moving in.

30

Twyla

I've never been this turned on in my life. Never felt so wide open and ready for anything. Everything. I want whatever Zion gives me. However he gives it. He can make Blade be a part of it, or not. I don't care. He can invite half a dozen friends to watch or, hell, take part. I don't care.

I've pushed past the point of worrying or caring or practicalities, into a place where I'm just the object and they're just using me and we're all getting what we want.

"Open wide," Zion says, as if my entire mouth weren't stretched out and waiting for his pleasure. I tear my gaze from his dripping cock and glance at Blade. *Their* pleasure.

My pussy pulses with want and I can feel the wetness just sliding from me, coating my inner thighs.

I focus back on Zion's massive erection. It's red at the tip, the skin so shiny and taut, it looks painful. But a good pain, I'll bet. Just like what I'm going through. It hurts, but it's pleasure and the two together are pure joy.

"Show me your tongue."

I obey and he rewards me by setting the hot crown of his cock right there. I moan, the sound low and guttural and ravenous.

Zion and Blade laugh. I strain to look up and catch them exchanging the kind of self-satisfied look I'd absolutely hate under other circumstances. And I hate it a little bit now, but it also hits me in that shame/pleasure spot that I'm just beginning to explore. I want more of it. So, instead of backing up, I move closer to him, edge his cock inside the metal rim of the gag and let it fill my mouth.

I push in and in and he throws back his head and groans, wraps his fingers in my hair and pulls me hard toward him and it's rough and so good. So good. I want hands on me everywhere. I want to be filled, I want more, more, *more*. I want to feel him take me every way he wants, every way he can.

"Whoa, whoa, baby." He uses my hair to pull me off him. A string of drool connecting us until he shoves himself back in, farther this time, more aggressively, and, holy shit, I think I'm going to come. You can't come from a blow job, can you?

As he presses deep, gagging me for a few uncomfortable seconds and then pulling out again, I barely notice my own hands at my breasts, pulling hard, squeezing, hurting them, which shoots electric currents to my core. I can't breathe. Can't breathe. Writhe to get away, and he lets me go. I gasp, the drool flows freely from my mouth, my eyes crying like I'd imagined they would.

I hadn't imagined how it would feel in my body, though, the full, swollen, open thing. The raw nerves and wide, wide realm of possibilities. The vague, but intense, somehow letting go and just *being* thing. That's what this is.

I'm here. I'm here and I *am*. That's it. That's all.

"What do you think, man?" Zion rubs his cock along the outside of my mouth, my cheek, my eye. "Lick my balls," he says and, god, I've never complied with anything as fast in my life.

It's not easy, but I get my tongue on him and with a grunt, he says, "Fuck, you've got to try it out, man. Come here. Give it a shot."

It, he said. It. Like I'm just a thing to be tried out and enjoyed.

I turn and see Blade, jeans spread open at the fly, apparently commando like Zion and I whimper.

He's big. Not just big, but scary huge. That thing is going to tear me open. And there's not a moment of doubt that I'll work to accept him in my body. Zion says I will and therefore, in this place, this liminal, out-of-world, out-of-body, out-of-mind place that we're inhabiting together, I will absolutely do it. No matter how difficult it may be.

No matter how much it hurts.

"Shit, bro." Zion stares, with what might be a hint of interest. "I forgot how big your dick is."

Blade shrugs one shoulder with an awe-shucks grin and walks over. I eye his cock, not convinced I can do it, but, in this frame of mind, totally ready to try. It's the size of my forearm, I think vaguely, from my fist to my elbow.

"Damn." Zion looks down at me, then over at Blade's erection. When he reaches out and slides a finger down the other man's length, the unexpected pleasure knocks an ugly sound loose from my lungs.

"Fuck, this is gonna look so good in her mouth," he tells Blade as he gives him a quick, efficient looking stroke, in the process making my insides swirl with a fresh fantasy. The two of them, on the bed or, no, no, against a wall, rough and hard. I'd want Zion fucking Blade, I think, but then the way he eyes his cock makes me picture it the other way around and...

The sounds I'm making go low and gritty and my pussy clenches hard on nothing.

"Think she likes you touching me, man." Blade reaches for Zion, his gaze smoldering. "You like this, too? Huh?" He weighs my husband's balls and I shudder at how good it looks.

They're both watching me, drinking in these uninhibited reactions.

"Go ahead," Zion says, nudging Blade toward me. "Get in there, man. Go for it. Use that mouth."

My eyes roll back at those words.

Blade adds to the fire with an easy, "Thanks, man," like he's just accepted a plastic cup of beer at a keg party. And then, he's here, pressing inside.

I'm overwhelmed with the smell of him—different from Zion's. Not bad, but unfamiliar, which makes it a little scarier. He's staring down, feeding himself into me one thick inch at a time and I get to the gagging point so fast, he has to pull out. He *tsks*, grasps my hair tighter, and forges inside again and I strain to watch him through my tears while he does it.

I want approval. I want to please him. To be the thing he expects me to be. To take him, however he wants. However Zion wants, really. Zion's in charge here. He decides.

"That looks good," Zion says from somewhere behind me. "The two of you."

I try to look back at him, but Blade's sinking into my mouth again and filling it and my throat and *tut tutting* like I'm a bad girl and I really, really don't want to be a bad girl. "Eyes here," he says, his voice sterner than it's been, his face deadly serious now. "You watch me when I fuck your face."

I try to nod, which isn't possible, though I think he appreciates the effort. And that's important in this moment. So important.

"Fuck, this is real good, man," he says, sinking so deep I don't have air and then ignoring my struggles—or pretending to. I think he sees everything. They both do. "So goddamn good."

"I know," Zion says, as if he's somehow responsible for this. For the pleasure my body brings this other man. "I'm gonna fuck her cunt."

I don't have time to react before Blade pulls out, drops to his knees, and Zion pushes me onto all fours and slams inside me.

My entire body jolts from the shock, the fullness of

the plug and my husband's cock. Is he bare? I want him to be. I hope he is. I want his come filling me in some kind of ancient, instinctive rite, old and primitive and right and also wrong in the way of so many of my desires.

I let myself picture both of them coming in me, others, too. Sharing me, using me. The reality would be too much, but I imagine it, revel in the sensations flowing through me, while my own hoarse moans wrack my body.

My jaw aches as Blade eases his massive erection back into my mouth and suddenly, I'm being spit roasted between them, and it's a mess. Or, I'm a mess, my body pushed and pulled, their rhythm matching quickly.

I've fantasized this exact thing, many, many times, in the safety of my own bed. The reality of actually doing it sizzles through me, complete with smells and a sound-track I'd never in a million years imagined.

"Fuck, baby," Zion says, low and rough. "You're a goddamn dream." He pounds into me, while Blade hits the back of my throat and, within minutes, one of them says he's coming. Blade, I think. I can't tell.

"Pull out," says Zion, which I only vaguely notice, because the mother of all orgasms is barreling toward me and there's nothing I can do, nothing *to* do but hold on.

There's a helpless split second when Blade goes still, looks at Zion behind me, and his face changes from that smoldering, sexy concentration, through almost annoy-ance and then, understanding, maybe. He nods, as though he gets whatever's going on, though I'm lost, and pulls out.

In the next moment, Zion thrusts deep inside with a fresh fierceness.

Blade steps back, watching. Hungry.

What was that? What happened? Whatever was said in that unspoken exchange led to an understanding and, though I can't see Zion, I get the meaning.

This is for him only. He's changed his mind, maybe. It's a predator thing and, on that level, I think Blade knows exactly what his place is in this dynamic.

There's play time and then there's ownership and Zion's just staked a claim.

And, fuck, fuck, it satisfies something deep inside me and now, as he fucks me so hard, all I can do is take it, watching, eyes wide open, soaking it all in, as if it'll be the one and only time.

I shove that thought away and focus on how I'm his and he needs to be the one to mark me. He's possessive and, damn it, so am I. I like that about us. It's part of who we are.

Blade, who's stared hard until now, turns to the side and jerks himself off two-handed. When he starts climaxing, it's a volcanic eruption spewing all over the sheets. His shaft actually vibrates. He lets out a pained grunt with each fresh spurt of come.

Behind me, Zion slows down to watch, I think, which turns my crank just enough to send me over the edge and, as I do, he pumps harder, his grip tight enough to bruise, his voice raised in incomprehensible shouts of ecstasy. No words, just sounds, brutal and beautiful and terrifying.

I join him, my insides compressing and releasing with pure violence. My arms give, I drop.

Vaguely, from outside myself, I see my body convulse and go rigid as a bow, feel it work hard to split, fracture, change before coming back together again. It's nuclear fission. Worlds bursting apart.

When my heart beat finally slows enough for my brain to kick in, I crane my neck to watch Zion finish. And, god, he looks good as he pulls out, rips off the condom—which I'm weirdly disappointed to see he's worn—and strokes himself right over that butt plug. He grunts with each spurt, his balls high and tight, the electric shock of his relief palpable. All I can do is it let my head hang and live it, let this whole thing take me over, wishing I could see more of him, wishing there was more for him to give. For me to give.

With his last hot jet of come, his chest finally expands, and I let myself breathe, too, feeling oxygen deprived and brain-dead and alive. After a while, minutes, maybe, he gives my bruised hips one last squeeze, shifts back to tie up his condom and then, as if he can't help himself moves in again to run his fingers through his semen on my ass.

I collapse fully onto my front and one of them removes the gag, which is suddenly unbearable, something's spread over me—a blanket, maybe? Someone goes to the door, talks to Max, who sticks her head in, grins and waves, and disappears. Finally, two warm bodies slide into the bed, one on either side of me. With a happy groan, I curl into Zion's side, put my hand over Blade's on my hip, and pass out.

Zion

The room is still, but my insides are a roiling mess. Questions, wants, doubts I've never let myself have, all jumbled up, fighting for position.

I guess this is just the way now. I want things. Human things. Affection, attachments. Meaning.

Twyla shifts and I move my arm, bumping into Blade on her hip in the process. He doesn't pull away. Instead, he threads his fingers through mine, tightening until we're palm to palm, and waits for my gaze to land on him.

"What you two have? This connection? Let it be special, man," he whispers, over Twyla's sleeping head. "I know you've got... Fuck, just let yourself love her."

I want to pull away, but I can't. Not with the way he's watching me—so pure and open in a way other people rarely are. His honesty's magnetic and a little repulsive. Too much, too real.

Blade's gone through some shit of his own. He knows what it feels like to love and lose and that's what opens my mouth and pushes the words out. "It's so hard."

"I know." He squeezes my hand and lets go of the awkward hold. "Means it's worth it."

I pull back a couple inches and look down at Twyla's slumbering face—smeared makeup, rosy cheeks, bruised lips—and something in my chest twists and cracks, flooding wide open. Tears rush my eyes, so suddenly it hurts. "How do you deal with the fear? The idea of losing her is... Fuck, how do you survive this shit?"

He presses his mouth into a tight smile and shakes his head, his eyes the most tragic thing I've ever seen. "It's terrifying, man. But that's just it. Life has meaning because it ends. Love has meaning because you could lose it. Impermanence makes shit more real, in the end."

My gaze slides back down to Twyla, like a compass to true north, and I let the protectiveness I feel for her swell and swell until there's literally nothing else. I can't imagine having cared about anything, ever, but this. Her.

"Fuck," I say, to which he gives a sad smile.

"Yeah." He sinks back onto his pillow with a shuddery sigh.

I reach out again, grab his hand again, hold it, feeling his strength and giving him mine. He tightens his fist around mine and there's something like comfort here and, with a start, I realize I've shut myself off to more than romantic love with the way I've lived my life. Friendships I could've deepened have stayed flat because I've never committed to either version of myself. To this. Him. Friendship.

I must fall asleep for a while, because at some point, one of us moves, a body twisting, another turning. My cock's fully hard by the time I open my eyes and see Twyla on her back between us, stretching hard, like a happy kitten. I glance toward the door and see no light seeping under it.

It's still night, which is a relief. It means more time here.

Our gazes meet. She smiles. A soft, dreamy expression that reaches her eyes, lights her up from within. Still waters run deep. That's Twyla. Layers and layers and layers to uncover. I want that. Those layers. This smile. And every other kind of smile she's got in her. I want them all.

And that's it. I fall. Hard, fast, forever.

I love her. The feeling's huge, wide open, painful, like Blade said, because it can be taken away, but also, unbearably light. Unbearably good.

I glance at her mouth, flush hot all over, start to lean in and—

"What time is it?" Blade asks, coming awake on his side of the big bed.

With a groan, I sink back down, flush with nerves and adrenaline. Fuck Fuck, I want to kiss her.

I turn and she's still watching me with the sort of naughty, secret smile I want to see every morning for the rest of my life.

"Don't know."

Blade sits up, one hand casually set on my wife's naked thigh. I don't say anything, though I can't stop staring at it. He turns, catches my look, and lifts it off with a huge grin. "I see how it is, bro."

"You don't have to—"

"Nah, I like a little jealousy. Just that extra dose of spice." His grin softens. "Y'all wanna be alone or are we going for a second round?"

We both look at Twyla, who stills, her eyes huge on me and then him and back to me. "I'm a little hungry, but I could, um..."

We wait. She bites her lip and pulls the sheet up to her shoulders, eyes wide.

"What, baby?" I whisper.

"I could do that again."

My cock pulses.

"What part?"

Her smile is full-on. "I liked it all."

All three of us grin.

"But I still have this...thing in my butt and..."

Oh, fuck. Both Blade and I tense up like we've been electrocuted. I'm guessing his excitement's not quite on a par with mine, but a glance down tells me that the man is ready.

"How do you want it?" I ask. "Want to feel used again? Or just..."

She shrugs. "Maybe a little. It's pretty..." A shy smile. "Satisfying."

Blade and I laugh low. My stomach muscles tighten as I let myself take in her body, then his. He turns to give me a better view of his cock and, damn, the man would give me a complex if I weren't naturally confident.

"Want to get dinner together with me, Blade?" I ask, swinging out of bed.

"Sure."

Naked, we head toward the kitchen area, leaving Twyla sputtering on her own in the bed. "Hey!"

I point at the other door. "Bathroom's in there. Get washed up and join us in the kitchen."

"Yes, sir." She salutes, sashaying off with an extra dose of wiggle in her walk, and I grin and the easiness of the whole thing seems like a dream. Too good to be real.

A shiver of unease runs through me. I do my best to ignore it.

In the kitchen, the two of us pull out a cheese plate and a half-bottle of champagne. Most everything's ready, but I suddenly like the idea of being busy while she services us. I'm unnecessarily rewashing grapes when she appears in the doorway.

"Okay," she says, a little bratty around the edges. "I'm here. What next?"

"Suck his balls," I say, without looking up from what I'm doing. I hold my breath.

She lets out a comical little peep/gasp, clearly hesitant. As soon as she moves, I release my lungs and exhale. She steps into the tight space, sits on the rough floor, and edges between the cupboard and Blade's legs, without a bit of help from either of us.

Blade, who's cutting an apple, pauses when she strains up to lick him, but then just carries on with his job. She makes little noises while seeking a better position, using the cabinet and his legs to lean on. No reaction from him.

I glance down, my cock going rock hard at the sight of her mouth wide open around him. "You played with anyone good this week?" I ask, nonchalant.

"Few people. You know that Primal couple teaching

workshops this year?"

"The ones who do the drumming? With the film crew?"

"Yeah. They've been fun." On the floor, Twyla scoots a little, wedging herself between us. One small, warm hand lands on my foot. "Shit they get up to is..." He blows out a breath.

"That good, huh?"

"Hoo, yeah." He gives me a sly look. "You should play with them. Three of you would be something. Anaya's got this ass obsession. You'd go wild."

I glare at him.

Twyla shifts again, moves away from him. "Get the other side, too," Blade says to her, grabbing his cock and holding it to the side to give her access. And, if that's not treating her like an object, I don't know what is.

But she complies. And she likes it, I think, from the way she's squirming. After a second, I think back and remember what we were saying, turn to Blade and say, "Nah, I'm keeping it close to home from now on."

He looks surprised. "Yeah?"

"Yep. The wife's a little possessive."

He laughs, turns back to the counter and moves shit around, since there's nothing left to do.

"Seems to me it goes both ways," he says, while my wife literally sucks his balls. Yeah, I see what we're doing. I feel the wrongness of making myself jealous like this. It's a new fetish for me, but man do I fucking love it.

"Yeah. She's mine." Without looking down, I gather up her soft, wavy hair, side step close to Blade, and hold my cock up so she can get her face in my balls, too. Because, fuck that looks good.

"Look at that," he says, finally acknowledging her. "Got almost all of it in her mouth."

"Good girl," I saw, in awe of this woman who is every-thing—everything. "Suck it deep."

She complies, moaning, already playing with one of her nipples. We're going to have to deal with that, at some point. Do I let her play with herself while she takes care of us? Tonight, yes, but in the future, I might have to edge her orgasms a bit, see if she likes that. "I rawdogged her, man," I tell Blade, who shuffles to the side and watches her take care of me.

"Shit, I miss that part of being married."

"First time for me." She latches that mouth onto the end of my dick and I throw back my head with the shock of pleasure. "Both of us," I manage to grunt out. "Suck us both. Get as much as you can in your mouth."

Okay, so we're pushing way into humiliation here and I'm not sure it's what she wants, but she's eager when she reaches for Blade, slides our fat cockheads together, and does her best to put them in her mouth at once. It's almost impossible to watch without blowing my load, but I do. Because, whatever happens next, now, here, in the future, between us, I don't ever want to forget this. Ever.

After a minute of her struggling to do the impossible, I notice her hand drop to her pussy.

"No touching that pretty little pussy, Twyla," I say, pulling away. "You come only when I say."

I guess we're doing the edging thing today, after all.

31

Twyla

I can't believe how fast I fall into this state of pure, mindless debauchery. This place where nothing can hurt, and everything feels, feels, *feels*. Like I've grown a fresh crop of nerve endings and they're all bursting to life at once.

Zion could tell me to do pretty much anything right now and I'd do it, quickly, automatically, enthusiastically. It's a dangerous place to be, I guess, but it feels unbelievable. And, I realize again, that I *do* trust Zion. And not just now or yesterday, when he opened up about himself. Or when I went and made the seemingly unwise decision to have unprotected sex, maybe even before then. And that's possibly—no, definitely—why I was so hurt when he went out and cheated. We had no love contract between us, no sexual agreement within the confines of the marriage, but I *trusted* him. And that hurt.

I'll never do it again, Twyla. I promise. On my life.

I think of his words, his emotion, his raw intimacy with me and sink back into the scene.

Now, I'm so worked up, so loose and lost and under his spell, that when he tells me I can't come and it's suddenly so close, I can't stand it.

Instead of complying, I impale my mouth on his cock and reach for my clit. A brat is a brat is a brat, I guess.

"Whoa, bro, what's she doing?" asks Blade, clearly stifling a laugh. "You see that?"

With a martyred sigh, Zion, pulls away, leaving me empty and frustrated and bereft. I reach for him and he bends just far enough to grab my face, squeezing my cheeks with his fingers and, in the process opening my mouth. It hurts, but I keep rubbing my clit. He'll need more than this to stop me.

"Fuck, Zed, I had no idea."

"Right?" Zion's cock slaps me across the face, drawing a gasp straight from my lungs. Forgotten, my hand falls away from my clit and, before I know what's happening, he bends and picks me up in the same fireman's carry he used to drag me here.

I squeal as Zion hauls me over to the bench and drops me on my back. "We need the bigger plug," he says.

Blade moves, his stride smooth and graceful, and returns with another plug and lube in hand. "Fuck, she's dripping."

Zion sighs again. "Yeah, but she doesn't listen."

"Sorry, man. You've got your hands full. Brats are tough."

I start to roll off, thinking—or not thinking—maybe I'll run so he can catch me? Maybe I'll piss him off and see what comes next, because I absolutely love this game. But Zion stops me with a hand on my chest. "No coming. No running away. Those are the rules, got it?"

I turn my head away. Zion leans over me, his cock pressed against my abdomen, too high to do any good, and does that face grab thing again, pressing my lips into the plumped-up O of a blow-up sex doll. "You stay still, you don't come, and you do what I say, or..."

"Or what?" I ask, spittle hitting him in the face.

"Or you get treated like the little brat you are."

A thrill runs through me. I want that. I want to be treated that way, even though I've got no godly idea what that is.

So, I twist out of his hands, of course. I struggle, hard, to get off the bench, fall to the floor, crawl to the door, as if running away's what I want. It's not. I don't want to leave. I want to stay here in this cocoon with Zion. I want what he wants to give me. I want the punishment, I want the pain, the anger, the emotion, harsh and pure, beautiful.

I make it outside, which I think they might have allowed, to be honest, get to the top of the porch steps, grab onto the wooden post, and get flattened by Zion, who wraps a hand around my throat, not to choke me, but to hold me.

I look in his eyes, expecting anger, I guess, but it's not there. Not at all. What I see instead sends a flutter to my belly, tightens my chest, and makes me want to kiss him. To take care of him.

It's the earnestness, probably, more than anything. Earnest and sort of shocked, like he's taken a bowling ball to the stomach and he's out of air and doesn't know how to get it back and, the thing is, I'm the same way. I am.

"I feel so much," I say, without meaning to, tears gathering in my eyes.

"Me, too," he replies in a whisper.

"Is it always like this?"

"Never." He shakes his head, brings his face close to mine, shuts his eyes through a series of breaths, and opens them again. "I want to kiss you."

I nod. "Do it."

He leans in, so close his breath licks at my lips first, then his mouth, which he presses, for a quick, urgent moment before pulling away. "Why are you like this?"

"Like what?" I ask, the hurt creeping inexorably in.

"Better." He gulps and runs his hands through his hair, leaving it a mess. "Than anything. Anything I could ask for, think of, dream up. It's like you're..." He grimaces, looks out into the teeming darkness, then down at me again. "Like you're the fantasy I never dared have. Never let myself. How could I, when I didn't even know?"

I nod, caress his face, test the stubble on his jaw, the softness of his lips. "I want to...I want to postpone the scene. Okay?"

He blinks and backs up, giving me way too much space. "You all right?" He looks me up and down, leans in and runs his hands over my waist, arms, shoulders, flanks, as if searching for a wound. "What do you need?"

"I'm good." My mouth twists into a smile. "I just...I want to... I want to be with you. Not a scene. Just...with you."

Blade appears, as if from nowhere, fully dressed, while the two of us are totally naked out here on the porch. "Hey." He walks up and puts a hand on my cheek, his other hand on Zion's. "Love you two," he says, leaning in to kiss my forehead, while he strokes Zion's cheek. He gives Zion a long look, filled with a cryptic message I can't begin to decipher. "You got this, Zion. You do." With a final squeeze, he takes off down the porch steps, leaving the two of us alone. It's a goodbye, a benediction.

I watch him stalk down the dirt path and disappear into the night.

Suddenly nervous, I look up at Zion. "What now?"

Zion

Hell if I know.

She's the one asking me what to do next? I'm the fetish expert here. I can tie a Prusik Head Knot with ease, cut a rope in a jiffy, and come up with any number of filthy scenarios, but she wants me to tell her how to do *this*?

Except, when I stop thinking and check in with my body, my breathing's even, my pulse regular, my brain... content, I guess.

This calm isn't something I've experienced before. It's not the calm I step into before walking onto a set or the quiet emptiness of a hard run. This is a peaceful thing. Serene and wide open.

"Now, we go home."

"To your cabin?"

I shake my head. "To Liev's place. It's where I stay when I'm here. It's like...my family home."

"Okay." She grins. "Can I take this thing out of my butt now?"

"Fuck, baby. Yeah. Here. Let me." She bends forward and I breathe through the desire that swamps back over me when faced with her gorgeous, soft ass in all its fucking glory. I pull her cheeks apart and admire the view. "Fuck, you're amazing."

"Yeah?"

I knead her ass cheeks and breathe deep. "You're so goddamn beautiful."

"Says the man making eyes at my booty."

I give one cheek a light, playful bite, gratified when she lets out the kind of low *ooh* that tells me there's potential for more fun there, and ease the toy from her body, sighing at the sight of her all stretched out and open. "Any time you want to try this again..." I say before planting a quick kiss on her and standing. Something else occurs to me. "You know, I found a shoe the other night. It's back in my room at Liev's. Reckon it might fit you."

"You *do* have my shoe!" She slaps me lightly on the arm. "I knew it!"

"I um, kind of didn't want to let it go? Is that weird? Like, as long as I had it, I'd find you or something. I had a piece of you. I know. It's silly." I shrug.

"It's not silly, it's sort of lovely."

"Come on. Let's get some clothes on."

"I don't have any clothes." She sounds put out, but in a pouty-lipped way that strikes every goddamn chord in my soul. "You ruined my dress."

"I'll buy you a new one." I take her hand and walk her inside.

"That's not the point, Zion. The point is that I've got nothing to wear. Right now." She still sounds annoyed, but she's not pulling her hand away, and that—just that— feels meaningful.

"Here," I bend and pick up my T-shirt, turn it right side out and slide it over her head. She purrs a little, which isn't a thing I knew humans could do.

It makes me smile.

"Okay. But you can still buy me a dress."

"All the dresses."

She rolls her eyes.

I look around and straighten up a few things, head into the kitchen and grab the cheese and fruit tray, along with the champagne, and shove them both into a picnic basket. "Come on."

She slips on her shoes and I close up the shack behind us, planning to come back to clean before the next scheduled scene in the morning. Around us, the air is charged, the humidity high.

"Smells like rain's coming," Twyla says.

"We need it." I pause at the top of the porch steps and suck in the heavy air, listen to the night creatures, all stirred up, and look at Twyla. "I want to do it again."

Her eyebrows lift high. "The kidnapping?"

Lighting strikes, somewhere in the distance, startling us closer together.

After eyeing the sky for a minute, I shake my head, let my eyes slide to her mouth, let the heat take me, and the need. "I wanna do the other thing." And then, like the good kinkster I am, I spell it out for her. "I want to kiss you."

"Do it," she says, stepping closer.

"I will. I need...a second."

"Okay." She watches me, those eyes big and dark and luminous.

My gaze roams her face until it settles on her mouth. It's a wide mouth, plump, but not quite bee stung. I love the little divot at the top, so neat and pert. I want to lick it, taste it. Taste her tongue, smile, sip at the moans she makes when all her pleasure overflows.

"Got to get home before the rain," I say. To extend the moment? To put it off out of fear that I'll get it wrong or it won't live up to expectations or maybe there's an edge of that other thing that says I'm not fit for love. That love's for other people, this kiss is a commitment and—

Throughout my inner diatribe, she doesn't budge, her attention unwavering, the weight of her stare as warm as a blanket. "Let's go, then."

I'm on her before my brain gives me more excuses.

I grab her face, press my mouth to hers, and it's *nothing* like an on-screen kiss. It's electric, wild, and so goddamn frightening. Her lips are warm and soft and it's not like anything else at all. On set kissing's just a movement. This is a delving inside myself, inside her. It's reaching in and plucking out all the tender parts and sharing them between us. It's beautiful and it hurts and I tear myself away for fear of losing my mind just as lightning lights up the sky and sets my hair on end. Up high, the treetops dance with a sudden gust of wind that hints at more than a little summer storm.

I want another kiss, but my wildly thumping heart needs a minute to recover from the first one.

"Fuck, Twyla. That was—"

Thunder cracks around us—under us—and we've suddenly got no choice but to go back in or race home and I need to be inside my woman the next time I kiss her. In my bed. Our bed.

"Take this," I say, passing the basket to her. "Hold it tight."

"Why?"

Before she can protest, I bend over, and throw her over my shoulder again, enjoying her surprise and the slight struggle, then the soft, perfect feel of her body laid over mine.

"What are you doing, Zion?"

Thunder rolls over our heads.

"Carryin' you home?"

"Why?" she squeals.

"Storm's coming and you can't run in those shoes."

I take off into the night as fast I dare, more careful of my giggling wife on my back than I've been of anything in my whole life.

I've never had anything so precious. And never wanted anything more.

32

Twyla

"Put me down!" I yell again, laughing like a kid.

Zion tightens his hold and snarls, "*Mine*," like a lion with a fresh kill. Or, I don't know, a six-year-old with a new toy.

"You're acting like an ass," I yell at him from where he's got me slung over his shoulders. "Put me down!"

"Yeah? Well you're..." He cranes his neck so his eyes meet mine and whatever he sees makes him change tacks. "Only with you, Twy. I'm only like this with you."

"Oh, I'm so honored," I say in a high, fake voice. But really, I kind of am? Not honored, exactly, but sort of... proud? Is that weird? Yes. Yes, clearly it is, but when I think of it, as I grip the basket in one hand and rub the thick muscle along his shoulder with the other, I really do enjoy feeling like I'm his prey. I mean, along with most everything we did today, this works for me. A lot.

By the time we make it to the top of a long, steady rise, he's out of breath.

I twist in his hold. "Come on. Seriously. I can walk barefoot."

"No." He slaps my ass and I wriggle harder. "I'm carrying you home. It's a...a rite of passage or something."

"How much farther is it?" I ask, struggling in earnest to get out. I swear the creatures in the woods around us ramp up, too, like we're in sync and then, like the whole world's in on it, thunder rumbles. "I'm hungry, it's about to storm, and—"

"And we've got kissing to do. Lots of kissing."

Oh, yes. I want that.

My breath's shuddering. My entire body's trembling, despite the heat, the humidity, the closeness of our bodies. Every piece of me, every cell or fiber is shaking with excitement.

Our last kiss wasn't nearly enough, barely a kiss, even and somehow still the most passionate thing I've experienced in my life.

It occurs to me, as he pounds up the path leading between empty craft stalls, that I've never felt this way with another human being.

This week alone, I've been through pretty much every emotion with Zion: anger and jealousy and hurt. *So much hurt.* Excitement and anticipation and tenderness and this other thing. This deep pulsing thing that I've never felt. Not once, despite a life I'd say has been pretty well-lived.

It's *him.* Zion Mason. The only human alive who's

capable of turning me into a writhing, hissing monster one minute, and a slave to desire the next. As if to underscore my feelings, the sky rumbles, low, but close, the wind sending the entire world into turmoil.

"Let me go."

"No." The refusal's final, solid. I crane my neck and arch my entire body for a glimpse at his smug expression.

Our eyes meet. "Do I have to safe word you right now?"

With an irritated sigh, he shifts my weight to his front with annoying ease and slowly releases me, sliding my front down his with an erotic, languorous friction that directly contrasts with the wild, frenzied storm brewing all around us. I've got to force myself not to react, because if I do, we'll end up doing it right here and then we'll definitely get caught in the rain. Probably get brained by a falling branch. Also, our cheese plate will get soaked and I really want that cheese.

He grabs my hand and we set off just as the sky above flashes bright, the lightning close enough to raise the hair on my arms.

"God, you're beautiful."

"Beautiful?" I snort. "I'm passably pretty, but beautiful, I am not."

He stops and turns me toward him and, even in the dark, I can see that he's unhappy. "Pretty? Are you kidding?" He makes an ugly scratching sound, low in his throat, echoed by another rumble of thunder. "You'll never be pretty, Twyla."

"Wow." I blink, gobsmacked. "That's not very—"

"Pretty's *nothing*. What's pretty?" He's close now. His face inches from mine. All thoughts of racing for shelter are gone. "Pretty's forgettable. Easy."

I wait, breath held. The sky lights up, the storm so close, I see the jagged imprint out of the corner of my eye.

"No, what you are is...is...devastating, but in a good way. In a deep way, to my soul. Healing, moving, like music. But not the commercial shit they play on the radio." He steps in so close I feel the humid heat pumping off him, smell his sweat. "You're one of those songs you can't help but listen to over and over. Those songs aren't fuckin' pretty. *Hell*, no." More thunder and the wild hiss and chirp of insects ramps up, their song a frantic counterpoint to the rushing in my heart. "They're the ones that make you feel *everything*. They tear you open at the belly, rip out your guts and rearrange them before sending you on your way, a changed man."

His hand comes up and skims the side of my face, from my forehead to my chin. I don't move. I can't. The caress is so tender, it nails me in place.

"You're like that." His voice is low, pained. "I knew the first time I saw you, you were the most... *Pretty?*" He scoffs. "Dammit, Twyla, you're not some little storm, you're a *hurricane*. You're a goddamn earthquake, rearranging the face of the planet."

I open my mouth, but he moves in tight, our body heat sizzling. "You don't sail a thousand ships, you *pulverize* them." Every word puffs hot against my lips. "Cast them against the goddamn cliffs 'til there's nothing left but dust." He pulls away, just an inch or two, his stare takes in my face like a rock skipping on water—light touches to my nose, my eyes, down to my mouth. "You've destroyed me, Twyla. Rearranged me, wrecked me. I'm ruined. *Pulverized.*"

Throughout this speech something inside me has broken off or opened up. It's almost painful how deep he's hit with his words, but like the pain he's described, it feels right.

The best things in life aren't skin deep, after all. They inhabit every cell, every atom of our being. That's what Zion's just done with his words. He's taken me over, moved straight in—to my heart, my bones, my soul.

"Zion," I sigh, not knowing what to say and then, for some reason I can't fathom, I apologize. For hurting him? For making him want me this way? For seeing the real man behind the many masks and tearing them off one by one?

"I'm sorry," I manage to whisper again, though it's hard when our mouths are almost touching and the wind's whipping up. I want to kiss him, but I won't break his golden rule again. *He* has to do it. It's his choice. I'm hobbled by our closeness. If I move, we'll touch.

"You should be sorry." His hand slides forward, digs into my hair, holds my head perfectly still. Clouds skitter above us, blocking out the moon, closing us in.

I don't fight it. I don't move at all. I breathe out of sheer necessity.

"You should be sorry, doin' this to me." I feel more

than see his mouth flatten, curving down at the edges into a bitter smile. "Making me feel all this..." In the next flash from above, I see his expression edging toward disbelief. "All this *shit*." Those lips turn up, adding a little sweet to the bitterness. "Eloquent, right?" He sighs, leans in, rubs the tip of his nose to mine. His breathing's shaky, cutting in and out the way mine does when I'm nervous, when something matters. Like right this second. "I want to kiss you again. Again."

I stare at his big, dark silhouette. "I'm not stopping you."

His nod's just a nudging of noses. He huffs out a pained, silent laugh. "I'm terrified, Twyla."

"I won't hurt you," I whisper, with a smile he can't see. "Want me to..."

"I've never done this before. I mean, earlier didn't count, right? Just a brush. Just learning. I've never done the real deal."

"Remember the red carpet?" Thunder shakes everything and in the ensuing burst of light, my eyes seek his. It's odd, this close up. Like seeing a different person, or a younger, innocent version of him. "That was a kiss."

"That was for show. Plastic. I've never..."

"Never what?" My breath's caught tight in my lungs. I swear the night noises stop. Not a cricket stirs around us. Even the sky takes a breath.

"Never cared." He inhales, smelling me, I think, taking more of me in. His hands tighten in my hair, making my roots sting, sending my already frantic pulse into overdrive. "God, Twyla, you're so fuckin'..."

Thunder shakes the entire world as he dives that final inch and puts his lips to mine. It's another perfect first— stiff and awkward and so thrilling I might faint. The cool, dry friction of skin, just a hint of movement, just a brief exploration. I shut my eyes, working hard to memorize this, to bottle it up inside me, enclose it in my heart.

He moans and the sound's like nothing I've ever heard—heartfelt and deep and wounded and *mine*. Mine in a way nothing's ever been.

My hands, which somehow found their way to his shoulders, wrap around him, pulling him closer, my nails digging deep, marking his flesh.

Another sweep of our mouths, another, another, so tender, so focused, holding back, making it last. Where'd all these nerve endings come from? Each touch is tearing at my insides, twisting my heart, and it hurts, it *hurts*.

"I need you," he mutters against me, his mouth opening the slightest bit, our kiss getting wetter, warmer, deeper, digging roots inside my heart. He pulls away, I chase him a bit, then he tilts his head and consumes me like a man starved.

The sky bursts open. A prayer answered.

We're soaked in seconds, the rain cool and enveloping and barely noticeable when his tongue slides against my lips.

"Oh, fuck," he says, with another slow slide, then another, more urgent. "Let me in, baby. Let me taste you."

With a heart-wrenching sob, I open up, just enough for his tongue to ease in and explore and, this, oh, this isn't a mere kiss, it's a plundering, an invasion, a transfer of fucking ownership. I'm his now. All his.

And he's *mine.*

My tongue sweeps out to meet his, to tangle and tease, tasting the essence of Zion, smelling the mineral perfume of rain sizzling on dry earth, the thrilling burst of ozone from a strike that's much too close for comfort. As if we cared about something as inconsequential as weather. How can we, when we're a part of it?

We are the spark that lit up this night. We are the crack of lightning, the boom of thunder.

Growling, he bends at the knees, letting go of my hair long enough to slide those big arms down my back. He squeezes my ass and then scoops low. I gasp and shriek when he picks me up again, my legs going instinctively around his waist. He looks over my shoulder, moves a few steps and presses me against a tree.

"I want to fucking *eat* you," he says before diving in to devour my mouth. He's snarling and groaning, biting and licking and consuming like if he could, he'd do it.

But I don't want that. And maybe that's what's so good about us together. I won't go down without a fight.

"I want to *own* you, you little brat."

"Yeah?" I reach up to pull his wet hair, lose my grip and twist in order to shift his head to where I want it, then bite his lip so hard it draws blood and a long, delicious *oooooh* from his lungs. "Not if I own you first, you big jerk."

His delighted laugh's the best sound I've ever heard.

The pungent scents of blood and rain and rich dirt forever entwine in my body as his. *Ours.*

He opens his mouth and, for a split second, the world goes quiet, as if even the storm's leaning in to hear his next words. And they break me wide open.

33

Zion

"I love you, Twyla." I tap my breastbone, working to catch my breath. "I fucking love you."

There. It's out. As soon as I've said it, I'm lighter, my chest isn't quite so tight, the ball in my gut's unwinding. The tree we're leaning against shakes, the woods around us strobing bright and fast, but nowhere near as frantic as the beating of my goddamn heart.

"I've loved you forever. Before camp, even. Before everything."

All I can do is kiss her hard, the taste of rain and copper pure poetry in my mouth. The snap of ozone in the air proof of the alchemy happening here—the two of us coming together the way nature intended. The way we were meant to, from the very start. From before we ever met. Sanctified by blood and Mother Nature.

"Fuck. You mean so much to me, Twyla," I say, each word punctuating a kiss, digging all this emotion out of me, like pulling splinters from my skin, shards of glass from my soul. The streaming water washing me clean. "You're everything. You're beautiful." A kiss, another. It fucking hurts, but in the best possible way. Like the sting of my palm to her ass, like the pain of rope burn or the dull ache of a good bruise. It's a hurt I'll seek over and over. I'll never let it go.

It's mine now. *Ours*.

"You're my wife," I tell her, as if she doesn't know that. As if that piece of paper we signed bestows anything more than this night's blessed us with. "Will you stay my wife? Give me a chance to show you who I am and how much you matter to me?"

I'm blathering at this point, but who can blame my brain for not functioning with all these endorphins flowing through it? I laugh at how high I feel and push my denim-clad erection into the snug cradle of her crotch, which is bare under the soaking wet T-shirt, now molded to her tits. She's a wet dream, literally.

I kiss her again, deep and tender and real, then pull slowly away. For a split second, I worry that if we stop, we'll come to our senses—or at least she will—and this'll be over. Just a dream. A fantasy, here and gone before we know it.

"Put it in me," she says, an out of breath siren. A succubus, sucking all the bad from me and leaving nothing but good. "Come on."

We reach for my button together, work the zipper down, and I rub my crown through her slippery heat before pressing in.

"God, yes." She tilts her hips and I push deeper and the warmth of her, the pure, painful bliss, envelopes me.

I shift her weight, shove her thighs up and back as far as they'll go and sink deep with a groan. Then, fuck, then she grabs my face and puts that mouth on mine and turns this into something I've never had in my life.

That sets me off, raging like something primitive and bestial. All I can do is take her. Hard, rough, but uncomplicated. Pure. She tilts her head against the tree, claws my back, clenches tight around me as I pulse hard inside her, coming before I've given my body permission.

"Oh, fuck."

She leans in and takes my mouth, pulls my hair, clasps my cock with her cunt, moans and takes me.

"Fuck, baby. Fuck, you feel good."

"Zion," she cries. Just my name. My real name, on her mouth, as she kisses mine, and that's it. We're done. Gone.

Eyes screwed shut, I tighten my ass and plunge deep, emptying my aching balls inside her, picturing a future with babies and kisses and love, so much love. A home full of it. It hurts to imagine it, see it, feel it in my bones and balls, but I let it come. I couldn't stop if I tried.

We're soaked, I notice, vaguely, as I come back to reality. I slowly pull out. We groan and share a smile. I look down at my goose bump covered chest, her dark nipples highlighted by the see-through T-shirt, lower, to where I'm dripping from her. If I had a free hand, I'd reach down and push it back in, put my sticky fingers in her mouth, make her lick me off while I kiss her.

She looks soft and lost, her already plush lips red and swollen. All I can do is watch her. All I can do is hold on.

Twyla must see all of this on my face.

Slowly, her expression changes. "What's wrong?" she asks. "What is it?"

And here's where it gets hard. Harder. Impossible. The moment when telling the truth has the potential to hurt me the most and simultaneously give me what I want. I had no idea it would feel like this. None. Although, maybe that's a lie, because you don't avoid kissing your whole life out of fear that it'll be good and quick and easy before moving on to something else. But, hell, who am I to hold back when this woman took the scary-ass step to follow me to camp?

"I'm scared," I admit, out here being baptized by the rain and her lips. "I don't know how to be with someone. I'll fuck it up. For sure."

She smiles. "Of course you will. We both will. But not like you did before, okay?"

"I'd rather die."

"I know that now. I know you. I trust you." Her nod is slow and thoughtful. "What if whatever we do, we do it together? We discuss and agree before scening or bringing someone else in?"

"I don't need anyone else."

"But at some point, you might *want* someone else." Her eyes dance. "I saw the way you looked at Blade's dick tonight."

"He's hot," I say with a grin.

"Well, you two touching opened up a whole new world of fantasies for me."

"Yeah?" Excitement rises, fresh and new from the ashes of the half-man I used to be.

"Definitely."

Her hand plays with my soaking wet hair and cups my ear before she moves in. It takes me a second to realize she's giving me her lips for a kiss.

I plant one on her—quick and casual, as if we do this every day.

She leans back with a happy sigh. "My parents mess up constantly, Zion. It's what happens when you try hard at anything. You mess up, right? But then you apologize and you try again, harder. It's work. Yeah?"

"I'm a hard worker," I tell her, a grin springing up from out of nowhere.

"Oh, I know." She nuzzles me and then pats my shoulder until I release her fully. Her feet slide to the ground.

I don't move away, though. I love boxing her in. And then, because I'm allowed to, because it's easy and feels right, I lean down and move in to kiss her and she tilts her head back, the way I've seen people do, and we kiss, the zing so bright it resonates in my spine, my eyeballs, the tip of my cock.

"You know what feels good?" she asks, that secret smirk twisting my insides up in the best way.

"What, baby?"

"Dinner. And sex in an actual bed. Oh!" Her expression goes bright, as if she's just gotten an amazing idea.

"And kissing." Her lips pull at mine, releasing me with a wet sound. "Lots..." Another kiss. "And lots..." Another. "Of kissing. Just kissing and—"

I don't let her finish the sentence. She's already slung over my shoulder again and I'm stalking toward the big house, where my bed's ready and waiting, the sheets messy from one too many tortured nights of thinking of her and wanting her and not getting that *keeping* her was what I'd wanted all along.

"Put me down!" she wails, giggling and slapping my thigh.

"You safe-wording?" I ask over my shoulder.

When she doesn't make a peep, I laughingly smack her thick ass and grab it tight, then turn my head to kiss and bite it. "Mine. *My* gorgeous ass."

She uses her free hand to grab onto me, twists her body like she's trying to get down, and makes a frustrated sound. I tighten my hold. "What are you trying to do? Fall on your head?"

"I want to bite your butt, too!"

"Later. In my bed. I'll let you bite me."

She snorts. "No you won't. You'll make me fight for it."

I smile. "Damn straight I will. And you'll love it."

With a loud theatrical sigh, she smacks my arm, then squirms until she can sink her teeth into it.

"You're a pest."

"But you love me," she says.

I can do nothing but agree, although love seems like

such a tepid word for the way my insides are being annihilated by all these *feelings*.

That's it, isn't it? I get it now. The messed-up, wonderful, unavoidable truth: You've got to raze yourself to the ground before building back up again.

And the pain? The pain's the thing that tells you it was all worthwhile.

Twyla

I don't think I've ever been wetter than I am right now. Soaked and chilly, but warm inside with a glow that's got nothing to do with Zion's body heat and everything to do with his heart. He's given it to me and it's the most precious gift I've ever had.

I sigh happily as he carries me, caveman style, through a gate, up a slick set of paving stones edged with old boxwoods, then up a few steps, onto a porch. Inside, the house is lit up, but out here it's dark and sheltered from the rain and it feels like a private little world only the two of us inhabit.

In the soft glow of the window, with the rain pelting the porch roof, our bodies steaming in the night, he slowly drops me and, without thinking, I strain up for another drugging kiss. Just one more out here before heading in and bursting this perfect bubble.

The overhead light comes on, the door flies open. Cringing, I turn, and startle at a silhouette that definitely should not be here.

"Gigi?"

"Surprise!" yells my best friend with an apologetic grimace. "I, um. Wow. Whoa. Stop the presses. Look at you." She blinks down at the shirt that felt like more than enough coverage when we left the shack. Right now, it's like a window pane into my new debauched existence.

"What are you doing here?" I ask, too destabilized by her presence to act anything but shocked. "How'd you get here?"

"Aaaaaan airplane." She looks up at Zion and puts out a hand. "Hey! Sexiest Man Alive. We met at the wedding, but I'm not sure if you—"

"Gigi," he says, sounding calm and collected, which is totally unfair. "Good to see you again."

"Oh, my god." Gigi grins, wide, as she takes us both in. Zion, naked from the waist up, his hair clinging to his skull in a way that only highlights those cheekbones of his, those lips. God, those lips. I'm sure I look like a drowned rat. "You two... This is so much better than anything I could have imagined. Hold on. I need a picture, just for—"

"No pictures. Come inside." Liev's voice cuts through, from behind Gigi. "Let's get you a shower." He looks us up and down, his face somehow conveying humor or happiness without actually cracking a smile. "And some clothes."

"Is it them?" Lamé calls from farther inside the house. "If it's them, make them wait! I want to catch the post-coital glow before it fades into sad domesticity. Move. Move, I want to see the hedonistic mess of their..."

Their voice trails off the minute they pop around the doorframe, joined a second later by Grace.

"Here we are!" I say, wishing they'd all disappear and give us a few more hours alone.

"Shoulda stayed at the shack," mutters Zion out the side of his mouth.

They all grin. Every last one of them. And, yes, it's all kind of funny in a way, but it's also really freezing and this has been a big, big night for the two of us. I'd really rather be—

"Wait a second." I look at Gigi, my brain coming back online. "What's going on? Seriously. Why are you here?"

She hesitates, which is so unlike her, a sense of foreboding takes me over.

"Tell me. What is it? My parents? Are they okay? They're on the cruise, right? I told them I'd be off-line and out of—"

"No. No, they're fine. I talked to Esme and she's..." Gigi gives a tight little smile with a wink and a shimmy, the whole move so very much my mother that I huff out a laugh, despite the tension that's taken everything over. "She's great. They're great. Happy as larks, dancing their way through retirement like a pair of rabid teenagers."

"Okay. So?"

Nobody speaks.

Zion goes tense and hard behind me. "This about me?"

"Well." Gigi glances at Liev, then looks up at Zion. "Kinda."

I feel him nod, his arms drop, he steps away. I shiver harder the moment I lose his body heat.

When I look up at his face, it's gone hard, jaw set, his features blank. "I'll take care of it." He gives a single, stoic nod and moves toward the door, leaving me alone on the porch.

Everybody shifts aside to let him in except for Lamé. "Okay, sure, Kinky Crusader," they say, stopping him with a long-nailed finger to the chest. "Except you might want to find out what happened before throwing on the old studded cape and revving off to save the day in the Kink Mobile."

"What happened?" he asks, without a hint of curiosity.

"They're here."

"Who?"

"Come inside and we'll tell you." Liev leans out to grab my hand and Zion's shoulder and hauls us in before slamming the door.

"Shower first," says Grace, bless her heart. "Then talk."

"Would you all mind..." Zion sweeps his arm out and everyone parts to let us up the wide, wooden staircase. He stays close behind me the whole time, keeping my backside hidden from their view.

We make it up and into a bathroom, where he gets out a pile of soft towels. "I'll bring you clothes." He glances down at my bottom, then back up, a little heat back in his eyes. "You need help with..."

Every muscle in my body wants to melt into his arms,

but we've got a crowd waiting for us downstairs. "I've got it." I bite my lip. "For now."

"Okay." He starts to go and turns back, eyes clear, expression earnest. "I'm gonna fix this."

Something happens in my chest, expanding, opening, sparking with this new life we're choosing for ourselves. "I know."

"And then I'm fucking your ass."

Heat washes over me as I grin up at him. "You'd better."

"Just so we're on the same page."

My smile widens. "We are."

"I adore you."

"Me, too."

"Okay. Bye."

I give him a finger wave and move to turn the shower on.

He watches my butt like a lion on a hunt then, with a pained groan, turns to go.

34

———

I stare at the phone, feeling empty inside—blank.

There I am again, only this time, I'm not the one caught with my pants down. This time, it's Twyla, on the day of the spanking workshop, caught in all her lush, well-lit glory. She's bent over the bench in that fluorescent yellow bikini, her beautiful ass presented for all the world to see while I smack it with my open palm.

It's an out of body experience seeing that moment again. The pain and possession and jealousy of it, along with a good dose of pleasure.

Now, all I feel is rage that someone stole that moment from us.

The irony is that the site that "broke" the video, claimed it was that other woman, not Twyla, getting her ass beaten. They don't even realize it's her.

That's one blessing, I guess, because watching that video has made my insides gritty and rough. And the click-bait headline—***Slut takes spanking from Zion Mason—at private adult Sex Camp: click for full video***—makes me want to smash the world.

I've destroyed everything. Not just Twyla's career and my own, but the entire camp experience.

For everyone. Anonymity, privacy, security. Those were the cornerstones of this place. And now, they're gone. Poof. With a leaked video that should never have been taken, much less gotten out.

"Who did this?"

"We've tracked it and, well, it's a combination of things," says Grace, looking annoyed. "First off, people are filming you because you're you."

"Which everyone already knew, apparently."

She shrugs. "This getting out was a mistake, from what we've gleaned. You know how it is."

"Yeah, well, we've got a no phones policy for a reason. They took the video and posted to their private FetLife account," says Liev. "Got screenshotted. Gossip site picked it up. The culprit's already been asked to leave and banned from camp, but, the damage is done."

"I'll go," I say, feeling dull inside. "Get the PR people to create a distraction someplace else. Keep the media from finding the camp and bringing—"

"No." Liev gives the room's other occupants a long, slow look. "We've discussed it and that's not the solution."

"Look. This is *my* problem, I created this. I need to handle it. And I can. I will." I look at Twyla, dressed in

Grace's clothes, a sweatshirt of mine on top, all wrapped up in a blanket, seated on the sofa between Gigi and Lamé. She's pale and tiny and exhausted. Big surprise, right? After the intense scene we lived through, then the kissing and everything that happened between us. Now this nightmare. "I won't let anything bad happen. I'll distract the tabloids with some bigger fiasco. That's the—"

"There's no *I* here, Zion." Twyla's staring right back at me. "There are two of us now. That's how this works."

"*All* of us," says Grace.

Gigi overlaps with, "There's no I in team."

"Or in family," Lamé joins in.

"Well, actually, there's an i, but the idea's—"

"We need to—"

"Stop!" I explode to standing in the middle of Liev and Grace's cozy living room, with its simple furnishings and warm lights, and art everywhere. It's much too civilized an environment for this. For me. "I'm going. Now."

Liev gets up. "Sit down," he growls, looking at me with low-level intimidation in his expression, if not actual aggression. It's the sort of look I imagine a dad might give his kid before telling him he's grounded. A no-nonsense mix of exasperation and affection that I've never been on the receiving end of.

"We need a plan." He points at the armchair I've just left. "If you could hang out for a few more minutes, we'll discuss it like the family we are, and take it to—"

A loud banging starts up from the front of the house.

"Shit," Liev mutters, following as I stalk down the hall to get it.

I throw open the door to see Benji and Max, looking deadly serious. "We've got visitors."

"Where?"

"Front entrance," Benji says, a muscle ticking in his jaw. "Couple men in a rental car. They're doing their best to get in."

"I saw cameras."

"Paps." I nod once. "I'll go. If I distract them, give them the shots they want, we can get campers out the back way. Give you time to evacuate."

"Like hell," says Liev who's come up beside me. "We do that, they'll be back next year. We'll have people trying to get in every summer. This place'll turn into a circus. We'll have to shut down."

"Or move," Grace adds from behind me.

"This is ridiculous. They're here for me. I'll go. That's it."

"*We'll* go." Twyla sidles up beside me, all cute in Grace's too-tight sweatpants and my oversized hoodie, wearing an expression that says she is not to be fucked with.

"*Oooooooor...*" Suddenly, Lamé's sliding into the front entryway. "We could trick them."

"How?" asks Liev, watching them through narrowed eyes.

"Make them think we're something else."

"Like what?" I ask, disbelievingly. Even in casual wear, there's a look to us that says we're not an average group. No way can the mix of campers down there pass as anything but kinksters. "A corporate retreat?"

"Like one of those team building things." Gigi, Twyla's friend and agent, whose presence at camp seems to surprise no one but me, pops out from behind Lamé. "Except instead of a tree course, you get beaten by Barry in accounting."

"Oooooh, I like that," Lamé says excitedly. "Or, or... What about like a motorcycle club?"

"Family reunion?" proposes Gigi.

"Knitters' convention?" Lamé throws back.

Gigi yells, "Kinky super heroes!"

"Come inside." Grace's voice rises above the others. "You're letting the bugs in."

"Oh, shit. Sorry," I say.

"Is it still storming out there?" asks Grace.

"Drizzling," I tell her. "Supposed to keep going all night, though."

"And tomorrow."

"Yeah?" I consider. "That's good."

"Why?" Grace gives me a curious look.

"It'll keep people indoors. They can't catch anything on their telephoto lenses if everyone's staying inside."

"Good point." She nods.

"And that might buy us some time," Twyla grasps my elbow.

"For what?" I ask her.

"Lamé's idea," she says. "I think it could work."

"How?" I look at all the faces.

"You know those cameras filming the documentary?" Lamé asks. "With the Primals?"

"Yep." Liev's nodding. "That's right."

"There's a sound person and everything," Twyla says.

"They got permission," says Liev. "I don't think they're the ones who leaked the—"

"Oh my god..." says Gigi, who, like me, has caught on.

"What is it?" asks Max. "What am I missing?"

"What if... we make them think we're shooting a film?" Twyla grins at Lamé.

"Like, this whole place is a set?" Max is catching on.

"Exactly."

"We've got a ton of extras." Twyla's spitballing.

"Other roles, too." I look at Benji, who's in jeans and a T-shirt. "You could be crew."

"I call costumes!" yells Lamé. "I was *born* to do costumes."

As everybody shouts out ideas, too fast to keep track of, my brain starts rolling through options. We could transform the camp pretty easily, make the spaces into things they're not. We'd take down the pet pens and turn the Sex-o-drome tent into an outdoor eating area. Cast stays in the cabins, the tents are extras. The only overtly kinky areas, like the Dungeon, would have to remain what they are.

Which is fine, given the leaked footage. The film will have to have a kink element.

"What if you're undercover in a kink club?" Twyla asks, proving that we're headed in the same direction. "It's a big ask. Can we make it stick?"

"What if we go on the attack," Gigi joins in. "Say, I get both your PR teams to reach out to one or two outlets. Like, I don't know, *Entertainment Tonight* or something.

And let them come in and film." Liev opens his mouth and Gigi pushes right through. "Specific areas only."

"Show the bench where I was spanked. Set up lights and so on to make it look real."

I meet Liev's gaze. "It's a lot of work."

"We can do it." Lamé stands tall.

"Everyone'll pitch in," Benji agrees. "Hell, aren't BarbieMoll and Kenwah roadies for some huge band? Isn't that their day job? Those people get shit done."

"This means trusting everyone," Grace says, watching me closely. "This means opening your life up, to the other campers, at least. It means going to them with the problem and letting them help solve it."

I nod. "I know."

"It means sharing the load, Zion. Opening up. Being real. Can you handle that?" Liev and Grace and Lamé wait, knowing what a huge step this is for me. They want to be a big family? Where I come from, family's equivalent to nothing but pain, loneliness, shame. On a baser level, it's hunger and filth. Dirt poor's an expression for a reason.

I look from one face to another—Benji, Max, Gigi, Lamé, Grace, Liev...Twyla.

"We can handle it," she says in the steady, rich voice that feels like floating on my back in warm waves, looking up at the stars. She's watching me, her eyes blazing with their singular combination of soulful and kind, bratty and strong. There's an inner power to Twyla that shines through, no matter what she does. A strength that's bone-deep.

And she's mine. Not just to play with and pretend with like we do here, like we did out there in an entirely different way, but for real. Right here, in this moment, she's giving me something greater than just her body, her career, her pleasure. This is faith. Belief. In me.

"Yeah?" I ask and then, because she's so damn solid, I turn and look at the others, too. "We can do this."

Twyla smiles and I swear the crash of thunder overhead's a direct response from the sky. An agreement. A confirmation. "We can. Together." She strains up and tilts her head back and, without thinking I bend down and meet her lips with mine. I ignore the gasps from the people around us and focus on the hot press of her mouth, the quick flick of her tongue, the scrape of teeth and then one word that seals my fate to the end of my days. "Mine."

The room breaks out in applause, Twyla smiles against my mouth, which turns into a giggle that I sip at like fine wine. "Mine," I whisper back, certain, for the first time in my life, that everything I want is right here.

"Y'all better wrap that up if we're gonna do this," says Gigi, grinning like a fool.

"Yeah." Lamé gives me a slow up and down. "Someone needs to make you look like a movie star."

Eighteen hours later…
Twyla

"This won't work." I sink onto a lounge chair beside the pool, completely exhausted. And discouraged.

"It'll work." Gigi hands me a glass of water and flops down into the chair beside me. "Shit, why didn't you tell me it was wet?"

"Everything's wet. It's been raining all day."

"Ugh. Great. I'll have to change before the *ET* people get here. No way I'm getting caught on camera looking like crap."

"So, Enid Connor's here? For real? Like *the* Enid Connor?" I still can't believe Zion convinced her to come here, at a moment's notice. But then, I had no idea she was a closet kinkster herself. I mean, now that I know it, some of her filming choices make so much more sense. But I guess Zion knew—or had an inkling—and his people called and asked for a favor and then she and Zion talked on the phone for an hour last night and she flew out from California. For the cause, she said. But also, I'm guessing, because this is the kind of thing that would push her career into the stratosphere. As long as none of it implodes.

"Yep. In her cabin, just getting ready for our fifth day of shooting."

"First."

"Fifth," Gigi corrects me. "You've been shooting since you left DC, remember? That's the story." Someone beyond the pool area yells, another voice replies, and a group of people goes by, carrying something. They're dressed in day clothes, which is so weird to see it takes me a second to realize I've seen most of them in various states of undress—and probably in flagrante, as well.

"Right. Crap." I squeeze my temples and bend over, wishing we had more time or more options or, I don't know, a real project to work on. "We've aimed too high, Geege. Something's going to give."

"Mm mm." She sips at her soda and eyes the empty pool. "Soon as all the industry people leave, I'm stripping off and diving in there. Rain or shine." She turns my way, sliding her sunglasses down to give me The Stare. "And you are gonna put on whatever costume Lamé throws at you and just, you know, be the kinky sex goddess you are. For the cameras this time, instead of for your annoyingly gorgeous husband." Her eyes go narrow. "And Blade. And whoever else your husband decides to share you with in the future."

"Hey, it was my choice. I'm the one who wanted to do it with two men." I sniff and then, just to bug her, mostly, I say, "And maybe I'll ask for more in the future. Maybe I'll let him share me with—"

"Goddamn it, Twyla, I'm just jealous."

"Jealous? Why? You're not into this stuff, are you?"

She gives a nonchalant shrug. "Might be."

I sit forward so fast I spill water down my front. "Serious?"

"If I'd known they looked like Blade and Benji around here, I'd have come sooner."

I snort and sink back into the chair. "I'm just..." I shake my head. "Nobody's gonna believe that it's *me* in that first video."

"Oh, didn't I tell you? It's all over. Boom. Done. You *are* the woman in the video. We leaked the news this morning. It's everywhere."

"They bought it?"

She nods, looking happily sly. "Aaaaaaand, the assface responsible for all of this is catching a lot of flack on social."

"Hey! I've been looking for you everywhere." Max runs up, breathing hard. "We've got news."

"Okay." I brace for whatever's next. Good, bad. Life-changing. "Okay. I'm ready."

Max gives me that cheeky little snaggletooth grin that I love so much and I instantly relax a notch or two. "Two big studio execs showed up and, guess what?"

I pop out of my seat like a jack-in-the-box, all nerves and excitement. "What? Who? Why are they here? What did Zion do?"

"He signed on for a fourth *Everwars* movie."

In the next breath, all the stress pours out, leaving me almost boneless with relief. "They're doing it? They agreed?"

She nods, her lips going tight with suppressed glee. "And guess who's headlining with him—at their request?"

I stare. "Who?"

"You, you dingdong." Gigi slaps my arm and squeezes it tight. I stare at her hand for a few numb seconds, still not getting what this means exactly. "She means you. That's what I was trying to tell you. They reached out to me a couple hours ago and we finally hammered things out. A little rushed, but as of the release of yesterday's video, you're a hot commodity."

A hot commodity? Headlining with Zion? My *actual* husband, Zion? Slowly, the cloud of confusion lifts and in its wake, there's fear and intimidation, the notion that I'm not good enough or big enough for this. "What? I'm not an action star. Oh no, am I going to have to wear a harness and jump and—"

"Hey." Gigi puts her hands on my shoulders, steadying me with her presence and the literal hold she's got on my body. "Today, all you have to do is be sexy."

I'm shaking, still in denial, though something like elation's edging its way in. "Sexy? I'm not Bond girl sexy, I'm the character actress who—"

"Bullshit," says Gigi, clearly pissed now.

"Agreed." Max crosses her arms over her chest. "You are totally Bond girl sexy."

"Only better, because—"

"Because there's more of me." I repeat Gigi's tried and true phrase and let the thrill take hold and kick me back into gear. "Holy shit."

"Yeah. Yeah! Because there's more of you, babe. Because what you do at camp isn't just about getting your rocks off. It's about physical acceptance and sexual freedom and being the sexiest fucking woman alive."

"You're hot." Max leans in. "I'd totally do you, Twyla."

"Me, too," says a camper walking up. I've seen them around, but we've never met. The last time I saw them, they had clamps on their nipples and were suspended ten feet in the air. Right now, they're wearing enough clothes to walk into a fast-food place unmolested. "We need you on set. You ready?"

I suck in a breath. Am I ready to do this? To step into my new role like I was born for it?

"You are sexy," says Gigi. "And you are beautiful."

"You're hella talented," Max joins in.

"We need more plus-sized rep on the big screen," says the newcomer. "And then maybe just be called actors instead of getting labeled by size like we're fucking articles on a rack."

"Shit," I say, looking at all three of them. "You're making this seem real."

"It's real, babe," Gigi says. "You just need to accept it."

Rolling my eyes, I squeeze her hand before heading up to the dungeon to shoot the most important scene of my life.

35

———

Zɪᴏɴ

"Sound!" Enid's AD calls out, followed by the sound woman's response of, "Sound rolling!" The fact that she usually films porn flicks didn't bother Enid—or the director of photography she brought in—at all.

I'm standing by a well-lit Saint Andrews cross to which my scantily-clad wife is currently cuffed, like Fay Wray in the remake: Kink Kong. She's in this very racy, barely-there, bright orange lace negligée, selected by Lamé, of course. It looks about as comfortable as the thigh-hugging leather pants they've put me in. I'm slightly out of breath from the fifty push-ups I just did to get my muscles pumping and my veins popping and my skin—like Twyla's—has been oiled to a sheen.

I accept the flogger from Tage, our props person—aka Steely Dan when camp's in session—and weigh it in my hand. It's not mine, but it's a good little tool, with wide, soft falls in a shimmering silver that will look great on camera. I do a quick figure eight in the air and nod at Tage's unspoken question. "Perfect. Thanks." They smile and step out of the shot and I breathe deep and look at my wife.

And pop an immediate boner. Thankfully, the fucking anaconda pants have got it in a stranglehold, which I realize, with a flash of inspiration, was Lamé's intention. God, how well they know me. I peer around, catch sight of them, and nod a huge thank you. Lamé winks in response. They know.

Everyone here knows.

Except for the two execs in the canvas seats against the back wall, along with their small army of assistants and the television folks we've invited in for an exclusive first look at the next picture in the *Everwars* franchise. Possibly also the Director of Photography. But that's it. Everyone else is a kinkster at heart. Everyone else is in on it.

My God, if we get away with this, it'll be...

I swallow.

Shit, don't think about it. Just do your thing.

I cast a quick look around at the "Extras," played by real kinksters, of course, but looking like the tamped down Hollywood version of themselves. I get a few nervous smiles in return, which is funny, given that this is their world.

Not anymore, it's not. Right now, we're on a movie set, masquerading as a dungeon. It's weird. But it looks good. This is my world. Both of them, actually, blended. Kink and film.

The Lifestyle, meets the Industry. And it's not so bad.

To my right, Blade's wearing jeans and a mesh top, looking absolutely camera-worthy as he prepares to pretend to have sultry for-the-screen sex with someone. If our visitors' reaction is any indication, audiences will go wild over Blade. The fact that he's unbothered by the attention makes him even more magnetic.

In the few seconds before the director calls action, I let my gaze travel to my wife, who is pure, unadulterated sex on a cross. Her expression doesn't change when our eyes meet, but I see the message there anyway.

I adore you, it says. And *mine*.

I beam it back to her, loud and clear and strong and forever. Whatever happens here today, we're a unit. Together. Mine, hers. Ours.

"Action!"

I breathe deep and settle into this new, unexpected role, totally tired and wired but also content and more relaxed than I've been since this whole thing blew up.

How weird is it that, of all times, *this* is when I'm suddenly happy?

But I guess that's what happens when you're surrounded by people you love—people who'll watch out for you and care for you and step in to save you no matter what. My people.

This set right now is what it looks like when kinksters come together. Kind of. There's no real sex happening, after all. No penises out, no cages on testicles or clamps on labia, needles or—oh, wait, there is someone actually puncturing skin with needles off to the side, but I doubt Enid will focus on it too long. I can already imagine audiences complaining about how fake it looks.

If they only knew.

There's a chance none of this'll ever see an audience, of course, but that doesn't matter. What matters is that we convince these people this is a film set, not a private adult camp.

We've got one chance. One.

Better make it count.

I lift the flogger and strike.

Twyla

Zion's magnificent, as always, but with the cameras rolling, that otherworldly light inside him comes alive and he's positively riveting. Not just to me, but to everyone. To the people on-set and the people who will one day sit in a theatre or at home, and watch, breathlessly, as Matthew Kincaid, the lead character in the blockbuster *Everwars* movies, goes undercover in a BDSM camp, hidden somewhere in the southeastern United States.

Yeah, so we did it. All of us. Together.

It was a gamble. A *huge* gamble that will only work thanks to Zion's connections and influence—and his willingness to make a movie he's been avoiding for years.

No, this isn't the film Zion wanted to star in next and no, I never expected to get a sexpot role in a high budget action flick—or in *any* film, for that matter. But here's the thing: Gigi and Max are right. I am sexy. I *am*. I'm a large woman, with big breasts and thighs and a wide ass, a wobbly belly, and arms that jiggle and I'm goddamn *sexy*.

And maybe it's time the world understood that people who look like me are sexy and beautiful and worthy of attention, on-screen and off.

There.

In my hastily thrown together character, I twist enough to glare at Zion, who's holding the flogger with the ease of lots and lots of practice.

Fans will notice that. Especially the ones in the know. They'll see the way he flogs me and they'll get it. They'll know.

The falls flick out and catch my half-bare ass and, while I might have been irrationally annoyed by Zion's vast previous experience a few days ago, I'm very appreciative of it right now. When he hits me, it looks good for the cameras, but it only hurts a little.

Unfortunately, it's turning me on. A lot.

Which is fine. Good, even.

We *want* the cameras—both the crews' and the visitors'—to catch my reaction and, if all goes well, they'll show it online and on TV and... Okay, so there are issues with our plan.

Camp will have to be cancelled this year. Or kept indoors, at the very least.

We can't risk over the top fans trying to break our perimeter and finding out what's really happening here. That still hasn't changed.

But we're hoping this'll be enough to convince people

that the land's just been rented out for the shoot, which will let us come back here next summer with additional security.

It'll work. It has to.

And if it means that Zion and I owe a few favors to a whole lot of people, well, what's a few favors compared to a thousand kinksters outed, their lives destroyed?

The flogger flicks my ass and I don't have to pretend to like it when Zion leans in and whispers—perfectly audible to the fat microphone hanging over our heads, "I'll break you, Anna Madura. And you'll love every second of it."

A line that's a little ridiculous. A line he'll probably hear over and over again for the rest of his career—his life—like poor Arnold with *I'll be Back.*

"You'll have to try...*harder,*" I reply, half taunting, half begging, and completely breathless. Anna Madura, the sultry spy character the exec team created for me is designed to be the perfect foil to Zion's intrepid, falsely easygoing Matthew Kincaid.

The scene goes on for a few more minutes, with Zion—skin oiled to a shine and muscles pumped up to some modern standard of perfection—pretending to beat the crap out of me and me greatly enjoying every second, before we cut and rerun it a few times. Enid's a perfectionist, I've heard.

Oh my god, I'm working with Enid Connor.

Various crew members rush the scene, but Zion insists on undoing my cuffs himself. He starts with my ankles, caressing me in the process, then my wrists, which he massages one at a time. Lamé throws a robe over my shoulders and Zion helps me slide it on, then ties up the sash, finally using it to pull me closer.

"You're fucking beautiful," he whispers. "The love of my life."

Tears rush my eyes. "So are you, Mr. Mason."

"You gonna take my last name, now that we're—" He pauses and flicks a look over his shoulder. And rightly so. I wouldn't put it past that *ET* crew to be recording everything we say.

"Why would I?" I ask, giving him a wicked little smile. "I've already got one."

He grins, wide and happy, and leans in. "I fucking love you, Ms. Hernandez."

"You can call me Mrs."

"Oh, you minx. Keep talking like that. Say it again."

"I'm your Missus."

"Mine," he whispers, so quiet you'd have to read lips to know what he's saying.

"Yours," I say in response. "All yours."

"Fuck, I need you now."

"Right here?" I tease, wishing... Oh, whatever. We can hold off for a bit. Anticipation, I've learned, can be as good as the real thing.

"I'd do it, you know."

"I know."

"Ahem," says Enid, her scratchy voice bringing us back to the present. "Y'all should probably get a room."

I hide my burning face in Zion's chest for a second before stepping back and facing our new director.

"So, uh, we're gonna call it a night." She glances left at something. Or...someone? and looks back at us. "I heard the Craft Services here's pretty good."

"The best," says Zion, with a huffed laugh.

"Yeah," she says, looking left again. "Yeah. So, uh, let's talk, okay?" With that, she heads over to Max, who laughs outrageously at something she says.

"Is she flirting with Max?" I ask, shielding my eyes from the lights.

"Looks like it."

"Well, as they say, you can take the kink out of kink camp..."

"How you planning to finish that sentence?" Zion asks, wrapping his arms around me and bending to give me a quick peck on the lips.

Just a peck, to anyone watching, but we both know it's more than that. A whole lot more.

"You coming for your interview?" Gigi leans in, eyes blazing with excitement. "She's dying to ask how you met."

"You're enjoying this, aren't you?"

"Are you kidding me? Dahling, I was *born* for this." Her grin's contagious and, when I look up, I'm not the only one who's caught the bug.

Zion's looking on with a big smile and something that looks an awful lot like love on his face.

"My heart's never been so full," I tell him and Gigi and, frankly, anyone else who'll listen.

"Yeah. Well, I didn't know I had a heart. So..." He leans in and plants another kiss on my lips—this one deep and wet and sexy—and pulls back. "I'd say we've done pretty well."

"You got that right," says Gigi, slapping us both hard on the back. "Now, come on. Let's spread the love, shall we?"

EPILOGUE

Eighteen months later...

Zion

"Quiet everybody! Quiet on the set!" Lamé yells into a pink gold microphone. The feedback has people squealing and laughing and throwing popcorn in return.

"Sheesh, sorry." They flick their hair behind their shoulder and turn to me. "I guess this is your show, Z. Come on up here." Quietly, they add, "Tough crowd today."

Laughing, I give Lamé a one-armed hug and accept the mic, then wave Twyla up onto the Dungeon's stage.

She shakes her head, but I just wait her out and, after an eye roll and a stuck out tongue, she gives in with a sigh, stomps up on stage, and slides herself under my arm, like I knew she would.

My woman. My wife.

"Hey, y'all," I say to the gathered crowd.

"Hi Zion!" They reply, like we're at a goddamn puppet show. And that's about the atmosphere, I guess. A few hundred kinksters gathered to watch the fruits of their labors for the first time, in a safe, happy place.

Twyla, dressed in finery like the rest of us, giggles, her body a soft, sleek piece of heaven pressed tight to my body. Her dress is this... fuck, I don't know what you'd call it, but it's long and sort of slippery and it hugs her tits and makes me want to bite her arms and the whole thing's this bright blue waterfall that I want to dive face-first into.

Later, though. Later.

Right now, we've got things to do.

I put up a hand to stop the crowd's totally unnecessary applause.

"All right. All right. First off, I want to thank each and every one of you for everything. And by everything, I mean for saving my goddamn life." A few hoots are quickly shushed. "But much more importantly, I want to thank you for stepping up and correcting my mistakes, for making sure that we've got a camp to come to every year, when I just about went and blew it for everyone." I wave off a few good-natured catcalls. "For that, I want to apologize." I suck in a deep breath. "And, ah, I want to, uh, shamelessly piggyback on this moment to, uh..." I turn and take a step back from Twyla, leaving her standing alone onstage, which is hard, dammit. I don't like leaving her there, though I know the woman can handle the spotlight.

She narrows those dark eyes at me, one brow curved

up in a question and an *I'm gonna kill you when this is over*, but I ignore all that and reach into my pocket and pull out a box.

I'm shaking. Like a leaf. But I guess that's okay, 'cause if there's one thing I've learned it's to trust these people, Twyla first amongst them. They'll rib me, but they won't tear me down.

And hell if they don't have my back like nobody's business.

"Twyla, baby. I know we're already wedded."

"Happily," she leans over to say in the mic.

The crowd goes wild.

"God, yes. But this..." I swallow and her eyes soften as she watches. "This is about much more than that. You know?" I grab her hand and run my thumb over the rings on her finger. "These symbolize a partnership out there in the world, where I lived a half-life 'til I met you."

The peanut gallery lets out a loud *aaaaaawwwwww*, and I scoff and wave them away and shuffle my feet and look up, my face hot as hell, and say, "Will you wear my collar, sweetheart? Will you do that for me?"

She gasps, her eyes wide, her cheeks the dark pink they get at the start of a scene. "Yes," she whispers, then clears her throat and, for the people in the back, projects like hell. "Yes, Zion. I'll wear it."

With relief, I open the box and hold it out for a second, like a total dipshit and then, tense as hell, I grab the delicate gold collar and wrap it around her neck, clip it in place, and step back, my heart thumping a mile a minute.

I run my finger over the ring at the base of her throat, then dig my hands into her hair, and finally look into her eyes.

"Don't cry," I whisper. "Baby, *don't*."

She smiles and half laughs and a tear leaks from the corner of her eye and races down to meet her lip and I wipe it with my thumb and lean in for the kind of clashing kiss you only ever see in movies.

Except it's real, this time. It's deep and hot and so full of love, I swear we're making music with our mouths.

We kiss for way too long like this, which would be weird anyplace else, but given we're at a special camp session and these people don't have a problem with sex or intimacy or pleasure or pain or, hell, seeing a grown man cry, then I guess they don't mind. Even as my tears overflow to join Twyla's, I don't feel a moment's shame or embarrassment or any of that shit designed to keep us in line.

No, I feel loved.

Loved and seen and goddamn proud to be here.

With a shuddery exhale, we pull away from each other.

"I love you," I whisper.

With a shaky exhale, I give that collar a final look and turn to the folks I know and love and will forever be grateful to, and say. "All right. It's a rough, early cut. Still got months of post-production to go, but I figured you all deserve to see the movie that, uh, saved Camp Haven. So, sit back, enjoy. Don't rib us too much. It was mostly improv. And..." I look down into the front row. "If you've got any complaints, the director's sitting right here, so, take it up with Enid. I'm sure she'll be happy to listen."

Enid blows me a raspberry and yells, "Start the damn thing already! We're here to see a movie."

Laughing my ass off, I step offstage and sit in my seat, gathering Twyla close to me. I tilt my head as it opens on a shot of her looking like a dream in latex and stilettos, whipping a well-known older actor in a Paris apartment, and say, "That okay? I hated to spring it on you, but..."

"You felt like we never got our wedding."

"Exactly." I'm relieved. Goddamn, the woman gets me.

"And," she whispers directly into my ear. "If we're thinking of this as, say, a wedding night, maybe we could do something special?"

I turn full now, ignoring the whispers of the people sitting behind us. "Such as?"

She inhales, long and slow and mysterious, sort of like the woman up on the screen. "I was thinking I might be ready to try that *thing* we were talking about."

My pulse quickens. "Yeah?"

"Yep..." She glances around, as if anyone here gives a shit. "I'm ready."

"Oh, baby, I could..." I drop my forehead to hers. "I could..."

"You can," she says, with a sultry smile. "And you will. But for now, how about you lift up my dress and finger me while we watch this *stellar* film?"

"You're *such* a brat." I squeeze her thigh.

"You love it." She squeezes my arm.

"I really do."

"And I love you." Her squeeze turns to a caress.

"I know." I kiss her, long and soft and with every ounce of my filthy little heart. "I'm the luckiest man alive."

Read on for the Possession Bonus Epilogue...

WHERE WE BELONG

A CAMP HAVEN BONUS EPILOQUE

1

———

Twyla

We've done everything.

Except this.

Okay, maybe not everything. There are things I'm not into and things he'd rather not subject me to. And then there are the things we've been saving for sometime in the future.

Like the double penetration thing.

And apparently the future is now.

Honestly, I'm nervous. Like really nervous.

But fine. Mostly.

We've set up the scene in our cabin at camp. It's bigger than the one we spent the night in all those months ago and built higher up in the trees. There's a hot tub on the back porch and sitting in it's like taking a bath in a treehouse. Which we do together all the time. I love it.

I set out a bowl of chips and check again that the

fridge is stocked full of beer. It is. Beers and white wine for me. Although maybe I should have a vodka. Two drink limit, of course. Not that I need it with how worked up I am.

As with pretty much everything we do in the bedroom (and out) it's not just a physical scene. It's mental, emotional mindfuckery of the best sort.

So, I'm nervous and I'm amped and I'm everything in between. Because—and here's the mindfuck part—tonight's a competition. A big one. Entirely based on my desires.

I rub my palms down my denim-clad thighs, then head back to the kitchen to wash them. And then, because I've still got a minute or two to wait, I use the restroom, check my face in the mirror, check my teeth. I look fine.

No. Zion would say I look good, not fine. He'd say I'm beautiful. Gorgeous. Sexiest Woman Alive is his new favorite, so of course Gigi started referring to me as The SWA, pronounce *Swah*, which Lamé changed to *La Swah* and now every single person at Camp has picked it up, so now my camp name's French for silk. Zion and Gigi, who love the name, both believe they should get credit for it, so there's a little rivalry happening there and... I love it so much. Almost as much as Zion loved Christmas at my parents, with the dogs and the ballroom dancing, and the "Port course" which they picked up on one of their cruises.

And Mom obviously loves Zion. I've never seen

someone get so babied before. *Never*. Not once. It was so damn sweet I almost died.

Oh, God, where *are* they?

I check the time on my phone and sigh. Okay, now they're late by two minutes. He's doing it on purpose. It's just the kind of thing he likes to do. Prolong the wait, the pain, the pleasure. Edging me already. The jerk.

Footsteps on the cabin porch.

Uh oh. I look around, wishing I'd thought of something to be doing when they get here and then, frantic, I pop into the kitchen, to give myself an extra minute.

The door flies open, loud and fast, the way only Mean Zion would open it.

Mean Zion's a real bully. And I fucking love him. I dream of Mean Zion, masturbate to him when we're off on location and can't get in a video call. The grittiness of his voice, the way his eyes go stone hard and uncaring.

I shiver, already turned on at just the thought, and wet my hands at the faucet and put my cold hands to my hot cheeks for a second, before breathing deep and calling, "Babe? That you?"

Mean Zion doesn't answer. Obviously. He's such an asshole. Instead, he loudly tells the guys to come in and get comfortable. I hear heavy footsteps and imagine construction workers in workboots, coming home after a long, exhausting day on some job site. A lot of footsteps. How many are there?

Adrenaline revs and my pussy clenches on nothing.

Crap, I need to calm down or I'll come the first time

someone touches me. And though I complain about Zion's constant edging, I'll to enjoying the wait.

"Want a beer?" Zion asks in that meathead voice.

A couple grunted response.

"Babe. We need a beer in here. Stat!"

Oh, that gets me going. A clenched-stomach annoyance joins in with the excitement and nerves to make a cocktail I couldn't begin to explain. Why? Why do I love Zion the Asshole so much? Why don't I get off on flowers and praise, the way some folks do? I mean, I'll take those things—and I get a lot of them—but that's not what sends my libido spinning into the stratosphere. No. Humiliation, objectification, a little pain...those are my drugs of choice.

And I'm married to a man who knows just how I like it.

"Babe. The fuck?"

"Sorry!" I grab a bag of chips and empty it into a bowl, snag two cans of beer from the fridge, spin, and crash right into Zion, standing in the doorway.

He looks me up and down with a slow, familiar fervor that I'll never get used to. It turns me on and lights me up and tells me all the things he's holding in for this scene. All the things he'll verbalize when we're done. And then after and after. When we get up and a million times tomorrow.

My man loves me.

"Here," I press the bowl of chips into his wide, sweat-clad chest and he just stares down at it like he's got no inkling why it's there. "Could you grab this?"

"I want a beer," he says, half petulant, half puzzled.

I barely contain the smile trying to pinch up the corners of my lips.

He leans in, gives me a quick peck on the mouth, and whispers, "You good?"

I nod. "Yeah."

"Nervous?"

"Yes, but good. Don't stop."

He smirks, mean and slow. "I'll take that beer." He glances back into the main room. "A beers for the guys."

Guys. That revs me up. I knew there'd be more than two, but I've got no idea how many. Three? More?

"Sure," I say, breathless and shaking.

He grabs a can from me, pops it open and takes a long, slow sip with a final up and down look before heading back out. "It's coming," he says, dehumanizing me with two simple words.

Let's do this.

I set the bowl on a tray, along with two more beers, then snag a glass of wine, just in case. I turn the corner... and stop.

There are Three. Four, counting Zion, who's the only one not to look up when I enter. He's telling some story about a famous poker game he played a few years ago with a legendary line up of Hollywood bigwigs and politicians and sports stars. He hated that game. Every second of it.

But to hear him talk about it today, it was not only the greatest moment of his life, but he was the best player there—by far.

Oh, Mean Zion, how I love thee.

My eyes move from him to scan the other guys. I know them all, except for one. He's white, big and wide, with the kind of solidity that comes from hard labor, not the gym. His dark hair and beard could use a little taming.

They all look up, Blade and Benji and the new guy, and I swallow, half intimidated, half jumping out of my skin with excitement. They're gorgeous—Blade all shiny, dark brown skin and hard, defined muscles that we now know for a fact look amazing on-screen. He's a born actor and, though he's been fighting it, he'll wind up in another movie someday. I know it. Benji's beauty is more subtle, though no less beautiful. He's of Korean heritage, I've learned, and he's got an open, friendly face, his features straight and sharp, the thick hair falling over his forehead shiny and soft. The other guy, the white, bearded one... Well, he's a big, intimidating mystery I'm not quite ready to face full-on yet.

"Hey," I say with a shy smile.

Blade smirks, Benji grins back. New guy just nods. Shit, he's...I don't know? Scary? Hot? Daunting.

The four of them together are sort of terrifying.

It's a good thing that's the exact sensation I'm going for.

"Here you go," I say, handing out beers and setting the bowl of chips on the coffee table between them.

Benji nods, Blade gives me a full body scan, with a soundless Hey. New guy just dead-eyes me and, here's the thing—I feel safe. I know Zion. I know these men. I know they won't hurt me, unless I ask for it. I know they've gotten extensively tested for STDs and they're all experienced kinksters and kind people, but this one? He's got presence. If I saw him in an alleyway or, hell, a bar? I'd run.

"Hey," I put out my hand and it's shaking. "We haven't met."

He looks at it, waits a breathless beat, and then clasps it with his big, warm, dry hand, gives it a quick, almost comforting squeeze, and says, "Vicious."

"Oh. Is that, um..." I shake my head. "Never mind."

He holds my hand a second longer, then drops it, grabs a beer and pops it open. "Thanks."

"We good?" the big man asks. Vicious. What does that kind of name say about a person?

I look him up and down this time, scan the other two, then turn to Zion. "This is good. I'll safe word if I need to."

"Good," Zion replies. The others just watch me.

After a last nod and a quick smile, I escape to the kitchen, out of breath, to lean on the counter and let my lungs and stomach and brain catch up with my soaking wet pussy.

"Babe," Mean Zion yells, too loud to be my real husband. Too abrasiveness and uncaring. "Get back in here."

I look up, catch my reflection in the window above the sink. It's showing me a pale, hollow-eyed version of myself that can't possibly be real, given how hot my cheeks are right now. I must be blazing.

"Yes?"

"Get in here." Oh, Mean Zion's annoyed. Probably exchanging a look with the others. It's so degrating, it kills me and at the same time, my libido loves it. I revel in it. "I want to show the guys something."

Okay. Wow. I inhale and put my clammy hands to my cheeks. "Coming."

I step into the room to see all four of them lounging, two on the sofa, two in the big, overstuffed leather armchairs. Three of them are watching me.

"I told the guys about those big, fat nipples of yours, babe." Zion's rooting around in the chip bowl, as if this is no big deal. Just another day at the office. "Pull up your sweater and show 'em."

And just like that, it's on.

Zion

The day Twyla Hernandez agreed to be mine, she took two half-men and made them one whole person. I mean, yeah, I've had months of therapy, too, but Twyla's been there every step of the way. She's the reason for the change. My sweet little catalyst. And the magic of her love is I feel right this way, not cobbled together and wonky. I'm as solid and true as Liev now. Rooted in this woman's life like I've always been here. Like we share the same trunk. We're strong as hell together.

But that's just it about Twyla. She's strong and, still, she's the kindest, softest person I've met.

That she's as dirty as I am in the sack just means this whole thing's as fated as it's felt from the moment I first saw her face on-screen.

This isn't just two souls hanging out. We're meant to be in a way I'd never have believed in my other lives. We're a love story. I grin. Two perverted souls getting their happily ever afters—and their rocks off while they're at it.

I mean, I loved her before. I know now. But when she came to camp and bared her own pervy little soul, well, I never could have imagined a better gift. A better life. What could be better than a soul mate that completes you, in all the ways?

"Come on," I say, knowing that she needs me to be the shitty boyfriend right now, not the gushing partner. "Show 'em. They don't believe me."

The guys—bless 'em—squirm and shift a little in their seats, but, aside a low grunt from Vicious, they make no other sound.

"I..." She looks at me and down at the floor, then glances at the guys and blushes so hard, I come close to stopping the scene right here.

She'd kill me, though.

"Jesus, babe. It's not a big deal. They're my friends."

"I just met Vicious tonight," she says, as if that's what would hold a person back.

"Fuck, babe. Vicious? We've known each other for years. Come on."

All four of us watch closely as she reaches down and pulls the hem of her sweater up, with shaky hands.

Underneath, she's wearing a cute, sweet light pink, lacy bra. It's see-through enough to see just how hard her fat little mouthfuls have gotten.

"Shit," Benji whispers. Blade adjusts himself in his pants. The only part of Vicious that moves is his light eyes.

"Yeah. Come here."

When she obeys, quickly this time, I meet her partway, grab the flimsy-looking cups of the bra and pull them both down, baring her to every eye in this room. At her gasp, I tweak both nipples, hard, and scoot over to give the guys a look. "See? Fuckin' cherries." And then, to ramp up her already gaspy breathing, I add, "try 'em out. You'll see."

Right away, Blade's up and walking toward us. He doesn't spare Twyla's face a glance, just watches her tits until he's close and then, like I knew he would, he grabs two handfuls. "Fuck, man. They're nice."

"Right?"

Benji stands, but Vicious stays right where he is, the way I knew he would. This, right here, is so totally his jam that I wouldn't be surprised if he asked to make this a regular thing.

Which is a big, fat no. I'm fine sharing Twyla with a person once, but my possessiveness doesn't allow for repeat performances. I don't doubt my woman, the way she doesn't doubt me, but we've established rules. And one of them is that we're exclusive to each other and that's it. Aside from this one time with Blade, we will never play with the same person twice. And we only ever play at camp.

In a place we trust, with people we trust.

"Go on, babe," I urge. "Show Benji."

She turns and arches toward him, still holding that damn sweater up, which is so fucking hot I have to unzip my jeans to make way for my erection.

Benji's smooth—always—his hands long and slender. Different from mine. That difference does two things: it pisses me off and it turns me on, a combination which, to this day gets me wilder than just about anything else.

Possessiveness, it turns out, after everything I've done, is my kink. And Jesus does it rile me up.

"Vicious's turn," I interrupt Benji's intense examination.

Without pausing, she turns. And waits. Vicious—the dick—doesn't move from where he's sprawled on the chair. "C'mere," he says in his low, caveman rumble.

Twyla takes two hesitant step toward him and, when he doesn't even shift to make way, slides between his wide-spread legs.

Vicious pats his thigh and, with a quick glance my way, Twyla perches on it.

His hand rises, so goddamn slow, and finally, gently, plucks at her. One side, then the other, his movements lazy, though I can see he's pulling hard, then twisting tight. All the while, he watches her face.

Oh, she likes it. Likes the lazy way he didn't move, likes the shininess of it, but also that single-minded focus on her responses.

"You were right, man," he murmurs, looking at me, before nudging her off to grab some chips from the bowl.

"What do y'all wanna watch?" I ask, leaving her to stand there like part of the furniture.

After a minute's discussion, we put Speed up on the big screen. I settle in my armchair, Vicious in the other, Blade and Ben on the sofa. "Sit on the sofa, babe," I tell her. The guys make room between them. The movie starts. We drink beer and eat chips. She sips daintily at her glass of wine, breathing so hard I can see her chest rise and fall from here.

I make her wait. Two minutes. Five. She's fucking suffering now. I'll bet she's soaking wet.

"Babe."

She looks over at me, her eyes glassy. "Yes?"

"Take the sweater off. You're making us uncomfortable."

"Oh." She glances around at the others. "Okay." Pulls the sweater off. Benji grabs it and throws it my way. Within a minute, he's playing with her tit, like it's his to play with. Blade's doing the same on the other side.

On-screen, Keanu's climbing an elevator shaft.

"Vicious, you good?"

He lifts his chin in a move that's neither yes nor no. Doesn't matter.

"Look, man, let me know if you need something."

He nods, watches the TV, then slowly turns to take in the guys as they nonchalantly play with my wife's body.

"Look, man, if you need anything...anything at all..."

He shakes his head, slow and calm, his eyes focused

on where Twyla's trying not to gasp and squirm and show just how much she loves every second what those two are doing.

"Babe," I say. She turns vaguely my way. They don't let up. "A little hospitality."

"Oh," she says, eyes at half-mast, her mouth hanging open. "I don't..."

Vicious's boner's tenting his jeans, like the rest of us.

"Look what you did to him," I say. "He's hard."

"I'm..." Pinch, twist.

Benji bends and takes her nipple in his mouth. Blade does the same. They're licking and biting now, squeezing and weighing. She writhing in her seat, her legs crossed to give herself pressure at the crotch. The whole scene's a fucking fantasy.

I palm my cock.

"Get over there and suck him. He needs it."

"Okay," she says, not moving.

I look at Vicious and shake my head. "Doesn't fuckin' listen." I'm working the total prick thing that gets my baby so wet.

"I got this," he says, standing up to his full, impressive height, and walking across the room. On the sofa, the movement stops. Twyla's head drops back to look up at him.

"How tall are you?" She asks.

"Six eight. Weigh Two sixty." One eyebrow goes up. "You okay with that?"

She nods.

"Good. Now get up. I want that seat."

She scrambles to standing, which is hard given that he's in her way, but it works for the scene. He grabs her by the hips, turns, and drops between the guys, who have to shuffle away to make room for Vicious's bigger bulk. He spreads his legs, catching her between them.

"On your knees. He worked hard today," I tell her. I'm sprawled out in the other chair, looking lazy and bored, but inside, I'm as tense and worked up as I've ever been. "Take him out."

"I don't..."

Blade shakes his head and looks across Vicious at Benji before glancing up at me. "You still got that gag?"

"How about you guys just hold her mouth open?

2

———

Twyla

I give a full-body shudder at the idea of being used the way Zion's suggesting.

"I can do it," I say, though I'm not sure why. I *want* what they're threatening.

"Take his cock out," Zion says again.

With an eagerness I can't hide, I push up high on my knees, glance at the big man's face, and then set to work opening up his fly.

He's hairy, though he's clearly well-groomed. And his cock's thicker than any of I've seen. It's big and hard and a little scary-looking. I glance at Zion, who's back to watching the movie, as if it's more excited than what's happening here.

Vicious shifts, getting his jeans farther open, and pulls himself out, slow and threatening. "You got her?" He glances at the guys and, without missing a beat, they bend forward and reach for me.

Hands behind my head, fingers prying my mouth and stretching it wide open. Someone pushes me forward, not giving me time to adjust, and he's in my mouth.

Filling it, pushing in, deep, my eyes water, my mouth, too.

Up close, I smell his musk. It's clean, salty/sweet. Not Zion's ambrosia, but not bad. I try to pull back, but they're not having it. I choke, wiggle, fight a little, and they let me up. I pull back and stare at the mess I've made of that thick, dark purple, swollen cockhead.

"That's good. Again."

A fist tightens in my hair, my mouth's stretched and he's pressed inside again. I fight it a little. I can't help it. I want it, but that other thing kicks in—the instinctive thing that tells me it's not safe. Someone pinches one of my nipples. My other breast is manhandled. Kneaded. My hair's twisted, hard, my head pulled back. Pushed forward again, the cock fucking into me, hard, now. His hips lift and push, push, breach my throat, my face pressed tight to his abdomen. His hips move, thrusting, thrusting, hitting the back of my throat. I'm gagging, my mascara probably smudged. I picture the black running down my cheeks in rivulets as my eyes water and over-flow with the force of the deepthroating. My body's crying out and suddenly, another hand joins in.

Zion. "I got this," he says, low and mean, before grab-bing my hair and using me like a rag doll. "There you go. Take it. Show him what a good little fuck toy you are."

I moan and struggle and they laugh—all three of them.

"You've got to taste her pussy, man," one of them says. Zion? Maybe. I don't know. My brain's gone, my mind blown wide apart.

"Bed."

I'm pulled back and I try, so hard, to suck that cock again. I want it. Need it. Someone grabs my face and shoves a thumb in my mouth, chuckling low. Someone else slaps my breast. I'm pulled up to standing, dragged to the bed.

A hand wraps around the collar I never take off. A body, hard behind me. Solid, warm.

Zion. His hand. His comforting presence. I open my eyes, turn and look up, meet his stare. See the affection, behind the asshole mask.

"I love you," I tell him.

He smiles—a real Zion smile, not this version's slimy smirk. "Love you so much, Twy." And then, closer, quieter. "You okay?"

I close my eyes, drop my head back to his shoulder, and consider. Is this okay? No. No, okay's not the word for it. It's not fine or okay or whatever. It's something else. It's something dangerous and fierce. It's a game, but it's also a way of life. It's an acknowledgment. An acceptance. It's digging deep and pulling out the most basic, animal part of myself, and letting it free.

It's real.

It's us.

I nod, smile, lean back for the soft kiss I know is coming, and then say, "Yes. I'm good."

"All right. Now get on the bed and give these guys

what they need." The smirk's back. "They worked hard today."

Quickly now, and awkward in my haste, I undo my pants and drag them off, get to my underwear and hesitate.

"Leave it," says Zion.

I obey, stand there lost for a second, and then gasp when he picks me up and throws me onto our massive play bed. "Gotta taste that pussy, man," says Mean Zion, just giving me away. "So fuckin' sweet."

The men converge on the bed, fully clothed. First Blade, between my legs. He bends and brings his face close to my crotch and sniffs, audibly. "Fuck, she smells good."

"You should lick it."

Without waiting, Blade swipes the crotch of my panties aside, pulls my lips apart, and just stares at me for a second. His gaze flicks up to Zion. "Looks so fuckin' good."

"It is," my husband replies. "Fuckin'...heaven."

A quick swipe of Blade's hand through my wetness, and he dips down for a long up and down lick. When he comes up, he looks at the other guys, grinning. "This pussy's soaking. I gotta get my cock in here."

"You will," says Zion, his eyes on mine. "You all will." He gives a long, slow, evil grin. "But I get to come inside."

Someone groans. Weight shifts on the bed. Zion stays standing like a master of ceremonies or a conductor or something. He pushes his hand to his cock and watches, his expression ferocious. I see the ownership there and feel the irony in my bones.

Possessive, jealous, mine, mine mine, and yet, he's sharing me with his buds. It's a paradox, I guess. Sexy and dirty and obscene. "Her mouth's empty," Zion says to me, to the room. To Vicious, I guess, when my body's hauled to the edge of the bed and my head's hanging off it and that cock's prodding at my lips, demanding entry and there's nothing I can do but open up.

"Look at that pink," says Zion as someone licks my cunt, hands on my breasts. My mouth's full of cock, my breasts being pulled, hard, to the point of pain, but the pleasure's there instead.

My ass is lifted, thighs spread. A tongue back there, then... oh god, cold. Cold, dripping.

Something toying with me there, while the mouth devours my pussy, a tongue probing my hole, a finger flicking at my clit, then another tongue? Maybe?

I don't know.

I'm choking on cock. It pulls back and I lick the salty droplets of precome and a groan rumbles above me, low and angry and the next time he fucks into my face, it's aggressive, a domination, not an exploration. I'm lost, just a body. Just cells. Just taking it all. Taking.

Hands holding my head, my breasts being tortured. Something clamping a nipple, the pain so unexpected and bright that my spine flexes. I'd scream, but I can't with my mouth full.

What? What's that cold on my ass? I struggle a little. Don't know why. Lube, dripping, and...

I'm gagging again, that fat cock pressing deeper and deeper, while something presses into my ass, stretching me... a finger? I think. Two? I don't know.

For minutes, I suck and take, struggle to catch my breath, drool, sob. It's not sexy, I guess, but I'm so behind sexy it doesn't matter. Nothing matters, but the stretch of my lips and my ass and the fingers fucking into my cunt, the tongue lapping me up and up until I'm so close to coming it hurts.

"I want to come," I say when I get a chance to breathe.

"Fuck. Lift her up." Zion, that was Zion.

I'm hauled to the side. Hands everywhere. I don't know whose. I know there's more skin than before and I want to see their bodies, but it's all so blurry. I can't focus.

Someone on the bed, beside me, beneath me.

"I got you." Zion whispers in my ear. "Got you, baby."

I blink and turn, let him take my lips. Work hard to focus. There's Blade, his body familiar, but geez is he beautiful. He looks warm. His cock looks like it'll split me open.

"Think you can take him?" Zion asks, from where he's lying face-up beneath me.

"No," I gasp.

"You will."

He nudges my face toward Benji. Face flushed, his eyes shining black, a muscle ticking in his jaw as he takes in my body, sprawled out over my husband's. "Look at

Benji's prick, baby. Did I mention all those piercings? I think I forgot to tell you about those."

Panting, I let my eyes descend his flat-planed chest, smooth and polished-looking, to a sparse happy trail and at the end... "Oh...wow," I say, staring at the Prince Albert piercing studding the tip of his cock. It's beautiful —and painful looking. "I don't know," I voice, for the first time aloud. "I'm not sure..."

"He'll fuck you," Zion says, with absolute certainty. "Now, look at Vicious. You've seen that cock. You've tasted it. You'll take him, too."

"I can't," I gasp, drooling a little as I take in the man's massive body, the dark, wiry hair on a chest so massive that it can't possibly be real, biceps as big as my head, hands like catchers' mitts. "Oh, please."

Zion sighs, kisses my temple, and drops his head back onto the mattress. "You're such a good girl, baby."

I hum happily, my inner brat way too overwhelmed to lift her head.

The guys agree, shifting into some predetermined position, all three of them stroking themselves. Hands rub my legs, my feet. Someone touches a breast, flicks my clamped nipple.

I cringe and moan and shimmy my ass on my husband's hard cock.

"You still want this?"

"God, yes," I say, blurry, but present enough to know just how good it'll be. "Yes, I want it."

"Good," he says, reaching down to pull my legs up and open. Expertly, he eases his cock through the wetness between my legs and then down, down, to my asshole. "Gonna fuck your ass, baby."

I shut my eyes and moan.

"Head on my shoulder."

I squirm and drop my head back.

"Open your mouth."

I open, just as Zion's cock touches my asshole and then, oh god, then, he pushes in.

My body tightens up.

"Legs open," orders a deep, angry grumble from above.

"And your mouth," says someone else.

Close to coming already, I obey.

Zion

My cock's aching with need as I push, push, push inside her tight little asshole. It takes a while to get it stretched out, but that stretch is part of the process. And I enjoy the fucking process.

To our right, Benji crawls over, dick in hand, and stuffs that intimidating cock into my woman's mouth. Her asshole tightens around me in response. I catch sight of his clean shaven balls, imagine how soft they feel against her chin, shut my eyes, and breathe.

At the end of the bed, Blade shoves her legs wider, stretching her open for another invasion.

My pulse picks up speed. I push, Twyla whimpers,

and I'm fully in. "Fuck, baby," I say, low in her ear. "You feel that? So fuckin' good."

"Tight," she moans.

I smile, thrusting up into that perfect little fuckhole. "Gonna get a whole lot tighter with Blade's fat cock in your pussy." And then, because I'm the asshole tonight, I say, "Brace yourself."

She clenches. I laugh. Someone smacks her ass and she goes tighter still.

"Again," I order.

Another smack. Another. The hands graze my thighs as they thwack her. It stokes my need.

Beside and above me, Benji stuffs her mouth full of cock again, which I'll admit is fucking beautiful from this angle. His balls slapping her face, his thigh pressed up against the top of my head. The smells drive me wild here. Sex, lube, sweat. It smells like summer and sin and goddamn paradise.

"Blade's up." I grunt, then pant through a few quick pumps. Fuck, I love this.

"Yep," says the man who's been waiting an awful long time for this moment. With a grin, he puts on a condom, snaps it in place, then edges up onto the bed between our legs. "I'll take it slow."

I pause, grab Twyla's thighs and pull them as wide as they'll go. An offering.

"Fuck, that looks good," he says.

"One time only," I tell him, though he knows this. "You fuck her once and you never touch her again."

"Yeah, I got it." The grin he throws me tells me he

knows exactly how possessive I am and he's getting off on this dynamic, too. We all are. "Still looks fucking incredible."

Vicious pulls a chair up to the bed and settles in it, thick cock in hand. "Sure does," he rumbles low.

And then, the moment we've waited so long for...the moment she's begged me for a million times in bed.

Blade rubs his tip up and down a few times, then, after a split second's eye contact with me, slowly, slowly, eases inside.

Between us, Twyla makes a sound that raises every hair on my body.

"You okay, baby?"

Benji pulls out of her mouth.

Everyone goes still.

She whimpers, shifting. Blade slips inside another inch. The stretch is unbelievable from inside her ass.

Her groan goes lower, more bestial. It sounds like it originated in her bone marrow. Or her soul.

Beside the bed, Vicious's hand speeds up on his cock.

"I need a yes, baby. Just tell me it's good and we'll continue."

Another groan, echoed by sounds from the others.

They're as deep in this scene as I am, as mesmerized by it, immersed like they've dived deep and don't ever want to reach the surface.

"Yes," she whispers, moving her hips just a fraction of an inch. "Yes, don't stop. I want this." A pause. "All of you."

Immediately, Benji's in again. Vicious moves the

chair closer and leans in to play with her tits and—oh, fuck, there it is.

"I feel you," I tell Blade, who's probably only a third of the way inside my wife's tight pussy, but already likely hitting bottom.

"Not gonna make it much farther," he says, in some kind of pain. A shift back, a pump in. "This thing's tiny."

I laugh low at the way Twyla's body responds to those words. My sweet little woman, just dying to be objectified. To be used.

"Stretch it out," I say, though he knows the limits we've already set. No hurting her. At all.

She's not into fisting, not into the idea of a vaginal DP and she doesn't want to hurt. Not really.

Aside from a little soreness tomorrow, of course. Enough to remember this by.

"I'll try," he says, gritting his teeth as he pulls back as if it's his job and he'll take care of it, dammit. Even if it kills him.

I shut my eyes hard against the pleasure, fucking back into her whenever he pulls out. In and out, the rhythm slow and mostly steady. After a while, Blade gets into a series of drawn out ooooooohs. I look up to see him watching Benji fuck her mouth. Damn, I can't look or I'll come.

"I'm close," he says.

I nod. "Any time."

Between us, Twyla's humming around Ben's cock, the sound rising, louder, more frantic. I reach out and run a hand down his thigh, needing to close the circuit between the three of us or something.

"You can come, baby. Let it out."

She wails.

"Any time tonight, remember? This is your night. Come all you want."

Her sounds change as Ben mutters that he's almost there and I picture him coming in her throat or on her tits, in her cunt, but I can't let it happen. Not for a second. Not now, not ever.

That's mine.

One hell of a hard limit to have, but there it is.

"In your hand," I tell him, as if he doesn't already know this. As if we haven't gone over this scene in great detail.

He nods, his brow wrinkled up as he concentrates, hard, and without warning, he steps back, grunting, and fills his hand with come.

Within seconds, Vicious is back, sliding into her mouth like he owns it.

She gags and he pulls out and that inner voice tells me he's stepped over a line, though I can't say what it is.

No. No, I know what it is. It's the possessive bear inside me, growling to let loose. A scene like this is a dance between Twyla's desires and mine and the goddamn bear, who's jealous and pissed and wants everybody to know just whose woman she is.

All I hear in my head is *Mine. Mine, mine, mine,* and I know better than to ignore it.

"Not now," I tell him, straining to keep it together.

With a nod, he pulls out, steps back, and catches my eye.

"Fuck. This is it. Fuck. Fuck." Blade's up on straight arms, looking down at where his cock's pumping into my wife and rubbing mine in the process.

Suddenly, he looks up at me, and grins. "Sure feels good to be a deviant, doesn't it?"

I let my head fall back and laugh.

3

———

Twyla

I'm stuffed full of them, my body stretched to its limit. "Zion," I try to say, though it comes out as just "Zah."

"Yeah?" He tilts down to look at me and I crane to look up and the second our eyes meet, we smile. My heart, God, my heart's just as tight and full up as I am.

"I love you," I say.

He grins. "I know, brat."

I laugh, the sound scratchy and weird, and arch back as Blade slams deeper inside me. "Oh, shit," I say, working my hand down between us, to where my clit's this pulsing, throbbing thing. Just an achy bundle of nerves on the edge of something very, very big. It won't take a lot. Just a touch. Just a...

"Fuck. This is it." One last pump and Blade pulls out, yanks his condom off and strokes himself to orgasm in the palm of his own hand. Zion's rule. And it's so damn hot, I moan.

I watch with hot fascination, feeling Zion's interest, as keen as my own. He loves watching people come, loves the moment of need so strong the control flies out the window. And his semen fetish, well, that's a whole other story.

It's so perfect, I could expire just from watching.

"Benji," barks my husband, no longer Mean Zion, but not the calm guy I live with every day either. "You got it in you?"

Benji, sitting beside the bed now, lazily jerking his half-hard erection. He laughs. "I think I'm done, man. That was..." His eyes meet mine. "Fucking beautiful."

"Vicious. You're up."

Oh god. Oh *God*, without missing a beat, that massive rough-looking brute walks over with his condom-wrapped erection tapping his abdomen. The bed shifts under his weight and I wonder if Zion's recent reinforcements were enough.

"Get ready," the man mutters, his voice nothing but a rumble, and I swear it's almost enough to get me there.

He's the one person in this room I've never met before. A complete mystery. Which scares me and turns me on in equal measures.

Zion chuckles, his breath warm against my temple, and then Vicious puts his weight on the back of my thigh, the move so proprietary I feel Zion stiffen.

In the next moment, Vicious's against my opening and then...

All the air leaves my body as he sinks in.

Right where Blade just was.

And he's wide. Wider than Blade. Wider than anyone or anything I've ever taken.

I whine as he works to get inside. Beneath me, Zion goes still. "Want to stop?"

I shake my head. "No. God, no. This makes me feel so..." *Dirty? Loved? Surrounded? Taken?* I don't even know what to call it. But it feels right, despite the pain. Because of it. It feels like us and our specific brand of perversion. *This* is where I'm supposed to be right now.

"Touch yourself," he urges. "Do what it takes, baby. Got to give the man a turn. He gets his fucking turn." His voice dips for a second into Mean Zion territory. "Everybody gets a turn on you."

Those words twist me and wind me up and ramp it all back to an electric buzz.

I no longer question why this is what turns me on. It doesn't matter in the slightest. The fact is, it's bodies and sex and it feels so damn good and, with Zion, it all feels healthy and open and honest.

"Go ahead, man," Zion says, clearly working hard to get the words out while they battle for space in my body. "Use that hole."

And there it is. Those words, filthy and wrong, rev me up high and fast and over that invisible barrier and suddenly Vicious is in and he's pumping and I'm making inhuman noises as I climax like I've never once climaxed in my life.

It's a bestial thing, rough and ugly. I sound like an

animal and feel nothing but pleasure and, for a short time, I swear I leave my actual skin behind.

When I come to a handful of seconds later, I whimper. Zion reaches out and grabs Vicious by the arm. "Hold up. She needs a sec."

The big man nods and goes still, watching me closely.

I've never felt so much like prey as I do under his intense glare. He's big, heavy, hot as hell, and thick in a way I'm not used to. Not just inside me, but all around. Overwhelming and intimidating and not entirely at ease.

In the silent stillness, I feel the width of his hips and their heft against my inner thighs, the rough friction of his chest hair against my breasts. He's levered up onto his hands, his arms straight, and his shoulders are unimaginably huge.

"Are you, like, a football player or something?" I ask, not thinking about the rules here and how real life's the most taboo subject of all.

The man apparently doesn't mind, though, because as I watch, his face morphs into not quite a smile, but something close. Something easier, warmer. "Rugby," he says in that low, rumbling voice before pulling slightly out and pushing home again, the stretch just this side of painful. Over the next few slow thrusts, he lets his gaze take in my face and my breasts, then lifts up to look at where he's penetrating me. Beyond that sight, his attention lingers on my thighs, Zion's thighs, then back up. A last, lingering look at my face, almost warm, if that's something this man can experience, and finally, he looks at Zion.

"I'm close."

"Good," says my husband, possessive as always. "Hurry up. I need to unload."

Oh, he's so crass. So freaking vulgar. It sends a fresh shudder of excitement through me. I can tell that Vicious feels it by the way his pumping goes faster, more haphazard.

"Yeah," he grunts, looking from my face to Zion. "You gonna fill her up."

"Sure am." Zion gives a pained smirk. "I nut inside her every chance I get."

I shut my eyes, hard, at how he's talking. Not because I hate it, but because it zings through me like a million extra pinpricks of excitements.

"Fuck. Fuck, yeah." Vicious thrusts hard and fast now, his body the biggest, strongest I've ever felt. I shudder and let myself take it. "So goddamn good." He slaps my thigh, hard, and I gasp. Another slap has me tightening around him, my body clenching, clenching...

In the next second, Vicious is up and out, the condom off, his arm furiously working. Only I don't get to see it, because Zion leaves my body and I'm up, flipped onto my hands and knees. Wobbly. Every muscle weak.

The plastic sound of another condom ripped off, only this time, it's immediately followed by the hot press of Zion's cock to my pussy and then he's sliding in, quick and rough. His harsh, gasping breaths tell me he's close, close... Hands digging into my ass, pulling me apart, and then...

Zion

I'm coming, hard. Hard enough to see stars. Hard enough that the groan my lungs release gets caught in my throat and for a handful of seconds, I'm not sure I'll make it out the other side.

Through the rushing in my ears, my instincts or need or whatever the fuck it is tells me to open my eyes as I pump deep inside her. I pull out just enough to watch as another jet shoots from my tip and that gets shoved into her sweet, pink cunt, too. Instinct's the word, because the need to fill her isn't coming from my brain, it's from deeper inside, from a primordial place, so intense and basic, it might as well be blood pumping from my veins.

"Fucking mine," my mouth growls as I slide the last hot spurt inside her. "Mine."

I open my eyes, shocked to find that I've closed them, and stare down at where we're joined, up over her round ass and thick waist, to where her head's pressed into the mattress. Slowly, I pull out, watching her body shudder.

Behind me, the door closes.

I don't turn. I can't. I'm here. With Twyla. Joined in something that feels deeper than love. At least the kind of love I thought people had. This connection doesn't feel like a thing outside of me. It's as deeply ingrained in my body as my heartbeat, as entrenched in my being as my soul.

I look down in time to see the first drop of semen oozing from her and immediately, my half-hard cock's there to catch it. With a long, slow sigh, I ease my dick and my seed back inside her.

"Where I belong." The words come out on a whisper.

Twyla backs up getting me deeper, our bodies closer. She releases a long, happy sound as she stretches her arms and turns her head to look at me over her shoulder.

I reach out and grab her hair the way she likes, tense my hips, pressing them tight to her body, and let all the pleasure I feel sail out into the quiet room. "I...."

"I love you, Zion," she says. The words are mine, along with her sigh and her smile and the hot, sweet pull of her bare pussy.

"I feel complete," I tell her, finally, almost shocked at the realization. "So fucking happy."

She smiles and I lean over her body and give her a deep, dirty kiss. The kind with tongues and lips and biting. The kind that draws blood and singes my soul and proves that true love is never too much to hope for.

ACKNOWLEDGMENTS

I want to thank you, dear reader, for being here. I'm so grateful to you for giving these sweet, kinky books a chance. Thank you for reading and reviewing and talking about my stories. You make every moment of this amazing journey worthwhile.

A huge, messy kiss to Kettle Macauley, who I've spoken to pretty much every day throughout this process. Just having you here has made all the difference. And to my other daily writing zoom peeps, Joanna Bourne and Sofie Couch, y'all are the best. I love seeing your faces.

As always, Alleyne Dickens, you've stepped up and been there when I needed you. I hope I do the same for you.

To Michelle, aka: The Best Decision I Ever Made™. You know I wouldn't have finished this thing without you. You're amazing, not just as a stellar PA, but as a friend.

Annika Martin: I'm so grateful for your help and insight and also that you're willing to eat all the food and drink all the wine while we talk writing.

Becca Mysoor: your input on this book was so very spot on. I will always and forever come to you for help.

Nicole McCurdy: you are a natural. Truly. Your edits

were thoughtful and precise and absolutely instrumental in shaping this book. Let's do this again.

Leigh Kramer, you are amazing. Your insight and perspective are so very precious. I can't tell you how much I value your opinion.

To Varinia, sister-in-law, friend, and fellow Romance reader: Thank you for reading this book, even if I know much of it is probably way past your hard limits. Your opinion means the world to me.

To Kim Cannon, copy editor extraordinaire, not only are you quick and efficient, but you polish my books to a shine. Thank you.

Zoe York, you're just The Best. I honestly don't know how you do everything you do, but you've got some kind of magic. I'm so glad to count you as a friend. To Sierra Simone and Nikki Sloane, thank you, thank you, thank you. You're both so freaking generous and gorgeous and talented. I appreciate you stepping in and calming me when everything hit the fan.

To Jacqueline and Esther: you're amazing Beta Readers and I will forever harass you to read my books early. Oops. Did I not mention that before? You've signed on for life now. You'll never stop hearing from me. Sorry.

And lastly, to my lovely family and friends: Thank you for bearing with me every step of the way.

Et Bb, merci pour tes bisous et tes poulets rôtis au citron confit et mes petits cafés au lit. Je t'aime.

ALSO BY ADRIANA ANDERS

Camp Haven/Kink Camp Series

Kink Camp: Hunted

Paris Je t'Aime Series

We'll Never Have Paris

The French Kiss-Off (coming soon)

The Survival Instincts Series

Deep Blue

Whiteout

Uncharted

Love at Last Series

Loving the Secret Billionaire

Loving the Wounded Warrior

Loving the Mountain Man

The Blank Canvas Series

Under Her Skin

By Her Touch

In His Hands

Standalone

Daddy Crush

ABOUT ADRIANA ANDERS

Adriana Anders writes award-winning Romantic Suspense, Contemporary Romance, and Erotic Romance. Her books have received critical acclaim from the New York Times, OprahMag, Entertainment Weekly, Booklist, Bustle, USA Today Happy Ever After, Book Riot, Romantic Times, Publishers' Weekly, and Kirkus, amongst other publications. Today, she resides with her husband and two children on the coast of France, writing the love stories of her heart. Visit Adriana's Website for her current booklist: adrianaanders.com

BB bookbub.com/profile/adriana-anders

X x.com/AdrianasBoudoir

instagram.com/adriana.anders

pinterest.com/adrianasboudoir

facebook.com/adrianaandersauthor